Last Lovers

LAST
LOVERS

WILLIAM WHARTON

Farrar, Straus and Giroux

New York

Library of Congress Cataloging-in-Publication Data
Wharton, William.
Last lovers / William Wharton.
I. Title.
PS3573.H32L37   1991   813'.54—dc20   90-46117

To my wife, Rosemary

This tale takes place
between April and November 1975.
Location: Paris, France.

Believing is seeing.
W.W.

Last Lovers

Chapter 1

ZAMBO!! Suddenly I'm on my hands and knees down on the asphalt next to a bench near the statue of Diderot in the small Place beside the boulevard Saint-Germain, across from the Church of Saint-Germain-des-Prés.

My precious thirteen tubes of paint are scattered all over the place. My prize easel, my hundred-franc easel I bargained for in the Marché Aligre, is knocked all galley-west with one leg bent under and another splayed out like a spavined camel trying to stand up in a windstorm.

Shit! This is just what I didn't need. I'm still holding a paintbrush in my hand, the top of it is snapped off about three inches above my knuckle. Luckily the canvas landed with the painting side up, so it could be worse.

Then I notice. There's an old lady all dressed in red on her knees beside me. We must look like two elderly clochards chasing after the same butt someone just flipped. My first reaction is, this whole thing is her fault; why the hell doesn't she look where she's going?

So, still on my knees, trying to ignore her, I start scooping the tubes of paints toward me, before some other idiot steps on one of them. That'd be a *real* mess, colored footsteps tromping through the Latin Quarter, yellow, green, alizarine crimson. I scramble over to pick up my canvas and lean it against the bench, no serious damage I can see. Next time I'll cozy myself up in the lee of that bench, safe from kooky old gals wearing red costumes.

Then, finally, I go over. She's swung herself around and is sitting on her duff rubbing one knee. Both her stockings are ripped where she hit the ground. One knee is bleeding and she's licking her finger and rubbing it, the way a cat would. But she's not looking at her knee. She's looking at *me*.

"Est-ce que vous êtes peintre, monsieur, artiste-peintre?"

What the hell else does she think I am, a surveyor taking measurements of Saint-Germain-des-Prés so we can make a copy and build it out in the desert for some Arab prince to convert into a mosque? Hey, maybe they'd let me house my chevalet there, a horse turned camel. The French call easels *chevalets* for some reason, sounds like something to do with horses, at least to my semiliterate French-American ear.

I lean down and try straightening my box up, lengthening the collapsed rear leg, slowly twisting one side leg that's sticking out all cockeyed. Nothing seems to be broken, thank God. It could just possibly end my budding career as artist. Maybe that's "grafted" career, more accurate, probably.

"Oui, madame, je suis peintre, artiste-peintre."

"Ah, and you are American, too. That's very interesting."

Then I see the cane. It's white. I feel like a real asshole. It's the kind of insensitivity, unawareness, that's my greatest problem. I get down on my knees again beside the old lady.

"Est-ce que je peux vous aider?"

She seems to look right through me. I realize only then she's spoken in perfect, practically unaccented English-English.

"Ah, ha, you have seen my cane. I can tell by the change in your voice. Yes, you may assist me. Would you help me pull myself to my feet? If I try getting up myself, I shall need to roll onto my knees again and that would be rather painful."

She stretches out her hands. They're small and smooth. I gently pull her to her feet. Actually, she more pulls herself up, using my hands as support. She has strong arms for an old gal.

I lean over, pick up her cane, give it to her. She brushes herself off, all over, not knowing where she's dirty, with the thoroughness of a blind person. Then she starts swinging her cane in arcs around her, close to the ground, like a radar scanner or somebody hunting for money at a beach with a metal detector.

I see what she's looking for, a purse, more like a satchel, about two yards nearer the church. I go over and pick it up. I step inside the radar sweeps and touch her hand, push the leather straps of the satchel out so she can grab them.

"Ah, sir. Sometimes it is difficult being blind. Thank you for your kindness. I am very sorry I bumped into you. Or should that be crashed? Any- way, I am sorry. You see, I have my little private paths where there is the least chance I will stumble

into anything or anyone, and you were in the middle of one; I did not expect you, you fooled me.

"You must work very quietly, monsieur, or I would have heard you. Of course, there is the noise of automobile traffic out there."

She waves her cane at the boulevard Saint-Germain.

"But I should have smelled you, at least, the wonderful smell of turpentine. I should have smelled that. Yes, I must be getting old, it is hard to realize."

"Perhaps the wind was blowing the wrong way."

She leans back, smiles, looks me in the eye, that is, if a blind person can *look* someone in the eye.

"Ah, an American, an American painter, with a sense of humor. This is very interesting. It is something I did not expect, a pleasant surprise. There do not seem to be very many pleasant surprises left in this life."

I notice then she isn't completely in red, not anymore, anyway. She *is* wearing a red pillbox hat, the kind Jackie Kennedy was wearing in Dallas, only red, not pink; a bright Santa Claus–red skirt, sweater, and coat. But now the coat is well dabbed with several colors from my palette. It must have brushed against her in the cataclysm, bump, crash, or collision; whatever it was.

"Excuse me, madame, but there is paint on your coat. If you would stand still I can take it off now with my turpentine. If I don't, and it dries, it will stay there."

"Is it a good design, the paint on my coat? If so, I should like it to remain. It would be lovely *having a hand-painted coat, painted by an American artist here in Paris, n'est-ce pas? Even though I could not see it, would it not be exciting?"*

"I'm afraid, madame, it is only a smear of burnt sienna, yellow ocher, alizarine crimson, and a touch of ultramarine. Even in the Salon de Mai it would not be considered much of a composition."

I'm not usually so flip, so verbal. Perhaps it's because I don't get to speak much English these days and I'm enjoying the freedom of my own language, but I think it's the nature of this woman, the situation. I want to continue our wordplay, our game, practically a flirtation.

Or maybe it's because I sense she's lonely, too, wants to talk with someone, practice her English.

"Then perhaps, monsieur, it would be best if I take off the coat so you can obliterate, transform, or remove your work of spontaneous art. At least, then I shall have the smell of turpentine following me around for a day or two, a souvenir of our meeting. I think I should like that.

"I am sure definitely it will be better than going into one of the art galleries. I always feel so unwanted there. Some painters seem to feel a blind person staring at their paintings is an insult; perhaps it is. I am only looking for something I should want to see. From what my sister, Rolande, has told me, it would not make much difference if I could see; I am not missing much. Oh yes, sometimes there are advantages to being blind."

She starts to unbutton and shrug the coat off her shoulders.

She's a slim woman, straight, neat. I go around behind her and take the coat, slipping it down her arms. She transfers her cane and satchel from hand to hand as I remove the coat.

"Won't you be cold, madame? I could lend you my jacket, but it is almost *completely* covered with paint. It might just well *be* accepted in the salon."

"No, I do not think I shall be cold. I am going over to the stone bench there at the foot of Monsieur Diderot. It is where I was going when we met so precipitously, or, perhaps, fortuitously; no, that has too strong a French derivation. What would be a better way to say that in American, monsieur?"

I swear she looks me in the eye again. Maybe she's only partly blind, or likes to pretend she is and for some reason enjoys carrying a white cane. Maybe she isn't even French. She speaks English better than most English or American people I've known, so precise, with such an elaborate, thought-out vocabulary.

"Would you accept 'propitiously,' madame?"

"Oh yes, wonderful. An American with a sense of humor, and so gallant, as well. Oh yes!"

She walks away directly, quickly, toward the statue, not tapping her cane or in any way indicating she's blind. No wonder she crashed into me. If she was going at a pace like that, it's amazing either of us survived. In a football game, they'd definitely have given her fifteen yards for clipping.

I manage to gather my stuff together. Except for a swipe across my palette and the broken brush, I'm in good shape. I spread her coat over the bench and start working on it with turpentine and one of my paint rags.

Yesterday I found three towels thrown out in the trash over by where I stay near the Bastille. The centers had the toweling worn thin, but they make perfect paint rags. I've torn them up into foot-square pieces. I use one of my best rags.

The problem is not to spread the paint any more than is necessary and still get it off. I work about ten minutes, a separate part of the cloth for each color. When I'm finished, the only stain that shows is the dark wetness of the turpentine.

It's an early spring in Paris. The chestnut trees are only now sprouting leaves, limp baby leaves, just out of the bud, no blossoms yet. The famous song talks about April in Paris, chestnuts in blossom, and so forth, but actually the blossoms usually come in May. Today is April ninth, and although the sun is out and it's just possible to paint without the paint and my fingers stiffening up, that old lady must be freezing without her coat. I make a final inspection.

I look over. For Christ's sake, she has pigeons all over her! There are pigeons sitting on her shoulders, on her head, on her lap, and she's actually holding one in her hand. How the hell can a blind woman catch a pigeon?

I scurry over. When I come close, most of the pigeons fly up and away, a few retreat to the ground at her feet, watching to see what happens next.

I hate pigeons myself, and if she's going to have them *squatting* on her like that, I've just wasted too much time and turpentine removing paint spots. She's going to have pigeon shit all over her, so what difference could a few dabs of paint make? Pigeons, dammit, flying rats, that's all they are!

She turns toward me when I'm still about ten feet away.

"Ah, the American painter comes to visit with me. Do not worry, my feathered companions here will fly back when they know you are a friend of mine."

I've been promoted to friend. Does that translate directly from French as *ami*? As far as her pigeons are concerned, I just don't want them shitting on me or my painting.

"I've removed the paint from your coat. The smell will go away rather quickly. I hope it doesn't bother your pigeons."

It doesn't hurt anything trying to be nice. She stands and I slip the coat over her arms. She snugs it against her shoulders, feels with her hands if the collar is straight, fastens the buttons. She does everything with smooth, easy movements, no hurry, but very efficiently. She turns her eyes toward me. There's nothing I can see wrong in those eyes. They're clear; I don't see any cataracts, no film over them. They look like perfectly good eyes to me, regular doorways to the soul.

"Please will you not sit down with me a minute, Monsieur le Peintre? I do not have a chance very often to speak with anyone, especially a painter, an American painter. It is strange, but I begin to have the feeling I might be in one of those films, those moving pictures I have heard about."

She sits, I sit beside her. The stone bench is cold. I notice she's sitting on a small inflatable cushion. She reaches into her bag and pulls out another, rolled into a small package about the size of a cigar.

"Here, you may sit on this. If not, you are liable to develop pain in your kidneys."

God, she sounds like my mother! And it seems she can read minds as well as "see" when she's blind. I feel somewhat foolish, but I blow up the cushion and slide it under my duff. It's comfortable and does keep off the cold as well as being softer than the hard stone. This old lady really knows how to do things.

It's one of those days when, if the sun is shining, it's warm. However, when the sun is blocked by the many scudding white and dark clouds overlapping each other, immediately a cool breeze springs up and it's cold. Right now the sun is bright and lighting the tops of those beautiful French clouds, the kinds the Impressionists painted, that I've never seen anywhere else. I hope someday I can work up enough nerve to really try a crack at those clouds.

The damned pigeons have come back. They don't seem to mind me, as if this old lady gives some kind of magic protection. She's devoting herself to them now. I watch. It's the weirdest thing I've ever seen.

She has a small leather roll-up kit, the kind a good mechanic might have to store his wrenches, only smaller. She has it open beside her on the bench, that's on the other side from where I'm sitting. In the kit are small scissors, two pairs of tweezers, both large and small, various little metal picks, toothpicks, tiny sticks with cotton wrapped on the end like Q-tips, miniature bottles with the smell of alcohol, and several small files. There is also a bottle of antiseptic.

I don't know how she manages, but she puts out a finger, no food on it, just a finger, and several of those crazy pigeons fly down to land on it. She selects one of the birds by putting her hand over its back, slowly, carefully. As it hunches down, she picks it up. She then gently spreads out a wing and runs her finger along its length, checking the feathers. If there's a twisted feather, she tries to straighten it, or, if it's badly twisted, she quickly pulls it, checking the feather socket with her sensitive fingers and with a Q-tip applying a touch of antiseptic.

She goes over the entire body of the pigeon that way: probing, feeling, adjusting. Each pigeon seems to enjoy this, like a Swedish massage. There's no fluttering to get away, no panic, they just relax and let all this happen. She then checks the feet, feeling for scales, I think, smoothing or filing rough spots with one of her small files, clipping the toenails if they need it, cleaning out the space between nail and toe, washing the whole foot. I wish somebody would take care of me like that. I wouldn't shit on their statues, either.

One bird has an infected joint, where the toe joins the leg. She cleans this thoroughly, gently, expertly touching, feeling for swelling, and puts both alcohol and antiseptic in the sore spot.

As she finishes with a pigeon, she deftly reaches into each of about ten little bags she has lined up close to her thigh. She chooses individual grains, as if they're vitamin pills, and feeds them, one at a time, to the bird on which she's just worked. The pigeon, meanwhile, is fluffing out its feathers, doing a quick little inspection with its beak, checking any repair work that's been done.

The pigeon takes the grains from her hand as she offers them, then she gracefully swings away the pigeon on which she's been working, gently off her finger. They usually fly up, circle a few times, then land on the statue of Diderot for a quick rump-thumping crap. The favorite places seem to be the pen in his hand, his hand itself, and his head.

There are pigeons all over Diderot. He has even more pigeons on him than the old lady, but then he's about ten times bigger. He has a patina of white pigeon shit over the dark green patina of his bronze to show for it, too.

I watch through about five or six pigeons. I'm too fascinated to even think about getting back to work. I've never seen anything like this. I had canaries when I was in high school and I loved to hear them sing. But pigeons only make that gargling noise all the time, could make you vomit just listening to them. However, I must admit, I've never seen anybody handle birds the way this old lady does.

While she works on the pigeons she talks to me, mostly asking questions. She never takes her mind from her work with the birds, but once in a while she "looks" at me and smiles. I begin to realize she's guessing at the location of my eyes from my voice, my smell, something. I feel she does it so I won't be uncomfortable with her blindness. She's pretending she can see, for me. But I *am* uncomfortable, I can't help it, I still can't figure how she can look directly into my eyes, read me. It's weird.

"*Are you long here in Paris, Monsieur le Peintre?*"

"Yes, I've been here almost five years now."

"*But you have such a heavy American accent. After so long in Paris you should speak better French.*"

God, I think I only said about fifteen words to her in French. I didn't know it was *that* bad.

"I don't seem to have a good ear for languages, madame. I try to learn French, but it is difficult. I speak much better now than I did a year ago, so that's something."

She's concentrating on a flight feather which is dangling and must be removed. She could be a surgeon, her hands are so sure and quick.

"So you have good eyes and I have good ears. Together we would know much about this world if we could share. Almost no one uses the gifts they have. Only when one loses one gift does one begin to find and appreciate the others."

There's a long pause as she carefully extracts the feather, puts antiseptic on the feather socket.

"Now, Orlando, that will be much better. You will be able to fly faster away from the automobiles and soon a new feather will grow in."

She turns to me again, smiles.

"I hope you do not mind if I talk to my pigeons. I have a name for each of them and they are my only friends, my only family. Being an old, blind woman is sometimes quite lonely."

"I've talked to pigeons myself, also, madame, sometimes they are the only creatures with whom I *can* talk."

I don't tell her how mostly I'm cursing them when they make that sudden flurry of stiff feathers from behind me when I'm trying to concentrate on a painting. A person could have a heart attack when a flock of pigeons soars off in a bunch like that.

"But I don't know them the way you do, madame. When I talk to them it's as if I'm talking to myself and seem to learn nothing. I've never been as close to pigeons as you are."

"Well, you see, monsieur, I have been coming here every day from about ten in the morning until the midday bells ring, for thirty years, since the end of the second great war. The pigeons in the flock change but the flock itself remains. Even the young new ones, or a pigeon who joins this flock from another, know me. You see, pigeons are some of the kindest, most trusting, least hostile creatures on this earth. I am convinced they communicate with each other, can talk in a special way, but hard as I have listened, I have never learned their language. However, humans could learn much from them as to how we should live."

Being out in the streets, I run into all kinds of loons, but this may be my prize catch, a blind old lady in a red suit who wants to talk to pigeons because maybe they can tell her how humans should live.

I'm beginning to feel I might be getting involved with another nut. I've developed a sort of sixth sense for sorting out the real crazies. But this woman seems different. Except for all the pigeon business and her blindness she seems more normal, more clear, intelligent, than anybody I've talked with in a long time.

But also, I'm beginning to feel itchy about getting on with my painting. I've decided to paint this woman in at the base of the statue. I definitely could use a strong color there in the foreground and red would go great against the green of the trees in the park next to the church. I've already decided to treat Monsieur Diderot loosely, with suggestions of the bronze, a few pigeons, and the thrust of his leaning toward the church across the street.

"Well, I'd best get back to work, madame. The light is changing fast and I want to finish my underpainting today."

"What are you painting? Is it the church?"

I still can't get used to her being blind. When she comes out with something like this I almost feel as if she's kidding, but then I've had this happen often before, with people who can see. I'll be sitting directly in front of something that interests me, making what I consider a fairly good representation of what I'm seeing, and they'll stand there, looking all around, puzzled, and finally ask me what I'm painting. It can drive me up a wall, it also isn't very good for my confidence.

I thought they were kidding at first, but no, it just isn't what they're good at, the way I can't seem to learn French. But, of course, with this woman, she's *really* blind. She only knows I'm beside the statue of Diderot. I could be painting the café or even the Hôtel Madison.

"Yes, madame. It is the church, but much more. I have the statue of Diderot on the left side of my painting, then I'm looking up boulevard Saint-Germain with Le Drugstore, and across the street, Les Deux Magots, then the opening to rue Bonaparte. In the middle is the tower of the church, with the nave going across the painting to the fountain. In the foreground, I have the little garden where children play, and in front of that, le boulevard with the bus stop."

She stops working on her pigeons and listens to me. She closes her blind eyes the way a person with sight would close theirs to picture something.

"You describe it all very well, I can see it in my mind. I do wish I could see your painting. I have lived in this quarter all my life. I feel you are prob-

ably a very good painter because I think you are a good man. Thank you for cleaning my coat and then keeping me company. I hope you are happy with your painting when it is finished."

As she speaks, the bells of Saint-Germain-des-Prés start their beautiful, hollow, hallowed gonging, ringing. The first few notes, then the crescendo as they pick up speed, are so comforting. The bells are one of the things I've learned to love in Paris. Not far away, I hear the deeper bells of Saint-Sulpice start their welcoming answer to noon, invitation to the important French déjeuner.

The old blind lady has been gathering her tools together and fastening them. She puts away her small sacks of feed, then pulls out a larger sack and strews some grains on the ground in front of her. She turns to me.

"This way, they do not notice I am leaving and it is not so hard for them. Tell me, are there any small birds there with the pigeons?"

I look and there are sparrows darting in front of the pigeons, getting their share and more.

"Yes, there are sparrows."

"Are any of the pigeons fighting them for the food?"

I look. Sure enough, they aren't, they're pushing each other to get to the grain but there is no pecking or fighting among themselves or against the small sparrows.

"No. There's no fighting. They allow the small birds to take what they want."

"You see, monsieur, the pigeons have much to teach us."

With that, she picks up her cane, stands, and reaches out her hand toward me. We shake hands.

"Will you be here tomorrow to work on your painting?"

"Yes, if it isn't raining or too cold."

She lifts her head, turning it left and right like a pointer trying to get a scent.

"No, tomorrow will be like today. I hope to see you then."

I watch as she turns and walks away quickly, using her cane only occasionally, She said she'd "see" me. It must be strange to be blind and still use the terms of seeing.

I go back to my painting. I block in where I'm going to paint her. I must consult her to see if it's all right. There's no way she could ever know, but it seems the right thing to do. It's the kind of lesson I'm learning, slowly but surely. Something that might seem perfectly right and logical to one person can be a terrible violation to another; we're all different. I wish I'd learned this earlier. I'll ask tomorrow before I start painting her in seriously.

I work away at the underpainting for several hours. Usually I go more quickly, but in the few oil paintings I've tried so far, I've discovered that faults of drawing or composition which might be acceptable, even invisible, early on become glaring as the painting comes to conclusion. I'm trying to eliminate all such awkwardness.

Still, I can already feel I'm going to have the same trouble I've had with the others. Even if I manage the drawing right, not only accurate, but well designed; even if the selection of forms and colors for the underpainting seems vital, appropriate, there's no *excitement* in the painting. I don't seem able to incorporate, build into my paintings, the strong emotional feelings I have about my subject, about Paris, about life itself. There's something missing, a wall of fear, of timidity, between me and what I want to say. Also, there's an arrogance. I don't seem willing to let go, to fall into the painting, become part of it. Perhaps it will come with practice, when I'm less concerned with technical problems; I hope so.

At about five o'clock, the light is too far gone. I feel the under-painting is finished and a night of drying will get the surface just right for my impasto tomorrow. I'll start with the sky, make a stab at those constantly changing, magic clouds against the blending blue of the sky. It's where my cerulean blue should come in handy.

Someday, I'd like to try wet-in-wet, go right from the under-painting to the impasto with no drying time between. Rembrandt did it and so did some other great Dutch painters, some of the Italians, too.

I pack up my box, hang the painting on the back of it, and start my walk home. I could take the number 86 bus almost directly to where I'm living, but I like walking in Paris. It's what kept me together over the worst days. Also, at this time, the buses will be filled and it's easy to smear a painting on someone, even if it's only underpainting.

I walk down boulevard Saint-Germain, across the Pont Sully, up Henri IV to the Bastille. I go along Roquette and cut off down a narrow street called rue Keller. It's about a forty-five-minute walk. The painting box is light enough so I hardly notice it. The walking helps keep me in shape, too. I'll really enjoy my dinner tonight.

I come onto the passage des Taillandiers, the street where I live. It's still early, so the buzzer to the door isn't set. I slip past the loge de concierge without any trouble. I know the name of a painter in the building, and if the concierge ever asks anything, I've decided to say I'm going to visit him. Actually I've never met this artist and hope I never do.

I go up Escalier C, the least used of the staircases. At this time, most of the artisans, furniture builders, and carpenters have all gone home. I, quietly, but with a casual step, as if I belong here, jiggling a meaningless ring of keys in my hands, go to the very top, past the last legitimate door, up one more flight, and through a heavy fire door into the dark attic, le grenier.

There's *no* light up here. I find my hidden flashlight, flick it on, and feel my way down the narrow hallway, between the individual attic rooms, to the one I consider my own, although I'm only a squatter. I reach for the key hidden over the door and let myself in.

The smell of old dust, of dry stored wood coated with sawdust, of stale air, is home to me. I stand my box with the painting at the far end of the room. There's a skylight in the slanted ceiling with a metal brace. I push it open to air the room. I block the cracks in the door with an old curtain so no light will show through, and light two candles. I unhook my painting from the box and put it between the two candles. I look around and see nothing's been disturbed. I think it's been years since anyone other than me has come into this room. I don't even know which of the carpenters' workshops below uses it for storage.

I pull down my piece of foam rubber and my sleeping bag from up in the rafters where I hide them during the day. I get out my tiny butane cooker and one of the sealed one-liter mason jars with my supply of cooked vegetables. I take out my bottle of wine and the half a baguette I hoard over two days. I only eat once a day and I'm really hungry. I was about ready to snitch some of those grains from the pigeons.

I turn on the cooker and warm up my Mulligan-type stew in an old pot. I pull my spoon from behind a supporting post where I store it and pour myself the one small glass of wine I allow myself each day. The six-franc bottle of wine I drink has to last a week. Aside from the costs of my painting materials, this wine, the butane, my baguettes, and the candles are the bulk of my expenditures.

I sit in the gathering dusk with the candles for light and slowly eat my portion of stew. I, who all my life have been a meat and potatoes man, have, perforce, become a vegetarian. At first I bemoaned the fact, but now, after several months, I sometimes think I couldn't face a steak, or even a well-done hamburger. I *feel* a lot better, too. But that could be from the running.

I look at the painting. In this light, away from the subject matter, it looks better. I probably *won't* paint in my sleep tonight. The whole idea of me painting *oil* paintings, considering everything, especially the cost, is an insanity; but I'm hooked. I don't know how I'll ever sell these things for enough money to pay back the cost of paint and canvas, let alone make a few francs. If I have to return to drawing and watercolor again, I'll feel as if my legs have been chopped off. But I'll do it, to keep my freedom.

I bought the paint box for a song. It's a genuine collapsible easel made with hardwood, dovetail joints, brass fittings. This box has to be at least fifty years old, older than I am. It doesn't have a metal inner liner as the new ones do, nor a second drawer underneath, but it's sturdy and light. It's constructed so the legs fold out and can be tightened to give strength. It's all there, storage for paints, palette, brushes, turp, varnish, oil, paint cloths, and it opens to hold the canvas, any canvas, up to size 25F. Also, it's smeared with paint and the air of authenticity. Just going out to paint with it gives me a thrill. I walk along feeling in tune with Monet, Pissarro, Cézanne, Sisley, a real painter in the field.

I thought carefully when I bought my paints. I found a place called HMB near here. It's not an art store but a real paint store for the artisans around this area. The paints and brushes are about half the price I'd pay anywhere else. I decided on Le Franc Bourgeois paints, because they're not too expensive, yet aren't packed with filler or too much oil. I bought studio-sized tubes. I tried to stay with the cheapest colors, colors listed 1 or 2 on a scale of 6. I bought titanium white and ivory black. Those I remembered as my favorites from when I was back in school at Penn, with dreams of being a painter.

Then I bought earth colors. If necessary, I'd paint with them and black and white only. I bought burnt and raw sienna, burnt umber, yellow ocher. Next I bought a tube of ultramarine light. That was seven colors. To fill out my spectrum, at not too great a cost, I bought ultramarine violet, the cheapest violet; the other violets were 5s or 6s. Next, chrome yellow, chrome orange, both substitutes for cadmiums, which are 6s. Then alizarine crimson. For green I bought sap green. It's transparent and can be used in the underpainting and also added to the yellows and earth colors for foliage. Last, I splurged and bought cerulean blue as a thirteenth color. Painting skies in Paris without cerulean would be a real challenge.

For brushes I bought pig's bristles numbers 4, 8, and 10 and, luxury of luxuries, a number 6 sable. That last brush alone cost 42 francs, enough for me to *live* two weeks.

I make my own varnish from Damaar crystals I buy at HMB. It's there I also buy huge cans of white acrylic house paint for sizing canvas, also turpentine and linseed oil by the half gallon. I usually have some crystals soaking in turpentine inside a woman's nylon stocking up here in the attic. I try for a five-pound cut, but it's mostly by guess and luck.

It's the canvas that's expensive. I shot half my whole wad buying a roll of raw duck canvas at a shop where they sell canvas drop cloths for painters. I snitch boards from up here in the attic to make stretchers. I tack canvas to them with carpet tacks and a hammer. I found the hammer, with a broken handle, in a trash can down the street. The short handle is enough for me, short-handled hammer and now a short-handled brush.

I use my fingers to stretch the canvas. I can get it tight enough that way. One trouble for me was figuring out *when* I should hammer the canvas onto the stretchers and heat the glue for sizing. Since weekends practically no one's around, also the concierge leaves Sundays, I decide that will be the best day. The hammering makes noise and the glue stinks to high heaven.

I worked all last Sunday, that is, after I'd gathered my vegetables and some fruit when they closed the market at the Marché d'Aligre. They just throw away anything that's started to rot. I cooked up my weekly stew at the same time I stretched canvas and made glue; all the smells blended together.

I built five stretchers, sized and put two layers of acrylic paint on the canvases after I'd stretched them. I pulled them nice and tight and have them stored in the rafters. I built them to the standard French dimensions. Two were 15 Figure and the last three were 25 Figure, or about two feet by three feet. It's the first of those bigger ones I'm working on now, after getting frustrated with the 15s; they were too small. I'm getting to be a real big-shot painter; I'm just not making any money.

Even with all these cheapo solutions it's going to break me soon unless I can figure some way to sell these damned paintings. I calculate, materials included, but not my time or labor, that I've got a hundred francs in each canvas when it's finished. This means I need to recoup at least three hundred francs a painting. There aren't many people walking around with that kind of money in their pockets, especially to spend on paintings by some nobody. However, the tourist season is coming soon. Probably I'll sell something during the summer. I've *got* to!

I'm not complaining, though. Things have worked out so far and I'm feeling great. I know it'll all come around okay. I have the feeling my life is beginning to make some sense again, despite everything.

The worst thing is loneliness. I try fighting it off, but it keeps sneaking up on me. I also try to keep myself clean. Once a week I go to the public baths next to the police station near the Marché d'Aligre. I scrub the worst dirt off my body and stomp on my clothes to get them clean. I wring out those clothes, put them in a plastic bag, and hang them in the attic to dry. I have a second set of clothes I wear out of the bath. But I still look pretty much like a bum. Maybe it's the beard. I try scissoring it so it's sort of neat, but if you're wearing foot-stomped clothes, not ironed, and a beard, even if you're clean, you can't help looking like a clochard. It's tough shaving every morning with no warm water. Razors would increase expenses, and besides, I've begun to like my beard. It takes the MBI curse off me, aims me in the right direction, the direction I want to go the rest of my life.

Once every month or so, I take my clothes to a self-service laundry. I shove them all in one washer, except for a sweat suit I wash by hand, then put them in the little spinner for a franc a shot. Together it costs seventeen francs, with drying. But after that I smell like an angel for a few days. My T-shirts glisten and my jeans almost have creases.

After I finish eating, I blow out my candles and stare for a while through the attic window. I keep thinking I'll climb up and clean the grime off so I can see out to the sky, but I'm afraid of tipping off whoever really owns this place to the idea I'm up here, so I don't. The weather's getting good enough now so I can leave the window pushed up at night and have a good look at the stars when there are any. I've discovered from experience just how far I can push it up and still not have rain come in.

Before I fall into a deep sleep, I remember that tomorrow I should stop at American Express to see if there are any letters from Lorrie or the kids. Also, I want to write and let them know I'm all right and how well my painting is coming along.

Blind Reverie

His smell is so different from that of most men, not only the turpentine. And his voice, sometimes calm when he answers me, but there is excitement in there. At the same time, this is a sad man, an alone man. I think he is probably a good painter.

He was kind to join me under the statue. The feet of Monsieur Diderot had a moldy smell today, could it be from the rain and the pigeons. It was stronger than usual.

I do not think Monsieur le Peintre cares for my pigeons. It was in his voice, in the way he sat, even with my pillow, I felt he was uncomfortable. I must teach him to love them as I do. I hope he comes back tomorrow. I can smell his turpentine in my coat all the way in the other room.

I hope I was not too brash. It is so rare to

find someone with whom to talk, who is not always thinking about my blindness. That is _their_ blindness. I so often feel sorry for those who must live inside the world and not outside it as I do. It must be so hard and cruel for them.

Chapter 2

I wake with the first light. I slip on my running costume: a pair of shorts, a T-shirt, and a sweat suit. The best thing I took with me when I left were my two pairs of running shoes. These running shoes I'd had at least three years and never ran in them. I dread to think of when they wear out. These things cost fifty bucks a pair. Now I use one pair for everyday, for painting, and the other for running only.

I sneak out the gate downstairs. Nobody is up at this time in the morning except garbage collectors and Algerian street sweepers. I start my usual warm-up, run down Ledru-Rollin and across the river to the Left Bank quai. I run through the little park there and the sculpture garden.

I stay with the quai even when I have to go up steps and down the other side. I take the steps quickly and two at a time. I want to make my blood really bubble. I run till I get to the Pont Alexandre III and cross it. Now the light is coming on stronger and traffic is picking up. I don't like to run when there's too much automobile smell.

I run along the street above the Right Bank quai. Sometimes I need to run up here along where the bouquiniste stands are, because of the road they've built along the quai. I cut in through the Marais to the Bastille. Traffic is picking up seriously. I go down the rue de la Roquette, the way I came home yesterday, and up rue Keller and home. It's only about an hour's run but it wakes me up. There's no trouble getting through the gate, the concierge sleeps until seven-thirty or so. I'm dripping as I quietly run up the stairs, my usual two at a time, to my hideout.

I take off my sweat suit and hang it on a hook behind the door. I spread my soaking shorts and T-shirt on a piece of string along the back wall behind some long pieces of wood. I stretch out on the floor until I stop sweating. I have a little piece of rug I found in the trash by the rug store at the corner of rue de Charonne and avenue Ledru-Rollin. I'm flat out on it, getting my breath back and trying to relax.

After about five minutes, I start my one hundred, deep-breathing, sit-ups and then do a few yoga exercises. I finish with fifty slow push-ups, hands lifted off the floor each time.

I don't think I've been in as good a shape in my life, not since high school. I'd *better* stay in condition, I have no backup, no social security from the French, no health plan, no MBI. I've *got* to stay healthy. The best part is it's such fun staying in shape.

When I first started living in the streets, almost a year ago now, I was slowly going downhill. I didn't eat right, I didn't keep myself clean, I'd put down a bottle of red wine every night so I'd sleep, and then it'd be noon before I could shake my head without hurting. I was well on my way to becoming a *real* clochard. It's hard to believe how quickly one can go down when one just doesn't care enough.

I splurge this morning and give myself my usual Sunday treat, even though it's only Thursday. At least, I think it's Thursday. I still have the end of my baguette saved from yesterday and dunk it into a cup of coffee I brew on my stove. Real luxury. I sit against my bedroll and look across at the painting. I'm anxious to get into it again. From the look of the sky as I was running, that old, blind lady was right, we're going to have another great day, another painting day.

I hide everything, tuck away my running clothes where they can't be seen but will have room to dry, wash myself off quickly with the water I pack up in wine bottles. I don't have any soap. I tuck my key and flashlight in place and quietly go down the staircase. Nobody really gets to work before eight, so I'm okay. The concierge's door is still closed, too.

Out on the street, the sun is up, long slanting light making everything clear and shining. There are the usual morning Paris sounds of garbage trucks, water running in the gutters, pigeons gurgling and splashing in the dirty water as they're just waking up. Then I watch as they glide against the sky. I guess the flock around here lives in the tower at Sainte-Marguerite's. I think about the blind old lady and what she said about pigeons. What a nutty idea. I've got to admit, though, they look great against a sky, and I'm going to start using them to hold things together, tie the sky to the earth.

I decide to walk straight down Henri IV the way the bus goes, so I can get the long view of Notre-Dame from the back. It's a special view from the bridge, with the little garden tucked on the end of the island.

I get to my painting spot at about eight-thirty. I put down my box and sit on the bench just soaking up what I'm going to be painting, trying my damnedest to let it happen to me. Letting it really come into me is something I'm trying to learn. I'm too aggressive, keep forcing the subject matter too much, not changing it but trying to make it mine instead of letting me become it. I breathe deeply, trying to relax, have confidence in things. I've had too many years where if you were caught relaxing, "goofing off," it was held against you. Every day it was a race to see who'd be first in the office and last to leave. I never even realized it was happening, either. And it wasn't happening just to me, it was all of us.

When the bells ring nine, I'm into it. I've set up slightly to the left of where I was painting yesterday. There's no chance anybody will be crashing into me and I can use the bench to store my varnish and turpentine bottles.

I start with that sky, working from the top, buttering it between the trees, around the tops of buildings. I like having the sky established before I start lighting the rest of the painting. I'll let the other parts of the painting happen to the sky, later. Also, the sky's up where it doesn't get in the way, doesn't get smeared as I work.

I'm lighting the top of the tower when she sneaks up behind me. I actually jump. I didn't hear or feel her near me at all.

"Ah, Monsieur le Peintre, you are here. That is good. Are you happy with your painting this beautiful day?"

She's holding out her hand to shake. My hands are relatively clean but with some dabs of blue and yellow ocher. I quickly wipe them on my paint rag and shake with her.

"Oh, it does not matter if you get paint on my hands from yours, monsieur. I could feel it and wipe it off with a tissue."

She smiles. I try to think how she knew. Of course, it was the slight delay before I shook hands with her, she knew I was painting. She's a regular Sherlock Holmes.

"Yes, madame, so far the painting is going well. I am just now painting the tower of the church against the sky."

"It must make you feel like a pigeon flying up there. Sometimes, as I am falling asleep, I try to imagine myself as a pigeon in the open air, close to the bells, the sky, above the trees, the streets. It is lovely."

She pauses.

"Do you know, often I dream of it. In my dreams I can see. I see all of Paris below me, glowing, glistening in magic light. I am never blind in my dreams. Is that not interesting?"

It tells me something. It tells me she hasn't always been blind. The company-trained psychologist strikes. Or else it tells me she likes to lie, also interesting. I start painting again. She stays beside me.

"Monsieur le Peintre, is it possible that I could make an arrangement with you?"

Oh boy, what's coming next. I step back from the painting but

I keep my brush in hand. I'm ready to take the en garde position. I can just see it spread on the front page of *Le Soir*:

American artist arrested
for attacking old, blind woman
with paintbrush

This would be in French, of course.

"You see, I know each of the birds in my flock, all forty-six of them, but only by feel; I should like very much to know how they look: what color they are, how they are marked, striped, checked. Since you are an artist, trained to see, truly, clearly, you could describe them to me."

She pauses. I wait. What's next? She said something about an arrangement. Is she going to offer money?

"If you will do this for me, monsieur, I shall prepare for you a very good meal today at midday. I assure you I am an excellent cook. I like to eat. As I said, when we lose one gift, other senses become stronger. My senses of taste and smell are very strong. I think you would like my food."

How can I say no? It means I won't get much painting done, but I'm in no hurry. I'm for sure not going anywhere. She can't live too far from here if she's blind.

"I live just there, behind the statue of Monsieur Diderot, just past where the Italian restaurant is. It is called the rue des Ciseaux. I live at number 5 and on the second floor. There is only one door

on that floor. If you come, you need only knock."

My God, maybe she has a *sixth* sense as well. She seems to read my mind.

She stops and now she waits. I know the rue des Ciseaux. It's a street of restaurants. I never thought of anyone *living* there.

"Of course, madame. It would be a joy for me to watch you with your birds again and, if you will have me, I should very much enjoy my déjeuner with you. Thank you."

"Thank you, monsieur. I hope you do not think I am being too forward, but it means much to me, also I shall enjoy having someone dine with me to whom I can speak in English."

I start painting again. I think I'm taking advantage of her blindness, that she won't know, but she knows immediately. It's probably the direction of my movements or even the sound of the brushes.

"Yes, you keep painting until it is a good time for you to stop, perhaps when you have caught the beautiful light on the tower against the sky. I shall wait for you."

With that, she turns away. I continue painting the steeple and heavy stone of the massive tower. Her comments about being a pigeon, flying up there, the openness of the sky, the strength of the tower, all seem to flow into me. I'm painting it with much more force and at the same time a new sensitivity. It's amazing how an idea can affect the way you see.

I paint for perhaps fifteen minutes or half an hour more and it's good painting, some of the best I've done. I put down my brushes and walk over to sit next to the old lady.

She turns toward me, smiles her quiet, not quite sad smile.

"I hope I have not interrupted you at an important point. I do very much appreciate this help you are giving me. I have not yet worked on any of the birds, but as you can see, they are waiting for me."

Sure enough, there are pigeons all over the place, all over her. It's amazing no sparrows or any other birds come. But then, come to think of it, only pigeons seem tame enough, friendly enough with humans to come close. They're either very stupid, or very trusting, as she insists.

She opens her little satchel and unfolds her kit. This is some kind of signal. She holds out her finger and two birds fly down; one lands first, so the other veers away. She puts her hand over it.

This is a really peculiar-looking bird for a pigeon, smoky-dark, with some remnants of checks on the back. It's slightly lighter on the chest, with a few almost white feathers on the thighs. Its beak is yellowish, with a streak of blue or violet, and its legs are a dark yellowish pink, almost salmon color. I describe all this to the blind lady while she does her inspection and files off a few scales from one leg.

"This hen is not young, she must be more than five years old. Her name is Nicole. She has been in the flock a long time. She has had at least fifteen nests and most of her young have grown. Some of her sons have left the flock. She is becoming thin and I do not think she will have more than one nest this year. From the way you describe her, she is

not a very beautiful bird, is she? I had always thought she would be one of the most lovely. I imagine what we think is beautiful in a pigeon is not necessarily what pigeons might feel. Perhaps sometimes it is best to be blind, so one can see the way things really are, and not be blinded by the way they look."

She gently launches Nicole away and another bird flies down to her hand. This bird is almost pure white but has irregular blue-gray markings. It is big, with a tinge of iridescent color around its neck. It has beautiful pink, almost scaleless legs with bluish nails. I describe this one as best I can.

"Oh yes. I always felt he must be white. He is so bossy, even though he is only from one of last year's nests.

"Almost always he is one of the first to come to me, not because there is anything wrong with him. He only wants the grains I give."

She's started feeding him his individual grains and he picks them quickly from between her fingers. She more brusquely lofts him off into flight.

I sit and describe each of the birds as they come. It takes more than an hour. I'm enjoying myself, enjoy trying to describe the birds accurately. There's something in it of the careful seeing one does while painting. But I'm also wanting to get back into my own work.

"Well, Monsieur le Peintre, I suspect that is all we are going to have today. There are two who did not come, perhaps they are with another flock

or perhaps something has happened to them. It is terrible the number of pigeons killed by speeding automobiles in this city. The automobiles never stop, so the pigeons are smashed into the street and are totally destroyed. There should be a law against it."

I don't tell her how they seem to lose their color, how the feathers become spread under the tires so that, in the end, the pigeon disappears into the asphalt. In one day, on a busy street, a pigeon can turn into nothing.

"Well, I shall go prepare our meal. If you stop painting when the bells start ringing, I shall expect you about ten minutes later. You can bring your box with you and place it on the palier or in the vestibule. It is at your disposition."

She bows her head slightly in dismissal and begins to gather up her equipment. I go back to my painting. The work I've just finished is even better than I remember it. I start painting across the long façade of the nave, trying to vary the color of the stone with the shadows, with the staining of age, with the flashes of light through the trees, at the same time fighting to make it all hold together. I also begin working the foliage of the trees against this light. When I have a color I feel would be good in another place, I put it there. The statue of Diderot takes careful but loose painting, as I bring the color of the sky down into the color of the pigeon shit, as it blends to the color of the oxidized bronze. I'm beginning to feel that, in parts at least, I'm entering the painting and being inside it. Time seems to fly.

Then I hear the bells of the church ringing. I don't remember hearing them start, I was that much out of things. I quickly pack up my box. I put the bottles of turp and varnish into my pockets, rapidly clean paint off the brushes. I'm packed in no time. I look around to see if I'm forgetting anything. I have it all. I start off behind Diderot, to the mouth of the rue des Ciseaux, and down the hill of that small street toward the rue du Four.

On the left, I find number 5. It's an old building with walls slanted in from the time when mortar wasn't strong enough to support straight-up walls. The stairway is narrow, so I need to take the painting off the easel on my back to maneuver the tight corners. At the second floor, I put down my box and painting. There's a place under the electric box for me to store them. I knock.

Almost immediately the door is opened.

"I heard you coming up the steps. You had to stop because the painting was too big to come around the corner, am I right?"

I nod, then realize I must speak. It takes time getting accustomed to a blind person.

"That's right. I almost knocked the corners off the walls."

I go inside. It's a nice apartment but dark. It opens onto the court. Of course, for her, the darkness would be no disadvantage. Although it's neatly kept up, no disorder, everything in its place, the plaster is hanging from the ceiling, the wallpaper is loosened from the walls, hanging in strips, and the woodwork is unpainted, dirt-stained from constant handling.

The rugs are worn. It's a strange contrast between this well-kept woman, her carefully set table, the general order of the room, and the overall squalor of the apartment.

Also, to make it worse, on the two windows opening onto the

dark court are hanging ragged green curtains, faded with age into yellowish stripes. I see five doors I imagine enter into other rooms. The old lady is wearing an apron and she's smiling.

"Please, if you would like to wash up or if you have any needs, the water closet and the salle d'eau are over there."

I actually *am* awfully filthy, both from the way I live generally and because I've just come in from painting. I bow (invisible), smile (invisible), then, to compensate, say thank you. I move toward the door where she's pointed.

I go in, close the door to find it totally dark in the toilet room. I open the door again to look for the light switch and find it. I flick the switch, but no light. I look up and find the light bulb hanging on a cord from the ceiling with a green metal shade. I screw out the bulb, classic, French, old-fashioned, bayonet bulb. I can see through the clear glass that it's burned out.

I get myself oriented, close the door, lift the toilet seat, and, lining myself up with the toilet by my knees, let fly. Knowing her supersensitive ears, I pee against the side of the toilet so I won't make any noise. I hope I'm not peeing over the side onto the floor. I flush and open the door. I inspect. Luckily, I managed to get it all inside the bowl.

Then I go to the salle d'eau, a room with a basin for washing hands, cold water only, and with a bathtub, one of those tubs made from enameled metal and standing on lion's feet.

Again, the light switch doesn't work. I don't even climb up on the side of the tub to check the bulb. I imagine after years of someone blind living alone in a place, either all the bulbs get burned out by being left on with nobody to see them, or the thin wire in the bulbs goes bad and burns out the first time somebody happens to switch one on. French electricity tends to have surges which burn out light bulbs anyway, no matter how careful you are.

This time I leave the door open while I wash my hands. The tub has hot water as well as cold and there's an old-fashioned water heater hanging over it. I'd give a medium-sized watercolor just to soak for half an hour in sudsy water filled to the top of this tub. Instead, I do my best, washing up at the sink. The mirror above the sink has a layer of grime and flyspecks over it, so there's no way I can see myself. I'm not all that interested anyway. I just want to check and see if I have paint on my face. I often hold brushes in my teeth, not very professional, but I do it often, and paint smears on my cheeks.

I come out. The old lady is bustling about from the kitchen corner where she cooks, to the table where we're to eat. It's as if she never knew what it was to be blind. I wonder if the light bulbs work in *this* room. I'm willing to bet there's not a functioning light bulb in the entire apartment.

She indicates where I'm to sit and I do. There are clean cloth napkins and an hors d'oeuvre of coquilles Saint-Jacques, hot in the shell. This is the kind of haute cuisine I used to get at all those business lunches. Of course, when we were dealing with the French, it would be almost absurd, the food would be so good, and the prices were impossible, but I wasn't paying. OPM, other people's money, was what we were all spending.

There was one place called the Coq Hardi, about a fifteen-minute drive from my office, where we'd eat often, and they'd practically hand-feed us, a waiter standing beside each of us, passing different cutlery, different goodies. The bill after all that cosseting would be enough to keep me for six months now.

But this, right here, in this dark dingy room, is a good start toward one of those fancy meals. The old lady has taken off her red costume and is dressed in a dark blue sweater with a white collar showing and a dark blue skirt. The dull light is coming through the window behind her and shining through her hair. She wears it in braids tied tight around her head almost like a crown.

"Bon appétit, Monsieur le Peintre. I hope you like the coquilles."

"Bon appétit to you, too, madame. I'm sure I will. This is one of my favorite hors d'oeuvre."

"I am mademoiselle."

"Okay, mademoiselle. Bon appétit."

We eat slowly, carefully. These are some of the best coquilles I've ever had. It's a mixture of scallops, a white sauce, mushrooms, and Armagnac. There are also small shrimp, each about the size of a fingernail. I wonder how she manages.

"Have you been painting for a long time, monsieur?"

"It's a complicated story, mademoiselle. I studied painting a long time ago and then was in a large American corporation doing business, first in America, then here in France. Now I am back to painting again."

"Have you retired?"

"Yes, probably one could say I've retired, but I actually feel as if I've just started my work after a long interruption."

She's quiet. I don't really want to go into all of it. It's still damned painful. I remember I want to stop to check for mail at American Express, and write a letter. I'll stop by before they close.

To change the subject, I figure it might be time to bring up the idea of including her in my painting, at the foot of Diderot. For some reason, I've been putting it off.

"Mademoiselle, I hope you don't object, but I would like to paint you in my picture. I'd like to have you sitting with your pigeons on the stone bench at the base of Monsieur Diderot's statue."

She stops with her fork halfway to her mouth. She puts it down and wipes her mouth carefully with her napkin. She looks me directly in the eyes and I can see the beginnings of tears in hers.

"Thank you very much. I would be most happy to be in your painting. One of the worst things about being blind is the sensation, the conviction, that no one sees you. Most of the time I feel terribly invisible.

"Monsieur, it will give me great pleasure to know I am there in your painting, in the world I can no longer see, to be visible to all."

She looks down at the table and wipes her eyes gently at each corner with her napkin.

I had no idea it was going to be such a big deal. Normally, I'd start to get nervous. Sometimes when I was doing a watercolor people would ask me to put them in and I was always sure it would ruin the picture. Painting people isn't really my thing. Mostly, I guess I just haven't had much practice. But since she can't see, she'll never know, I can relax. No matter how I might botch her, it won't matter. I can even paint her out if it's too bad. Only the painting will know, and it's part of me. But I'm glad I mentioned it.

She stands up, comes over, and faultlessly takes my dish with the eaten coquilles and the small three-pronged fork, then moves into the kitchen corner. I can smell something delicious that's been simmering in a frying pan there. I'm hoping it won't be some half-raw red meat cooked the way most French insist these things must be done. I'm not sure I could handle it after all my vegetarianism.

But no, it's one of my favorites again. She *must* be a mind reader. It's escalope à la crème champignons and beautifully done, the cream sauce lightly flavored with the same Armagnac as the co-quilles, blending the two together. She brings some pommes frites allumettes to go with it, and thin white asparagus. I'm really getting the best of this deal. At this rate, I'll describe every pigeon in Paris for her if she wants.

And it's pleasant being with her, eating such good food in such a civilized manner. We eat, comment on the food, talk about pi-geons, something about my painting, nothing too serious. I know she's curious concerning me, but she's a real lady, no probing questions. It can be hard with women sometimes, especially Amer-ican women. They'll ask about anything, before you even get to know them. This is a wonderful woman of the old school, a true lady.

After we're finished with the escalope, she brings on fruit and cheese. Again, everything is perfect. How will I ever go back to my Mulligan stew again?

Finally, there's coffee, and she goes to another, tall cupboard, climbs on a small stool, and pulls down a dusty bottle. She wipes it off, then puts it in the center of the table.

The coffee, of course, is outstanding. We sip at it. She looks, if she *can* look, over the edge of her cup at me.

"Tell me, monsieur. Is there really a pear inside that bottle?"

It's one of those fancy bottles of Poire William. It looks as if it might be the *original* bottle, it's so dusty, faded.

"Yes, there's a pear inside."

"It is the last thing my father sent home to us before he was killed. My sister, Rolande, insisted we never drink it, that we keep it there, locked in the closet, in honor of his memory."

"That was very thoughtful of her."

"Monsieur, I should like to drink from this bottle with you today. It has been too long; it is time."

It's her decision. I really enjoy this particular liqueur, one can actually taste the gritty, pithy quality of the pear when it is properly aged, and this liqueur is certainly aged, in fact, I think it has even evaporated a bit.

"That would be very kind, mademoiselle. But are you sure you want to drink it after all these years?"

"Yes, I am quite positive."

She looks at me with those clear, sightless eyes again.

"Do you know how the pear gets into the bottle, monsieur?"

I'd never really thought about it. I know one can soak an egg in vinegar and then, when it's soft, slide it through the neck of a bottle, where it will harden, but I've never tried it. I guess I just wasn't curious enough. I don't imagine one could do that with a pear, anyway.

"No, mademoiselle, I have no idea. It is interesting to think about, isn't it."

"*I know how it is done. They wait until the blossom on the pear tree has been fertilized by the bee, then they place that blossom inside the bottle and tie the bottle to the tree. The pear is born, grows inside the bottle.*

"*When it is grown, they cut the stem of the pear, take the bottle from the tree, then pour liquor made from other pears on top. They close it up tight with the cork, and the pear remains in the bottle. It can never come out. Is it not a lovely idea, even though it is so sad?*"

She stands and goes deftly over to a drawer. She pulls out a tire-bouchon, a corkscrew, and hands it to me.

"*Would you be so kind, monsieur, as to open the bottle, and we shall drink this liqueur which has been waiting inside with this pear for over fifty years just for us today.*"

While I center the corkscrew and twist it in, she goes to the cupboard and comes back with two small glasses. They are etched on the sides with tiny cupids frisking in an encirclement of leaves. She watches, or appears to watch, as I pull the cork. I sniff and there is an aroma through the room. I hand the bottle across to the old lady.

"Please, would you pour, mademoiselle? I know the man is

supposed to do it, but this is such a special occasion, a private celebration, it seems only right you should be the one."

She takes the bottle from me. Her hand is steady. As she pours into each glass she has the tip of her thumb just inside the rim of the glass and, as the liqueur reaches it, she stops pouring. It's something I wouldn't've thought of. I guess, if I were blind, I would. We all have so many blindnesses.

When she finishes pouring, she carefully puts down the bottle. She holds her glass up to me and looks across into my eyes.

"Please, before we drink, would you tell me your name, monsieur. I do not want to be impolite, but it seems proper that when we share this we should know at least that much about each other."

That's natural enough. But I don't think anyone has asked me my name in almost a year. I'd almost forgotten I have one.

"I've been called Jack most of my life, mademoiselle. My real name is John, spelled J-O-H-N in English. But this past year I've been calling myself Jeán, J-E-A-N, the French way. It sounds better to me."

"I like your American name, Jack; like the English villain Jack the Ripper. But may I call you Jacques in the French style? I know it means James in English, but I'd like to call you Jacques."

She doesn't ask my last name, but I would have told her, for whatever it meant.

"And may I ask your name before we drink this delicious liqueur. this fateful beverage?"

"Call me Mirabelle, please, Jacques."

"But that seems so impolite, mademoiselle, I mean, Mirabelle. What is your family name?"

"That does not matter. I shall call you Jacques and you call me Mirabelle. You know, Jacques, there is no one left on this earth who calls me Mirabelle. My sister was the last one, and she has been dead for fifteen years. I do not want Mirabelle, the idea of Mirabelle, to die. Please, Jacques, call me by the name of my childhood, Mirabelle."

There are tears in her eyes again. We touch glasses, they clink with the sound of true crystal. I know I'm expected to say something.

"To the two of us, Mirabelle and Jacques, on this wonderful day, drinking to the dreams of our past."

"And to the dreams of our future."

She drinks and I drink with her. It is absolutely incredible. Never have I tasted a liquid so filled with nectar. It is as if the pears have been compacted, distilled, heightened in flavor until only the essence is left. We both sip, close our eyes, let the warmth flow through us, then, simultaneously, open our eyes and smile. It can only be coincidence. She could not match my smile and I know I am not consciously trying to match hers. She holds the glass against her breast.

"It is as if my father lives again. I can almost feel, hear him. Thank you so much, Jacques, for this wonderful moment."

We drink the rest of our glasses and I ease the cork back into the bottle. Each sip was like the first, an experience into another world.

"Jacques, I shall drink the rest of that bottle with no one but you. Is it too much if I ask you to déjeuner with me tomorrow?"

I'm slow to answer. One part of me doesn't want to get involved with anyone, even if it is only an old, blind lady. But another part does want to share time with her. I'm feeling ice clots breaking up inside me.

"Yes, Mirabelle, and thank you. But you must pass the test first."

She leans forward, obviously puzzled.

"Tomorrow you must tell me the color and markings of each bird when it comes to you. Show me what you have learned today."

Mirabelle smiles, the most spontaneous smile yet.

"I have learned much, Jacques. You shall be surprised."

Soon after, I rise, ease myself toward the door, pick up my painting box in the hall, and leave. Mirabelle "sees" me to the door. She's refused my offer to help her clear the table, help with the dishes.

"No, Jacques, I want this time to myself so I can savor the pleasure of our meal. Also, it would be wrong for you to stay in here on this beautiful day, when you have your painting to finish. Goodbye for now. Au revoir."

On the way down the stairs I start smiling about my new name, Jacques. I'm not even sure I can spell it. I know the way Mirabelle pronounces it, it sounds a bit like Jock in English. I never thought I'd ever be a "jock."

There are about two hours of good painting time left. I have some trouble handling the street in the foreground and the bottom right-hand corner. I think of putting in a bus at the bus stop, but that's against my idea of what I'm trying to paint. I don't want to put in any cars either. What I'm trying to paint is a Paris that transcends time somehow, a Paris which will always seem to be; yet, in another way, never was. I don't put in TV antennae, automobiles, or motorcycles, not even bicycles. When I paint in people I make them vague so there's no problem with dated clothes.

Also, I've found, if I put in a figure, no matter how hard I've worked on the entire scope of the painting, people will see it only in relation to that figure. I noticed this with my watercolors. I'd do an entire composition of buildings with shadows cast upon them, shutters, chimney pots against the sky, a sense of space, then I'd make the mistake of putting in a woman hanging out some clothes from one of the windows. People'd look at it and call my painting *The Woman Hanging Clothes out the Window*. But they'd buy it, much more frequently than if there were no woman at the window.

I'll probably have the same trouble with this painting. Nobody can resist ignoring the sky, the trees, the entire Church of Saint-Germain-des-Prés, Les Deux Magots, Diderot, the entire composition; it'll just be *The Lady in the Red Suit with the Pigeons*. So it goes. In this case, because of all that's happened, I can live with it.

I more or less solve the lower right with shadows cast by the trees in the garden and by putting in cobblestones, the cobblestones that used to be there but have been smeared over with asphalt. It isn't the best of solutions, but it's the only one I can come up with.

I find, in my paintings, I have the most trouble composing the upper left and the lower right areas. I never even notice I'm going to have this same problem again until I get there. Sometimes I think I'll never learn.

I scratch my signature and the date on the painting. It's almost invisible, just a scratch using the top of my brush. Then I turn it over, title it *Mirabelle with Diderot*, date and sign it. Mirabelle really fits in the painting. It's as if she's always belonged there.

The sun is off the front of the church when I pack up and start for home. Tomorrow I'll use another of my 25F canvases. I'm not sure just what subject I'll paint but I know it will be near to where I've been painting. I found when I was doing drawings and watercolors that each little quartier has its particular quality and one painting tends to lead into another. I'm half thinking I might try the Place Furstenberg. It's a beautiful Place and I've painted it three times with watercolors and drawn it at least four or five times. When things were desperate I could always sell a few watercolors or drawings of the Place, and it was fun doing them, it's a real challenge in its simplicity. There are a fair number of tourists who go through there but at the same time it isn't exactly a tourist trap.

I stop in at American Express just before it closes. There's nothing. I pull a folded sheet of paper and an envelope out of my jacket and use my drawing pencil to write a reasonably long letter. I try describing the painting I've just finished, and also tell something about the blind old lady named Mirabelle. I finish by assuring them

I'm fine but miss them all. I sign it with "all my love." I mail it to Lorrie at her new address.

The next morning, after my run, as I beat my way crosstown, I realize I'm looking forward to seeing Mirabelle, not just enjoying some more of her wonderful food, but spending time with her, absorbing her strength, vitality; feeling her concern, sensitivity, empathy.

The day is beautiful. More sun and fewer clouds, but there are still some soft, floating, spidery ones drifting quietly across the sky. Unless you stop and line them up with something on earth, it's hard to tell they're moving.

I'm wearing my usual painting outfit, a falling-apart, multi-stitched denim jacket I bought for twenty francs at the flea market. I didn't put on the green check woolen shirt I usually wear under it. The shirt's missing more than half its buttons but it's warm. When I ran this morning I realized today I wouldn't need it. I'm beginning to think I don't even need the jacket. Paris is giving us a little taste of what spring will be, real spring, maybe with a touch of summer.

I get to the site and elect to paint the Place from the uphill side and to the left of the street leading into it. I set myself practically *in* the Place because I want the lamps in the middle to be the center of my painting, sort of a focus around which the rest will swing in three dimensions; I'd like something of a merry-go-round feeling.

I do a rather careful drawing, keeping in mind the painting as I go. It's amazing how one can paint something several times and it's always different. I'm about to start putting paint on my palette for the underpainting when I begin to think of time passing. I don't have a watch. I forgot it, left it behind on the night table in our bedroom when I packed up, more than a year ago, so I ask the time from somebody passing by. It's just five minutes to ten.

I break down the box, swing it onto my back, and move up behind Saint-Germain-des-Prés to the Place in front of the church. I look across the street and there she is sitting in her usual spot. I try to see how close I can creep up on her before she senses me. I walk carefully. If anybody was watching, they'd think I *was* some kind of Jack the Ripper with a specialty in old ladies, because I'm practically walking on tiptoe. Before I get within six feet, she turns to me, smiles.

"I thought you might not come, Jacques. I knew you were not here and I was disappointed. It is so very good of you to come after all."

"It was the smell, wasn't it. You smelled me coming. Is that it, Mirabelle?"

She smiles and pulls out her second inflatable cushion for me.

"No, there is something on your painting box which jiggles when you walk, it sounds like metal hitting wood. I did not smell you until after."

"Do I smell that bad? What do I smell like, anyway?"

"Oh, Jacques, you want to know all my secrets. All right. You smell like turpentine, of course, and you smell something of perspiration because you concentrate so hard. And you smell . . ."

She pauses.

"You smell like a man. You have a special man smell about you. It is not the smell of tobacco as with my father or some other men, and it is not the smell of the different perfumes so many men wear these days. Sometimes it is hard for me to tell the men from women except for the sound of the shoes they wear, and even that is changing.

"You have a very special smell. I cannot describe it but I like it. The closest thing I can think of is the smell of horses."

I've finished blowing up my cushion and I sit beside her.

"I'd better not sit too close, Mirabelle. I never realized I was so smelly."

"No, Jacques, I like you sitting close to me. Remember, I enjoy your smells. They are very healthy, hardy smells.

"Now, are we ready for my test? I shall touch and feel my pigeons and then tell you how they look, is that right?"

"That's right. But I was only teasing, Mirabelle. It will be impossible."

"Let us see."

She puts out her finger and one of the pigeons, which had been hovering around her, lands. She picks it up, turns it over, inspects it.

"This one is a tannish brown with two brown stripes across the wings. It has yellower eyes than

most and its legs are a nice persimmon red. You admired the look of this bird and said it was almost acceptable, even for a pigeon. Am I right?"

She's right, all right. She's so right she's telling me things I don't even remember telling *her*.

"I don't believe it, Mirabelle. Come on, try again."

Another bird flies down. This time it's a heavy, dark blue bird with stripes on its wings, an ordinary-looking pigeon. Mirabelle strokes its neck with her finger and massages the feet and legs. She looks at me.

"This one is bluish gray with two darker bars on each of her wings. She has a sheen of color on her neck almost like a cock. She has pale pink legs and darker than amber eyes."

She lets this one fly away, after giving her grains from her little sacks.

"I am not sure what color amber is, Jacques. Is it more an orange color or yellow?"

We go through the entire flock. The only interruption to her perfect replay of what I told her yesterday is one bird, a small-sized, gray one, which had not come the day before. Mirabelle tells me immediately when she handles her that she does not know the markings of this bird. She knows it is one of the birds who didn't show up yesterday, that she is probably brooding an early nest.

An hour has passed and I'm ready to go back and start my underpainting.

"Where are you painting, Jacques?"

"I'm on the Place Furstenberg. I'm painting down the hill with the rue Jacob at the end."

"Oh yes. That is a lovely Place. I would play with a ball there when I was a child. It is one of my special places."

"What do you mean? Is it one of your favorite places?"

"Yes, that is true, but more than that. It is very complicated. You go paint now and I shall explain to you while we déjeuner. I must go now to prepare. The food for the week was delivered from the market this morning, so we shall eat well."

With that she begins putting her things together.

One of the strange aspects about being with a blind person, I'm finding, is when they stop talking to you, you *do* sort of disappear yourself. I stand, watch her a few seconds, and walk back across the boulevard. I'm still astounded at how she could describe all those birds in such detail. How could an old lady like this have such a remarkable memory?

On the Place, I'm soon into the painting. It seems no time at all before the bells of Saint-Germain-des-Prés start ringing, I have the sky and the left side of the Place with the bare trees roughed in. It's a good time in a painting, everything still seems possible.

We have another wonderful meal. I try to talk about my enforced vegetarianism, how I don't eat as much meat as before. She's served small tournedos of beef with fresh string beans and pommes Dauphine. It is magnificently prepared. This time I notice how she must be cleaning things up as she goes, because there's no mess in the kitchen, everything except the absolutely necessary pans and dishes is soaking in hot water in the sink.

Then she asks where I'm living. I tell her about my squatter's attic, how I cook, where I get my food, about my running, just about everything concerning the life I lead, even to the stink from the glue and noise of my hammering. I try to tell it as humorously as possible. If you think about it, considering everything, it is all damned funny.

She keeps staring into my eyes. There is a concentration beyond sight.

"But why do you live like this? What will you do in the winter when it becomes cold?"

"I survived last winter and then I had no attic in which to live. Now I have a home. This winter I'll buy an extra blanket at the flea market and be just fine."

We're finished eating. She goes over, picks up her stool, and reaches into her closet for the Poire William. I move to help her, then settle back. She's too quick for me. As she stands on the stool, stretches, slightly lifting one leg, I see her legs are thin like those of a young girl, perhaps a girl thirteen or fourteen years old. She wears thick old-lady stockings, lisle, I think it's called. She comes to the table. I know where the glasses are and take them down. She hands me the bottle.

"Please, Jacques, this time will you pour? I want to feel spoiled, taken care of, treated like a young woman, just a little bit."

She sits, ankles crossed under her chair. I pull out the cork, the smell of pears fills the room again, she inhales. I pour three-quarters of a glass each. I hand one glass to her, pick up my own, and we touch glasses.

"To Jacques, one of the finest painters in the world."

"How can you know that, Mirabelle?"

"Because I am blind? Most of what I know, I know because I am blind. I know you are a fine painter."

"All right, then: to Mirabelle, the best blind critic of paintings in the world. May all critics have such a depth of perception."

We sip. I remember.

"Mirabelle, you called Place Furstenberg one of your special places. What did you mean by that? You said you would explain."

She sips again, tilts her head toward the table, then looks up at me.

"You know, Jacques, I am not really blind."

She's looking me right in the eyes. I'm not surprised. I'm only wondering why she pretends. Why in heaven's name did she smash into me when I was painting, actually hurt herself. Am I involved with another total crazy?

"No, you see, I have perfectly good eyes, there is nothing wrong with them. I have perfect nerves to carry what my eyes see to my brain."

She pauses.

"But my mind, it will not let me see. I am what is called hysterically blind, aveugle hystérique. I have tried everything, but since I was fourteen years old I have been able to see nothing."

"You mean you don't see me now, here in front of you? You don't see this room? What do you see?"

"I see only the visions which are in my mind. I have my own world of things I see, but they are all ancient images, visions of when I was a child. Many doctors have worked with me trying to make me see again. My sister took me to psychiatrists and others. I was hypnotized many times. But I cannot see. Sometimes I think I shall never see.

"One of the things I was supposed to do, helping me see again, was to remember places of my childhood, places I loved, enjoyed, and then go to those places, close my eyes, try to remember everything that was there. After, I was to open my eyes and hope I would see these things of the real world, but they were never there for me.

"I have twenty-two places, all here in the quartier, which I have in my mind. They are almost like personal picture postcards, postcards I can bring before my mind. For many years, I would go to those places and concentrate, trying to see, trying to see anything, even the slightest light, but it never happened. Place Furstenberg was one of those places."

"What happened? How did this come to be, Mirabelle? It's terrible."

"It is terrible to you. But it is not terrible to me. The doctors tell me I do not see because deep inside I do not want to see. I am afraid."

"What are you afraid of, Mirabelle?"

"I am afraid of what I will see. I have learned to enjoy this private world in which I live. Yes, it is inconvenient being blind, but it is also very comforting."

"My God, whatever happened? Why are you afraid?"

She sips again and holds the drink against her breast. I've never seen anyone do that before, until she did it yesterday. Maybe it's a way to protect the glass from being knocked from her hand by accident.

"Perhaps another time, Jacques. I should like to talk with you right now about something important, if I may."

What could be more important than why she's blind? I wait.

"I should like you to paint my portrait. Since you have created me in the picture at the foot of Diderot it has given me much comfort. I feel I exist in the outside world, not just in the world of my imagination, inside my mind. Please, will you paint me?"

This I hadn't expected. It's so embarrassing. I sip some more of the Poire William, trying to figure what to say, how to refuse without hurting her feelings.

"I am not really a portraitist, Mirabelle. Since I was a young man, a student, I've tried painting portraits of people. I couldn't do it then and I don't think I could do it now."

"Yes, however, with this painting, you have no one to please but yourself. I cannot be a critic. I do not even know how I do look. I only want to

have you make a painting, an object, which says something about the way you see me, feel about me. It would mean much to have this happen."

"But, Mirabelle, it's so expensive. I'd be happy to paint you for nothing, but then I'd want the painting myself. Also I am running out of francs."

"You may have the painting for yourself, in any case. I would prefer that. But you cannot paint it for no money. I want you to charge me a regular price. This is a commission."

"It would be my first commission, Mirabelle. But you have no idea of the cost. I must charge three hundred francs for each painting to have enough to live."

"I will not pay three hundred francs."

She pauses. I'm off the hook. She just has no idea. I see her differently now, though. I see her as a painting. I *would* like to paint her if she would be willing to pose. I'd like to paint her inner calm, vitality, separateness, courage, if those things can be painted. It'd be more money down the tubes, more paint *out* of the tubes, but I still have a few francs left and then there'll be the tourist money this summer. Maybe I'll go up onto the hill at Montmartre, play animal with the others in the artists' zoo; I'm sure I could sell something there.

"Jacques, I must pay at least a thousand francs or you cannot paint my portrait. I would gladly pay more if you want it."

Hell, I'm not off the hook! In fact I'm *really* hooked. Mirabelle gets up and glides in that special way she has, not dragging her feet but hardly lifting them, feeling forward with them, as if she's sliding her feet into slippers with each step, moving quickly to the cupboard again. What other delicious goody will she pull out?

She takes down a metal box with pictures enameled on it. She pries the lid open, reaches inside, and feels around. She pulls out one, then two, five-hundred-franc bills. She closes the box and puts it up on the shelf again. She comes back to the table.

"Now you know where the blind old lady hides all her money. She does not hide it from herself."

She holds the bills out to me. I don't want to take them.

"Wait till I'm finished with the portrait, Mirabelle. This is crazy."

"No, but it is crazy waiting until the painting is finished before I pay you. What is the difference. This way you can have the money now and I would only keep it in that box doing nothing. You can buy paints with it so the painting can be better. That makes much more sense."

She leans the money closer to me, looking into my eyes the entire time. I take the money. She's right.

"If I come over to where you are painting now, on La Place Furstenberg, may I stay beside you? I will not be a bother, I want to feel you painting, know you are seeing, really seeing, that which I can only remember. Would that be all right?"

It's okay with me, but how's she going to get over? It means crossing boulevard Saint-Germain and that's a fast-moving, wide street, not exactly the kind of street a blind old lady should try to cross.

"You can come with me if you want. I'll help you across boulevard Saint-Germain."

"No, I shall clean up here first. You would be surprised how I can find my way. I go anywhere in Paris I want. At the boulevard, I listen to the feet. When they start moving across the street I go with the others. Also, there is always someone to give an arm to an old lady in a red costume with a white cane. I can sometimes almost see myself in my mind. Of course, the boulevard was completely different when I last saw it, but I can tell much from the sounds and smells."

So I take off. The light should be just right now. I'm realizing that, in the end, I'll be running two paintings at the same time if it's going to take me several days to paint each one. I'll need one canvas for morning light and one for afternoon. I'll really have good use for that thousand francs, just keeping myself in paint and canvas.

I've been painting about an hour when I look beside me and there's Mirabelle sitting in a little collapsible chair. She smiles.

"Oh, now you see me. I have been here awhile and you have been so busy looking, you didn't know I was here. Sometimes looking so hard can make one blind. Is that not interesting?"

I'm just getting into painting the globes of the light stand in the center of the Place. I swear each one is a slightly different color. If you didn't look closely, you'd think they were only white, but one's slightly bluish white, one's greenish, one yellowish, and the other has a violet tinge. I never would have guessed it until I tried painting them. I try explaining this to Mirabelle. Again she closes her eyes as I talk as if she's trying to cast up the images in her mind. We're quiet for a while.

"Jacques, do you mind if I talk about what I am seeing here, myself, in my mind, listening to the wind against the trees, smelling the street, the paint, you; remembering from when I was a little girl?"

"No, I'd like that very much, Mirabelle."

"Well, first I remember it was like a giant room, as if it were not outside at all. The trees make a great cover like an umbrella. There were benches on each side of the lamp and I would sit and stare at each of the globes, moving my head back and forth to watch my reflection move in each of them. The walls then were gray, blue-gray, violet, brown-gray, and when the sun would shine on them, they seemed to glow with a white luminescence not much different from the white in the sky between the leaves.

"Now I understand the walls have all been painted white and yellow and light colors of brown. It must be beautiful, but it is not what I have in my mind.

"It seemed then, as a child, that the street down to the rue Jacob was very long. We would roller-skate down that street, our skates strapped to our shoes, and we would roll hoops. There were very few automobiles and many horses. Only part of the street was smooth, the rest was stones. The rue Cardinale was only dirt. The windows were mostly open and will always be open in my mind, with

flowers at the windows and clothing hanging on little lines, like butterflies against the green of the trees.

"Also, at certain times, the trees would have purple flowers, the flowers would then fall, and we would gather them in our skirts and throw the petals at each other. It was a wonderful time."

She stops. She still has her eyes closed. She's brought such a freshness, a dreamlike vision to what I'm seeing, I find I'm integrating some of her feelings into my painting. I have alternatives for almost any decision I make in the painting now. There's what my eyes see, there's what my mind is seeing, the selective vision of the painter; and then there's the vision of Mirabelle's mind. It's the same as it was with the pigeons against the sky over Saint-Germain-des-Prés, I'm flying in her dream, painting her desires.

She keeps on talking, resurrecting the memories she's stored, cherished, all these years, speaking of the way it was, and it seems so much more real than what I'm seeing before me.

I begin to think I'm going blind myself, then realize it's only getting dark. I have no idea what time it is, but the painting is almost finished. I never believed I could get so far along on a painting in a single day. And what I've done is good, it holds together; more than that, it sings out the feelings I have, about Paris, about Mirabelle, and in many ways her feelings about Paris as a young girl, and now as a blind old woman.

I pack up the box. Mirabelle has some grains with her for the pigeons. Many from the flock at Saint-Germain-des-Prés come here to this Place and pick up bits of food tourists or others leave on the ground. When my box is packed, I lean against the wall beside where Mirabelle is sitting. It's a great little folding stool she has, I wish I had one for myself, sometimes my back gets tired standing. She turns to me.

"I feel it growing cooler. Is it really becoming dark? Is that why you have packed up your paints?"

"That's right, Mirabelle. It was getting so dark I was beginning to think I might be going blind myself."

"No, Jacques, that is not the way one goes blind."

She still sits there. The pigeons are all around her. It is evening and I guess that's when pigeon mating instincts come to the fore, because two or three cocks are doing the old courtship routine, puffed out, head bobbing, flight feathers dragging, rattling, on the ground, going round in tight circles.

"Are they dancing their love dance, Jacques?"

"That's right, Mirabelle. I guess pigeons spend more time courting than any other creature I know."

"But you know pigeons are mated for life. They do their dance around almost any hen, but they are mated for life."

"Somebody told me that once, but it's hard to believe. It certainly would be nice if it were true. I like the idea."

"Honestly. Have you ever seen pigeons mating in the streets, in public, as cats, dogs, even other birds do?"

"No, now you mention it, I never have. Maybe you've got something there, Mirabelle, about pigeons teaching humans how to live."

"They are only flirting with the hens, showing how they care for, admire, value them. I think it is most beautiful. I thrill to hear their cooing song, hear their feet pounding on the ground, listen to their feathers bristle. It is such a dance of meaningful, purposeless passion."

She looks up at me in the blueing dusk.

"You know, Jacques, there is not enough love in this world. Sometimes I think the pigeons are the last lovers in Paris. There seems to be much of sex in these times, but very little of true love, of love that makes all creatures come closer together, that allows one creature to express an inner feeling toward another creature so they know they are important and valuable to them."

She stands and I help fold her chair. I throw it over the top of my box. I offer her my arm and she takes it.

"Jacques, would you be my guest at La Palette on the rue de Seine? We can have a cup of coffee or something there. It is a place where artists have long gone. I have not been there for more than ten years, since before Rolande's death. Please, take me there. It would be such a pleasure for me to hear and feel the excitement of that place."

I've passed the café tens of times but never gone in. Café sitting just doesn't fit into my budget. I hope I'm not spending Mirabelle's savings. It doesn't seem fair or right.

"If that's what you want, Mirabelle, let's go. But I must pay. I'm a rich man. I have a thousand francs in my pocket right now."

I smile down at her, knowing the smile means nothing, is invisible, she cannot see it, but it makes *me* feel good. I'm smiling for myself.

She holds tighter on to my arm, not clutching, only tucking herself in closer. It's a lovely evening and we must make quite a pair walking into La Palette. We find a table in the back and both order a Cointreau. It seems the perfect thing to finish off a good day's work. It's going to cost more than a week's living but it'll be worth it.

Mirabelle has all her antennae out. I can tell by the almost ecstatic look on her face, the smile, the inner concentration. She's probably "perceiving" more of this ambience than I am, by far. I close my eyes and try to experience the way she does. While I have my eyes closed, the Cointreau arrives. I can tell it's there even without opening them. The smell of oranges surrounds us. I wonder if I would have smelled it if I'd been sitting there with my eyes open.

"Is it not wonderful, Jacques?"

She is fingering the round ballon of Cointreau, spinning it around in her small, pointed, thin-skinned, dainty fingers.

"I feel everything so strongly it's almost like seeing."

We clink glasses, she makes the first move, of course. It's been a long time since I've had Cointreau, and this isn't the best but it tastes good, not as good as that Poire William, but good on an early spring evening.

We sit sipping and listening. I'm also watching the coming and going, the flirting, the general horsing around of the young people. Why do artists always feel they need to make such a scene all the time? Probably it's what makes them artists, or makes them want to be artists in the first place. They want, need, to be *seen*. For some reason, they aren't sure they *are*. I wonder how much of that is in me. Probably anyone who has all the love, acceptance they need would never actually create, *do*, anything. They'd be complete within themselves. That would be the end of writers, poets, painters, singers, musicians, politicians, most of the people who help make the world go around, at least who strive for human communication.

It's dark when I escort Mirabelle home. She invites me up but I don't feel like sitting in a dark room while she wouldn't even know it. I'll have to buy a few light bulbs and slip them in around her place if I'm ever going to spend any time there.

I have a great walk home, I use the gate code number I learned by watching others punch it in, sneak up the stairs quietly, and settle in. I watch my painting for a long time in the candlelight as I eat a light supper. With all the lunches, I'm not eating up my stew for this week.

Blind Reverie

I feel so brazen. I wonder if he feels it, too, but he means so much to me. He must have some idea of my feelings, even if he can see.

I am confused. Knowing how my pigeons look has taken so much away. I thought my love for them would be more, but it is somehow less. I should have known. I think he is convinced I am childish, calling them by name, but they have been my only companions for so long. I hope he doesn't mind my calling him Jacques. He cannot know it was the name of my father.

I felt something negative when he came into the apartment. Can it be so dirty, unkempt? I must ask him. But I must go slowly. It was much, asking him to paint me. Now I am glad I did it. I wanted something we could share, a way to keep him near.

I think he likes my food. I could tell by the sounds as he ate. I am so happy to have found him. It is wonderful to have someone with whom I can share my pear in the bottle.

Chapter 3

The next morning I'm finishing the painting of the Place Furstenberg. I feel in control. The strong movements I established yesterday are holding up as I move into the more descriptive elements.
The light is coming through the trees and I'm using a tremendous
variety of color to capture the sense of light on the paving of the
Place. The painting is somewhere between Impressionism and
something different, a new kind of vision for me, a highly personal
vision such as Vincent van Gogh had, a conviction that the way I
see is valid.

I work all morning and then I feel Mirabelle beside and behind
me.

*"I can tell you are happy with your work,
Jacques. The bells are ringing, will you déjeuner
with me, and then perhaps we can start the portrait."*

How can she possibly know I'm just about finished? Do I give
off some kind of "satisfaction vibrations"? I scratch my signature
in the lower right-hand corner. I pull the canvas off the easel and

print in the title, *Place Furstenberg*, date and sign it on the back. I'm almost tempted to sign it "Jacques."

"Yes, I'm very happy with the painting. But I don't think I can start with your portrait because I have no other canvas here with me. I didn't realize I'd finish this one so quickly. I wish you could see it. It's the best painting I've done and you helped very much."

"Thank you. It means much to me to feel I could help. Can you understand what this must mean to someone blind such as I?"

Her face is very serious, then it breaks into a smile and she "looks" down at her feet briefly. She finds my eyes again.

"Could you not buy a canvas near here? I do not think the shops are closed as yet."

"It is very expensive to *buy* a canvas, Mirabelle. A canvas stretched, of the size I would need, could cost over a hundred and fifty francs."

She reaches into her purse. She pulls out two hundred francs.

"Here, please, Jacques, buy it. We do not know how long I shall be around to be painted and every day I am getting older. I should like to be painted as soon as possible, while I am still young."

"Okay. I'll give it back to you this afternoon from the thousand francs when I have it changed. That's only fair. All right?"

"Yes, if that is what you want. But you must hurry now to find a shop open before they close. I shall go home and prepare our food. It is mostly ready, but there are some last little things to do. I shall meet you there."

She turns away. The art store is just around the corner, not far from La Palette, where we had our Cointreau. I decide to leave the box standing in the Place. I put the painting back on the easel. I take off right away. Nobody will steal it in the few minutes I'll be gone. I start running, holding the two hundred francs bunched in my hand.

The bells are still ringing when I get there and they're open. The canvas, real linen on a good stretcher, 20F, with portrait linen, is a hundred and ninety francs. I feel like a rich man. But at this rate I'd be a candidate for the poorhouse in no time.

I dash back to my box and everything is fine. There are two people looking at the painting, a well-dressed French couple. The man asks me if I want to sell the painting.

I do and I don't. He's pretty insistent and I'm busy cracking down the box, putting things away. At the sound of my crappy French, he switches into good-quality, heavily accented English-English.

"But you must be in business, monsieur. Do you have a gallery where I may see your work?"

"No, I have no gallery."

"But you are a professional, yes. The painting is of very high quality."

"Thank you."

I don't answer the first question. I guess I am a professional but I don't think of myself that way. It sounds like a prizefighter or a whore. The French word *amateur* means "lover." I think I'm more an amateur, at least when it comes to painting.

"How much money would you take for your painting, monsieur? My wife and I like it very much."

I figure I'll name a big price to shut him up. I'm sure he thinks it's like Montmartre, where paintings are knocked out for nothing.

"The painting would cost fifteen hundred francs, monsieur. I must live."

He reaches into his inside jacket pocket, slides out a dark, shining leather billfold, and separates three five-hundred-franc notes. He hands them to me.

I could kick myself. I haven't had enough time to enjoy this painting. But, God, fifteen hundred francs, I can get through the entire summer with that. But I'm going to be very professional about all this.

I lift the painting from the place where I've leaned it against the wall and hold it at arm's length for a last long look at it. I feel I'm selling part of Mirabelle at the same time. I hand it to him.

"Be careful, monsieur. It is still wet. It will be a week or more before it is dry."

"That is quite all right. We live near here. We love this Place and thank you again for selling us your work. You are very talented."

With that, the two of them walk away carrying our painting. She's wearing a white fur coat and white stockings with clocks in them, slightly off-white shoes. Her hair is perfectly coiffed. He looks as if he could be the Prime Minister of France. Hell, I wouldn't know the Prime Minister if I fell over him.

Inside myself, I'm really torn. I need to tell Mirabelle. I've sold *our* painting. How will she feel about that? I put my paint box on my back, empty, and start the walk to her place. I'm carrying the new canvas in my free hand. Now I'm late.

I put the box outside and her door is open. I knock and go in. She's in the kitchen.

"I began to think you were not coming. Please,

let us sit down. I have little crêpes with mushrooms and a cheese sauce. I have just finished making them."

I go in to take a leak. I use the same "knee-locking" system as before. Then I go over and wash my hands, leaving the door open for light again. I've taken several sheets of toilet paper from the toilet room and I wet them. I try to wipe off some of the grime and specks from the mirror. The dirt's really ground in. I manage to clear a circle in the center of the mirror, enough to see myself. I haven't actually looked at myself in a mirror, up close, in a long time. I don't look as bad as I thought I would. I definitely look younger than I did two years ago. If it weren't for the gray in my beard I could maybe even pass for forty.

I sit down. Mirabelle puts three beautiful crêpes on each of our plates. They smell delicious. Again I close my eyes and let the smell come into me. It's getting to be a habit. Before I know it, I'll probably go blind myself.

"Mirabelle. I have something to tell you."

"The art shop was closed and you could not buy the canvas."

"Worse than that."

There's no way around it. I must tell her, I owe her that, at least.

"I sold *our* painting, the painting of the Place Furstenberg."

She's quiet on her chair, looking at me. She hands me a bottle of white wine, a Pouilly-Fumé, to open. I start turning the corkscrew.

"But that is very good, Jacques. You said you must sell paintings to live. We can always paint the Place Furstenberg again. It is in my mind, all of

it. It makes me feel happy to think we have shared our vision with someone else."

And I suddenly feel released. Mirabelle's right. I can paint it again. I'll paint it better than last time. I just didn't have enough confidence in myself. And I really do have over twenty-five hundred francs in my pocket, the thousand from Mirabelle and now the fifteen hundred. I reach in my pocket. I hold out the thousand francs.

"Here, Mirabelle, take this. I don't need it now. All you need pay is the money for the canvas, and you've already done that. We're even."

She pulls away from the money as if it were a snake.

"Do not do this, Jacques. You have a commission from me. I could never feel right if you do not take this money. Please, take it away. I can smell it in front of my face. It smells sour, a blend of dirt, cheap perfume, the inside of pocketbooks, and perspiration, as does all money. Please, take it away, or I cannot eat."

I put it on the table beside me.

"Well, we can discuss that later. For now, I want to eat these beautiful crêpes and drink this wonderful wine."

I hold out my glass and there's just the slightest delay until she realizes what I'm doing. No one would probably have picked up the slight pause, but I'm getting more closely tuned to her now.

"Yes, Jacques, we drink to the sale of your beautiful painting. I knew you were a very good painter. You should sell your paintings for much more money, you sell them too cheaply."

"I have more money than I can use now, Mirabelle. I know that doing things to make money can pollute life faster than anything else. I'm happy to have this money, but it must not become the *reason* why I paint. This is something I've learned."

"You will never paint for money alone, Jacques, only when you are hungry and desperate. Before that, you can come live with me."

We drink. The wine is dry and cooled just properly. It has a deep raisin taste, yet is light and almost effervescent. It's time to change the subject.

"Where do you get these wines, Mirabelle? This kind of wine costs almost as much as that painting."

"They are not mine. These are the wines of Rolande. Where she worked with the Ministère des Finances at the Louvre, she would always receive cases of wine at Christmas. We hardly ever drank them, so there are many cases stored in the cave. I am glad I can share them with you. I think Rolande would be happy, too. At least, I hope she would."

After the wine, we have a wonderful soufflé. To think of all I've heard about how hard it is to make a soufflé properly and here this elderly blind woman has pulled off one to match any I've ever had in my life. Mirabelle is a constant wonder. I find myself sneaking glances at her. In my mind I'm already starting to paint her portrait.

We finish off with our usual Poire William. We're coming close to the bottom of the bottle. I wonder what Mirabelle will want to do with the pear when it's all that's left.

She clears the table and pours two cups of coffee. Again, she makes some of the best coffee I've ever had. Perhaps this is partly because I have the chance to drink coffee so infrequently. I've heard it said that the best way to ensure yourself compliments as a cook is to keep your guests waiting until they're practically starved, and I'm sure in my past I've been victim to this theory, but with Mirabelle, everything seems to arrive just at the appropriate moment.

I watch as she so efficiently, gracefully, removes the dishes from our table, slides them into soapy water, rinses them, stacks them in a rack. It's like music, calming, just to watch her. I know I could never dance to her dance, so I stay seated, talk to her about the people who came up to me and bought the painting. I tell it with the kind of detached elation I felt, and it comes out as so funny, we're both laughing. Mirabelle comes over from the kitchen, drying her hands.

"Now, Jacques, are you ready to paint my portrait?"

"Yes. First I'll bring in my box and the new canvas from the palier. I think I'll paint you by the windows so I have enough light on the canvas."

I move toward the door. I struggle the canvas and box inside, closing the door behind me. There are only two windows in the room, both opening onto the court, so there isn't much light. But worst of all are the raggedy drapes, three-quarters drawn across the windows. They block just about any light that might come in.

"Mirabelle, would it be all right if I take down the drapes on the windows, or pull them back? I need more light to see."

"Oh yes, please do. I had completely forgotten

they were there. You must have been sitting here with me in the dark. Why did you not say something?"

For the first time, including when she'd bumped into me and fallen, she seems generally nonplussed, embarrassed.

"Oh, I could see enough to eat. But if I'm going to paint you, I must have more light."

"Please take them down. There is no one to peer in at me and I would like it if they did, at least somebody would be seeing me. We had those drapes up for Rolande."

I use the stool she's been using to reach up into the cupboard. I stand on it and find that the mechanism for moving the drapes is completely jammed. I lift the entire contraption off its hooks, lower the curtain, and step down onto the floor again. The drapes are coated with dust and so fragile they tear in my hand.

"I think these drapes are finished, Mirabelle. Do you want me to save them?"

"No. Please throw them away. The smell of the dust makes me feel as if I am dead already. Put them out on the palier. Later, I shall take them down to the poubelle."

I climb to lift down the other set of drapes. Same thing: jammed, rusty, dusty drapes, faded, falling apart. I lower them as I come down from the stool, wrap them around the valence. I take both of them to the door and shove them out onto the landing, the palier, where my paint box had been.

"I'll take them downstairs when I go home, Mirabelle."

Now I look at the windows. They're as filthy as the mirror had been. But I'm not going to clean them now. The weather is mild, maybe I can open them.

"Do you mind if I open the windows, Mirabelle? It will clear the air. If you feel cold you can wear another sweater, perhaps."

"Oh yes. That will be fine. What would you like me to wear for this portrait?"

"I think just what you are wearing now, your dark blue sweater with the collar."

"Is my hair in order?"

She feels over her head, shifting bobby pins and maybe hairpins over and around her head.

"You look wonderful."

I move one of the chairs from the table and place it so I have a three-quarter light falling on her face. It gives enough penumbra, but not too much. I can pick up the features on the shaded section, even in this limited light.

"Shall I sit in the chair now?"

"Not yet. Perhaps you can finish cleaning the pots and pans from our wonderful meal, if you want, while I open my box and prepare myself."

I'd noticed that in her cleanup she'd left some pans soaking in the sink.

I wedge the long back leg of my box under the window. I want to have enough light on the canvas and still not have the canvas block my view of Mirabelle. I want the eye level of the portrait at my eye level and at just about the same eye level as Mirabelle. I'm going to paint her one and a half times life size. Painting on the vertical dimension, this should fill a 20F just fine.

I'm all settled in when Mirabelle sits in the chair. I need her head turned more to the light with her sightless eyes seeming to look at me. I want the dynamic of the two directions. I wonder if when I paint her, her eyes will seem empty, they don't seem that way to me at all. I have the other chair set up in front of my paint box. I stand and go over to where she's sitting. I put my hands on each side of her face and turn it so the light is just right. I think it's the first time I touch her face.

Usually, from the little experience I've had with painting portraiture, one asks models, after they've been posed, to pick something and fix their eyes on it. But this is obviously impossible in this case. She does the mind-reading trick on me again.

"I can hold my head still like this because I know where you are and I can feel the open window."

I start my pencil sketch with a 3B pencil. I'll move up to 6B later on when I'm more sure. I really don't like working the drawing with charcoal and then blowing fixative on it the way they taught me those long years ago at school. I draw with the pencil and correct with a soft eraser. I begin drawing and concentrate for at least fifteen minutes, getting her placed on the canvas, having the right relationship between head, body, and negative space. I want her placed up high on the canvas but not too dominant. I make quite a few erasures before I get the proportions and angles I want.

"Please tell me, Jacques, how I look. No one seems to look at me, or, if they do, they have never told me. Many times I would ask Rolande how I looked but she would only say I was quite pre-

sentable, or sometimes when she was cross, that I was too pretty for my own good. But that was a long time ago.

"I can feel with my fingers that I am getting older. There seems nothing one can do to stop that. It is only natural, is it not?"

She pauses. I'm trying to concentrate, get it right, what's she talking about now?

"Do I have gray hair, Jacques?"

This is going to be hard but I want to be truthful. I look away from the painting, up at her.

"White, Mirabelle, you have white hair. There are some dark hairs in your eyebrows, but the hair on your head is practically white."

"Oh dear! I have begun to think so. At first, twenty years ago, I could tell some of the hairs were stiffer and were hard to manage. I imagine they were the white ones. They were not like the kind of hair usually growing on my head. Now they are all the same, all stiff and straight. You know, it is hard for me to think of myself with white hair. Is that not silly? Here I am, seventy-one years old, and I actually almost did not believe I had even gray hair. I feel like such a fool."

"None of us ever really look at ourselves, Mirabelle, even if we can see. Perhaps it is best, it helps us sustain our illusions."

She's quiet for a while. I'm working on the relationship between her eyes and nose. She has a lovely, thin aquiline nose with visible, slightly flaring nostrils. Her eyes, her non-seeing eyes, are set wide and are large. It's so hard to believe she sees nothing.

"Yes, you are right; perhaps that is why I do not allow myself to see. But tell me, do I have wrinkles in my face? Of course I do. Would you please tell me about them? I want to know, I really do."

It's hard to concentrate because that's not the part of her face I'm working on yet. I can see this is going to be quite a problem painting her. I lean back and look.

"Yes, Mirabelle, you have wrinkles. So do I. I'm forty-nine years old, so naturally I have wrinkles. Without wrinkles nobody's face would be very interesting.

"You have a wonderful line of concentration, slightly to the left, between your eyes, and a smaller one just beside it. Then across your forehead you have four questioning lines, unevenly spaced, going all the way across. Two of them intersect on the left side. There are lines coming out of your eyes on each side, mostly smiling lines, lines from avoiding the glare of the sun. No, that can't be, the glare of the sun would mean nothing to you. They must only be smiling lines. You do smile often, you know, Mirabelle.

"There are lines down the sides of your mouth from your nose. These are the deepest lines in your face. They come right down past your mouth to your chin. Those are the main lines on your face, the most visible, but not the most important."

She's quiet some more. I get back to work with my drawing. Again, by having explained to her, I'm seeing better. The spacing between the eyes and the mouth is better related to the length of the nose. This can always be a problem in doing a portrait.

"*And what other lines are there?*"

I don't stop drawing this time.

"Well, there are all the lines that come with aging, with the gradual loss of skin tone, small crosshatch lines, the lines from the pull of gravity on the skin. These are the usual lines which don't really tell much about a person, what they are, the way they've thought. They're only the lines that come naturally as anybody gets older, lines of normal skin aging."

I don't mention the lines I'm drawing in now, those lines that run down into the upper lip, the lines of a shrinking face, the most prominent aging marks on almost any face. I hope she doesn't question me anymore.

"*Am I ugly, Jacques?*"

This is asked in a very low voice.

"No, Mirabelle, you are quite a handsome, mature woman. I'm sure you must have been a very pretty girl and a lovely young woman, as well. I'm quite proud and happy to be painting your portrait."

I can say this and really mean it. There's something mystical, almost childlike in her face, her voice, and all her moves, which denies her age. Maybe blindness helps people not get old too fast. Perhaps she's been protected from so much of the distraction, the impact, the stress of ordinary city life, she's been preserved in some way. There's a strange quality, so fresh, new, clean, about her.

"*Do you think anybody could ever love me, Jacques? Be honest now, please.*"

What a question! I finish up with the curvature of her cheek before I answer.

"*I* love you, Mirabelle. You're one of the finest, most intelligent, sensitive, and interesting people I've ever met. I enjoy your company. I feel like a better person when I'm with you. Does that answer your question?"

And I'm not lying.

"*Thank you, Jacques.*"

I hope that's the end of it.

"*But I mean, really love me; want to make love, faire l'amour with me. Do you think it is at all possible for some man to feel that way?*"

Well, this stops me. Maybe I'll just pretend I didn't hear her. But I can't, the intensity of her question demands an answer.

I sit back, look at her, look at the drawing. Actually, it's coming along pretty well, considering everything. I'm beginning to realize there's a young girl locked up in this old woman's body. It seems sad. It's like the pear.

"It's not impossible, Mirabelle. You are really a most attractive older woman. It is only because you are blind you do not have enough opportunity to make contact with enough men, and Rolande was so protective of you. I'm sure some intelligent man your age would want to have an intimate relationship with you."

I lean forward to work again. How much more does she want? I'm surprised at how embarrassed I am. Then she comes straight out with it.

"*When I was younger, when I was thirty years old, I wanted very much to have a baby, to be a mother. I thought if I had my own child, maybe*"

I would want to see it so much I could let myself see. I was sure that, given a chance, I could find a man who would make one with me, even though I was blind. He would not have to marry me, or even see me again, I didn't care. I just wanted my own baby.

"Oh, how I wish I knew you then, Jacques. But you would only have been a young boy in America. Ah, it can be difficult, these things, time is strange.

"Rolande was so shocked, so angry. She said it was immoral and where did I get such ideas? She said I could not take care of a child, that I could not even take care of myself. She said all the responsibility would be hers. So I stopped talking about it, but I did not stop thinking about it."

She stops, smiles, "looks" at me, slightly turning her head in my direction.

"And now it is too late. I am a virgin, Jacques, and I do not want to die a virgin. I feel I have great capacity for giving and receiving passionate love but I have never had a chance. It does not seem fair."

There are tears rolling out those wrinkles from the sides of her eyes, and down the outside of her face. This is more than I can handle. I'm feeling sorry for her, at the same time I'm feeling boxed in. I try to keep my hand steady as I develop the line of her jaw.

I've stopped working. We're staring into each other's eyes. She, of course, can't see me, and I'm not seeing her as a subject for a portrait. I guess I'm seeing her as a woman for the first time.

"I know you are a good and kind man, Jacques, someone I can trust, or I could not talk to you like this. I am surprised at myself. Please forgive me."

"There's nothing to forgive, Mirabelle. It must be terrible for you to be so alone. I must tell you, I'm a married man. I have a family, I love my wife, my children. Even though I am separated from them now, I feel responsible to them."

There's a long time while she's quiet. She's stopped crying. I lean back into the canvas, my drawing starts coming alive again. I wouldn't think I could keep drawing with all the emotional stress I'm feeling.

"I am sorry, Jacques. I did not know. We know so little of each other. While you are drawing me I should like to tell you something about myself. You deserve to know."

Blind Reverie

It was so exciting for me when he called the Place Furstenberg "our" painting. It is the way I felt myself, it was something we did together.

I do not think he particularly noticed when I suggested he could live with me, perhaps he did not believe what I was saying. I almost did not myself.

It is so strange being painted. I can almost sense myself being seen, I have a sensation of his eyes upon me. It made me feel very real. I could not help myself. I wanted so to know what he was actually seeing. And then, more, what I looked like to him, as a man, not only as an artist. Am I truly a woman, yet, still? I hope I did not scare him by almost offering myself, but I have known from the first moment we came together, this was a man I could love with all my body and soul, give of myself and feel gifted.

I must be more careful or he will be frightened away. I did not think he was married, at the same time, I could not think of a man like him being alone. He feels, seems, the way my father was, a true family man, a man a woman could love deeply.

I hope I am right in telling him about myself.

Chapter 4

"We were a very happy family in this house, Jacques. Perhaps it is only because my memories are so old, so worn down by wishes, by tears, that it seems so. Still, I remember many wonderful things.

"My father worked in reliure, book binding. He had a beautiful reliure on the rue des Canettes. It had been the place of his father and his grandfather before him. He loved his work. Sometimes he would bring it home with him to share with us. It was wonderful to feel the smooth leather and rub our fingers over the mounds of string bindings and etching of titles on the spines of books.

"He was kind to us. Always on Sundays and Mondays he took us to the Jardin du Luxembourg, or the Jardin des Plantes, or the Parc Zoologique at Vincennes. He loved life, he loved us, and he loved our mother. I do not think it is only time which makes it seem this way. I remember so clearly. It is one of the things about being blind, there is not so much to cloud the vision one has of the past.

"Our mother was a nervous woman, she was afraid of many things, but when my father was there, she was never afraid. We would row in the wooden boats in the Bois de Vincennes or in the Bois de Boulogne. We had picnics and played games. It was a very calm, beautiful life.

"Then, when I was only ten years old, came the Great War. My father had to leave immediately. My mother cried for days. When she stopped crying, I never remember her smiling again, except when she received letters from my father, or on the two times he came home to us on leave.

"My sister and I went to school at the Alsacienne on the other side of the Jardin du Luxembourg. Rolande was three classes ahead of me. We were happy students.

"It was October eleventh and I was released from school three hours before Rolande, because she had piano lessons on that day. Each of us had our own key around our neck, under our uniforms. I had my books in my arms. All this I remember very well.

"I came into the house, calling for Maman. It was the time when she always had a goûter for us. In the kitchen there was nothing. I could not imagine Mother not being home. She rarely went out, especially after Father was gone. I looked into each of our bedrooms and there was nothing. The door to the WC was open. I carefully knocked on the door to the room of my parents, then pushed the door open. There was nothing. I was beginning to be frightened. The only room left was the bathroom, la salle d'eau. I knocked and no one answered. I pushed open the door, it was not locked.

"There was my mother. She was in the bathtub and the tub was filled with blood! Her eyes were open. I went down on my knees beside her. I still did not know what could have happened. I was so young. I had just had my fourteenth birthday and also had begun with my règles. My first thought was that somehow my mother had had her règles and was bleeding to death.

"When I touched her she was cold. The blood in the tub was only slightly warmer. I saw the razor of my father on the edge of the tub. I still did not know, could not understand. I only wanted to lift my mother out of the blood. I reached down into the depths, staining my school uniform, and pulled the plug to let the blood and water drain. As it drained, my mother sagged into the depths of the tub. I started running fresh water, crying, scream-ing, but nobody came. I washed the blood from my mother, calling her name over and over, not her name but Maman, MAMAN!

"When she was clean, I lifted her in my arms and somehow struggled to her bed. I stretched her out as best I could, crying and screaming all the time for help. I pulled her nightgown over her cold, naked body. I wanted so for everything to be all right again, for my mother to be warm, to speak to me. I remember I could not fit her arms into the sleeves, so I pulled the nightgown down over the tops of her arms. I opened the covers and slid her into the bed. I pulled off my own clothes, down to my chemise, and crept in beside her.

"I wanted to warm her. I had seen the slits, the gaping wounds of her wrists, but they did not seem bad enough to kill. They were not bleeding and they were water-shriveled. My only thought was to hold her in my arms and make her living, warm again, bring her back. I held her to me and cried until I went to sleep.

"When Rolande came home, that is how she found us. Afterward, she told me she almost backed out and closed the door, thinking we were only taking a nap, but then saw blood on the floor, went into the wet, still-blood-soaked bathroom, and came out screaming. She was three years older than I and knew enough to be aware that something terrible had happened.

"She tried to waken us and I woke, saw her first, then looked over and saw the eyes of my mother, empty, staring, not seeing. It was the last thing I remember, the last time I saw. It was her eyes, open and not seeing. I did not want to see any more. Inside, I think I wanted to be like my mother, my eyes open but not seeing.

"I do not remember the funeral. It was as if I were dead. I did not want to eat, to breathe, to live. In the bedroom, they found a telegram saying my father had been killed. It seemed everything I loved in life, my mother, my father, was gone, and I wanted to be gone, too.

"The mother of my mother, our grandmother, came to live with us and take care of us. Her husband was also dead. She was always tired, and Rolande had to stop school before graduating, in her 'Terminale,' and help with the house and help take care of me. When I was twenty, my grandmother died, too. The shock of losing her husband, then her only daughter, my mother, had killed something inside her.

"At first, it was assumed my blindness was temporary, that when the first shock wore off I would see again. I remember then, as I still remember now, how I did not want to see. I see often in my dreams the eyes of my mother, open eyes, not seeing, and yet I know she was seeing all that others could never see. I wanted to be with her, to see with her, to see my father.

"For many years, doctors tried to help me. I did everything they asked, but there remained deep in me the terrible fear of seeing. My mind did not want any more of this world to come through my eyes. It did not trust them, I suspect I still do not trust them, and that is why I do not see. It is difficult to understand, yes, Jacques?

"Rolande managed to pass her baccalauréat and obtain a position in the Ministère des Finances because our father had been killed in the war. She worked all her life there.

"She had a man friend whom she loved. He also worked at the ministère, but he was married and had a family. He could never marry Rolande and she, because of me, could never marry, either.

"We lived together here, the two of us, in our family apartment, all the years. Rolande and I were never close as sisters. There was the age difference, my blindness, and also we were quite different people.

"She was not a happy person. Her work was boring to her and, aside from her friend, she had no pleasure. I am not sure how much pleasure she had with him in later years. She never talked about it to me. We did not talk to each other very much at all on any subject. She treated me as a child.

"I filled my days by taking care of the apartment the best I could, by doing the cooking. I started with my pigeons. I became interested in learning languages, using records, then tapes.

"Rolande was usually home with me evenings. She would read her newspaper, or listen to the radio, *later watch television. Sometimes she would go to a film or go to meet her lover. On nice evenings we would sometimes walk on the boulevard together.*

"Her friend went on retraite into the country with his wife when Rolande was only fifty-five years old. He was ten years older than she. It was very hard for Rolande.

"Rolande died fifteen years ago. She died of a stroke which killed her almost immediately. She was at work when it happened and only a few months from her own retraite.

"Since then I have lived alone. People from the Sécurité Sociale come once in a while to see if I am all right. I receive a benefit from the death of my father as a soldier. I also receive a benefit because I am blind. Rolande left her money to me, this apartment is mine, and I am comfortable.

"During the years, I have found ways to fill my time. You know there are the pigeons. Then, although Rolande objected, twenty years ago I began to do yoga and to meditate. It gives me much comfort, and my blindness helps me obtain very high states of inner calm.

"I have continued my study of languages. The Mairie on the Place Saint-Sulpice has a wonderful selection of disques and tapes from which I can learn. Also, through the Bibliothèque Nationale I borrow tapes of many kinds, including much music. Through them, I have learned to speak English,

Italian, German, and Spanish. In this way, in the streets I can understand the tourists and it is a pleasure for me.

"I also learned to love music and am familiar with much music from the seventeenth, eighteenth, and nineteenth centuries. I have a special interest in music of the Baroque period, especially music for the harpsichord.

"I never learned to read braille. I still keep in mind that I am really not blind and someday will see again. Therefore I am not willing to take the time necessary to learn this method of reading.

"As I said, I love music very much. In what was once Rolande's bedroom, I have my harpsichord, I also have now a large collection of my own tapes. It is a passion for me. I play, not at a professional level, but proficiently. I perform, make a tape of it, and listen to what I have done, that way I can improve. I do the same with my language lessons. I listen, then I speak, trying to perfect my accent. Then I listen to myself. I think, in my life, I have heard myself speak more than anyone else in the world. Is that not strange, Jacques?

"But I am very lonely. I want to tell you a story which will give some small idea of my aloneness.

"When I had learned to handle the pigeons so they trusted me and would come to me, I began crocheting little holders I could slip onto their legs.

In the holders I would put the same message. It said:

I SIT EVERY DAY UNDER THE STATUE OF DIDEROT BETWEEN TEN AND TWELVE IN THE MORNING. IF YOU WOULD CARE TO SPEAK WITH ME, PLEASE COME. I WEAR A RED COAT AND HAT.

"*I sent this message out on all my pigeons over more than ten years and no one ever came. I thought perhaps the pigeons were too shy or afraid and people could not catch or hold them. Perhaps some came but did not speak with me when they saw I was blind. I do not know. I never told Rolande about this. It was my secret.*

"*Then, one day, I was sitting alone on the bench when I smelled a man coming toward me. He had a very strong smell of man, almost as strong as some of the clochards. He touched me on the shoulder.*

" '*Here, madame, I believe these are yours.*'

"*He reached down with rough hands and took my hand. He turned it palm up and dumped into it what turned out to be more than fifty of my old crocheted leg bands with the messages still in them. The holders were falling apart with age. Sometimes the paper of the messages had become stiff, and when I tried to unroll them, they would crack.*

"The man sat beside me. He was a very kind person. He told me he is the one who cleans out the bell towers for all the churches in Paris. He cleans each major church about once every ten years. He scrubs and rubs linseed oil into the great oaken beams which support the bells. He oils and greases the mechanism of the bells, checks for cracks or other faults in the bells, replaces worn parts. He also cleans out the bell tower. He has been doing this since the war, the first war, that is, and is looking forward to his retraite. He told me many things.

" 'Madame, most of the pigeons that die in Paris die up there in the bell towers. They become so weak they cannot fly down and then fly back up. So they roll into a ball and die on top of the major support beams for the bells. There are sometimes hundreds of pigeon skeletons and feathers I sweep into sacks and carry away. There are often birds who are dying, but there is nothing I can do for them. They would be eaten by cats or run over by cars if they flew out of the tower.

" 'Up there today, with the dead pigeons, I found all these little bits of wool packets with paper in them. I opened one and read it. I looked down and saw you. So here I am.'

"He would not come home to eat with me, but he unpacked his lunch box and ate his lunch on the bench beside me. He has a wife and two children.

Both of his children have gone to southern France. When he goes on retraite, he and his wife will go there to join them.

"He ate lunch with me several days while he cleaned out the tower. The main brace on one of the bells needed repair and it took two days to forge a new piece.

"As a final gift, he gave me the key to enter the tower. I have kept it these many years. He said it was just in case I ever wanted to go up there and feel what it is like to look down on everything. He said he would be on retraite long before anyone else went up to clean the tower again.

"I think he meant I should go there and look down to see the Place, Diderot, the café, the Jardin, all the places where I live. I do not think he ever really appreciated what it is to be blind. He knew I could not see, but he was not the type of man to understand truly what blindness is.

"I have kept that key in my silverware drawer for more than ten years, but I have never gone up. It would be too difficult to climb alone, and dangerous. Perhaps you would like to go up there sometime. There might be much to paint. If you would take me up with you once, I should like that very much, too.

"So now you know something about me, Jacques. I do not think I have spoken with anyone about these things since Rolande died. Mine is a strange story, is it not?

"I have been quite content in my own way. It is probably bizarre learning all those languages for nothing, but I enjoy it. Also, sometimes I can help tourists when they are lost. I hide my cane and try not to appear blind. Probably my vanity makes me do this.

"Does any of this make sense to you, Jacques? I only want you to know why you mean so much to me; why I could be so bold as I have been.

"If you do not understand, I understand. I sometimes do not know just what it is I want. My life seems empty and dry, lately. As I said, I feel that something is coming to an end and I have been only an unseeing spectator. I have not really been a part of real life. I am always on the outside looking in with my sightless eyes.

"Am I complaining too much? I do not like people who complain. It is so easy to be aware only of personal problems and not let the problems, cares, of others be important to yourself."

I haven't been able to draw since she started her story. I slowly squeeze onto the palette the paints I'll need for the underpainting. I scrape another clear place from which I can work. I'm in shock.

Mirabelle had stopped crying while she was speaking. Her story's so terrible, so hard to believe. I look at her and am moved as I don't think I've been moved in years, perhaps since our first baby was born.

I stand and walk over to Mirabelle; I drop to my knees. She puts her hand on my head.

"I'm so sorry, Mirabelle. Except for your blindness, none of this suffering seems to show. You are so positive about life, you live as if nothing had happened. How do you do it?"

"It was all a long time ago, Jacques. I only wanted to tell you so you would understand. I didn't want this which I carry in my heart, which makes me the way I am, to be between us. I hope it can bring us closer."

I stand and look down at her.

"Do you feel strong enough to continue posing or should we say this is enough for the day? I feel now I can paint a much better painting of you than I could before you told me about your life. I even see this apartment differently, knowing the good life that went on here, the suffering, the long time you've been alone. I should have known it, but I didn't think about it deeply enough. It is a bad problem I have, Mirabelle, I can know things and still not feel them."

"Is there enough light for you to continue, Jacques? I should like to stay here with you this way some more. I think the blind learn how to be still more than most people."

I walk back to my box and look around at her. She seems so small, so fragile, so alone. I've known only her strength, her courage, her incredible skills, and now I feel I know her much better, more profoundly.

I start with the background, I choose a blue modulated with alizarine crimson. I had thought to do the background in warm colors, with burnt umber and burnt sienna. Now I know this would not be right. Those are not the colors of blindness, of aloneness. They give too much warmth, intimacy; the intimacy I felt for her, still feel, but that would never be enough to make the painting true. I know now this part of her must be painted *into* her, not around her. She must stand out in her aliveness against the coldness she has known.

"Jacques, you spoke of your wife and your children. Would you be willing to tell me about them while you paint? I should very much like to know about you, what life you have behind you. In my blindness, I feel I do know you, but only the you which is here right now. You have not told me much about yourself except for the way you live, and that life does not seem appropriate for the man I feel I know. Would you tell me what you can?"

I know I won't to be able to paint while I talk, but I start creating movements of paint in the background to the painting of Mirabelle.

"Mine isn't a very interesting story. It is so ordinary, so much like thousands of others, it is almost not worth the telling. I've told no one about my past life before, partly because I wasn't sure what has been really true and what I've made up, or didn't notice.

"Often we are deceived more by what we don't know than what we think we do. But if you want to hear this, I'll try to put it together in my mind and tell it as accurately as possible. It might be a big help for me to tell you. You're the one person I know with whom I can try to be honest or even really care to."

"Please go on. You do not need to keep painting unless it will help you tell your story. I understand. If you want, I can make some tea or coffee."

"No. I want to stay like this in this dying light, Mirabelle. I'll stop painting when my eyes tell me to. If you become tired of sitting, or listening, only tell me. If you want to sit in a more comfortable chair, say that also, or just move."

Blind Reverie

At first it was so painful to bring it all back, to tell Jacques of what had happened. But I knew I had to do it if we were ever to be close. He had to know me as no one had known me, not even my family or the doctors.

Then, as I spoke, it was as if a light were being shone into all the dark places. It did not make the darkness any lighter, but it made it more visible in my mind. I could look at things I had not been able to face for many years; in some cases, since they happened.

I wondered if this might be the beginnings of sight again, if I will lose my desire to hold on to my personal darkness. But as I went on, I realized I was only sharing my darkness with Jacques. I was still safe, only not so alone. I felt his heart beating with mine, feeling my pain, and my life already seemed richer, more valuable, worth living.

I hope I have not given him such a terrible share of pain to carry that he will become afraid. What can be in his life that makes him so unhappy? In one way I want to know, in another I am afraid of what I will learn.

Chapter 5

"I don't know where to begin, Mirabelle."

I put down my brushes and slide down on my chair, staring at the canvas or at Mirabelle, but mostly at the painting, at this effort to bring her alive through my eyes, my brain, my hands.

"To tell something of how I came to be here in Paris, in the streets, painting, I need to go way back in my life, if anything is going to make sense at all."

"Begin at the beginning, please."

"I was good in school, Mirabelle. I had loving parents and two loving sisters, both older than I. Maybe it started there. It was as if I had three mothers and they all loved me, made me think I was wonderful.

"From the time I can remember, I wanted to be an artist. My mother and sisters encouraged me; it was all part of my being different, exceptional, for them. But in high school, because I did well in mathematics, in science, there was no chance for me to take art. I was scheduled into college preparatory classes. I enjoyed them, it was challenging, and I was in classes with the more interesting students.

"I don't know if any of this can mean anything to you, Mirabelle. It's all so American, so much a part of a different way of life."

"No, Jacques. Tell me. You know, because of my eyes, I cannot read. Hearing you tell about another life in another place is very interesting to me. More than that, I want to know you, how you became what you are. One wonderful thing about being blind is I can enter into your voice, feel your feelings, see the things you tell me about in my mind, with nothing to interfere. Do you understand?"

"Yes, Mirabelle, I think so. Now I'll try to tell everything that had to do with my life which I think had some part in bringing me here to this place in this moment.

"Back there, in school, I joined the art club, it was after school. I was more proud of this than of my good grades.

"My father, who was an electrician, worked for Westinghouse. He wanted me to be an engineer. He labored every day in his dirty overalls and always had dirty hands. He worked with men, engineers, in white shirts, who wore suits and ties, whose hands were never dirty.

"He wanted his only son to be like them. He'd show me his beaten-up, dirty hands and that was enough. It was his personal badge of failure.

"World War II was going on during my high-school years. As part of a speed-up program, I was selected to go three days a week in a bus with five other students to a technical school called the Drexel Institute, in Philadelphia, to study engineering. My father was intensely happy about this. Somebody in the family was going to be *somebody*.

"I enjoyed the studies, but even then I knew I would never be a happy engineer. Too much of it was so predictable. Engineering was making everything as predictable as possible, eliminating all room for error. Art is living with the possibility of error.

"By a series of strange accidents, too complicated to describe, I found myself, in September of 1943, at eighteen, in the infantry as a private. By chance and good luck, I didn't get killed as your father did. I did, however, learn one thing: if I survived, I was going to be an artist, not an engineer. I had my *own* one and only life to lead.

"My parents were so happy to have me home in 1946, after I'd been gone three years, they didn't complain much when I told them my decision. I think I could've said I wanted to be a trapeze artist and they would have agreed.

"My father said, 'After you've spent six months with all the weirdos in art classes you'll be happy back in engineering.'

"I studied art at the University of Pennsylvania. My grades got me in and the government was paying the high tuition with the GI Bill. It was the chance of a lifetime."

I start lightly indicating the darker areas of her face. There is a concentration, an empathy, I want to capture in my painting.

"My father wasn't completely wrong. The art department at Penn was mostly women, and the men, except for a small contingent of veterans, were borderline. The overt sensitivity, theatricality, and inbred exclusiveness of the others were hard to live with.

"But I was learning perspective, color theory, learning how to use different media: pastels, watercolors, tempera, canvas, various kinds of paper. The government was paying for all my materials, too. It was truly a dream come true.

"A good part of the faculty shared their preferences with many of the students. Cliques formed. The teaching was very esoteric, with a sprinkling of pseudo-Picasso spread over dramatic, erotic, exotic abstraction. My own aesthetic did not fit. But I did learn.

"I was like a maniac in my excitement and joy. In order to pass my classes, I dealt in muted colors, flowing curves, breaking up any surface or area into prismatic bits and painting them with subtle designer colors. I learned to dramatize almost to theatrical levels when it came to painting. There was much Sturm und Drang, suffering, with a capital S, necessary in our drawings. One teacher wanted us to tie our hands to a doorknob and slump to the floor so we could experience *real* pain.

"It was all so artificial, but I didn't care. I did one kind of work for school to get by, but I was using the paid-for materials, the big well-lit studios, all these advantages, to work out my personal aesthetic on my own time.

"I was convinced, still am, that the world is intrinsically beautiful, and that I could see it and somehow show it to others, share my vision, without all the artifice, the theater, the intellectual rationalizations. I was almost like a missionary in my convictions.

"But I did begin to think I might have made a better engineer. Sometimes the simplicity, the cleanness, of draftsmanship would exert its appeal.

"I managed to survive the role of outcast in the art department, ate my own aesthetic, managed good grades, and became a member of the Art Honor Society. However, I was losing confidence that I was actually becoming an artist. These teachers at Penn were turning me into a designer, a member of a special fraternity or priesthood. I learned to outtalk almost anybody when it came to discussing painting: emphasis and subordination, plastic quality, transition, analogous colors, all kinds of nonsense which didn't have much to do with what I thought art was about. It was very frustrating. Do you understand, Mirabelle?

"I still just wanted to communicate from one person to another by making an honest personal statement about what I felt. This was not what 'art' at Penn was concerned with at that time. It was mostly trickery in an attempt to get attention, any attention.

"In school, in an English class, I'd met a wonderful girl who was studying at the Wharton School of Business. She was specializing in personnel management. She had no personnel to manage, no family business to go into, and it all seemed strange, meaningless to me, as removed from reality as what I was doing in the art department.

"But we had fun together. We both loved to dance, to row on the river, to visit the museums, the aquarium, but mostly we loved each other. We married when we graduated.

"She was offered a job in a pharmaceutical concern, somewhere between secretarial work and personnel management. I found an old garage in South Philadelphia, just across the South Street Bridge, not far from the University. I started painting seriously, painting the way I wanted. I sold nothing, no one was interested. I took a night job in an art agency, doing color corrections. It all looked dismal. Then Lorrie and I found out she was pregnant.

"I went back to Penn and took a teaching credential, a special credential to teach art in secondary schools. I managed to get a position in September; the baby was born in October. I tried to keep painting. Lorrie seemed happy as a mother, or at least convinced me.

"We'd found a small old house in a row of run-down houses, not far from my studio, where we could afford the rent. I was a reasonably good teacher but I still wanted to paint. I was becoming interested in some of the assumptions we'd all made as art students, about the communality of vision. The incipient engineer was striking back.

"The art department couldn't, wouldn't help me. I found a man in the psychology department who was interested in what I wanted to try. He managed to get me a grant for my project.

"Are you *sure* you want to hear all this, Mirabelle? The more I go on, the longer it gets, I'm practically telling you the story of my life. Besides, it's getting dark."

"It's always dark for me, Jacques. If you do not mind going on, I should like very much to hear you. It is growing cold, though; would you close the window? I shall make us coffee and we can eat some cake I have here."

She stands and goes into the kitchen. I stand and turn around to close the window. There's still a little light in the sky but not much. I hear the scratch of the match and its flare as Mirabelle begins heating water. In the near dark, I take down my painting box, then move the chairs back over to the table. Mirabelle brings the two cups of hot coffee and some cake on individual plates. It's even more astounding to me seeing her move so easily now it's getting darker. In half an hour I won't be able to see my hand in front of my face, but for her nothing will have changed.

The coffee and cake are delicious. I didn't realize how wound up and, at the same time, how tired I am. Mirabelle sits in the chair across from me, her eyes just visible in the dark. She's waiting. I take a long breath, let out a sigh, and go on.

"It was hard living for us. Lorrie's parents didn't have any money to help us with, either. Then, less than a year later, we find that Lorrie's pregnant again. The first one we named John after me; Lorrie said if this next one is a girl, she could have any name but Lorrie. She was never going to name a girl child after an English truck. It was another boy and we named him Albert, after my dad. I felt he'd been so disappointed in me, he deserved at least this.

"We were always short on money. I had to give up my night job at the agency so I'd have time to do my master's thesis. Even so, because I was teaching days in a junior high school, I was having difficulty establishing myself as a resident student at the University. In those days, things were much more rigid.

"I titled my thesis *Differential Visual Perception and Its Relationship to Certain Personality Variables*. Basically, this meant I was trying to demonstrate how people see differently according to the way they are. I think most people suspect this, but nobody except a Swiss named Rorschach, a long time ago, had tried to prove it. I worked a great deal with his set of ten ink-blot cards.

"Klopfer and Kelly, the main interpreters of Rorschach, became my heroes. I got my master's degree just before Lorrie delivered our third child. This one we named Helen, after Lorrie's mother.

"The thesis was well received and published in the most prestigious of the psychological journals. I received a few hundred dollars a year more from my school district because of the degree and was offered a period off every day to act as a grade counselor. I thought that was the end of it.

"I'd proven to my own satisfaction what I think I always knew, and now could shake off the encrustations of four years in art school at the University of Pennsylvania, maybe get on with my own painting.

"Mirabelle. You don't have to listen to this. It gets more boring before it gets better."

She stands. She walks over to the wall where I've stood the portrait. I can barely see it in the dark.

"How I wish I could see what you are seeing in me, Jacques. Please, continue with your story, I find it very interesting."

I know now I'm telling all this as much for myself as for Mirabelle. It's like sorting out cards that have gotten jumbled up and are spread on the floor. They're the same cards, but now, seen in order, they aren't so confusing, incomprehensible, to me.

"About a month after the publication of my thesis, I received a phone call from California. We'd just gotten our phone and I thought one of my buddies from the school where I was teaching was putting me on.

"It was from an organization called the Nard Corporation. It was what they called in America those days a 'think tank,' a place where supposedly intelligent people were brought together to solve problems and think together. They'd do something they called 'brainstorming,' where they'd take an idea and try to look at it from all sides.

"The man on the phone said they'd read my thesis with great

interest and wanted to know if I would fly out to California and talk to them about it. They'd pay my plane fare and a per diem of a hundred fifty dollars a day.

"I was shocked. I was only making slightly more than twice that a month teaching. I said I'd call them back. I told Lorrie and she said she'd be okay and I should go. I then called my school and had more trouble getting time off there, but they agreed, finally, to find a substitute for me for a week, but it would be deducted from my pay.

"I called Nard Corporation and said I was on my way. They'd already made plane reservations and scheduled a meeting with those who were concerned. I guess they're not accustomed to being refused at a hundred and fifty dollars per diem. I don't imagine they often were, especially in those days.

"It was January, and I arrived in California in bright sunny weather. Except for my military time, which was all cold, wet, and the wrong direction, I'd never traveled, never been in a warm-weather climate.

"I carried my overcoat on my arm and went to a hotel on the beach where they'd made reservations. I wasn't in the room fifteen minutes when the phone rang and someone at Nard asked if I would care to join a small group for dinner at a private home. It was like living in a film, and here I was in filmland. It was so different from anything I'd ever known.

"The dinner was comfortable, informal, my hosts and their guests never mentioned the subject of the scheduled meeting for the next day. It was only later I discovered that most of the Nard Corporation 'thinking' was financed by the U.S. Air Force and all these people were very secretive, very security-conscious. I was an outsider and being observed; but I enjoyed myself and the dinner.

"Next day I walked across a few streets to a low-lying brick building not more than a few blocks from the Pacific Ocean. I was stopped at the entrance. I was asked to wait and one of the guests of the evening before came down, signed a series of papers, gave me a little plastic badge to pin on my jacket, and I followed him inside, past guards, into an elevator, and up to another floor.

"The meeting was held in an ordinary-sized room with a long table and folding chairs. I was asked to sit at one end of the table.

"This sounds like a science-fiction story, doesn't it, Mirabelle. You can't be interested in all this."

"But I am, Jacques. I am truly."

"Well, to make a very long story short, they felt, from my thesis, that with my art background, and my experience with computers doing the statistics for the thesis, I was just the kind of person they were looking for.

"You see, Mirabelle, I'd done my analysis of the data for my experiment with an early computer, a miracle of that time, something that looked like a series of pinball machines or jukeboxes and cost four hundred dollars an hour to use. I managed to wangle a half-hour grant. The material inserted into it had to be organized on little cards with holes punched in them, then strung on spindles. It's amazing how things change.

"They wanted me to help man one of what they called silos on the DEW Line. DEW had nothing to do with water on the grass in the morning. It stood for Distant Early Warning system. They wanted to teach me about more sophisticated computers, then have me design programs of artificial situations to be flashed onto radar scanning screens. There would be men in these silos who would watch, scan, for unidentified aircraft, meaning planes or missiles, to bomb the United States. It didn't sound very interesting to me. It sounded too much like the engineering I'd abandoned. But when they told me the salary they'd pay, *five* times what I was earning as a teacher, I became interested.

"I would live in the silo for a month at a time, not leaving it. Then I would be rotated home and could spend two months with my family. My family was not to move from where they were. Before I could be used, it was necessary I be cleared for security, also Lorrie.

"One of the men there asked a series of questions about my background to see if there would be any problems. I've never joined anything, not even the Boy Scouts. My family couldn't afford the ten-cents-a-week membership fee. Politics have never meant anything to me, I'm still not interested.

"They said my training would start immediately. I would be trained in computers right at home, there at the University of Pennsylvania. Then, as soon as my security was cleared, I would have on-site training at a place unnamed and virtually inaccessible. I could tell my wife I was working for the government but no more. I was to tell no one else anything.

"It all happened so fast, seemed so overwhelming to me, Mirabelle, that I was uncomfortable. But those who were presenting all this information looked exactly like the people who had sat in for the oral defense of my thesis. There was the usual sprinkling of pipes, tweeds, beards, mustaches, heavy-soled low-cut handmade shoes. It was hard for me.

"That night, in the hotel, I called Lorrie. I was sure the line was being monitored. I was already becoming very paranoic about the entire business. But I was fascinated, too. I only told her I'd been offered a job at five times what I was making teaching, but I'd have to be away from home a lot more. I told her I'd work for the government, as a sort of artist-engineer. I explained I would be trained right there across the bridge at Penn, but then I would be assigned to a place, undisclosed, for a month, but then could be home two months.

"She was excited. There didn't seem to be any objections and she was sure I'd be home when the baby was born. It turned out she was right. I was still studying at Penn when Hank, our last child, came. Lorrie had her tubes tied. She wasn't yet thirty and felt four children were quite enough.

"And so that's how I started working for the government. The work wasn't too boring and I became fascinated with the new computers. Gradually, with my mathematics and art background, I developed a reputation as a specialist in computer graphics, at that time, in the mid-fifties, an almost unknown technology.

"I worked through C.S.D., a subsidiary to Nard Corporation, during the next three years. Then the concept of the DEW Line, as an effective means of defense, came under scrutiny. I came back to the Nard Corporation headquarters in California to help develop new approaches.

"I moved with my family to San Jose, California, near the Nard Corporation. I rode a bike to work every day. I was making even more money. We had a house near the hills. The children were going to good schools. We bought a new car. It seemed our lives were unfolding like a precast dream.

"Then MBI came into the picture. They offered me a contract

and a salary twice what I was earning at Nard. They offered security. I knew they were the biggest computer organization in America. At that time, it was difficult to even *buy* their equipment, they'd only lease it. There was tremendous opportunity for someone with a background like mine to advance. My friends at Nard encouraged me to make the jump and I did. We moved again, this time to White Plains, New York. This was in 1960, I was only thirty-five.

"During the next ten years, we lived in three different places, each time buying a new house, settling in, then being moved again. We lived in Atlanta, Georgia; Raleigh, North Carolina; and Minneapolis, Minnesota. Probably none of these names mean anything to you, Mirabelle, but they were all far apart from each other.

"My job was constantly changing. I was on what they called the fast track. They were training me for upper executive or management work and moved me around to see how I adapted. My performance ratings were good."

"But, Jacques, you were a big success. How does this story get you to being a painter on the streets of Paris where we met?"

"Be patient, Mirabelle, that part comes soon enough. Or perhaps we should wait for another time when I can tell you more of my life. It is dark now. I can see nothing. I'm sitting in the dark and I can't see you."

"Perhaps that is best, Jacques, to sit in the dark, if you do not mind. Please go on, you cannot just stop here. Have some more coffee, it is not too cold yet."

She pours without hesitation. I can just make out the cup in the dark.

"All right, now comes the difficult part. I don't know if I can tell this so you will understand. Listen carefully and tell me what I did and why I did it. Please, Mirabelle.

"During all this time, as my career progressed, as I became more and more important in the company, Lorrie and the children suffered terribly, and I didn't even notice it. I wasn't as aware as I should have been to the way their lives were affected.

"It's so easy to become involved in a way of life all day and, artificial as it is, it becomes your real life, taking the place of your family, your true life.

"In some strange way, MBI, the people I worked with, *became* my family. I don't know when the competition for getting ahead of the next guy, holding on to my position or improving it, began to become more important than the work I was actually doing, or, even more difficult to understand, how I lost contact with my wife, my *real* life, my children, making a home, love, being together, doing things together.

"I would be at work before seven in the morning, trying to be the first one there. I'd leave before the children were awake, then not be back until after eight in the evening. The children, usually, would already have eaten; sometimes, when they were young, were even in bed. Lorrie would wake with me mornings, then stay up to eat late-evening dinners. It must have been hell for her. And I wasn't even noticing!"

I try to pierce the deepening gloom of the room to see if Mirabelle is understanding. Her eyes are only dark holes in an indistinct paleness. I'm wishing I hadn't started this whole thing. Maybe there are some private aspects to life one should keep to oneself.

But that's what I'm trying to avoid now. I *want* to be vulnerable, to be known. I don't want to hide my feelings anymore. I'm sure it's part of what I did wrong. I sigh again, drink the last of the cold coffee in my cup.

"But I was making a considerable salary, Mirabelle, a salary I could never have dreamed of. In 1970, only five years ago, when I was forty-four, I was making over a hundred thousand dollars a year, plus stock options. We each had a car. I had a little Porsche and Lorrie had a big Chrysler station wagon. She needed it to haul the kids back and forth to all the softball games, dancing lessons, swimming lessons, tennis lessons, horseback riding; to deliver or pick them up at friends' houses. We had a five-bedroom, three-bath house in a good section of Minneapolis. It was the success about which we'd been taught to dream. We had it, or at least, *I* thought we did.

"Then one day my boss called me in. He came around his desk and shook my hand. I was suspicious. With a big outfit like MBI, it's a bit like being in the army; often the worst blows, the most horrible assignments, are delivered with smiles and congratulations. I waited.

" 'Well, it's confirmed, Jack. It's just been posted. You've been reassigned to . . . Paris, France. It should be at least a three-year assignment. You know what this means. This is the big test to find out if you're international-quality material. You'll be attached to MBI France and you'll be chief of personnel there. It's the big plum. You *really* are on the fast track, congratulations.'

"God, I'm wondering, how am I going to break this to Lorrie? She's just feeling settled in, here in Minneapolis. She has a group of women friends she meets with every two weeks or so, where they let their hair down, sort of work out all the things that bother them, she calls it her support group. The kids are all happy with their schools. Jack is supposed to graduate from high school this year. He has a good chance to be valedictorian and he's captain of the track team. I try to keep a smile on my face.

" 'Thanks for letting me in on the good news, Fred. Of course, I'll need to check it out with the family first. It's going to be quite a shock.'

" 'It's the chance of a lifetime, Jack. If you don't grab the brass ring now, you'll just be on this merry-go-round here, along with me, until they give us the old engraved gold watch.'

"I work my way out of Fred's office. I know he's keeping a stiff upper lip. This means he's been passed over, for me. I should be happy but I dread going home. I decide not to phone but just clean things up on my desk, and go home early. I want to be home at four just when most of the family will be there.

"And so, when I get home and everybody settles down, I tell them. Lorrie cries. Jack stomps up the stairs. The other three seem stunned. Lorrie recovers first.

" 'How soon would we need to leave? Will Jack have a chance to graduate?'

"I'd checked. They wanted me there before the end of April. That was only a month away. Like the army again, with MBI it was so often hurry, hurry, hurry, to wait. I was sure there couldn't be any great emergency or situation for which I was needed in Paris. I tried to tell Lorrie this.

" 'But it's so unfair, Jack. They're all happy here. We've paid our dues. You should be allowed to settle in for a while, especially with kids all in high school. Isn't there something you can *do?*'

" 'Well, I can say no, Lorrie. But then I'm ceilinged. This is MBI's way to find out if I'm top-grade material. I hate to miss the chance, but we'll do whatever you say.'

"That wasn't fair of me, Mirabelle, I know it now. Lorrie loved me too much, knew how involved with the company I was, to refuse.

"The next morning the kids stayed home from school and I stayed home from work. We talked it over. I tried to point out what a tremendous chance it would be to spend some time in Paris, to learn French. They'd go to the American School there, and it had a good reputation. Jack, our oldest, wanted to stay on, living with friends, but Lorrie said no, whatever we did, we did as a family.

"That week we started packing. I came over to France and found us a house in a place called Le Vésinet. It wasn't far from the American School and was a suburb not much different from where we lived in Minnesota, except the houses were more like little châteaus than modern ranch houses or English town houses. Everything was close together. But the house I found had a big lawn and it looked okay to me. The rent was outrageous, but MBI would take care of that. I came home with pictures from the realtor. Lorrie could have gone with me to make the choice but didn't want to. She said she had too many things to do at home first.

"So, by the last week in April, we were here. The company'd packed and sent all our furniture. I was swamped right away with the new job and began to find how hard it was to work here in France. I'd never really done any work in personnel before, either; that was Lorrie's specialty. The guy who had this job before me was French and all the Frenchmen I worked with hated my guts. I guess they were afraid for *their* jobs.

"Somehow, Lorrie had the new house fixed up in about a month. She's tremendous at that kind of thing. She says she hates it. Her claim is she always knows when MBI's going to transfer me. It's just when she gets the drapes hemmed. After the first two moves, she began hemming with temporary stitches. She said this time she wasn't even going to put up drapes.

"A bad part of this job was that I had to travel so much. There were branches all over France and I was the one in charge of all personnel: hiring, finding housing, arranging for French lessons, firing, making changes when there were severe personality clashes, and, more than anything, keeping the French and Americans from each other's throats.

"Most of the French were fairly reasonable. MBI has a good name and they were making outstanding salaries, with better in-centives and perks than they'd get with any French company. It was mostly the Americans who were trouble.

"Some of them couldn't adjust to the French way of doing things. A lot of them just hated France and the French. More often, it was the wives. They didn't know what to do with themselves. Some of them had held good jobs at home and were forced to give them up. There was much resentment.

"Then there was the adaptation to the schools. They had a choice of going to a regular French school, which was free, but awful by American standards. Or they could go to the Bilingual School, taught in English and French, but the kids had to wear uniforms. There was also the International School, which was small and in the center of Paris with no real campus. But the best choice, from what I could learn, was the American School of Paris. It was in the western suburb where we were living, but was expensive. Luckily, MBI paid the tuition. This American school was the only one run according to an American curriculum and was the one most of the MBI people chose.

"Our children were accustomed to a typical big American advantaged, suburban-type school and, to them, this school looked like a painted-over concentration camp, a narrow, pie-shaped campus with a muddy football field, no yard-stripe markings, and a track around it looking as if it had recently been plowed.

"The high-school classrooms were all about the size of closets compared to what they'd had in Minneapolis. Also, on one side of the school was a high-speed highway, and on the other, a railroad track with trains passing every twenty minutes. Our kids couldn't believe it when they actually saw it.

"But we were there. I felt guilty. I should have checked out the school situation better. From the beginning, I spent more time than I wanted fielding complaints about the school from other MBIers. I volunteered to serve on the board of trustees at the school and see if something could be done. It would also look good on my C.V.

"I talked to our kids and to Lorrie. I said it was something we'd just have to live with. I knew they had no baseball team, no regular football, only soccer, no swimming pool, and so forth, but it had a good reputation, academically, and after all, that's what school was for. I didn't get very far.

"We slowly settled in. Lorrie was great about it. She tried to make the best of things. The kids gradually were integrated into the school and enjoyed being big fish in a small pond rather than the way it was in Minneapolis.

"My work was a constant challenge, more than I really wanted, and there wasn't much reward. Lorrie wasn't very interested in Paris. We'd go in on weekends to visit the sights, but this was mostly for me. I was excited by the museums, the galleries, the *power* of the city. The kids, in general, were bored. They liked going up the Eiffel Tower, visiting the Arc de Triomphe, a few things in that category, but Minneapolis hadn't exactly prepared them for a cultural experience such as Paris. And there were no McDonald's or Burger Kings.

"One of the things they hated was learning French. The school had a rule everybody must take an hour of French every day. In general, they had French people teaching the French classes. That made sense except they didn't understand American kids. A good part of our kids' complaining was about their French teachers.

"Teaching French to the American MBI executives and their wives was one of *my* big headaches, too. MBI had hired a private firm to tutor our people on a one-to-one tutorial basis. Within the year, I began to see this was a serious problem. The company used attractive young women to teach the men and handsome young men to teach the wives. There'd already been some trouble before I took over the job, and we'd had to make two transfers back home to alleviate domestic situations. Mostly it was the men getting involved with the young, good-looking teachers, but there were two cases of the women having affairs with their French tutors.

"I had enough to worry about without this. I called in the man who ran the French teaching program for us. I suggested that, for reasons of domestic tranquillity, he assign men to teach men, and women to teach women. He gave me a classic French shrug.

" 'But, monsieur, they will not learn as fast. We have had much experience.'

"I checked the files and found my predecessor had run into the same problem, made the same suggestion, and it *was* as this professional had suggested.

"I pondered, and wrote a carefully worded memo regarding socializing with the French tutors. It was definitely to be discouraged. I hoped that would be the end of it, but feared it wouldn't.

"I was right. In two months, we had two good men, both with top-flight recommendations, records, get involved. I hired an American therapist, with a specialty in marriage counseling, to help out.

"Finally, I calculated that with the amount of effective work time being lost, the cost of the tutors, the cost of the therapist, and all the disturbance in the staff, it wasn't worth teaching French to our American employees and their wives. Most of the French who worked with us spoke English, anyway. But the powers-that-be in MBI were convinced a knowledge of the national language was necessary, so we continued. I was already beginning to look forward to *any* other assignment."

I sigh and look around at the dark surrounding me. I can hardly see Mirabelle at all. Those two narrow, dirty windows in this room don't let in much light even in the daytime; now it's almost pitch dark.

"Mirabelle, I'm tired, I can't go on. Maybe I can tell you more tomorrow while I'm painting you."

Her voice comes out of the darkness.

"As you say, Jacques. Your voice does sound tired and it begins to sound sad. When do you want to continue our painting?"

"I'd like to paint you in the morning light, or in the early afternoon light, whatever is convenient for you."

"I do my yoga and exercises in the morning, then I take care of my pigeons. Perhaps you could déjeuner with me and after we can do the painting. I remember the light comes in the windows better in the afternoon than in the morning anyway."

We agree to that. She suggests I leave the paint box and canvas; that's great with me. She asks me to stay and have a small souper with her, but I want to get home to my attic. Inside, I'm upset from telling what I've told. I feel empty and naked. I'm eager to leave.

"All right, Mirabelle, I'll see you there by the statue of Diderot, then, just as the bells are ringing."

I stand, start feeling my way toward the direction of the door, bump against the table.

"Oh, I am so sorry, Jacques, it is dark, is it not, you cannot see. Let me switch on the light."

She goes to the light switch and, of course, nothing happens. As I suspected, this light is burned out, too.

"Did the light go on, Jacques? I do not feel the warmth."

"No, Mirabelle, I think all your light bulbs are burned out."

She's silent for a moment. Then she starts making a strange sound. At first, in the dark, I can't recognize it, then know she's giggling, giggling like a little girl.

"Oh, is this not terrible, Jacques? I never thought about that. You have been sitting in the complete dark talking to no one. Is that not true?"

"No, I knew you were there, Mirabelle."

I start laughing myself. We giggle and laugh together in the dark. I feel her coming toward me.

"I am sorry. I did not think. Would you please buy some ampoules so you will not be blind with me. I can give you money now if you want."

"No, I won't need any money, Mirabelle. Remember I'm a rich man."

That starts us laughing again for no reason. She's close enough now so I could touch her. She reaches out with her hands and puts them on my arms. I smell her pale perfume, like a fading, light yellow rose.

"There would be nothing wrong if you kiss me on the cheeks in the French style, would there, Jacques? I would like it very much."

She leans forward, and in the dark without much to aim at, I kiss her on each cheek and she kisses me on mine. We stay just a moment like that.

"I must go now, Mirabelle. I am so tired I can hardly stand. Because I do not need to carry my box and paints, I shall take the bus. Thank you for listening to me."

"Thank you for telling me about yourself. I have

much to think about. I know it is hard for you to speak of these things from your past. I thank you, also, for painting me. A demain."

I find the door and open it. I push the button for the minuterie in the hall, and the stairway lights up. I feel as if I've regained my sight. I know she's at the open door listening to me go down the steps and I turn to wave, realizing, at the same time, she cannot see me.

At home, I just pull down my sleeping bag and stretch out. I light one candle but don't do anything else. I'm not hungry. I only want to stop my head from going, to find oblivion. I undress, climb into the bag, and find it more quickly than I thought I would.

Blind Reverie

It was terrible to realize that Jacques had been sitting in the dark while I was not noticing. He is such a gentle man and so kind telling of the happiness in his past life, telling it to an old blind woman in the dark. I do not know what I can do to make him know I understand, understand as only a blind person knows darkness.

It sounds as if he loves his wife and children very much. What could have happened to bring him here to Paris, living almost as a clochard in the streets? Perhaps there was a terrible automobile crash or something which took his loved ones. I cannot even think what it could have been.

He seemed so weary, so tired of everything, as he spoke, even at the happy parts, parts of which he should have been very proud. It is difficult to understand.

But the life he describes is so unlike the man I know, it is impossible to imagine him living it. And then, that company, MBI, moving them from place to place without considering the family, it is difficult to comprehend. How could he have let it happen?

Chapter 6

I wake late the next morning thoroughly refreshed, anxious to take my morning run. I run harder and faster than usual and don't seem to feel any tiredness. It's as if I really have sloughed away at least ten of my forty-nine years. On the way down the rue de Charonne, I stop in and buy a croissant, something I haven't done in months. I'm going to have a *real* breakfast. Boy, am I getting spoiled. Having a little extra money is going to turn me into a regular bon vivant.

I fill my basin with water and even heat it a bit on my cooker before I wash up. I have some almost fresh clothes and I slide into them. The jeans are stiff with paint, but that I'm used to.

The coffee with the croissant dipped into it is a delight. I pull out the paintings I've done so far and spread them around me. I just stare at them, try to pretend somebody else did them, be my own critic. I wish I had back that one of the Place Furstenberg, but then fifteen hundred francs is fifteen hundred francs. I stretch out on the sleeping bag and look up through my little window at a blue sky. Now and then a wisp of cloud appears and quickly disappears. It must be windy up there.

I think about the painting of Mirabelle, about Mirabelle herself, and about her story. I remember all I told her about myself. I wonder if I should go on. I could always duck some of the hard parts, just tell her the gist of things without going into it too much. I'm not sure I want to tell anybody, not even Mirabelle. I'm not sure I can. I've locked it so deeply inside me, I think I'm ashamed, also it was all so painful. At the same time I'm bored with it. It's over, finished.

I finish my croissant and the last dregs of coffee. I wash the cup and pot in my wash water, rinse and dry them off. I hide the paintings and tuck my sleeping bag up in the rafters. I listen, then go out the door, lock it, put the key in its hiding place, listen at the stairway, and lightly run down the steps. Living invisibly becomes a way of life. I do these things almost without thinking. I almost never come down this late, I'm getting spoiled all right, but it feels wonderful. I don't feel in such a hurry, rushed in my mind. The concierge still has her blinds closed and the curtain across her window.

Even after the hard run this morning, I feel like walking instead of taking the bus. The day isn't as beautiful as it was earlier. Dark clouds are drifting and that high wind is beginning to whip around the ground. It could even rain. But I think there'll be enough light for the portrait, even if it does.

That reminds me about the light bulbs. I drop into a Monoprix and buy four sixty-watt, 220 V, bayonet-fitting, frosted-glass bulbs. That's one thing about France, whether it's bread or light bulbs, there are always about ten decisions to be made.

I drop straight down to the quai on the other side of Pont Sully, where I usually run. I walk along the river looking at the boats. While I'm running, I don't see much. Most of the boats along here aren't working boats, people live in them. Boy, would that be a dream, living in a boat on the Seine, right in the center of Paris.

I walk up rue Saint-Sulpice to the Marché Saint-Germain. Inside, I find a small bunch of daisies for only five francs. She can't see them but she can smell them and feel them. The smell actually isn't so great, but I think it's the kind of thing she'd like.

I try again to sneak up on her. I don't have any box to jiggle behind me and I'm wearing my jogging shoes. Still, when I'm about three feet away, she turns.

"You are early, Jacques. The bells have not begun ringing yet, but I am almost finished with my birds."

"How did you know I was here, Mirabelle? How did you know it was me and not someone else?"

She has one of the brownish gray pigeons in her hand. She smiles at me.

"Well, first, I could tell from the sounds of the pigeons, the way they were acting, that someone was coming near me. But I did not hear anything and the pigeons seemed nervous, so I figured it was someone carefully sneaking up on me. Who else but you would be doing that? Also, I smell a new smell, something of cut grass. It smells like open places and makes me think of cows and vacations in the country, a lovely smell."

She has finished giving her grains to the brown pigeon and sends it flying away.

"You're amazing, Mirabelle. I can't even keep a secret from you. Okay, here, these are for you."

I hold out the daisies. She takes them from my hand and brings them gently to her face.

"Oh, Jacques, they have the smells of all nature in them, it has been so long."

She gently strokes one of the flowers.

"And they are my favorites, marguerites, how did you know? Are they yellow?"

She looks into my face, tears are at the corners of her eyes. I'm pleased and embarrassed at the same time.

"Don't tell me you can smell or feel the *color*, Mirabelle. That I won't believe. If you keep being this way I won't believe you *are* blind anymore."

"Would that not be nice? Please, Jacques, you must be gallant now. When you give flowers to a woman you must kiss her as well."

She turns her cheek to me and leans forward. I kiss her on one cheek and, almost simultaneously, the first gong of the big bell in the Saint-Germain-des-Prés tower chimes. She turns her head and I kiss her on the other side, a tear has run down the cheek and I feel, taste it with my lips. The bells are now beginning to ring. Rolling, almost cacophonic, deep resounding sounds fill the air.

Mirabelle leans forward and kisses me on both cheeks, her lips are dry, cool. The birds are flying, dancing around us to the increasing sound of the bells.

"Thank you so much for the flowers. No one except my father has ever given me flowers before. He gave me some he picked for my tenth birthday. I have never forgotten. They were yellow marguerites, just like these."

She puts them to her nose again, runs her hands across the top, brushing the tips of the flowers. Then she puts them down on the bench beside her and begins gathering all her pigeon equipment and little sacks together.

"We must go now. I have a lovely meal cooked for us and we want to have enough light so you can paint me properly."

"Please, Mirabelle. Can't we stay until the bells finish ringing? I'd never noticed before how beautiful they are, they're like sun and rain blended together, like a rainbow in sound."

I'm sitting beside her, my eyes closed and my head tilted back, listening. It's magic. I hear the wind, the flapping of the pigeons, the hum of traffic. Over all, blending everything, is the metallic, sour-sounding, soaring, yet strong thunder of the bells. Why haven't I ever really heard them before like this?

"You are becoming like a blind person, Jacques. It is something I enjoy doing very much, also. Sitting quietly and listening to the bells. They are quite different from the bells of Saint-Sulpice. The Saint-Sulpice bells are beautiful, too, but are more dignified, more religious, more sure of themselves. These bells are almost as if they are asking questions, questions no one can ever answer. Let us listen."

Then she's quiet and we listen through the bells until the last lingering final notes disappear. In the distance I hear Saint-Sulpice answering in deep tones. Mirabelle stands and I stand beside her. She puts her hand on my arm and I put my hand over hers, it isn't cold but not warm either. Mirabelle leans slightly into me.

"This is so nice, no one would have any idea I am blind. I am only a woman walking with a man. This is so comforting, you will never know, dear Jacques."

She goes ahead of me into the door to her apartment. She takes out her keys. Her pigeon things are tucked into her bag. She feels with one hand for the keyhole and puts the key, without faltering, directly into the hole and leans to open the heavy door. She hangs her coat on the rack beside the door we come in, pulls a drape across to keep out drafts, and slips off her shoes. She slides on slippers. I'd never noticed this before, but then I'd never come up into the apartment with her. She was always already here when I arrived.

I'm beginning to feel like a bull in a china shop. I sit on a chair beside the door and take off my running shoes. Mirabelle puts a hand on my arm.

"No, Jacques, it is not necessary for you to do that. It is only the idiosyncrasy of an old, blind woman. Your feet will be cold. No, wait, if you want, I have something. I sewed them a long time ago but no one has ever used them."

She turns behind her to a closet area closed off by another curtain. She reaches up high and brings down a pair of hand-sewn slippers, actually cloth sock-like slippers to slide over shoes.

"See, you can wear these over your shoes if you want."

"I have my shoes off, is it possible for me to wear them over my socks?"

"As you wish."

She turns to her kitchen. I slip the cloth slippers over my socks, they have elastic around the top and are comfortable. I line my shoes up beside the door.

While she's in the kitchen I figure it's a good time to screw in light bulbs. I start in the toilet room. I screw out the bulb and put in the new one, I flip the switch, "let there be light," and there is. I do the same in the bathroom, standing on the edge of the tub to reach the socket. Same thing, no problem.

The light in the main room is over the table where we eat. I know Mirabelle knows what I'm doing. I figure if she doesn't want me walking on the floor with my shoes she probably won't be too enthusiastic about my standing on the table where we're going to eat.

"Mirabelle, I have a bulb for the light in the ceiling here, but unless you have a ladder, I have no way to reach it except by standing on your table. Is that all right?"

"Of course, and thank you. It is kind of you to remember."

I climb on a chair and then onto the table. Even then I can just barely reach the socket. It's a double socket with two bulbs. I twist out the old bulbs, then fit both of the new ones in. The switch is on, so they light right up in my hand.

"Do be careful, Jacques, electricity can be so dangerous, do not hurt yourself."

"There, that's better. I didn't buy those bulbs for you, Mirabelle. You don't profit by them, so don't thank me. I bought them for myself.

"There, that's fine, Mirabelle. By the way, when the toggle switches are down, the light is off; when they're up, they're on."

"I have lived here more than seventy years, more than fifty years since I have been blind. I know the switches, Jacques, but thank you."

So the lights didn't burn out, they just died from disuse or temperature change during the years since her sister died. Or maybe they were accidentally turned on by someone else and left on. But then Mirabelle said she could feel the heat of the bulbs. It doesn't matter.

I sit at the table. Mirabelle is putting down the hors d'oeuvre. It's tarama. She takes off her apron and sits across from me.

"Today we are having Greek food. Have you had tarama before?"

"Yes. I like it very much, especially this way, with black olives and lemon."

"I bought it on the rue de Seine this morning. We shall have all Greek food today."

"I thought you did your yoga and exercises in the morning."

"I did them early and then went shopping."

She smiles at me, unfolds her napkin, I follow and lift the glass of wine she has poured. She holds out her glass.

"This is Greek wine, retsina, I hope you like it."

"To our portrait and to us, Mirabelle."

We take a taste of the wine. I've never been a great fan of retsina, it tastes too much like turpentine, but I don't say anything. When you're a painter, drinking turpentine is not a special treat.

We have moussaka and brochettes d'agneau for our main courses and finish with some sticky dessert. It's all delicious. If I keep eating like this I'm going to put my potbelly back on.

After we finish, while Mirabelle washes the dishes, I set up my easel by the windows and place the portrait so I have a good view of her and the best light. The weather is definitely changing for the worse. I hunt around and find some detergent, a cloth, and some newspaper. I start trying to wash the window.

"Is it really that bad, Jacques? I am so embarrassed."

"Mirabelle, when you're blind you don't need windows, but if I'm going to paint your portrait I need light. Don't feel badly."

I need to scrape off at least ten years' crud from that glass. Paris air is filled with pollution, and since she's cooking in the same room, the insides are almost as bad as the outsides with accumulated grease. I climb up on a chair and then up onto the windowsill so I can reach the high parts. It takes me at least fifteen minutes for each window, and Mirabelle has finished with her work before I get the last streaks wiped away with paper towels. To me it looks great but I know it doesn't mean anything to Mirabelle.

"Now we can really work. It's amazing how much light there is now compared to before."

"Jacques, in so many ways you bring light into my life."

"I feel the same way about you, Mirabelle."

It's a charged moment but we leave it there. I sit down and try to enter into the portrait where I was when I stopped, before I got all bogged down with my tale of woe. And the "woe" part hasn't even started yet, might not.

I begin the underpainting for her face and hair. I use a lightened version, thinner, of the alizarine crimson I was using for the background. I blend it with some yellow ocher. I've got to find some transparent yellow, maybe Indian yellow, for underpainting. I wonder what it costs.

Mirabelle sits there staring past me out the window with a slight smile on her face. She looks so frail, so fragile in a certain way, but now I know her indomitability, her vitality, her courage, I see her differently. She sits still as a mannequin.

"You don't need to sit so still, Mirabelle. I'm finished with the drawing now; if you want, you can relax and we can talk. I don't know how much sense I'll make because I get concentrated on the painting and I'm not much of a conversationalist."

I look up, she smiles and twists her head slowly around on her shoulders, a yoga exercise.

I'm working on the underpainting for her sweater now. I'm using a mixture of ultramarine and a touch of the alizarine crimson. I want to get it dark but rich in a cool way, then I'll bring it back up again when I start the impasto. The painting's coming along fine. I'm just drifting with it and I'm about ready to put some white and some of the yellows, oranges, reds, some more earth colors on my palette, to start the flesh tones.

"Jacques, would you be willing to tell me some more about your life in the past? Do not do it if it is too painful. I would not ask except I want to

*know more about you, how you have come to be
the impressive man you are."*

I stop and begin squeezing the opaque paints onto my palette.
One part of me wants to tell her, knows it would probably be good
for me, but there's a knot inside I've built over this past year or
so which has become something of my sense of security, of safety.
I don't know if I want to unravel it again. I begin with a stroke of
pale yellow ocher between her eyes. I look once more to get just
the right tone and then look into her eyes. She smiles as if she
knows.

*"When you stopped last time, you were in Paris
with your family. You did not like your work, but
your wife and children were beginning to adapt themselves to the change, the life here. What happened
then? I still cannot see how you came to be painting
in the streets, or sitting here with me in my room
on the rue des Ciseaux."*

She stops. What the hell, I'll start and keep painting. If she wants
to hear all this, it's okay with me.

"We were here in Paris three years, then before the third year
was up, I was asked to stay on for at least one more. Our three
oldest had graduated from high school and were back in America
studying at different universities. Still, Lorrie didn't complain, it
was almost as if she'd given up.

"As I said, Mirabelle, one of the difficulties with my work was
it was necessary that I travel more than I wanted. There were
subdivisions in several other cities, including Lyons, Bordeaux,
and Marseilles. I had to visit each about once a month. It kept me

away from my family too much, but at least the children seemed happier. When those at the university in America came home for vacations, they now seemed to love Paris.

"Unfortunately, Lorrie still spent too much time ferrying young Hank from one place to another and she didn't have much interest in Paris.

"My own big complaint was that here I was, an artist, in the city of artists, actually living in Impressionist country, and I had no chance to profit from it. I never even had a minute to do any drawing, except doodling while on the phone.

"Hank was scheduled for graduation in June from the American School. That was when I was told my assignment had been extended that fourth year. Either I'd done too good a job, or they were going to bury me here. I think maybe this was the straw that broke Lorrie's back.

"Up till then she'd remained a perfect multinational American wife displaced in a foreign country. She took care of the house, shopped, went to the school frequently as a member of the PFA, helping the kids adapt. She had practically nothing to do with French, France, or French culture. She had a tutor twice a week, as I did, but she didn't seem to make much progress, just enough to shop or get what she wanted. She avoided, whenever possible, social events associated with my work where most of the conversation would be in French.

"Then I started noticing subtle changes. First she changed her hairstyle. Just that was enough to make her look almost French, especially with her darkening beautiful auburn-red hair. Then she started buying very à la mode, high-style clothes. We could afford it and she looked great, really stood out beautifully against the other American women here with their husbands. She was still, even after four kids, a very attractive woman. Now she was stunning.

"Then she enrolled in a French cooking class at the Cordon Bleu cooking school in Paris. She started dancing lessons, classes in mime.

"We began eating very gourmet meals at home, just the two of us, with fancy sauces, candles, and white napkins with napkin rings on the table. It was overwhelming.

"She enrolled in a course at the Louvre on Sundays. When I wasn't traveling on business, we'd go to the different museums in Paris, and she really knew what she was talking about. And *I'm* supposed to be the artist in the family!

"Her French was suddenly improving incredibly. I was beginning to have a Frenchwoman, a very sexy Frenchwoman, for a wife. The guys at work even started kidding me about it.

"Lorrie and I'd always had a reasonably good sexual relationship, nothing to shake the world, but satisfying. Now she began to be almost insatiable. She was continually wanting to try new things, more sensuous, more complicated, more involved, intimate experiments. Nothing seemed too much for her to try and she brought me along with her. I guess that's nothing for a man to complain about, and I didn't, but I was confused. A twenty-two-year, ongoing, relaxed marriage was turning into something else. I felt as if I were living in a porno flick with my wife as director, cameraperson, and co-star.

"Then I started hearing more and more about Didier. Didier was her new French teacher. Her old one had transferred to Lyons. She asked me several times if it would be okay if she had lunch with him, she could practice her French and, at the same time, learn more about French cuisine.

"That was fine with me, although it went against my own memo. I was glad to see her so much happier, doing more than just keeping house, shopping, all the things that had to be done and had filled her time before. Also, with most of the kids gone, she had much more time to herself. It was pretty lonely for her when I had to take those damned trips.

"Then, one night, in bed, after we'd had a particularly strenuous sexual encounter, she began to cry in my arms. Lorrie was not the type. She hardly ever cried and it seemed such a strange thing to do after we'd just made love. I held her tightly in my arms. God, you'd think I would have known. I guess anybody else who was really paying any attention would have. I'm sure you've guessed what was happening, Mirabelle."

I'm still painting but my hands are shaking. I take a deep breath. Mirabelle wouldn't blame me if I just stop telling about it all here. Mirabelle's staring at me in that concentrated blind way of hers. Her face has turned white, so white I'll have a hard time getting her true colors. I put down my brushes and turn my hands over and over, looking at them.

"Lorrie told me how, that afternoon, after lunch, she and Didier had gone to a hotel and made love. He'd been wanting her to go with him for several months and they'd kidded about it but she kept pushing him off. Then, today, she had to admit to herself it was what she wanted, too. She couldn't believe she'd actually done it, that it was done, that she'd been 'unfaithful' to me.

"I didn't know how to take it. It was so much like the kind of thing I dealt with so often at work, I found myself listening, acting, feeling, almost as if it were somebody else she was talking about. This couldn't be *my* Lorrie. It just wouldn't sink in, I wouldn't let it.

"But she had to tell me. She wanted me to know all about it. Somehow, I think she felt if I knew, it wouldn't seem so wrong. At least, that's what I thought at the time. I was being too much the impersonal psychologist, not myself.

"Didier was married, too, was fifteen years younger than Lorrie, had two small children. She wasn't sure, but she thought she and Didier loved each other. According to her, it was all so beautiful and sad, sad for her, for Didier, for his wife, for me.

"She acted as if she actually wanted me to tell her what to do, as if I were a close girlfriend in whom she was confiding, or I were a marriage counselor of some kind, not really involved.

"I must admit this is part of my problem, has been for a long time. MBI values, very highly, employees who are cool, unflappable. I'd learned to live that lie. My first reaction to almost any news, good or bad, was to retreat into myself, to not react, to analyze the situation, figure out what to do next.

"I did it this time. I didn't cry. I held on to Lorrie while she cried harder. I was deeply hurt but couldn't show it, maybe didn't even know it. I'd learned to hide myself from myself so well I could easily do that.

"After she'd cried herself out and my insides had settled enough so I could talk, I asked if she was really sure she loved him, if she wanted a divorce. There was another outburst of crying, she said she didn't know. She shook her beautiful head, so nicely shaped, coiffed in the latest style, with little strands of lighter red-blond against the dark natural color of her hair. She said she loved me and the children; Didier loved his wife, his children. Maybe it was only an affair which would burn itself out.

"But she didn't want to lie to me. I appreciated that. I also began to think this afternoon wasn't the first time they'd been in bed together. I hated myself for thinking it, cringed inside to the betrayal I felt, but I tried to hold myself in. It was beginning to be almost impossible. I was losing my ability to see this for what it actually was.

"Simple, childlike jealousy, physical jealousy, was racking me so I felt I might vomit. Finally I got myself in control. I held on to her but I still wasn't doing what I wanted to do, just cry like a baby myself, scream, rant about the loss, the hurt I felt.

"I asked again what she wanted to do. She said again she didn't know. She was so miserable. She wanted to promise she wouldn't see Didier again but she couldn't, not yet. And that was the end of our first conversation on the subject. I've gone over it a hundred times in my mind, wondering what I should have done, should have said.

"All I did that night was lie awake, vacillating between feeling very angry, violated, cheated, as the French say, trompé, and, on the other hand, feeling sorry for, understanding, wanting to be supportive to Lorrie."

My hands have stopped shaking. I take up my brushes again and don't speak for a while. I try to bury myself in the painting of Mirabelle. Her color has come back. There are tears on her cheeks. I don't say anything. I'm doing my usual thing, trying to make the immediate go away by concentrating on something else. I work hard for at least half an hour. Then Mirabelle speaks in a voice so low I can barely hear her.

"Did you still love her, Jacques? Could you understand why she did what she did? What happened after that? Tell me if you can, please."

I try to keep painting while I talk this time.

"It didn't stop, Mirabelle. They continued to see each other. I changed her French teacher and didn't even consult Lorrie about it. That was stupid, it wasn't going to make any difference. I could tell from Lorrie's every move, her excitability, her almost manic desire to please me, the way she dressed, moved, slept, made love to me, even the way she cooked for me, that she was still seeing Didier and more than just seeing him. Her feelings of guilt must have been horrible for her and I had no sympathy. I felt myself growing away from her, from us. It was all too painful and yet I couldn't do anything about it.

"When I came back from a visit to Lyons which lasted four days, I finally got up the nerve to talk to her, try to clear things up.

"She was in bed. The plane had been late and it was after midnight. I was still wearing the suit I'd worn on the plane. I'd just dropped my briefcase on the floor beside the bedroom door. I don't know whether she was asleep or not when I came into the room. I knew I had to talk with her soon or I'd never be able to do it. I stretched out on the bed, on top of the covers with my clothes on.

"She didn't lie or even try to. She admitted she was still seeing Didier, that he made her happier than she'd ever been. She felt she'd never incited true ardor in a man in her life, this included me, especially me; that ours was only a 'comfortable' relationship, and had been from the beginning. I didn't, couldn't argue with her. I'd always loved Lorrie simply, nothing complicated, pure Philadelphia dumb love; there was no world-shaking event, it just snuck up on me bit by bit, as we went together and I got to know her, the way she was. It'd somehow lasted all these years. I hadn't even considered questioning it. It's amazing how naïve a person can be, at least, how I was.

"Then Lorrie begins revealing to me things I should have known all the time. She's really resented living in the slipstream of my career, moving continually, not having a chance to develop personally, totally immersed in caretaking, both of the children and of me. She's missed her support group of women in Minneapolis and now is feeling she's changed, so she can never go back. She has no idea what we should do.

"I lie back in the dark with my eyes open, at least, at last, I'm crying. But the anger, the resentment have receded. I'm crying the way you would cry at the death of a much loved parent or child. I'm crying in despair at the futility of it all. I think I'm even crying a little bit for Lorrie.

"More than anything it seems, my new assignment as personnel director here in Paris has annoyed her. She was the one trained to this work and I, a mere art major, have the kind of job of which she's always dreamed. She feels a lot of this is because she's a woman and women never get an even chance. She says she feels her early pregnancies interrupted her career for life, took her out of the real world. She feels cheated and that most of it is my fault. I should have taken more care.

"I listen in the dark and understand. She's deeply hostile toward the society, toward our family situation, everything, but mostly toward me. She feels I have not been a husband to her, only a provider; that the children hardly even know me, that I haven't actually participated in their lives, that she's had to bear the entire burden.

"She's up on the edge of the bed now in her nightgown with her elbows on her knees and her head in her hands. I look over but she won't look at me. I listen. She knows she's making excuses for herself in her guilt, but at the same time I recognize she's right. I was so busy with my own concerns, with making a success at Nard and then with MBI, over these years, I haven't paid enough attention to her or the family.

"I wait until she's finished. I want to say the right thing, be a loving husband, do the best for Lorrie, for myself, for the children. I'm having a hard time keeping my emotions from erupting, from drowning me, from forcing me to say, do things I'd be sorry about all my life. Finally I can say it.

" 'Lorrie, I'm not arguing. I'm only sorry I didn't pick up on this sooner, that you didn't tell me about your feelings over all these years. You're right; I haven't been giving either you or the children enough attention. I swear, if I get the chance, when this assignment is over, all those things will change. I don't really want to be a big deal at MBI. It's only part of a crazy competitive world that eats a person up.

" 'Look, we're going to be here another six months. I can probably even get another extension if you want. Enjoy yourself as you have been. Make the most of it. There are none of our parents, our relatives, our friends, to monitor your life. You have freedom. When Hank goes off to college in September you'll have your life to yourself, nobody to interfere.

"'Enjoy the freedom you didn't have. Make the most of this chance you have with Didier for romance, something you feel you didn't have. Life is too short, too important, to waste. I'm not sure I'm young enough, of the right disposition, to give you what you want here. Somehow I've become a real stick-in-the-mud and I don't know exactly how it happened.

"'We have a potential for twenty or thirty good years together. Let's not throw this all away just for our feelings now. We have our own twenty-two years of shared personal history. And the kids; think of all that, please.

"'I only ask that you save some time for me when I can be here, that you not tell me about the rest of your life. I'm afraid I can't take it. You might see this as selfish, childish on my part, but I'm the victim of male possessiveness as much as the next guy. All that psychology, the rest of it, only seems abstract now, no real help. Okay?'

"And that's the way we did it, Mirabelle. Hank graduated from high school and went home to school at my old alma mater, the University of Pennsylvania. I continued with MBI but tried to be home more, to give more time to Lorrie, to be with her, do things with her as much as possible.

"Lorrie was more radiant every day. I think, in a certain way, she loved me more than she ever had. I asked no questions. I only worked harder.

"Then, one weekend, Lorrie and Didier were going up to Honfleur for a little holiday. Somehow he'd gotten time off from his family. It was spring. Lorrie was lovely in a new dress, a light blue with tiny bluish flowers, almost like forget-me-nots, in a pattern all over it. She carried a small overnight bag and looked like someone from a modern version of a novel by Colette. I waved goodbye as she climbed into a taxi."

I have Mirabelle's face finished. It came up by itself without a single major correction. Portraits aren't what I'm good at but this time I know I've painted a truly beautiful thing. I stop again and just stare at her. Her absolute calm seems to be draining so much poison from me I know I'm going to have a hard time telling her the next part. I begin working her white hair over the dark underpainting. I'm deeply involved in the twistings of her hair where she's braided it in a crown across the top of her head.

"And then, Mirabelle, something broke. Maybe I went crazy or had a quiet, unobserved nervous breakdown. I don't know.

"I came inside after the taxi pulled out of sight, and everything seemed so useless, so meaningless. Life itself didn't seem worth the living. I looked around that huge house, practically running itself, in some way an adjunct to MBI itself, not really our house, just the place where we stayed, a semiprivate hotel.

"I took out a fifth of Bourbon we keep for company and sat down in the quiet. I started sipping. Generally I'm not a drinker. I don't particularly like the taste and definitely don't like the effect. The entire element of control has dominated my life and there has never been room for things like alcohol.

"I began wondering how Didier had gotten away from his wife

for the weekend. What excuses did he make, or does his wife know, and they're having a private laugh about the American woman who's all over him, and she's the boss's wife. I felt a deep disgust with it all, with myself. I cried a lot, a crying drunk.

"I sipped my way through that entire fifth and finally sank into sleep on the couch. I didn't even slide off my shoes.

"In the morning I took a long shower, some aspirin, and slipped into a sweat suit. I was surprised I didn't have a hangover. I picked up the phone and dialed our lawyer in Minneapolis. I spent most of the day on that phone working out the details. Milton, our lawyer, was convinced I'd absolutely flipped. He kept asking if I knew what I was doing, if I was all right. I assured him I was, but I wasn't.

"When Lorrie came home Monday morning, skipping up the three steps to the marble front porch, I was totally sober. I was shaking all over, but I was cold sober.

"I stayed quiet in the corner by my complicated, expensive stereo as she took off her coat, went into the bedroom to change her clothes. She wasn't expecting me to be home and I guess that's why she didn't see me. I was enjoying being invisible, probably watching her for the last time.

"When she came out again into the living room I stood up. I took her in my arms and said I wanted to speak with her. I asked her to please sit down with me. I must have frightened her because I've never seen her so pale, so rattled, so startled. She sat in the couch next to the one where I'd been sitting and I sat beside her. I took her hands in mine. She sat, knees together, her neat ankles crossed. She stared into my eyes.

———

"Do you know, Mirabelle, I can close my own eyes now and still see her there, so alone-looking, so beautiful, so scared. I'm sure this is easy for you to understand, because you have so many memories stored in your head, but I have only a few and this is one of them. I know I'm an artist and seeing is supposed to be my business, but there aren't many real scenes etched into my brain the way they seem to be in yours.

"Lorrie asked what I was doing home, why wasn't I at work. It was hard to start, to start all that would, before I was finished, be the end of everything we'd had.

" 'Lorrie, I don't work for MBI anymore. I've resigned. I'm supposed to go through a series of debriefing meetings, but I won't. I've called Milt and he's made all the arrangements at home. I know this is a shock for you, but I don't think it's good for either of us to go on the way we've been going. This kind of pretending will only, in the end, kill what we have together, and I still love you.'

"I wait for her to say something. If she had only said one word that would convince me this wasn't what she wanted, I'd have stopped everything, asked to be transferred home, started all over again. Whatever she wanted I'd have done. But she just stared at me, her eyes not even blinking. Her face was chalk-white.

" 'Everything we own is yours, Lorrie, the house, the cabin, the car here, the car there, our stock options, and some other in-vestments I've made. I've done the calculations and you can live your life out pretty much 'in the style to which you've become accustomed.' As you know, there are trust funds to put each of the kids through school, as far as they want to go. It's all yours, you're set for life.'

"Her face is a blank, an unanswered, unasked question.

" 'I can't keep it up any longer, Lorrie. I don't have the nerve, the courage, to carry through with our agreement. I want to search out the rest of my life, to see if there's anything left for me, any pleasure, any excitement, anything that still means something to me besides money, status, more money, more status.

" 'You see, I thought all this time I was doing what you wanted. I know now I was wrong. I got caught in some kind of mad race that had no ending except something like this. I'm not the only one, but that's no excuse.

" 'Would you believe it, but during these years, doing all the dumb kinds of things I've done, I've still thought of myself, in my heart of hearts, as an artist. Isn't that insane? But it's true. I've felt that all the rest has been a combination of accidents. Each step to where my life is now hasn't been so much a series of decisions but only taking the way which seemed sensible, practical, the easy way, the smart way. Well, it's finished.'

"Lorrie's still quiet. She opens her mouth twice, then starts quietly crying. I'm crying myself.

" 'Lorrie, I thought I could do it, I really did. You know what finally got to me?'

"I pause. I take a deep breath, trying to keep the aching sobs back down there where they belong. I don't want this to be a crybaby session.

" 'It was you, checking your watch all the time you were with me. It was like someone in a waiting room for a train, or a doctor's office, waiting for the waiting to be over. I knew you were waiting until I wouldn't be there, so you could call or be together with

Didier, get on with your real life instead of carrying off the private farce we'd created. I began to know how superfluous I was to your life, your happiness, that I was in the way, blocking what you really wanted.

" 'I want you to be happy, Lorrie, that's the main thing. By being around, I don't feel I'm helping at all.

" 'I need to get away, Lorrie. I've been thinking about this meeting with you all morning, wanting to do it right, not hurting you any more than I need to, trying not to hurt anybody more than is necessary.

" 'I have my bag packed. I'll be leaving soon as we're finished here. More than anything else, I don't want the kids to know what's really happened, if it can possibly be avoided; but it's up to you.

" 'I'd prefer you didn't tell them about you and Didier until you feel you have to. That's not only male vanity but what I think is best for them. I hope you'll agree, but it's up to you. Tell them anything that would be comfortable for you and you think won't be too traumatic for them. You can just say I'm going through some kind of male menopause, that I've run away with another woman, whatever you can come up with. I know now I'm not that important in their lives, anyway. It's a terrible thing to realize but it's true. How could I have been so unknowing, so stupid?

" 'But please tell them I love them and always will. I'm sorry if I haven't been much of a father. It was all a terrible mistake on my part.

" 'I have my carte de travail and carte de séjour. If I want, I can stay in Paris for as long as ten years. After that, I don't know what I'll do. I'm hoping to find myself as an artist again, go back to where it all started, the way it was the last time I felt alive and inside myself.

" 'If you want a divorce now, or at any time in the future, the papers have been drawn up by Milt. I've sent my signature, which will serve, along with his power of attorney, to make it legal. If it isn't enough, just mail me whatever needs to be signed and I'll do it.

" 'I'd like very much to know if you are all well, happy, how you are doing. If you want to contact me, write to American Express here. I'll check every two weeks. I'd appreciate very much hearing from you, but don't, please, any of you, feel you *have to* write to me. I'll write you here or at our address back home every two weeks to let you know I'm well.'

"I stand up. I have my bag beside me. Lorrie stays seated. I don't want to hang around. I want it clean as possible.

" 'I've taken five thousand francs from the cash we keep in the house. The checkbooks, insurance policies, and the rest are on the dining room table. It'll all be easy to figure out. If you get stuck, call Milt.

" 'Have a good life, Lorrie. Try to think of me sometimes. Remember I love you, always will. If you want me or need me, just write and I'll come, somehow.'

"I turned and walked out that big curved French door, walked to the RER station with the idea of riding the train into Paris. I was glad it all hadn't turned into some kind of impossible crying, screaming scene. I don't think I could have managed it. I felt numb, in shock, and at the same time as if I'd scraped a growth from my body which had grown all over and was suffocating me. I was experiencing a sense of being in charge of my life, whether I wanted it or not, a feeling I hadn't known since that phone call from the Nard Corporation."

My story is finished almost at the same time as I complete the portrait. I sit there. I know there's really nothing more to say and probably nothing more to paint. During the last parts of my story, I've practically forgotten about Mirabelle, except as the model filling the front of my mind. The rest of my mind, my soul, had been set free.

Now it's over, I feel strange, drained, embarrassed. Mirabelle stands and comes over to me. For the first time, I really wish she could see. Up till now, it has only been a vague desire. Now I wish she could see herself as I see her, know that, in another way, I know so much of her story, as it has been told in her face and then in the portrait. I know also that my own pitiful tale is somehow painted into the portrait, too.

Before I know it, Mirabelle has put her arms around my head and holds me against her. I don't even try to stop myself. I start crying. I cry, soaking the dark sweater she has pressed against my face. When I finally stop, it's practically dark again. The portrait looms in front of my face. Mirabelle steps away and across the room. She switches on the overhead light.

"Now it is time we have some light. Tonight you must stay and share my souper with me."

I'm not fighting her. I realize how tired I am of fighting, fighting my past, my present, myself. I feel a tremendous desire to just let go, be part of things, enjoy the little pleasures life has to give, pleasures Mirabelle has in some way made visible to me.

Blind Reverie

As I listen, I'm even more glad that I am blind. I have never, except for the death of my parents so long ago, been part of the hard, real world. How can Jacques stay so loving, so kind, after all that has happened? Yes, the sadness is in his voice, in his movements, but I had no idea. I do not think I could ever stand up under such troubles.

I am so glad he has been willing to tell me, but now I know there is nothing I can do and he is not available to me. He lives in his past, his loves, as I live in the world of my parents. Only his painting is what he lives for now. I am so happy to be a part of that world, if there can be nothing else. I wish I were young and beautiful so I could take his mind away from all his dark thoughts, if only briefly, give him some idea of how much he should be loved.

How could his wife turn to another? Perhaps it is as Jacques says, he was then a man who could not know love. I was impulsive to hold him in my arms while he cried, but it gave me such pleasure. I do think that now he is a man who could know how to love. Sometimes a loss such as he suffered can open doors of tenderness and passion.

Chapter 7

Mirabelle moves into the kitchen, takes her apron from a small hook just inside the door, and lights the stove. The kitchen is an alcove to the room where I'm sitting. This room is a cross between a dining room and a living room.

I guess, to the French, the place where you eat is the place where you live. I like the idea. I've always felt the American so-called living room was a remnant from the old-fashioned parlor and not a comfortable place to be.

I watch her. It's beautiful to see how easily, gracefully she moves. I'm feeling very passive, completely empty, not in a sense of being fatigued but as if sludgy motor oil in a car has been changed, or a boil has been lanced. I feel good. When Mirabelle turns her head toward me, I can't help but smile, meaningless as it may be. I don't know why she turns toward me.

"Jacques, I hope you are not sorry you told me about what happened with your wife. It is such a

poignant story, so difficult, that I am still thinking about it, trying to put it together in my mind, somehow wanting to understand the things that happened."

She starts setting the table, putting salt, pepper, butter, half a baguette, a plate with a bowl on it, for each of us. She sets these things on the bare wooden table, then brings out the napkins we'd used for lunch; each is in a napkin holder. I like the feeling of belonging, of having a napkin which is mine with its own holder. I, for the first time, really, since I left home, am ready to come in from the cold, be part of life.

She brings out a hot pad and places it in the center of the table, then carries a large metal pot from the kitchen and lines it up on the hot pad. With oven gloves she lifts the lid off the pot. Steam and a delicious smell pour from it. She goes back into the kitchen, then comes out with a large ladle. She takes my bowl and ladles soup into it without spilling a drop. It's as if she can see perfectly. She does the same thing for herself, sits down, springs up again.

"Oh, I forgot the wine. Usually I don't drink wine in the evening, but you've worked so hard you should have some."

She comes back and pours wine into our glasses, again without a single hesitation; only if you watch carefully can you see that her hands are doing what most people's eyes would do, locating things, determining amounts, distances. Her hands are like butterflies, yet they're calm, not nervous.

The soup is delicious. We eat without saying much, breaking off pieces of baguette and soaking them in the soup. I didn't realize how hungry I was. My Sunday Mulligan is definitely rotting on me. I look over at the painting leaning against the wall under the courtyard windows.

"Are you happy with your painting, Jacques?"

I don't even try guessing how she knows I'm looking at it. It's almost like living with a telepath.

"Yes, Mirabelle, I'm very happy. I didn't know I could paint such a good portrait. I've said everything I know about you in it, at the same time, it is a good resemblance *and* a good painting, a painting that would have value, even if you didn't exist, never existed."

"That makes me feel so happy. I only wish I could see it myself."

"I don't know if you would like it. This way, you can feel it is a good portrait just because I tell you so. I know it isn't very fair."

"No, it is the nature of my malady. Most of the time I am happier not seeing things. Usually vision is only a matter of convenience for most people. I have found ways to live without that convenience."

We finish the soup. Mirabelle begins to clear the table, carry the dishes and pot into the kitchen. I rise to help, she hears my chair scrape and motions me to stay in place.

"No, Jacques, I like very much cooking and caring for you. It is such a pleasure not to be alone. Eating alone is one of the hardest parts in my life. While I clean these dishes, would you be so kind as to tell me what happened in the year after you went out that 'curved French door,' leaving your wife, children, your entire life, and dropped into the

*streets of Paris? I should like to know very much,
but you need not tell me if it is too difficult."*

"Mirabelle, sometimes I'm even more ashamed of much of what
happened in that time than of what I did before. It is difficult now
for me to believe it."

She turns her head toward me, over her shoulder, and somehow
seems to look right through me.

"Please?"

"Well, first of all, I didn't take the RER; I *walked* all the way from
Le Vésinet, where we lived, into Paris. It was weather like this and
I enjoyed walking but I was terribly out of shape. I was carrying
a bag, not a big one, but it seemed to get heavier as I went on. I
was surprised to find how far from Paris we really lived. When one
only takes the RER, or drives, it is easy to forget how far apart
things are, how big the world is. I'd been locked into a tunnel kind
of life in more ways than I knew.

"So, when I finally arrived in Paris, late in the afternoon, absolutely bushed, with my feet blistered, I checked in at the cheapest
hotel I could find. It was thirty-five francs a night, no bath, no
shower. I washed myself off in the sink, took off the sweaty clothes
I'd been wearing, slipped on my sweat suit, and dropped off to
sleep.

"Mirabelle, how much detail do you want of all this? You see,
I've run it through my mind so many times I almost know it by
heart, day by day, minute by minute."

*"Tell me what you will. We have time. There
is no hurry, and I am happy listening to you, even
when what you have to tell is so sad."*

"Well, the next day I went out looking for a cheaper hotel. It was a good way to get around to parts of Paris where I'd never been, but my legs were so stiff I could scarcely walk.

"I knew I wanted to be within walking distance of the Louvre and the Jeu de Paume, but those areas are expensive. I finally found a fourteen-franc-a-night hotel on the rue Trousseau in the eleventh arrondissement, not too far from where I live now. I moved in there.

"For the first month, I only walked around Paris. I broke out one of the two pair of running shoes I'd taken with me when I left. The shoes I'd been wearing were the kind I've always worn to the office, expensive, handmade, hard leather shoes with rubber heels. They were definitely not for long walking.

"I only went to a museum once a week, but I arrived before it opened and stayed till it closed. I was astounded at what men had created, brought into life with their hands, their minds, their skills. I became aware that if I weren't careful I'd be spending almost as much money on museums as I was on my hotel. That didn't make much sense.

"For food, I'd buy myself Strasbourg frites at one of the places on the streets, or one of the Tunisian sandwiches, or, sometimes when I wanted to splurge, I'd order a jambon beurre at a café along with coffee.

"I was doing much thinking, a painful process. Sometimes I'd walk from the Bois de Vincennes to the Bois de Boulogne and back without even knowing where I was going.

"But I was looking, too, letting Paris sink into me. It was even more beautiful than I'd imagined. It was especially beautiful in the mornings. Sometimes, when I couldn't sleep, I'd walk in the early dark hours, after midnight, until the sun would come up. I was still numb, still not knowing what I was doing, what I was going to do.

"But I did know my five thousand francs was disappearing fast. Sundays in the Louvre were free, so I made that my museum day. Then, as the days got warmer, I moved out of the hotel and began sleeping down on the quai. I found two old blankets at the Marché d'Aligre, near where I lived, and learned to roll my few things into a bedroll which served as a pillow.

"At first, it was like camping. I learned to fight off the people trying to rob me. I kept my little wad of francs inside my Jockey shorts. I put a strong string through my wallet with my important papers and hung it around my neck.

"But I was getting dirty. I didn't bring that much in the way of clothes with me, and generally they weren't very practical. I was learning how I wasn't prepared to survive in this outside world. It was hard where I was living. There were perverts, sad alcoholics, drug addicts, thieves. These people were dangerous and totally unpredictable. But I began to look like them, live like them, and they started leaving me alone. During the days, I was still drifting in my mind as I wandered around Paris.

"Then, in October, it began to grow cold. I was down to my last thousand francs. I wasn't worried as much as interested. I wanted to know what I'd do when all the supports on which I'd built my phony life were gone. I protected my carte de travail and my carte de séjour around my neck, as carefully as my money. I wasn't asked by the police in all that time to show them, but several times I saw les flics just in time and escaped.

"I began trying to sleep on the benches in the métro, I could sleep there till the métro police would throw us out. I tried sleeping on the métro vents for the warmth, but the smell of sweaty old air was too much for me. I moved back to the quais, or sometimes I'd find a corner in a courtyard until a concierge would chase me.

"The worst of it was, I'd started drinking wine.

"It began as a way to make the ache inside lessen, then I used it to help me sleep when the ground was hard and the wind was cold. By January, I was drinking between two and three liters of cheap wine every day. I began to lose count of those days. I'd sleep more in the daytime than in the nights because it was warmer. I was in an alcoholic haze most of the time.

"Now, a good part of what I spent was going for wine, even at five francs a bottle. I wasn't eating properly. I began having sores on my legs and feet. My hands were swelling and cracking with the cold, from the general exposure, and the decrease of circulation due to alcohol. Strangely, it took a while before I accepted the fact I had become an alcoholic. It was the kind of thing I thought could never happen to me.

"I woke from my stupor one morning to find I only had two hundred and ten francs left. It was early February. I was down on the quai under the arch of the Pont Neuf. It was freezing cold, ice everywhere. I didn't want to beg. I resisted going to buy a bottle of wine. I actually *sucked* the last dregs out of the bottle I'd gone to sleep with. I had enough of my wits left to know I needed to stop *now*, pull myself together, or it would be the end. I would then have found myself, the self for which I was searching, and what I was finding was not very impressive. I guess it was plain old-fashioned pride which saved me.

"I rolled myself in my filthy blankets and didn't move for three days. It snowed. I tried to search for my mind, to think, to plan. I craved wine. The only way I could stop myself was to just hold tight on to my own body and not let go. I had deep black-and-blue marks on my arms from pressing my fingers into them.

"But on the third day I could think. I could think and I was hungry. I knew first, after eating something, I needed to clean myself, go to a public washhouse and take a hot shower, wash my hair, wash my clothes, try to organize my life again.

"I went to the washhouse up on Place de la Contrescarpe. I'd learned from some of the other clochards that this was the best place. I rubbed and scrubbed myself with my clothes and a small sliver of soap I found on the floor. I tried to get my filthy cracked hands clean, ran my fingers through my hair over and over to get my hair clean and my fingernails somewhat cleaner. I wrung out my wet clothes and put on my sweat suit, now filthy, and my other pair of shoes. I put the wet clothes in a plastic bag. I wrapped my blankets around me and went outside. I was wearing a wool knit cap I'd found in a gutter some days earlier. The wind was blowing and I was freezing cold.

"I went to a self-service laundry. It was warm and steamy. I washed everything except what I was wearing, including my blankets. I washed my first pair of jogging shoes, the ones I'd been wearing all this time. I sat there watching my clothes spin, wash, then dry, and I tried not to think of wine. I nibbled on a baguette.

"I took out my clothes, put the clean ones on my clean body, then shoved in my sweat suit and hat to be washed. This total washing used up seventy of my francs, but now I looked more or less decent.

"I borrowed a pair of scissors from one of the resident clochards

on the Place and cut my hair myself, the best I could. I was beginning to smell again, that's active 'smell,' not passive. The smell
of those clochards, which I hadn't noticed before, was horrible. I
don't think you would have liked to smell me *then*, Mirabelle, when
I was under that bridge or at any time during those months. I
smelled of my own juices, of alcohol, filth, vomit.

"On the rue Mouffetard I bought an orange and a banana. I
meandered down the hill eating them. I walked in the cold sunlight,
with snow still in the corners of buildings, across the river to the
Marché d'Aligre. I knew I could buy a warm coat there with the
little money I had. I found one, a heavy, wool-lined, three-quarter
denim jacket which I still wear. It felt good to be warm without
alcohol.

"It was Sunday and I walked through the marché looking for
anything cheap and nutritious to eat. My appetite was definitely
coming back. It was then I discovered there were other people of
the streets, artists and students, waiting until the market closed
so they could pick through what was being thrown out. I waited
with them. In the struggle I managed to get some slightly moldy
oranges, some very dark bananas, two brown-spotted apples, some
spongy onions, battered carrots, a bruised artichoke, and several
soft potatoes. I put them in the plastic bag I'd used to carry my
wet clothes from the washhouse.

"We scavengers didn't speak to each other much but there was
a certain comradeship. It wasn't vicious, the way it was under the
bridge, where nothing was safe. These were people without money
trying to survive. I'd joined a different kind of life.

"I began looking up at the windows and into the courtyards of
the buildings in the neighborhood. As you probably know, Mira-

belle, over there, in the eleventh, it's a neighborhood of artisans, ébénistes, tapissiers, vernisseurs, making furniture for the furniture stores on the Faubourg Saint-Antoine.

"I began wandering into various courtyards, up the stairs, avoiding concierges, searching, sniffing around for some place where I might hide out of the cold. It was this way I found my attic. It was in a dark hallway on the top floor of a building which was mostly used as ateliers for those furniture makers. In my wanderings, I discovered a key hanging on a rafter over the door to one of the attic rooms.

"When I entered, I knew right away this was an unoccupied place, probably never used. There was dust, untouched, over everything. There was a layer of dust on the floorboards so thick I left footprints when I walked. I put down my few things and moved in.

"Now, I had very little money but I still needed something on which to sleep. I didn't want the hardness and coldness of the floor to drive me to wine again.

"I went to the marché on Tuesday when it opened. For ten francs, I found an old WW II army-surplus sleeping bag, only slightly torn, with a broken zipper I knew I could fix. I also picked up a piece of foam rubber which had been torn out of a rotten mattress. I didn't ask, I just took it. I don't think anybody wanted it anyway, it was only trash in the street.

"I watched carefully for the concierge and, when she wasn't looking, dragged my things up to my little attic. It was nice having a place I could call home. I spent the rest of that day trying to figure how to cook my vegetables. I wound up, in desperation, eating them raw. I was down to under a hundred francs now. I'd also need to think up some way I could earn money. I definitely didn't want to beg, that would be like going back to alcohol.

"The next morning I felt full of energy. I broke out my second pair of running shoes and pulled on a T-shirt, slipped on a pair of shorts I'd foolishly packed when I left and had been lugging around all this time.

"I snuck down the stairs and started running. In about two hundred yards I had to stop. I was impossibly out of condition, my heart was pounding. I was a physical wreck, both from the years working at a desk for MBI and the months I'd spent letting myself sink to the bottom. But I started up again.

"I ran around in the little park on the Faubourg Saint-Antoine. I'd run a lap and walk a lap. There was no one there, but the policeman in the guard box in front of the police station kept an eye on me.

"Then I ran through the rue de la Main d'Or and home. I was sweating like a pig. I ate one of my moldy oranges and a brown banana. They tasted great and the sugar went directly to my blood.

"So it started, Mirabelle. I kept increasing the distance I ran and my soft MBI-clochard flesh started hardening. With some of my last francs, I bought a small tablet and a crow-quill pen. I began doing small, detailed drawings all over Paris of the things I'd found and loved. It was a week before I sold one. I sold it for twenty-five francs. At that time, my total resources were twenty. The next week I sold two and put the price up to fifty francs. I made a small sign and stood it beside the collapsible chair on which I sat when I drew. I'd found the chair at the marché for five francs. The canvas seat was torn, but I mended it, using thread and needle bought for another four francs. I was really counting my sous.

"At night, I began looking forward to my days. I found, abandoned in the street, a small butane heater. The canister was empty, but I bought a new one for thirty francs. The jets were clogged, and I cleaned them out with one of my needles. For sixty centimes, I bought a box of matches, and for five more francs, a box of candles. I was beginning to have the elements of a more comfortable life."

"Jacques, it could make me cry to hear you tell all this. Did you need to make it so hard for yourself? Were you so guilty, so depressed, you felt you had to punish yourself? It is impossibly sad."

"No, Mirabelle. It was only carelessness that let me sink so low. I didn't care anymore. But now I was learning to care again. I wanted to care for myself, make the most of my life.

"And I must say, my life seemed so beautiful. Spring was beginning to come but it was still cold. My hands would be stiff when I drew, but I was truly concentrating, trying to be part of something both inside and outside myself for the first time in many years.

"Also, I was beginning to have a little money. By the end of March, I could purchase a larger pad of watercolor paper, also a green folder with black ties and a box of watercolors with a good brush. I really began to *feel* like an artist. I put another, bigger sign on my green folder saying the watercolors were for sale.

"And these watercolors, which took no longer than the drawings to make, I could sell for a hundred francs. I sold almost every one I did. It was wonderful for my morale. I enjoyed meeting people and talking with them. I didn't feel quite so alone. I came to a time when I had over a thousand francs. I had a place to live, food to eat, clean clothes. I was clean myself and I was painting. I don't think I was ever so proud of myself.

"Then, one Sunday, I found an easel and paint box, chevalet, in the marché. It cost me three hundred francs; a new one would've been fifteen hundred. I had the money and I bought it. I spent three nights nailing in new nails, screwing in new screws, wiring together broken parts, scraping off the old palette.

"Days, I painted my watercolors until I had made enough money to buy oil paints, some turpentine, varnish, linseed oil, and canvas. I built stretchers from the wood in my attic, using ancient tools which were also up there. I used glue and house paint to size my canvas after I'd stretched it on my stretchers with tacks.

"Now I could go out with my chevalet on my back and paint. You'll never understand how good it felt to walk along, the weight of the box on my shoulders, ideas for paintings running through my head. I was feeling well, healthy, almost young again.

"I began painting my first oils since student days. I did two paintings, but it was discouraging. How could I sell these paintings for enough to buy new canvas and paints? Also, I was finding it difficult to express the deep feelings I have about Paris. The watercolors and the drawings were decorative, descriptive only, a light brushing of what my eyes could see, not what my heart felt. I wanted to do more with my oil paintings, something important.

"But I wasn't totally discouraged yet. I knew something of what was holding me back. I was too tight, too afraid to show my feelings, it was the old problem, the weakness which had ruined my life. I couldn't stop myself from closing down, protecting myself as if I were in danger, danger from something I didn't understand, couldn't know. Now, when I wanted to let loose, to be vulnerable, put my heart and soul out on the canvas, I couldn't do it. But I was willing to keep trying.

"The rest of the story you know, Mirabelle. I was painting my third oil painting when we had our collision, our crash, our encounter; we met each other. I was prepared to finish that painting of the church and then go back to painting watercolors in order to buy more paints.

"At home in my attic, I cook my food once a week on my tiny cooker. I have candles and can open the small, hinged window in the roof. I hide everything when I leave so no one will know I'm there. I'm actually living as an artist in Paris. It's the dream of my life. I have nothing to complain about.

"And, now, even more, I sold the painting of the Place Furstenberg we painted, for more money than I ever dreamed, and you've commissioned me to paint your portrait. I have money enough to paint maybe five or ten more paintings in oil. You see why I'm so enthusiastic? Also, I am happy because I've gotten to know you, Mirabelle. It is such a joy."

Mirabelle has taken the chair across from me at the table. She gets up and reaches into the high shelf for the bottle of Poire William. She brings over two glasses and sits down again.

"Please, Jacques, would you pour some for the two of us? We should drink to our good fortune. Is there enough in the bottle for us to drink? Usually I can tell by the weight and the sound when I shake a bottle, but with the pear inside it is difficult."

"There's just enough for the two of us to have one last drink, Mirabelle."

I take the bottle from her and pour into the tiny, fragile, decorated glasses. I hold my glass up to her. Only then do I see that tears have wet the entire sides of her face. Her face is constructed so the tears do not come down the front in the runnel beside her nose, but down the outsides. Her eyes are slanted and perhaps this is why, or maybe it's a part of her blindness. She makes no effort to wipe the tears away.

"To good times, Jacques, for us."

We clink glasses and let that wonderful aroma of pears surround us, bring us closer. I close my eyes and try to enjoy the whole of the experience the way Mirabelle does.

"I should like to do something for you in return for your painting my portrait."

"You've already paid, Mirabelle. It's yours."

"No, it is yours, Jacques. I wanted you to paint it for yourself. I can never see it, only as you have seen me is it important. And that can only mean something to you."

"But, Mirabelle . . ."

"No. I know what I am doing. I want to be with you, I want to be with you through your painting. But that is not what I want to talk about. I want to share with you a small gift in return for what you have given me."

She's holding her drink against her chest again, as before. She has her eyes fixed on mine, as if searching.

"I should like to play some music for you, Jacques. It is one gift I can give. This has been an entirely personal pleasure and I should like to share with you."

She stands and indicates for me to follow her. She leads me to one of the doors which has never been opened when I've been there. She opens the door. It's dark. I reach in for the switch, but, naturally, there's no bulb. She must sense what has happened, heard the switch and felt nothing.

"Oh, I forgot about that, Jacques, but it does not matter. Perhaps it is better so. Give me your hand."

She reaches her hand to me and leads me into the dark room. Some dim light is coming in from the light in the main room. She leads me to a chair and motions me to sit down. Then she goes back and closes the door through which we've come so we are in total darkness. If there is a window in the room, the drapes must be drawn.

"I hope you do not mind, Jacques. Forgive the vanity of a blind old woman, but I hope you will find it all worth the effort."

I hear her moving around in front of me. I hear the sliding of something clicking into place, there is the sound of panels folding or closing against each other. I think I hear Mirabelle sitting down. It is such a different world when one is blind. But then the blindness is over.

The resonant, clear, vibrant, intense sounds of a harpsichord come out of the darkness. It is the music of Louis Couperin and it is one of my favorites, the Thirteenth Suite. Music is the one delight of my life I have kept close to me through all the MBI years. I play no instrument but have a passion for music, especially Baroque. In general, I prefer Bach to most of the French. However, the Couperins are in close competition. Stereo equipment was where I spent more money than on any one item. It was a constantly expanding improvement in my life.

It is incredible, magical, that Mirabelle would know this of me, without my having said anything, perhaps it was only because I loved the bells' ringing. I listen. I don't think I have ever heard the precision blended with passion, which is the heart of Louis Couperin, played so well. In unmeasured music such as his preludes, the performer is very important, must find the harmonics, the timing, almost by instinct. I don't remember this particular rendition, the recording seems exceptionally clear, practically no white noise. It could be Ton Koopman, or maybe even Scott Ross, but it's different, slower, more delicate.

I find myself relaxing into a state of poised tension. The room is filled with sound. I'm *astounded* by the quality of the speakers, they're better than mine!

Then I realize, dumbfounded, that it's Mirabelle who is playing, playing in the *dark*, playing in the permanent darkness of her life, playing for me!

She finishes the Prelude and there is a moment of silence. I find tears in my eyes, I want to move toward her, to thank her. But then, before I can stand, she starts the Allemande. I can't believe it. I try to do as I did with the bells, just lie back in my mind and wait, make my heart seem to stop, listen to the music. I don't think I've ever felt so enthralled.

She follows with the two Courantes and then, with just the right pause, so I can breathe again, she begins the beautiful Sarabande. I know I've never heard it played so tenderly, with such vivacity. It could well be one of the most beautiful pieces ever written for the harpsichord. It lasts less than three minutes but it seems to fill my life.

Then, almost without a real stop, she goes into the Gigue. The change of pace, the grace of this sprightly dance are in beautiful contrast.

She plays the Chaconne and finishes with the well-known "Tombeau de Monsieur Blancrocher." I've never heard such a beautiful concert. Altogether, it couldn't have lasted thirty minutes. When the last note fades away, she doesn't move. I want to applaud but that would be a violation. I sit there totally overwhelmed.

"Thank you, Mirabelle. I don't think I've ever heard Couperin played so well. I can never tell you how much I've been moved. You are a genius."

"You know the music of Couperin? I would never have thought it of an American painter. Jacques, you surprise me all the time."

I surprise *her*! She must be kidding.

"Would you like to hear something of Johann Sebastian Bach, Jacques? Most Americans seem to prefer Bach, at least those who like harpsichord music. It is difficult for me because of the many voices, so I shall play something simple."

I sit silently. She begins a series of measured dances. There are several kinds, menuets, polonaises, marches. Her Bach is very good, but not quite as impressive as her playing of Couperin had been. She stops.

"You know, he wrote those for his second wife, Anna Magdalena. He must have been very kind

to his wife, but he was always teaching. I enjoy playing them very much. It must be like dancing. I have never danced, but with this music, my whole body starts moving to the music.

Then she plays a short prelude in C major that Bach wrote for his son Wilhelm Friedemann. Then an invention, number 4 in D major. I know it. It is one in which I can pick up the theme, sometimes carried in the right hand, sometimes in the left.

Although her Bach is not as good as the Couperin, it is still outstanding. This time I do applaud, and walk through the dark room, not so dark now my eyes are accustomed to it. Maybe blindness is becoming accustomed to the dark. I walk up to where she is still sitting. I lean over her fragile body and kiss her on the cheek. She turns her head toward me and I kiss her on the other cheek.

"It was the most beautiful gift, Mirabelle. How did you know I love music so, especially Baroque music? This is more impressive than even your usual magic."

She reaches with her hand and touches my face.

"You have been crying, Jacques. Are you so sad still? I wanted to make you happy."

"No, Mirabelle, these are tears of happiness, of appreciation, tears shed for the magic of your knowing me so well."

I straighten up and wipe my eyes. Mirabelle stands with me, closes the keyboard, goes around, and lets the sounding board down. I follow her out of the room.

When we come into the big room, the light in the ceiling, which had seemed so dull and dim before, seems bright as the sun.

There's nothing to say. I know it must be late. I've lost track of time.

Mirabelle sits at the table in her usual place, she motions with her hand for me to sit down.

"We could drink some more of our Poire William but it is all finished."

"I should leave, Mirabelle. It must be very late."

"For the blind there is no time, Jacques. Except for the bells of the church, I would never know if it is late or early, day or night, it is all the same. You may stay if you want."

"There is nothing I can think to say after your beautiful music. But I would like to ask how you learned to play. How have you become one of the most beautiful harpsichordists I've ever heard and no one seems to know? I have every tape and record I could buy of the French, the German, the Italian music played by Americans, French, German, English, even Japanese musicians. I have tapes and records by Scott Ross, Blandine Verlet, Ton Koopman, Kenneth Gilbert, Huguette Dreyfus, Alan Curtis, just about everyone, and you are as good as or better than they. How have you done it and does anyone know?"

There is a moment's silence. Mirabelle smiles at me. She looks at, or at least turns her head down to, her hands.

"I am not so good. You were only surprised. I started playing too late and my hands are beginning to become stiff and too weak to play really well."

She holds her hands out in front of me. They are small, with tapering fingers, pink, close-cut nails, but not knobby at the joints as most old people's hands are. Her little fingers curve slightly in, the first beginnings of arthritis, but no more than mine. There are veins on the back, and liver spots. The skin is dry-looking, almost scaly, but they are beautiful, capable hands. I reach out and take them in mine. She turns her hands so they rest gently on mine. She seems to look at them and then into my eyes.

"Fifteen years ago, when Rolande died, she left me a sum of money and her share of this apartment. I thought long about what I could do with the money. I was fifty-six years old. Except for the languages I have learned, I had no skills. I was already caring for the pigeons, but it was not much to offer in this world.

"My greatest love had always been music. As a young girl I played the piano and was considered talented. But with my blindness I could no longer read the music and so discontinued. Rolande sold our piano to get it out of the room where she slept. I decided that, more than anything else, I wanted a harpsichord. I visited three places in Paris where they are made and decided on a place not too far from where you live now, on the rue de Charonne. I would take a taxi over there every day and listen to the workers as they gradually built it. For me it was like having a baby. I wanted to be near for every heartbeat, every new breath of it.

"I'm sure, at first, the workers were not happy when I stayed so long in their atelier, but we became friends. They loved their work and knew I loved *music and would make music from the work of their hands. It was a good time.*

"Then we had the exciting day when my harpsichord, my baby, was delivered here. They could not bring it up the stairs, so they brought it into the courtyard and then on ropes through the window into the room.

"After it had rested in place several weeks and had been tuned, I approached it. For two days I only sat on the chair and rested my hands on the keys, feeling them, then feeling the strings, all of this magical music machine, this wonderful instrument of sound, without playing any notes."

"I have had a large collection of all Baroque music, Mirabelle, especially the harpsichord, but I have never played. The only way I have heard the music is through a very expensive stereo player system. I did not expect anyone could do what you have done."

"I listened carefully and hard to my tapes. I practiced, alone, without written music, until I knew where every note was on my harpsichord. I could sit, touch any part of the harpsichord, and know just what note my finger would play. I played until my harpsichord became a part of my body, my body part of the harpsichord.

"Then I started listening really carefully to my records and tapes. I wore earphones to keep out distracting noises. I played small parts over and over, translating them through my mind to my fingers. I lived inside the music.

"I had a second window put on the window in this room so I would not disturb anyone else with my practicing. Sometimes I would play all through the night; as I said, night and day are not so different for one who is blind. I so wanted to be alone with the music."

"And you play without music, then, Mirabelle, I mean written music. You play directly from the sound. Of course you must. My God, I hadn't really realized!"

"Yes, Jacques, but remember, the music is sound first, the notes are only a way of sharing it. Now, with the tapes, we can share these things more easily, I can know the music for what it is, sound. I do not need notes.

"Sometimes, especially with Bach, with the polyphonic pieces, two, three, or even four voices, playing with and against each other, it is very difficult. It would be easier, perhaps, if I could see it written out, but if I listen carefully, I can separate the voices. They are quite different, you know. I learn to play them independently, then put them together. It is a wonderful experience. It is almost like writing music myself."

I look at her with renewed awe. It's hard to believe the music I just heard was played "by ear," by someone who has never seen the written music. Like so many other people, I'd somehow become convinced that the written music was the "real" music and what I heard when someone read it and performed was only that, a performance. But Mirabelle's right, the real music is the sound, the sounds that came into the composer's head, the written music merely a notation, a way to share the sound from one musician to another, or from composer to performer. I wonder if there's anything like that in art of which I'm not aware. It could be the base of my problem in painting. It relates to something I've been thinking about.

If Mirabelle can't see because she's afraid of what she will see, would it be possible for me to paint from her descriptions of the pictures in her mind, as we did in the Place Furstenberg, so she would be satisfied, convinced, that what she would see, if she allowed herself to see the paintings, would be something she could accept? In a certain way, the paintings would be like notes of music, I would be the performer of the original images in Mirabelle's head, the same as sounds in the composer's.

Mirabelle is smiling at me, her hands are still resting lightly in mine.

"What are you thinking, Jacques? I can feel the turning and spinning of your mind, it is almost like something physical, I can feel the slight twitches in your hands, also. What is it?"

"Would you try something with me, Mirabelle? The painting we did of the Place Furstenberg: the combination of your memories, the strength of your vision, combined with my painting skills helped us create something I could never have done myself. It was almost the same as you listening to the tapes and then playing them. I was listening to your vision and painting it, combining it with what was before my eyes. You opened my eyes in some special way."

I stop. She's still staring sightlessly at my face. I go on, hoping what I want to suggest will not be considered by her a violation.

"Mirabelle, perhaps if I can paint paintings so much like the visions of places you carry in your mind, it might come to a time when you would have enough confidence in what we've done that you could allow yourself to see. Do you understand?"

"Yes, I understand. I would like very much to be there when you paint. I have twenty different places near here, all in my memory. We could sit together and make beautiful paintings. Also, we should paint again the Place Furstenberg. It is so beautiful and I have such wonderful memories.

"Now, Jacques, I would like to make a proposition to you, too."

"Okay, here we go again, another proposition. First it was a proposition about the colors of the pigeons, the way they looked in exchange for a wonderful meal. Then there was the proposition about me painting your portrait with you paying me a thousand francs. Then there was the proposition that we tell each other about ourselves, our past. So what's the proposition this time?"

I hope she can feel the smile in my voice. I hold her hands more firmly. God, I don't want to hurt those magical hands.

"You forgot one proposition, Jacques."

"What did I forget?"

"I almost proposed myself. Do you not remember?"

For one of the first times, I'm glad she can't see me. I think I actually blush. She keeps her eyes on me. Sometimes I'm convinced she *must* see.

"No, Mirabelle, I didn't forget. I didn't realize it then because I didn't know you so well, but it was the kindest proposition of all. But, as I said, I'm married. You know all about it now, I would feel wrong. I cannot live, yet, with the idea I would deceive my wife, my children, myself. Also, I think I would be taking advantage of you."

"Some of those things are true, but those are not the real reasons, are they? It is because I am so old, is it not?"

"That is part of it, Mirabelle, yes. But every day I know you, you seem to become younger."

"But actually, Jacques, I am becoming older. May I make my new proposition now?"

She smiles the broadest smile yet. Her speech is so measured, subtly modulated, and her smile so radiant. How can such an old woman have such beautiful teeth? They can't be false, they look so real. There is nothing of the tight-lipped smile which so often comes with false teeth.

"Yes, proposition away, Mirabelle."

"Does that mean you do or do not want me to make my proposition? I have never heard the phrase 'proposition away.' It seems to say two things at once."

The smile has left her face, the lines of concentration between her eyes deepen, her hands lie limp in mine.

"It means yes. Please make your proposition. I'm listening."

"Since you have been here, Jacques, I have become aware that my home is a shambles. All I can

reach I have tried to keep clean, but be honest, the rest of the house, the parts I cannot reach, is terrible, is it not?"

"Well, Mirabelle, yes, it is dirty. The ceilings are gray with old dirt and the wallpaper is falling off in pieces. The woodwork around the doors is dirty where you cannot reach it, but you do very well keeping your home clean."

"No, Jacques, I would like my house to be beautiful. Could you help me? Do you know how to do these things, painting, putting up wallpaper, all it takes to make a house clean and beautiful? You are an artist, you should know those things."

"It's been a long time, Mirabelle. I did much when I was young, but then twenty years have passed when I have done almost nothing."

"The proposition I would like to make is that you move away from your cold, dirty attic and come live with me. There is the bedroom of my parents which I never use. You could sleep there, it has a good bed and closets. I never go into the room, but I remember the way it was. The room of Rolande is for my music, but the room of my parents you could have if you would help me make this home beautiful again, even more beautiful than it was when I was young. Perhaps that, too, if it was beautiful, would help me see."

It's her last sentence that makes me reconsider my automatic resistance to this idea. I've earned my freedom, my privacy, and, as much as I'm enjoying the time with Mirabelle, I don't want to give up what I've gained. All the same, maybe if she could feel her home was beautiful, a place of joy and delight, it would help her want to see.

"Are you sure about this, Mirabelle? Remember, you have developed habits of solitude, as I have. We treasure our aloneness, much as we sometimes dread it. Do you think you could put up with having another person living so closely with you? Think about it."

"I have thought. You are right, we should only try this to see if it is comfortable. If either of us is unhappy, we can always go back to where we were.

"I need only the early mornings free for my language lessons, my music, my yoga and exercises. You tell me you run in the morning. We should not then be in each other's way. Next I go take care of my pigeons. During that time, you could do your morning painting. Then, perhaps in the afternoons, after our déjeuner, we could go paint together as you said. It sounds quite reasonable to me. What do you think?"

I can't help but smile and I can hear the smile in my voice and know she hears it as she smiles back.

"You have it all figured out, haven't you? What kind of scheme do you have in mind this time?"

"No scheme, you are quite safe with this blind old lady. But I do hope you can make this apartment more beautiful. I hope you can find time for that. I have the money to buy what you think it would cost for paint or rugs or even some new

furniture. I think it would be wonderful to do together."

"Okay, Mirabelle, you're on. But I'm not going to move my things from my 'cold, dirty attic.' I want to feel it's there. Could you show me the room where I would be sleeping?"

As I say this, I realize she can't "show" anything to anybody. She can "direct" or "present" but never show. "Show" has the idea of vision built into it. She stands and walks across the room to a door behind me, a door beside the door where she led me to hear the music. She turns the key which is in the lock of the door.

"See, Jacques, you can be completely private."

She holds out the key to me and I take it. She stands to let me go past her, into the room. I flick the switch, but, of course, there's nothing. There's a musky smell and the smell of dust even more than in my attic.

"I have not been in this room for many years, Jacques. I still have such terrible memories. It was a long time before I could take a bath in the bathtub. You do understand, yes?"

The light from the main room slightly lightens the dark dustiness of the room. I can just make out a large bed and a chest of drawers beside it. There are end tables on either side of the bed. I stand there with my memory of the story Mirabelle told me from so long ago. It's almost like Miss Havisham's dining room in Dickens's *Great Expectations*. Can I actually sleep in this room? I turn my head to look at Mirabelle. She has not passed through the door and stands silhouetted against the light in the ceiling of the main room.

"Is it so terrible? It is a dead place, is it not? Can you bring life into it?"

"I think I can, but not tonight. Tonight I'll go home and sleep in my 'cold, dirty attic.' Tomorrow I'll come in the light, buy more light bulbs, and begin to clean this room. I'll start here first, so I'll have a place to stay. Is that all right?"

"Thank you, Jacques, you are a most considerate man and I love you dearly."

She says it so naturally, with such a calm feeling, I know she's serious. I take it that way but don't respond. I know it must be very late. If I'm going to get a good night's sleep, I should leave soon. I can catch one of the last 86 buses going to my quartier.

"You are right, Mirabelle. It will be fun fixing up this place into our private nest. But now I must leave. Tomorrow I'll run, then prepare some more canvas to paint. I'll meet you by the statue of Monsieur Diderot."

Mirabelle turns from me and goes to a board with cup hooks hanging beside the front door. She feels on the board and takes a key off the board.

"Here, Jacques. This is a key to the apartment. I want you to have it."

She wipes the key off on her apron.

"This key has been hanging there since Rolande died. It is strange how time passes so quickly, how things stay in one place, alone, unused, when you live such a limited life as mine. It will be so good to have someone 'seeing' like you, really 'seeing' in this place. Good night, Jacques, do not let the rats bite you."

She puts up her face for a kiss. I lean over her.

"There are no rats to bite, Mirabelle. I hear them sometimes but they are only going about their own business."

I kiss her slowly on one cheek and she kisses me at the same time on the other. I kiss her slowly on the other cheek and she holds her soft, thin lips against my cheek near my ear, above my beard. I hold her by the arms and she rests her hands on my arms.

"Good night, Mirabelle, à demain."

I just catch a bus and ride to the Bastille. For the two extra stops after that, it costs another ticket and I enjoy walking down rue de la Roquette, still alive at this time of night. Also, I'm still not so flush with francs that I can tolerate paying another bus ticket for two stops.

Inside, I'm feeling confused. I hadn't realized how attached, how homed, I'd become to my attic, to this area, to the routine of the life I've been leading. I think Mirabelle and I can help each other, ease the emptiness and lone quality of our lives, but what will we lose? It will only be known with time.

Blind Reverie

It was so horrible listening to Jacques tell of his fall into the life of a clochard, of alcohol, of cold and dirt. I could not help but cry.

I was so happy to have my little gift of music to offer. It is wonderful that he, too, loves music, even the music I most enjoy playing, Baroque. That was a precious gift for me. So often, when I want to give to Jacques, it turns into a gift to me.

It was impossible that I asked him to come live with me. I cannot even think what Rolande would think, or my parents. But I am old now. I have this big apartment going to ruin and Jacques has nothing. I am sure he can make it into a beautiful place. Just having him living here, if he changes nothing, will make it beautiful for me.

I hope that living together, working together on the apartment, on the paintings he wants to do with me, will bring us closer. I want to be as close to him as possible. Never have I had such strong feelings. It must be terrible for an old woman like me to be like a little girl throwing herself at a grown man, a married man at that. I am becoming quite a hussy. I should be ashamed of myself. But I am not.

Chapter 8

After lunch the next day, I sit down and do a rough floor plan of the apartment. I use a tape measure Rolande had left in her room. I get to see the harpsichord when I look for the tape. It is enormous and painted a muted green, with gold ocher trimmings. It is really beautiful. I wish Mirabelle could see how gorgeous her instrument is, but she doesn't have to see it, she lives it, makes it sing.

When I finish my plan, I explain what I've done. She seems to understand. Although I'm going to start with the room where I'll sleep, I want to have an overall concept of what we'll be doing.

Mirabelle wants the main room, the room where we eat and talk, to be light and filled with the colors of sunshine. I decide to paint the walls a pale but slightly warm yellow, something on the order of cadmium yellow pale, with a touch of white. I'll paint the door frames and baseboard white, as well. All the woodwork now is a dim gray, or maybe it was once white. I'll have to scrub the woodwork before I start.

She wants the music room to be a combination of the colors in water, sky, and something of spring. I decide to paint the wall with the window opening onto the court a grayed blue. The other walls will be a medium green but light in value and not too intense. I want to suggest the underside of leaves in the shade. I'll put a darker green rug on the floor. These green walls will not be painted but will be covered with cloth. I'll put something sound-insulating under the cloth. It'll be a lot of work, but then I won't need to do anything about the filthy walls already there, I'll just pull off the sagging wallpaper and cover over it all. I'm going to put white acoustical tile on the ceiling. I'd love this room to be a good room for the sound of her harpsichord, without uncalled-for echoes and vibrations.

Mirabelle says she wants her bedroom to be an inside place, not under the ground, but as if inside something living. This sort of surprises me. She wants it to be in shades of red going almost to violet. I'm surprised she has all the names of the colors so well in her mind. I wonder if over the years her perceptions of the colors have changed, warped, slid into different percepts or concepts. But I try listening to what she's saying. There's an inner consistency to her ideas, as if she's been thinking of them a long time. There's a pause. I've been writing down her ideas and suggestions on a page of my drawing pad.

"I think, Jacques, I am wanting to go back into the womb of my mother. I had not thought of it before this moment, but I think that is what I am doing. For sleeping, I want the comfort of warmth and lifeblood. I know, considering what happened to me, this is a strange thing to want, but it is the way I would like it. Do you understand?"

"I don't know if I really understand, Mirabelle, but you seem to know what you want, and what you want you shall have. Would you like the walls painted, or shall we do these walls in padded cloth the way we're doing the music room?"

"Oh, padded cloth, please, it should be like the inside of a jewel box. And I'd like so much to have the bed in the center of the wall, with the head between the two windows. And could my bed be all in white with a quilted cover in white, too? When I'm in that bed, I want to feel like a queen, a queen of light in my darkness."

I look at her. This is the first time she's really revealed the little girl, the early adolescent, in herself. It is so charming to see, to feel the radiance of her dream.

"You *are* a queen, Mirabelle. If I've ever met a queen in my life, you are it, and so a queen's bed you shall have."

We agree my room should be a place where I can hang my drawings and paintings on the walls. I want it to be all earth colors, ochers, siennas, umbers. I am going to look for dark refrigeration cork and put it on the walls. That way I can tack or pin up drawings, drive in small nails to hang my paintings, without leaving ugly holes. I would prefer my bed to be a narrow single bed, but the bed in the room, the bed of Mirabelle's parents, is so large, with a canopy over it, albeit a rotting, hanging, dust-laden canopy; I just can't bring myself to throw it out. The mattress, oddly enough, is reasonably comfortable given that it must be over fifty years old.

I hang this mattress along with all the sheets and bedclothes out the window to air. My room has only one window, Mirabelle's two. The music room has one window as well. There is a direct opening to the bathroom from my room, but the toilet is across the room next to the kitchen. It's a classic old building, built before plumbing, with the plumbing installed later, according to where closets or pantries could be conveniently adapted. I think the toilet room was probably once the pantry. The bathroom has been carved out of the room where Mirabelle sleeps.

This room of Mirabelle's, because of the bathroom's intrusion, has an L shape. Her bed, if we fit it between the windows, will have just enough room for passage between the corner of the bathroom and the bottom of her bed. There is no opening to the bathroom from her room. If there were, since there is a direct opening from the main room, and from my room, there would be no place to put the tub. I could take the tub out and put in a shower so she could have direct access, but that would probably be beyond my limited skills.

I spend that first day just knocking down cobwebs in the room where I'm going to sleep, using Mirabelle's broom and a small ladder. I brush the worst dust and dirt from the ceilings and walls. There's dust everywhere. I leave the window wide open and close the door. Mirabelle is still nervous about coming in and stays outside in the main room.

Before I'm finished, it's getting dark and I've turned the overhead light on. Also, I've gotten one of the small end-table lights working now. I gather a set of sheets and pillowcases from those I've been airing out the window, plus some towels, and head for a self-service laundry down on rue des Canettes. Mirabelle says she'll have le souper ready when I come back.

It's dark when I come struggling up the steps with the wash.

I've also washed most of my own clothes. Mirabelle has the door open and is waiting on the palier for me.

"*Are you all right, Jacques? I began to worry.*"

"I'm fine. There was a line for the dryers."

I ease past her and put the laundry in the bedroom. Most of the dust smell has gone, so I pull the rest of the bedclothes inside, along with the mattress, and close the window; from now on, they'd only get damp in the night air. I'm feeling bushed. I collapse in the chair at the table.

"*Jacques, you did not do any painting today. I feel terrible about that.*"

"You're right, Mirabelle, but this was just to get things going. From now on, no matter what, we take off at least three hours to paint. I can paint by myself in the mornings while you're with your pigeons, then I can paint after lunch. In the late afternoon, I'll work on the apartment."

She's bringing in things to eat from the kitchen. This time it isn't soup at all, it's small crêpes with different jams, melted butter, and sugar. There must be ten or twelve crêpes. I can't help but wonder how she makes these things. Can she do it by feel? She'd burn her fingers. I look into the kitchen and, sure enough, there's one of those flat, sideless, thick sort of frying pans they use to make crêpes, and one of those wooden batter spreaders. I'm not even going to ask, just enjoy, appreciate the miracle, the miracle of Mirabelle.

After dinner we talk some more about the things we're going to do. I've brought along two of the canvases I'd stretched. Getting started on them is my first concern. I'll also look around for some wall paint and maybe cork for my walls.

It isn't even nine o'clock when I catch myself drifting off. Actually, Mirabelle catches me.

"Jacques, are you falling asleep? In my mind, I feel you slipping away."

"I think I am, Mirabelle. I'm sorry."

"Do not be sorry. You worked hard today, you deserve your rest. Go to bed and have a good sleep. I will clean up the kitchen, then go to sleep myself. I like to wake with the noises in the street. It is wonderful listening to Paris waking up, the first buses, the men sweeping the water in the gutters, the automobiles buzzing, the sound of people walking, and then, at six o'clock, the bells. It is the way I love to wake. Now you sleep and sleep deeply, we shall have a wonderful day tomorrow."

I stagger off to bed and just barely get undressed and into my sweat suit, which I'd brought over with me from the attic, and washed with the bedclothes, before I stretch out on that overly soft bed and fade away.

The next morning is glorious. I decide to run in the Luxembourg Gardens. It's something I've never done. I've been there when others were running but it's the first time for me.

I dress in my running suit just as light is coming through my window. I feel great, not even stiff from all the reaching the day before. I step out into the main room, quietly, on my way to take my morning pee, when I'm stopped in my tracks.

There's Mirabelle, in black leotards, standing on her head in the middle of the floor.

"Good morning, Jacques. It feels like a beautiful day. You have a good run."

I walk around her. She's steady as a rock in the yoga headstand position, her forearms on the floor, her fingers intertwined behind her head. I ease myself toward the toilet.

"I'm going to run in the Luxembourg Gardens, Mirabelle. It'll be the first time there for me."

"It should be lovely. There are still some crocus, and the spring flowers are in all the flower beds. The trees should be coming into blossom, too. I have not smelled them yet, but it cannot be long."

I step into the toilet room, close the door. I scrunch close and pee against the side to keep down the noise. I flush and come out.

Mirabelle is still on her head. I wonder how long she stays up there. I don't want to bother her, she might be trying to meditate. I've tried that headstand, but the only way I can do it is by having my feet braced against a wall. I cross past her to the door.

"I'll be back in about forty minutes, Mirabelle. I can buy croissants on my way home. Is that all right?"

"That would be fine. I will have some filtre coffee made for us and we can enjoy a peaceful breakfast."

I have ten francs and the key in my running-trunks pocket. I hurry down the stairs and run through the streets toward the park. There's practically nobody up and about on the streets. I run up the rue des Canettes, through the Place Saint-Sulpice, along Vaugirard, and into the park. Here there are quite a few runners going along the inside of the fence. There seems to be a regular route they take. I join the pack. It feels strange running with others. Running has been such a solitary thing for me. I'll have to admit

I'm guilty of pride when I pass some younger, obviously trained runners. For me, running has been a new lease on life. It starts each day as if I'm being born again. I wonder if I'll be able to run through the winter. I could run in my sweat suit but it'd be hard to dry out. I'll need to think about it some more.

The flowers are beautiful. I especially enjoy running in the less used parts of the park where there are espaliered trees and bee-hives. I look into the trees, and sure enough, the thrusting stalks of the blossoms are visible, just bits of pink and white showing, sometimes a few blossoms. Spring is really coming on. I can't wait to tell Mirabelle. I look into the center of the park and the fountain is spurting, blowing in different directions.

I listen to the clock on the Médicis Palace, now the Sénat, until I've heard it ring three times, that is, every fifteen minutes. Then I go out the same gate I ran in and back through the streets the way I'd run before. I stop at Mabillon and buy two croissants. I'll have to find out from Mirabelle what she prefers, croissants, butter or not, apple roll, raisin roll, pain au chocolat. For now, I just get two simple croissants.

I run up the steps to the room and Mirabelle is there to open the door. I'm dripping wet from sweat and still breathing hard. I hand the croissants to Mirabelle, the thin paper of the bag is already beginning to get wet from my sweat dripping.

"I need to take a quick washup, Mirabelle, then I'll be ready."

"I have drawn a bath for you. If it is either too hot or too cold you can put more water in."

God, she's too much.

"That's really nice, Mirabelle, but you don't have to do things

like that. It must interfere with your exercises and language lessons. I can take care of myself."

*"I know, but I enjoy taking care of you a little
bit. Is it all right?"*

"It's wonderful. I'll hurry right out."

*"Jacques, would you hand me out your wet
clothes before you get into the tub? I have some
hot sudsy water for them here."*

I go in the bathroom. It's steamy and warm. I don't know how
long it's been since I actually took a bath in a tub. Even when I
lived at home in Le Vésinet or anywhere, I usually only showered.

I strip off my running clothes, pass them out the door to Mirabelle, who must have been waiting for them because she takes
them right out of my hand. Am I ever getting spoiled! I ease myself
into the gigantic tub, trying not to think of Mirabelle's mother. It's
just the right temperature, a shade too hot, but as my body adjusts
it's tremendous.

There's good, strong-smelling soap and I suds myself down. I
feel like a Roman senator. I lower myself down till I'm completely
covered with water except my head. I wash my hair, there's no
shampoo. I feel guilty, keeping Mirabelle waiting, but I can't drag
myself out of that tub. I loll in it, long past any normal washup
time should take. I'm having a good, old-fashioned soak.

Finally, I get up on my knees, run some cold water over my
washed hair, and pull the plug. The water goes down fast and I
clean the tub with a washcloth as it drains. When it's empty and
clean I step out. There are big, heavy-pile white towels and I dry
off.

I use the direct entry to my room and quickly dress in my painting clothes. I'd washed them the night before and they smell fresh and clean. They're spattered with paint but they're clean. I comb my hair and go out with my shoes in my hand.

Mirabelle comes from the music room.

"Did you have a good bath, Jacques? Do you feel bumpy and clean?"

"I feel like a new man, Mirabelle. My body is clean and refreshed, my clothes are clean. I don't think I've ever felt so clean."

I lean over to put on my shoes. These shoes are beginning to wear out, the soles are losing all their tread and are splitting away from the uppers on both sides. I can never replace them and I'm so spoiled I could never wear the kind of shoes I used to wear. Maybe I'll find an old pair of tennis shoes in the marché. I'll keep an eye out.

"You do not need to be a new man, Jacques, the old man is quite good enough."

She brings the hot pot of coffee and pours for the two of us. This time, the coffee is so hot she doesn't allow it to reach her finger but just hovers one finger over the edge until the steam and warmth let her know she's poured enough. She sits across from me. She has the two croissants in a blue-and-white bowl between us. There are also some quartered pieces of orange on the plate before me.

"You're ruining me, Mirabelle. How can I ever go back to being a bum-type street painter after all this luxurious living?"

I bite into the oranges, peeling the flesh away from the skin of each quarter with my teeth. The taste is so strong, so fresh. After running, everything tastes good, and these oranges are out-standing.

Mirabelle holds her orange slices like a piece of watermelon and eats each slice sideways. I watch her. One great thing about being with a blind person is you can carefully watch what they're doing without being embarrassed, or feeling they're embarrassed. She nibbles slowly at her orange slices. I wonder what she'd think if she saw how I crudely rip the orange flesh out of its skin with my teeth. I'll bet she probably knows, from the sound.

The croissants aren't the best but they're good, especially with the butter and blackberry jam Mirabelle has set out on the table.

"I didn't know what you like, Mirabelle, so I just got these ordinary croissants. What do you like?"

"Oh, usually I only have some fruit and a slice of bread with my coffee. It is too difficult going all the way downstairs to buy croissants. Thank you, these are lovely."

"But what would you really like?"

"I like to be surprised, and these croissants were a wonderful surprise, thank you again."

After breakfast, I pack my box and canvas along with my turp and varnish bottles. I thought I'd go back to the Place Furstenberg and just do a careful drawing this morning, maybe get into the underpainting. Then, in the afternoon, if this great weather holds up, Mirabelle can come join me and help with what she's seeing, feeling, the way she did before. It sounds like a perfect day.

I have all the measurements for the walls in my room to buy

cork, or whatever I can find, as well as the paint. Mirabelle's already told me she has no brushes or rollers, so I'll get those at the same time, probably at the BHV department store over on rue de Rivoli. The best thing there is, I can see what I want, just pick it up and line up at the cashier to pay, no long explanations.

I'm out working before nine o'clock. The light is beautiful on the Place. I decide I want to take another position than the one I took the first time. I still want to paint downhill, the Place is on a slight hill, but I place myself on the other side and closer yet to the lamp in the center. I find just the spot, out of car's way, but still with a great angle. I set up the box, hook on the canvas, pull out my little canvas chair I borrowed from Mirabelle (she had two), and start. I do the beginning of the drawing with a 4H pencil to get things laid out, starting across the bottom of the canvas so I can see just what I'll be including. I'm working on a 25 Figure again, same size as the one I sold. I sure hope I can get as good a painting this time as I did with that one. Without Mirabelle, I feel almost like a kid sent to the store for the first time alone to buy candy.

I put in a good morning's work. In some ways, I think the drawing and composition are even better than the one I sold. It's in the actual painting where I feel Mirabelle most affects the work. In the intensity and sensitivity of her descriptions, she opens up a big part of me to the directness of color and texture which I don't seem to manage on my own. Up till now, I've been letting the drawing, the composition, dominate the paint. Somehow, with her, the paint takes on a life of its own.

When I hear the bells of Saint-Germain-des-Prés ringing, I stop. I sit there listening while they trace the sky, then pack up my box.

There's sun now, and shadows of leaves are across the Place. I look and wonder how I can make it appear to be lit like that on my canvas. Sometimes it all seems impossible.

After another wonderful lunch, Mirabelle folds up her own little chair, I throw it on top of my box and we start off to the Place. I go down the stairs first because they're too narrow for the two of us together. They're so narrow that, if you want, you can bump against the railing, then against the opposite wall as you go down, like a sailor or a drunk. My 25F canvas just clears on the corners. I look back and watch Mirabelle. She has one hand brushing the wall on her left and her right hand on the rail. For her, blind, this is the perfect staircase.

The sun is still out. She takes my arm and we walk around the church to the Place. We aren't saying much, just appreciating the warm sun after the long winter, and enjoying being together.

At the Place, I unfold and set up the two chairs first. Then I open my box, stretch out the legs, put paint on my palette, varnish and turp in my little pots, and look out. The shadows of the opening leaves on the trees have moved and a good part of the Place is in darker shadow. There's a gentle spring breeze blowing, but in general it's calm and quiet.

As I'm beginning the underpainting, Mirabelle starts talking about the Place as she remembers it, telling little anecdotes and giving brief, cogent descriptions. Most of the time she keeps her eyes closed, as if blocking the possible images in front of her from invading her personal vision. Once in a while, she'll ask about something she remembers, if it's still there; she wants me to describe how it looks now.

Normally, this would be an interruption of my painting, but

somehow we keep in tune. We talk and the paint flows out of my brush. I find I'm doing a much deeper, darker underpainting, at the same time with higher chroma, than I usually do. I feel as a coach driver must feel when he is driving a pair of horses who are well trained and know where they're going. Sure, I'm holding the reins, the brush, but the power, the direction are Mirabelle's. I almost feel hypnotized. I'm so much under her influence, I hate to stop the underpainting and put out the paints for the beginnings of the impasto.

I'll be working wet-in-wet, so I'll start with the sky and the leaves of the tree. I tell Mirabelle what I'm doing.

"How green are the leaves, Jacques?"

"They're about halfway out, Mirabelle. The leaves are just now getting their strength and are almost more yellow than green where the sun shines through them."

"Are they the way they used to be, with different colors of blue where the sky is reflected in them on top? Or when they have their real color, dark, thick, green? But best was the color looking up through them, sparkling bright yellow-green, almost like windows in a church."

I look up and it's as she says. It's so easy to miss such beauty. I sit there staring up through the leaves. I'm seeing how the sky, too, appears as different colors according to the colors of the leaves surrounding each space. Sometimes it is pale, almost cerulean, other times deep as violet. This can't be, because it's the same sky, but that's the way it seems.

"When I was a little girl, I liked to hold my hand against the stone base for the lamps and run

around fast as I could, round and round in circles. Then I would hold tight to that cold stone base and look up through the lights at the trees and sky still spinning above me. It was like being in the center of a carrousel. It was so beautiful."

I stop as I'm just starting to put in the first strokes for the sky and look up again. It all seems so still after hearing Mirabelle describe what she did as a girl. Did I ever do anything like that? I can't remember. I don't think I did. I put down my brush.

"Mirabelle, you've tempted me. I must do what you did all those years ago or I can never paint this Place the way it should be painted."

"Oh no, Jacques!"

She laughs, a little-girl laugh but with the soft gasps of an old lady.

"They will arrest you."

"No, Mirabelle. I must."

I walk to the center of the Place, put my left hand against the base, and start going round and round in a counterclockwise direction. It isn't long before I feel I'm going to fall and I wrap my arms around the base to the lamp tightly. I look up through the spinning lamps into the spinning sky. It's as she says. I feel as if I'm the center of the universe with the stars spinning around me. The trees and the sky bend and blend. I stay that way until it all stops, then I go back and sit down.

"You really did it, did you not, Jacques? I could hear you running."

I'm still dizzy and somewhat out of breath. My hands are shaking.

"It was just as miraculous as you said, Mirabelle. I feel now I can make an even more beautiful painting. You've opened my eyes and mind to many things."

We stay there, me painting, Mirabelle sometimes talking, sometimes asking questions, as I, almost incredibly, bring us all together into the canvas. It's a wonderful confluence of the paint itself, as paint, my vision of the Place, the Place itself, and Mirabelle's magical vision. As the painting appears, I almost feel sometimes as if it's happening independently of me. I find myself holding my breath, afraid to disturb the vibrations I sense around us.

It begins to grow dark. It's Mirabelle who notices first. I'm so lost in the painting I could probably paint until night.

"Jacques, is it not becoming too dark to paint? Are you not afraid the colors are changing too much?"

I come out of my reverie. I look around me, independently, as just me, American Jack, Mirabelle's Jacques. It's dark all right. I must've been out of my mind to keep painting with so little light.

I pack up, feeling so calm inside I could almost fall asleep right there on the Place. Mirabelle takes my arm and we fight our way across the evening traffic on the boulevard Saint-Germain, past Monsieur Diderot, down rue des Ciseaux, up the dark stairs, and into the apartment. I'm still adrift in my mind, in Mirabelle's, in the Place. I put away my paints behind the curtain covering the door and sit at the table.

Mirabelle has turned on the lights for me and is bustling about.

"Jacques, you should take a bath, relax, put on your sleeping costume, and then I shall feed you. You must be very tired."

I am. I follow her instructions, still in my dream. I'm not like

myself at all. I feel very relaxed, tired, but at the same time tuned
to everything, all the small things, sounds, shadows, smells. When
I go into the bedroom where I sleep, I smell the dust still, the
freshness of the clean sheets, the mold of an old house. I undress
in slow motion, feeling the air hit my body. I sit on the bed and
take off my shoes. I walk into the bathroom, start running water
into the tub. I strip down the rest of the way and ease my body
into the water as it flows up around me. I have almost no desire
to do the practical things one does taking a bath, soaping, scrub-
bing, rubbing out the paint on my hands. I only want to lie there
stretched out, practically floating.

But I finally do get myself more or less clean, into my clean
sweat suit, and go out to the room.

"Now you will be more rested, more refreshed. Come, let us eat. I think you will like my soup, it is pommes de terre et poireaux. It will give you strength."

We eat without too much conversation. We communed so
deeply there on the Place, ordinary talk seems just that, ordinary.
The soup is perfect. I break bread into it and eat with the large
soup spoon, slowly, almost methodically, for me. Mirabelle has
poured us each a glass of wine. It's a simple table wine and cuts
the thickness of the soup perfectly. I sit there staring at my empty
bowl.

"Do you want some more, Jacques? There is more soup in the pot."

I shake my head, then realize again she can't see me.

"No, Mirabelle. The soup was very good, but I've had enough."

I look up at her. She's concentrating on me, my every move,

every sound. I guess it's the blind person's equivalent of a concerned stare.

"I'm fine, Mirabelle, just relaxed, as you said I should be. I don't feel sleepy, only very calm inside."

"Would you like to hear some music?"

That sounds about right. Again I nod my head, forgetting.

"Yes, Mirabelle. I'd like that very much."

She takes the dishes from the table. I try to help her but it's difficult not to get in the way of a blind person who knows all the paths. I decide to sit down again and just watch her. I enjoy the efficiency of her every move, the revelations to me of the little techniques she's worked out to compensate for her blindness. She makes less clatter of dishes when washing them than almost any "seeing" person I know. It's as if she's washing dishes while someone else is sleeping.

"Now, Jacques, we shall have music. I want to play for you something I've been working on today."

I follow her into the music room. I don't turn the light on. There's no need. I prefer listening to music with my eyes closed anyway. She opens her instrument and sits quietly at the keyboard, no rustling of music. All the music is in her head. I settle back.

She plays François Couperin this time, starting with the "Tick-tock-choc," which has some polyphony in it but is not as difficult as the first suite she played. It's perfect. I find myself floating with the melody, the tinkling rhythms. And then I must have fallen asleep because Mirabelle is gently shaking me. She's dressed for bed in a clean, long flannel nightgown with a ruffled collar. I sit up suddenly, not knowing where I am, almost not knowing who she is, feeling like a little boy.

"You shouldn't sleep here, Jacques. It is very late, you must go to bed."

I struggle to my feet.

"I'm sorry."

"Was it so tiring, my music, that it put you to sleep?"

"No, it was perfect, beautifully played. Nothing could have been so wonderful. It was like going to heaven without dying."

"I could tell from your breathing you had gone to sleep and then you snored lightly. Rolande would snore sometimes when she was very tired."

She takes me by the arm and leads me out the dark room into the center room and then into my bedroom. She's turned back the covers on the bed. Sleep is taking me away. Why should I be so tired? I didn't work *that* hard.

I slide under the covers and Mirabelle stands over me. She has her hair down in a long braid hanging forward over her left shoulder. She touches me with her hand, then sits on the bed beside me. I close my eyes.

I feel her hand on my brow. It is cool, light.

"Now go to sleep, Jacques, and you will wake with the bells tomorrow fresh and ready to paint."

I realize she's in her parents' room, now my room, for the first time, probably, since she slept here with her dead mother those long years ago. That's the last I remember.

———

The next day, in the morning, I go to the BHV and order the cork, the paint, the rollers, brushes, all the things I'll need to do my room. I've decided to fix up one room at a time so the place won't be in a constant mess. At the BHV, they promise delivery for the next day.

I come back and tell Mirabelle. I tell her how much it's going to cost, going over the bills with her, so she knows what she's getting into.

"It is all right. I cannot understand all of it but I trust you and I have enough money. This is a wonderful way to spend it, making this place, the home of my parents and now of us two, beautiful.

"I even have my own checkbook and I can sign my name. I also have a way to write the numbers, names, and dates in the right place on the check. Do you want me to show you?"

She goes into her music room and brings out a checkbook. Inside, she has a small piece of celluloid cut so openings are aligned with the spaces on her checks. I wonder if she figured this for herself, and if she did, who cut the openings for her.

"You see, I can write the checks for money myself. Now let us have our déjeuner and then we shall go out to paint in the Place."

The day isn't as beautiful as yesterday. There are long periods when the sun is covered by dark gray clouds. Several times during the afternoon, I think it's sure to rain, but each time Mirabelle says no.

"I shall tell you when it is going to rain, Jacques.

I can feel from the air and the sounds of the trees and especially the birds. The birds know."

And she's right. We paint there four hours and I finish the painting. We've picked up just where we left off and the painting almost seems to glow when it's finished. More than that, I *know* right away when it's finished, there's no dinking around at the end, wondering if I can improve it. I can't. Also, Mirabelle knows when it's finished, almost before I do.

"I think it must be a most beautiful painting. I can hear the beauty of it in your voice. I hear the people who stop by, sometimes they say how lovely it is, and sometimes they are only silent, but I can tell. What a wonderful afternoon this has been, now I think it is going to rain very soon. Let us go."

That night, when I'm stretched out in bed, remembering the painting, I hear the door to my room open quietly. The light in the main room is out and very little light comes in the window behind me, so I can barely make out the form of Mirabelle in her nightgown.

"May I come in?"

"Please do, Mirabelle, come right in."

I slide over more toward the other edge of the bed. Mirabelle sits lightly on the edge. She's silent for a long time.

"I could not sleep. We were so close again today and then in the night I feel very alone."

A part of me is scared. I knew this would probably happen and I thought I was prepared for it, but now it's actually happening I feel very passive. This is Mirabelle, I admire, respect, love her. But I've felt nothing of passion. How can I tell her this? Must I?

"Jacques, I feel I know your mind and your heart so well, but I know nothing about how you look. I know nothing of men. The last man to touch me, except for doctors, was my father when I was a child and he was gone to the war before I was eleven years old. I know nothing of how a man feels. I can smell you, hear you, and when we faisons les baisers, I have felt the roughness of your skin, the stiffness of the hair in your beard, like the white hairs on my head, but that is all."

She's quiet again. I'm trying to think of what to say and nothing comes. I reach over and take her hand in mine. It's cool in the dark room.

"Please, Jacques, may I touch your face? May I let my fingers tell me what my eyes cannot, how your nose fits between your eyes, your mouth, your lips, how they are formed, so I can have a picture in my mind? Is it asking too much?"

I still can't speak. It's so sad to sense the completeness of her darkness. I lift her hand from her lap and place it across my mouth. She braces herself with her other hand on the pillow beside my head.

"Thank you, you are very kind."

At first, she only keeps her hand across my mouth, lightly changing the position of her fingers against my lips. It's almost like being kissed. Then she starts gently stroking my mustache with the tips of her fingers, gliding softly over the stiffness of the hair, down to the corners of my mouth. My mouth begins to tickle but I don't move my lips. The sensuality of her touch is incredible.

She explores the end of my nose, lightly penetrating my nostrils with the tips of her fingers, moving them tenderly over the outside edge, into the crease of the wings. She enters my nostrils again, seeming to search.

"Jacques, you have so much hair growing in your nose. Is that the way it is with men? I have some hairs in my nose but they are not so stiff and there is not so much."

I suppress a rising desire to laugh, to reach out and hold her.

"I don't think I have more hair in my nose than most men, Mirabelle. In the old days, when I went to the barber, he would clip any hairs that showed with the tips of his scissors, but I think it was normal."

Her fingers now are exploring the length of my nose. She lingers with thumb and finger along the tender sides as they go up to the corners of my eyes. I have my eyes closed. There's no way she's going to touch my eyeballs; they're about the most valuable things I have. It's as if she reads my mind. Maybe it's in some small movement of my face.

"I shall not hurt you. Only relax, I am learning much about you, about men."

Tenderly she passes each finger, in turn, over my eyelids, lightly tickling the lashes with her fingernails. I have to admit it feels fine. I don't think I've ever had anyone pay such close attention to me.

She rubs her thumbs along my eyebrows, pushing them so they stand up, then pressing them down again. She shifts her weight, so her side is against mine, then brings both hands up so she can rub her thumbs over each of my eyebrows at the same time, her fingers resting along the side of my head.

"I hope you do not object, Jacques, but I want to feel the differences of your face, one side to the other. I know the two sides of my face are not the same, and neither are yours. I think it must be an important part of how a face looks. Is that so?"

"Yes, Mirabelle, in painting a face, the artist always knows this. Everyone is two people in one face and body."

"You have such deep-set eyes, Jacques, and such a high brow over your eyes. Is this the same with all men? It must make you look much more primitive than women, if other women are like me."

"My eyes are deeper and my brow more prominent than many men's, Mirabelle. But most men are somewhat like that. Also, not all women have faces as gentle and soft as yours. I think it might be because you have been blind and protected. You do not have the hardness in your face so many women have."

She has her hands on both sides of my forehead now, gently tracing the lines above my brow. Her fingers follow the paths from one end to the other, each hand playing counterpoint to the other, the fingers moving independently. Only a blind person or a musician could have such a lightness of touch, independence of hand movement, and Mirabelle is both. Sometimes she rests her hands, her fingers, so deftly on me I can almost not tell they are there, except for the dry coolness of them.

She runs her fingers up into my hair. I'm lucky I have most of my hair. Baldness doesn't seem to run in my family. It's turning gray, marching up the side of my head from my ears and downward into my beard. I wonder if Mirabelle will be able to tell these gray hairs in my beard from the pubic-type hardness of the other hairs in my beard.

Her hands, her fingers, gently push through my hair, pulling my scalp slightly. It feels very calming, comforting.

"You have such lovely hair, Jacques, and it is cool, cooler than the rest of your face. I like very much the way it feels. It is like water and flows between my fingers."

"Your hands in my hair feel wonderful to me, too. You are very gentle."

She brings her hands down the side of my head to my ears, her fingers first running along the outside crest around to the lobes and under them. She does the same thing simultaneously on each of my ears with her hands. To do this, she is lying across me.

She explores the insides of my ears with her tender fingertips, tracing the whorls as the ear swirls down to the orifice. Now this is beginning to excite me. I have very sensitive ears. I feel a stirring but try to ignore it. I concentrate on the sensation as sensation and not as sexual stimulation. After all, it *is* only my ears.

"But, Jacques, you have even more ear hairs than nose hairs. Are you sure you can hear? Don't you ever try to cut these hairs out of your ears? When I feel any hairs like this on me, I cut them off. Don't you care for yourself?"

She's like a mother. I find myself settling down.

"I guess I'm just not careful enough, Mirabelle. But then you must remember, I've been living in the streets or in my attic. There wasn't much time to cut hair out of my nose or ears, and I didn't have a mirror."

"That is not an excuse; I cut my hairs off and I cannot see. Soon I shall cut the hairs out of your ears. You need not worry. I shall not cut you. I am very good with scissors. Remember, I live on the rue des Ciseaux."

I reach up and put my hands over hers. I slowly pull them away from the side of my head and in front of my face. I kiss the tips of each of her fingers, holding them tightly together, as in prayer, between mine.

"Now I think we should go to sleep, Mirabelle. We have much work to do tomorrow when all the materials arrive. They told me the delivery would be at nine o'clock, so it should arrive after breakfast. I'll run, you can do your yoga and exercise, then I will start to prepare this room to work in it. Do you have a ladder? I'll need one."

"Yes, I think there is a ladder in the cave. There are also some tools you might be able to use."

With that, she leans over and kisses me quickly and very lightly on the lips. She stands up.

"It wasn't so bad, was it? I feel I know you much better. You are really even more handsome than I thought you would be."

She turns and leaves the room. After about five minutes pondering in the dark, I go to sleep.

Blind Reverie

We are so close when we work together, I feel I know exactly what Jacques is doing, what he wants me to do. We become as one.

But what must he think of the way I want my bedroom to be? It is so childish, at the same time, wanton, the bedroom of a whore. I know he knows it is what I want and he will make it that way for me. He can help me feel like a queen, a much loved queen.

And then when we were in the Place Furstenberg and he made me feel he was painting my Place, the Place of my dreams. He can be so like a child himself. I suspect that is part of what makes him an artist, what makes me love him so. In a way, we are like two children playing.

I must be careful not to be too arrogant, too sure-sounding in my description of these personal worlds in which I live. He must not feel I am seeing his blindness. But no, there is nothing of that; I can feel it in our vibrations, our nearness.

It was so wonderful touching his face, feeling the hardness of his skin, the lovely curves of his nose, his ears, his mouth. The bulk, the strength of his body under mine made me almost want to cry, cry in happiness.

Chapter 9

The delivery from BHV comes right on time. I've had a good run, bathed, and we're just finishing our coffee when Mirabelle stops and lifts her head.

"I hear strange footsteps on the stair. Perhaps the delivery from the BHV store is here."

I can scarcely believe it. France is not notorious for delivering on time. But there they are. I open the door and a man in blue coveralls presents a bill of lading. I look it over and it checks with the prices I have, so I tell them to bring up the load. I give the bill of lading to Mirabelle and tell her how much the check should be written for. There's no delivery charge.

I don't haul the things up with them, because I want to inspect everything as it arrives, to make certain it's all there, and that it's the color and quality I ordered. It all squares out okay. I give the two guys ten francs as a pourboire and they stomp off down the stairs again.

After that, I go with Mirabelle into the cave, a kind of basement storage area. She takes keys from the key board by the door, goes down the stairs, and I follow her.

"It has been many many years since I have been down here. Before she went into a maison de re-traite, the concierge gave me these keys. One opens the door to the caves, the other is to our particular cave."

She turns back to me on the stair and holds out the keys.

"I believe the number of our cave is on this tab."

I follow her along a dark corridor to a door at the end. I switch on a light. There's a steep, stone, twisting staircase down into the cave. I search along the wall until I find the wooden door with the same number as the key. I insert the huge key and the lock turns rustily. Mirabelle stands beside me.

I find a ladder, a self-standing one, with eight steps, rather than rungs; it's made of wood. These days, they're just about all aluminum. I don't think I've ever seen a wooden ladder quite like this. The wood is oak and sturdy, so it's heavy. I also find a box of rusty tools. I pick out a claw hammer, a mason's hammer, a pair of rusty pliers that still open and close, two screwdrivers with wooden handles, a small saw, also rusty, and a scraper. There are some fascinating tools in that box including wooden planes and calipers of all sizes. I won't have any use for anything like that. At least I hope not. I wonder who ever did; they don't seem the kind of tools one would use in doing reliure.

"These are the tools of my father, Jacques. I do not think anyone has touched them since he left for the war. My goodness, it smells like a tomb down here. I had forgotten that. Before she left,

the concierge would often bring up bottles of Ro-lande's wine to me. See them there. Now, with both of us drinking the wine, my supply upstairs is almost depleted. Perhaps another time we can bring up more. But now please let us go upstairs again where there is fresh air and warmth."

I shoulder the ladder and pick up some tools I've separated onto the floor of the cave. This ladder is a brute. I watch as Mirabelle feels her way up the steep curving steps. When I go through the door, I turn to lock it. I shift the ladder and start up the stairs. At the first turn I realize I can't get the ladder around holding it under my arm. I'll need to use both arms, and hold it vertically. I put the tools down carefully against the wall on the step.

"Mirabelle, watch for the tools. I've put them on the left of the step, the sixth step from the bottom."

"Thank you. I could hear you putting them down. You are having trouble getting the ladder around the corner, is that right?"

"That's right, Mirabelle. I need both arms to pull it up."

I straighten the ladder. Closed tight, and stood vertically, it goes up just fine. I work it along till I get to the door. It's latched. I hope Mirabelle has the key. I completely forgot to bring mine. She comes up behind me; she has the tools. She puts them down on the floor and reaches into her tablier, a kind of apron she wears, and pulls out the key. She walks past me to open the door. I go in past her.

"You didn't need to carry up the tools, Mirabelle. I was going right back down to get them."

"It was a pleasure for me, Jacques. It was something I could do. You cannot know how much

pleasure it gives me being able to help. There is so little I can do in the real world."

Once I get started, I work all through the day. I only take a break for lunch. Mirabelle wants me to go out and paint in the afternoon but I'm caught up in the project. I'd forgotten how much fun it is to take a place and really work on it till it becomes the way you want it. I haven't done work like this since we lived in the little house by the South Street Bridge in Philly.

Mirabelle goes out to feed and care for her pigeons but she's back long before the bells ring.

"Do you mind if I stay while you work? It gives me great joy to hear you scraping and hammering. I try to figure from the sounds just what you are doing."

"Please do stay, Mirabelle. I like your company. I'll try to tell you what I'm doing as I go along. But won't your pigeons be disappointed? I don't want to steal time from them."

"Oh, Jacques. I know you do not like my pigeons. Please do not make fun of me."

"No, seriously. The more I know you and the more I think about it, the more I realize I was wrong about pigeons before. I didn't respect them for what they are, how they are so wonderfully innocent, trusting, tolerant. Maybe it comes from my working so long at MBI. There, they only value cleverness, competition, getting ahead. I really think I actually *am* learning from your pigeons the way you said I would. But even more, I'm learning from you, Mirabelle."

She's silent, standing there and smiling at me, a genuine guru smile, something I normally can't stand. I know she's happy. She probably thinks I'm just saying this to please her, but this is true. It's part of the whole change I can feel coming over myself. She breaks the magic moment.

"If there is some way I can help you with this work, only ask me. I would like that very much."

When she says it, I think it's simply a nice gesture, but when I start gluing the acoustic tiles to the ceiling, and then the cork on the walls, I find she's a great help, because I'm up on the ladder. She hands the tiles to me. I tell her what I'm doing, spreading mastic on the tile and fitting it in.

"Would it not be easier and quicker if I spread the mastic down here, then handed the tile up to you?"

"I think it would be too difficult, Mirabelle; the mastic must be just so thick and over the entire tile. It's a messy business."

"I have rubber gloves in the kitchen. Let me try."

She goes away and comes back pulling pink rubber gloves onto her hands. I climb down the ladder thinking this is really going to slow things up. How can a blind woman spread mastic when most people who can *see* can't do it right? I spread newspapers on the floor and pile tiles beside them. I let her feel the special serrated scraper I bought for spreading the mastic. I do one, then let her touch it with her fingers to know how thick it should be. She's on her knees beside me. She nods that she understands. I go up to place the demonstration tile. I'm starting from one corner on the wall with the windows and I'll spread out as I go. I'll trim along the other two walls. I look down, and Mirabelle already has a tile, perfectly spread, ready for me. I take it from her.

"Is it all right?"

"It's perfect, Mirabelle, you *are* a miracle woman."

"Perhaps, or maybe I am just a happy woman. Also, I feel like a real woman working with a man and it pleases me very much."

She's on her knees again, spreading, while she says this, and has the next tile ready for me just when I need it.

The work goes much faster. Mirabelle is down and up, spreading and reaching to me at the top of the ladder. I realize I've got the easy job, she's the one who's working. After about fifteen minutes, when we've covered the whole corner, far as I can reach, I move the ladder. I've already moved the bed out of the way. I have all the furniture on one side of the room now and covered with old newspapers.

"Mirabelle, do you want to take a rest?"

"Are you tired, Jacques? It must be very difficult standing high on a ladder and reaching up to the ceiling, I cannot even see it in my mind properly."

"No, the work you are doing is much more tiring. I was thinking of you. Aren't you tired?"

"I shall tell you when I am. I am not so old, you know, and I am in good condition."

By lunch, we're well past the center of the room, soon we'll be ready for cutting and fitting. The bells have just finished ringing. I come down the ladder, lift Mirabelle to her feet by her hands.

"Shall we eat, Mirabelle?"

"Oh yes, it is time, is it not. I have a wonderful boeuf bourguignon I started this morning, it should be finished by now."

She takes off her gloves and turns toward the kitchen. I smell the bourguignon as she lifts the top off her heavy black pot. The smell even overwhelms the smell of the mastic. I have mastic all over my hands and it's also dripped into my hair in a few places. I go into the bathroom to wash up.

When I come out, Mirabelle has already set the table, and is tossing a salad. She shows no signs of all the work she's done this morning, not a drop of mastic, not a hair out of place. I pull up a chair and sit down.

We dine like a king and queen.

"Mirabelle, how did you get to be such a wonderful cook? This is delicious, I've never had such a tasty bourguignon."

"I cooked for my sister when she was alive. She showed me many things she had learned from our mother. It was something I could do. Also, when you are blind, there is such a sharpening of the other senses. I like very much to eat, to smell the food, to taste it. I do not eat much, but I eat carefully. It would always annoy poor Rolande because I ate so slowly. I like it very much that you eat slowly, too."

"It is something I have only recently learned, Mirabelle. Sometimes, when I was living in the street, all I wanted was alcohol. Then, when I started to recover, when I was cooking my own food in the attic, I learned to truly taste things, trying to separate the tastes in my mouth so I could know the blends of different vegetables, the way carrots are next to potatoes or to poireau, or onion. For the first time in my life I was in no hurry and I took my time. I learned then that my time was my own, and the small pleasures such as eating and tasting were a good part of it."

"That is very wise of you. For a young man you have learned much."

"I'm not so young, Mirabelle. I told you I was forty-nine. That is not so young. Soon I shall be fifty, half a century old."

"Ah, that is young. You have much exciting life before you."

I'd forgotten how old Mirabelle is. By my calculation, she's twenty-two years older than I. It's hard to believe. I look across the table at her, daintily cutting and eating a piece of meat. She feels me somehow, looks up, and smiles. Then she looks down at her food again. Somehow we've said something, without a word.

We work the rest of that afternoon. I have a special tool for trimming the corners. I cut first, Mirabelle smears on the mastic, and I slide the tile into place. It goes fast, so we're finished before the bells ring six o'clock. I climb down the ladder and look up. The ceiling tiles are beautiful and the room is much lighter now with the reflected light. Mirabelle is standing beside me.

"Can you tell me something of how it looks? I know you are proud of it. It is as with the paintings, it is in your voice, the way you move. Try to tell me, please."

"It is a simple thing, Mirabelle. Now, instead of a stained, dark ceiling with cracks, it is all white. The squares fit into each other and there are holes in the tiles in little lines, as you probably felt with your fingers. Now the ceiling reflects the light coming in from the window and from the door. It is much more light than it was before and looks as if it is a new ceiling."

"It sounds wonderful. Thank you. I enjoyed working with you, Jacques. This has been another special day; let us now have our souper."

"First, I'll clean up everything and move the bed back into place. I'll pile the newspapers on the dresser so we can use them next time. By the way, Mirabelle, why do you have these newspapers?"

"The concierge next door gives them to me. You are finding out one of my little secrets. I shall show you what I do with them another day."

That night in bed I feel the muscles of my back and shoulders tight, from all the reaching. I also feel myself waiting. I don't have to wait long; the door opens just a crack, enough so I can see Mirabelle against the window in the room behind her.

"May I come in, Jacques? Are you too tired?"

"Come in, Mirabelle. To be honest, I've been lying here in the dark waiting for you. I've been trying to figure out what a blind woman can be doing with all those newspapers. Maybe you aren't really blind and all this is some kind of charade you're playing."

She comes into the room, shutting the door behind her.

"Do not be cruel, Jacques. I shall tell you about the newspapers another time. It is perhaps somewhat erratic, what I do with them, but when one is blind one must take advantage of all the possibilities."

She eases herself onto the bed beside me. Her eyes are open in the dark. I can just see them. It really is hard, here in the dark, to believe she's blind or that she's seventy-one years old. Her hair is braided and comes down over her shoulder on the left side, as before. She has a slight smell of roses and a pale scent of lilac. She's wearing a different nightgown. This one has lace trim at the end of its long sleeves and is not quite so tight around her neck. I reach out and take her hands.

"Do you want to explore me some more, Mirabelle? Is there more you want to know about me?"

"Do not tease, please. I want to know as much about you as I can. I want to know you not just as a man but as yourself. Is that wrong?"

"No, it isn't wrong, Mirabelle. I understand very well. It must be terrible for you being so alone."

"But I am not alone now."

I let go of her hands and she reaches across to put both hands over my ears. She holds each ear between her thumb and fingers, her thumbs blocking the holes, so I feel deaf. Slowly her hands slide down my neck, as if encroaching into foreign territory. She's lying across my chest again and her hands meet at the back of my neck. She interlocks her fingers there and pulls up gently, as if checking the weight of my head.

"Your head is so big. It must be twice as large as mine. I know you are taller than I am by at least thirty centimeters but I never thought your head would be so big, so heavy."

While she's saying this, she's drifting her hands over my head, across my face. It's so light, it feels like butterfly touchings and at the same time, because she enters every indentation, every crack and crevice, it's as if she's sculpting me, shaping my head. Her hands stop across my throat, her thumbs in the hollow above my sternum, between my clavicles.

"Would you speak, please, Jacques? I want to feel you speak. I know my neck vibrates when I speak, I think yours must, too."

"What do you want me to say?"

"Oh yes, it vibrates beautifully, more than my neck vibrates. Please, speak again, say anything."

I'm silent. I don't know what to say at first, then I know.

"Mirabelle is in my bed. She has her hands on my neck, exploring me. She is a wonderful woman, the most incredible woman I've ever known. She is making my life more exciting every day and I hope I can make her life better."

I stop. Mirabelle has dropped her head onto my chest, her ear against my heart, keeping her hands on my throat.

"That was beautiful, Jacques, both what I heard and what I could feel as you spoke. I can also hear your heart, it beats very strongly and very slowly. I've never heard a heart beat before. Sometimes I can feel my own heart beating in my head or on my wrist, or I can feel it in my chest, but I've never heard a real heartbeat. It doesn't sound like a beat at all. It is like a quiet roaring, a rolling, bumping sound, and it isn't the same each time. It is like Bach, with two voices, or maybe even three or four. It is so lovely, better than listening to water or even the bells. It is the sound of life, of things continuing in the dark, the way I do, living without seeing, without being seen."

I bring my arms up and rest them lightly across her back.

"I see you, Mirabelle, and I feel you, and I smell you. You are here with me this night in this bed."

She stays a long time like that with her head on my chest until I begin to think she's asleep. Should I lift her into the bed with me? No, that would be taking advantage. I budge a bit and she shifts her head. I put my hands over her hands on my neck. We intertwine our fingers. She begins gently to explore my fingers now with her head still on my chest. She takes one of my hands in both of hers and slowly rubs down the length of each finger, resting lightly on the ridges of the joints, pressing down into the webbing between the fingers. She holds each finger in turn in her hands, squeezing lightly, then squeezing two fingers at a time, starting with my thumb and little finger. She searches the inside of my palm, running her fingernail exploringly down the lines in my palm to my wrist, almost like a palmist. She does this with both of my hands, each of her hands moving independently, caressing, gliding on my palms. Then she turns my hands over and does the same on the backs of my hands, tracing the veins and knuckles, brushing lightly over the hairs on the backs of my hands, on the backs of my first finger joints. She, in the dark, is discovering for herself and for me things I didn't really know about myself, and it is so comforting, so healing, so relaxing.

She places her two palms against my two palms, her left hand against my right, her right against my left. She lifts her head from my chest.

"I think your hands are twice as large as mine. It, too, is something I had not thought about. Do

you sometimes find them too big to do certain things? And they feel so strong, as if you could crush my hand without even noticing, if you wanted. Men are certainly different from women, are they not?"

"I don't have particularly large hands, Mirabelle. I've known several women with bigger hands than mine, more graceful, with longer fingers, too. I do not have artistic hands, they are more the hands of a worker, it's just that my work is painting. People are usually disappointed to see I do not have long thin 'artistic' hands."

"I am not disappointed. I think your hands are perfect. I did not know hands could be like yours.

"Oh, I have learned much tonight, Jacques, thank you. I shall leave you now so you can sleep."

Still holding our palms together, she leans over and kisses me on the lips, gently but with a slight lingering. I try to kiss her back but she is gone. She stands by the bed a few minutes, then leaves the room. I feel myself slipping into sleep. I feel wonderfully cosseted, comforted in this big bed.

At breakfast the next morning, we decide we'll go out to paint in the afternoon. That morning we manage to mount one wall of cork, on the side of the room away from the court. It looks good. At first, I have a hard time matching the grain and getting the squares fitted level, without running mastic over the front, but I work it out after a while. Mirabelle helps again the same way, spreading mastic, handing me the tiles. I ask if she's stiff from all the crouching and standing up but she says no, all her yoga and stretching make her quite strong and flexible. I have to admit that when I go up on that ladder the first time, that second day, I ache in a few places, but as soon as we get going at it, I don't feel anything.

So, after a great lunch, we go out to paint. This time we're going to be on the rue des Canettes looking up into the Place Saint-Sulpice. It's one of her favorite memories. She wants us to be on the sidewalk about thirty yards away from the Place, on the other side of where rue Guisarde ends at the rue des Canettes. I set up there and am disappointed I can't see more of the Place. I'd like to get in something of the front of the church and the fountain, but they're blocked by the buildings in the foreground.

I sit a minute trying to figure it out, trying to think up a composition that will work. Mirabelle starts speaking.

"Is it not beautiful, with the columns of the church and the water splashing in the fountain and the light with the new trees. You know, they are some of the only chestnut trees in Paris with red blossoms.

"Why I like seeing the Place from here is looking down the line of dark buildings and then the Place opening up with all the light and water. It is like coming out of a tunnel into the sunshine, is it not?"

I wonder if I should tell her. But if I'm going to have the kind of view she's describing, I'll need to walk about fifty yards up the street closer to the Place.

"Mirabelle, are you sure this is the location you want to be, *away* from the Place on the other side of rue Guisarde?"

"Why yes, is it not beautiful?"

"Well, Mirabelle, to be honest, from here I can't see the Place very well at all. I can only see the towers of the church over the buildings and an open place between the columns and the fountain. Are you sure this is the position from which you want me to paint?"

"Oh, I am so sorry; in all the years, perhaps I have mixed things up. I thought I could see rue Guisarde in my vision. I know I can see it, but it cannot be, can it?"

"Maybe you've mixed up different views in your mind, Mirabelle. These buildings all look over a hundred years old, at least, and I don't think they've really moved anything. I'm convinced we need to go up closer to the Place."

"All right, if you say so. Would it be possible for you to change things? Could you paint the buildings from here, leaving a space for the Place, and then we can move up closer so we can see the whole Place and you can put it in. Can you do that? That way, in the front we can have the rue Guisarde going off to the left."

It's a wild idea. She's actually *composing* a painting without being able to see anything. At first it seems crazy, a real violation of the way things are. But then the possibilities begin to grow on me. There's nothing to stop me from doing it. If it exists in Mirabelle's vision, I can make a vision of it for me, for others. Why not?

I walk up the street till I find a place where I can see all that Mirabelle's described in the Place, then walk back to where I've set up. It'll be a good trick but it could be done. After all, I'm not trying to make architectural drawings of Paris. These are works of love, love for Paris, love for Mirabelle, her love for me. I sit down beside her and explain what I'm going to do.

"That will be marvelous, Jacques. This way you will make it so everyone can see my vision even though it is not really out there for people to see. It will be our private view of Paris, a Paris we created ourselves. This is wonderful."

I start. I widen the street a bit, leave out a few of the buildings so there's more space for the Place in the background. It's harder than I thought it would be. I don't want to distort the perspective and the proportion so much it's disturbing in the painting itself. This is for painterly reasons, not just verisimilitude. I finally get the "forward" part done to my satisfaction and we move up closer to the Place. I paint in all I can see there, the façade of the church with its columns, the towers of the church, each different, one looking like a mad spool of thread built with massive stone.

I draw in the Place, knock out the cars, squeeze in half the fountain. I'll have it gushing water even though it's dry now. I explain what I'm doing to Mirabelle as I go on. She also is describing things to me, what she remembers, the games she played here, ice skating in the water of the fountain one winter during the war. She tells me about the towers, how there had been a competition for the building of the second tower, after the first tower had stood alone for many years. The man who won the competition, upon whose design the stone spool was actually built, was so severely criticized by all when they saw it, he climbed to the top and jumped off. Mirabelle says his grave is just beside the ambulatory outside the church. Because he committed suicide, he couldn't be buried in holy ground. At least, this is what Rolande had told her.

It reminds me of the man who designed the opera house in Vienna. He forgot to put steps under it and in his disgrace killed himself, too. Architects are a screwball bunch, half artists, half craftsmen, caught between the imaginary and the real.

I carry my box and our chairs back to the location where I started, deeper in the street of rue des Canettes, and squeeze out paints to start my underpainting. It's nice having in my head a broader, more complete view of the Place as I'm working, looking up this long street with a slight twist to the left. Mirabelle tells me that the name of the street on our left, rue Guisarde, comes from when the Duc de Guise had his stables here and his personal bodyguard lived above the stables. It's hard to think of this old but posh little quartier being a place where horses lived.

Mirabelle asks what the sky is like, if there are any clouds. It's a pale blue sky with small streaks of white. It must have rained overnight because everything seems so clear. Even the buildings have a cleaned-down sparkling look, or maybe it's just me, I'm feeling sparkling and clean myself. Mirabelle is sitting in a little spot of sunlight coming through the buildings just behind me.

I do the foreground in dark, rich, high chroma colors, as I did the shadow under the lights of my Place Furstenberg. Then I move my box and chair up again so I can do the opening to the Place Saint-Sulpice. It's so light up there it's almost blinding. The fountain has started playing and there are people taking advantage of the sun at the little café on the corner where this street comes into the Place. People stop to watch, then move on. I wonder if they can figure Mirabelle is blind.

I use light yellow ocher and some burnt sienna with a pale almost-wash of the sap green for the trees. The contrast, even at this stage of the painting, is great.

All the while, Mirabelle is sharing with me her vision, as she did the last time. It isn't too far from what I'm seeing, except for the dislocation of place. Or maybe I'm beginning to see the way she does, her vision is displacing the mere vision of my eyes. I don't care.

Again, the paint seems to flow. The only interruption is constantly having to squeeze out new colors onto my palette. I find I'm painting with much more impasto, painting more quickly, knowing always what to do next, not having that fear of mistake which has been haunting me in other paintings. Something inside me is definitely changing. I feel less controlled by Mirabelle and more going along with her, pulling in tandem, working together at an even pace.

I work until five o'clock. The time seems to have disappeared. I've gone up, back and forth, to the Place several times, almost automatically, with Mirabelle following me. There's much foot traffic and too much auto traffic, but I'm almost ignoring it, they work their way around us. Then, when the bells ring five, I feel the light touch of Mirabelle's hand on my arm.

"You are working so quietly, Jacques, only once in a while I hear your chair squeak, or you whistle softly. I am certain you are painting something beautiful."

"I think we are, Mirabelle. This might even be more beautiful than the Furstenberg, it has so much light and space on such a small canvas."

I'm astounded to hear myself call a 25 Figure a small canvas. Only a few weeks ago, it seemed like an immense space to cover.

"Perhaps you should stop now, while you are still not too tired. It is a mistake to work until you are tired, then you will not want to start again. Let us go and sit in the café for a few minutes, have a nice cup of Viandox, and listen to the bells ring at six o'clock. You have worked hard, you deserve a reward."

I stand up and look at the painting. This is as good a place to stop as any. What I have to do now with the shadows of the buildings cast onto the walls of other buildings will need the light of the earlier afternoon, the light in which I designed the painting.

"You're right, Mirabelle. I want to have my concentration when I finish this one. It is easy, when one is excited, to rush and not do it right."

I fold up the box, the chairs, and give Mirabelle my arm. We walk right into the painting, up the street, the Place unfolding in front of us as we go. I'm sorry Mirabelle can't see it. How I wish she could share with me what I'm seeing and feeling.

We find a place outside at the Café de la Mairie. There is still a bit of sunshine, cool sunshine now. But it feels good.

"Are you warm enough, Mirabelle?"

"I am fine, but let me sit close to you. Maybe the coolness is only an excuse, I like to sit close to you, to feel your warm body and sense your movements. It makes me not so alone and it makes me happy."

She snuggles up next to me and puts her arm through mine.

The waiter comes and I order two Viandox. Viandox is a broth like a bouillon. It's usually served with a shaker of celery salt.

The waiter comes with it quickly and wants to be paid right away because the shift is changing. I give him the money, and a slight tip. He tears our little chit in half, sliding it under my Viandox. The Viandox is steaming and smells great in the early evening air. I watch as Mirabelle gets all her boundaries established. She lets go of my arm and finds the edge of the table, the location of the cup. I pass her the celery salt and she shakes a little in. She takes her cup by the handle, the fingers of her other hand lightly guiding it, and lifts the heavy white cup to her mouth. I lean forward over my cup and check the box beside me. It's okay, the painting, face against the wall.

"It is so nice and hot, Jacques, almost too hot for my lips. My lips are very sensitive."

I taste. It's warm, not hot to me, but then I can drink practically boiling coffee. It feels good going down my throat and warming me inside. I shake in more celery salt. I hold the shaker over Mirabelle's cup when she puts it down.

"Do you want more celery salt, Mirabelle?"

"No, this is fine, it is only too hot."

She twists her head around, sniffing, feeling the air, I guess.

"Do you think anyone passing by would know I am blind as I sit here, Jacques?"

"I'm not so sure myself sometimes, Mirabelle. I think you're experiencing more than almost anybody here, they all seem so locked up in themselves, I don't see a single smile around us. We're the only ones smiling."

She smiles up at me.

"Perhaps that is how they would know I am blind; also, perhaps, that you are an artist."

"With these dirty paint-splattered clothes and that beat-up box behind me with a canvas hung on it, they'd know I wasn't working in the Trésor across the Place there, that's for sure."

We sip away, the Viandox getting cooler as the air gets cooler. When Mirabelle is finished we stand up, I shoulder my box, and we start home. On the way down rue des Canettes, Mirabelle is humming. I recognize the Bach prelude she'd played for me.

"Yes, Jacques, it is going around in my head. I must listen to it again, there are parts I still haven't heard and played right."

Blind Reverie

Last night we were so close. I never thought I would, could, ever be so close to anyone. His hands became mine, mine his. It was all so clear. It was more than seeing or even feeling. Jacques is such a kind man. Sometimes I almost begin to think he loves me, too. But that is impossible. I must remember I am an old, blind woman.

Then, working together, feeling useful, part of something that is being made, it gives me such hope and joy. Jacques is not only being kind when he says I help. He would not do that, I really am part of the work.

Out in the streets, painting the Place from the rue des Canettes, we were together again, in another way. Our minds were bending together, forming a special private world, I felt I wanted to hold him, kiss him, make him love me, too. Do other people feel this way? Is this what people mean when they say they are in love? I cannot believe it, I know that what Jacques and I experience together is something very exceptional, something more than life itself.

Oh, how I desire to play for him again. The music is all I have to thank him for all he gives me. When I play, my heart goes out with the music, I can imagine it going into his ears, inside him, and I am with the music, I am his.

Chapter 10

That night, she comes again just as I'm stretched out and feeling good about things. I've also been waiting for her. I wonder what her excuse will be this time. I slide over and she sits on my bed. She's silent for a few moments.

"Jacques, be honest with me. Are you angry when I come to you like this when you want to sleep?"

"No, Mirabelle, it is very pleasant having you with me."

I wonder where it's going to go. I'm not lying, it is pleasant to have her there with me, so clean-smelling, so gentle, so girl-like as she softly explores me. I can't keep myself from wondering what more she wants.

"Am I being brazen, does it frighten you that I want to be with you and know you physically like this? Only be honest with me. I am very happy just having you live with me, you know that."

"Mirabelle, I'll tell you when you do something I don't want. It is sensual to have you touch me, it excites me. I'll tell you if it's too much."

"May I lie in the bed beside you, Jacques? I have never been in a bed with anyone except my mother. Would that be too much?"

I wonder if she's referring to the time when she took her dead mother into bed with her or if she's remembering times when she slept with her as a child. She did say that Rolande, when she came home and found them together in the bed, thought they might just be taking a nap together, so it could be only that.

I open up the covers, Mirabelle stands when she feels me pulling them away under her. Without a word, she then sits on the side of the bed again, on the undersheet, and slides her feet down under the covers with me. They're cold. I throw the covers over her and she turns in to me. I put my arms around her. Nothing is said for a long time.

"It is such a strong sensation for me to be like this with you, Jacques. I do not think a 'seeing person' can ever know how much touch and feeling mean to one who cannot see. I am so alone all the time."

I tighten my arms around her in response. She seems so fragile, so light. She snuggles against my shoulder and I feel her body shaking, she is crying. I hold her tighter yet and she lifts her head so I can just make out her face in the darkened room.

"This is not fair to you, is it, Jacques? I'm taking advantage of you, of your gentleness, of your kindness, of our friendship. I know I am an old woman and you are a young man."

"I'm happy, Mirabelle. I'm glad to have you in my bed with me, it's a long time since I've slept with someone."

"It has been almost sixty years for me, Jacques, sixty years alone in bed."

We're quiet for a while again, she lowers her head onto my chest. I know she's listening to my heart. She must know it's beating faster, harder than the last time. I whisper into her ear.

"Would you like to 'explore' me some more, Mirabelle? Is there more you would like to know?"

"I would like to know everything about you, Jacques, is that terrible?"

I reach over my head and pull the top of my sweat suit off. I hold her against me and she pushes away. She puts her hands on my chest.

"Oh, Jacques, you are hairy all over, like a cat or a dog, or some other beast."

She's running her hand over my chest, sliding it over my pectorals and into the hollow between them. I *am* more hairy than most men. I have hair down my back as well. Lorrie was always ashamed of me when we would go to the beach; she didn't say anything but it was in her eyes. Mirabelle is pushing my chest hair different ways, pulling it up between her fingers and letting it settle back.

"It is so long and thick. You do not really need to wear clothes, you could keep warm just with your hair. I never knew this about men."

"Not all men are as hairy as I am, Mirabelle; but there are parts of me which are not as hairy, so I would be arrested if I tried not wearing clothes. Also, I would be cold."

She slides over me with one of her legs between mine. She has both her hands on my chest now, stroking lightly from the hollow at the base of my neck, over my clavicles, then back over my pectorals again, cupping her hands under where they are delineated from my stomach muscles. Simultaneously, with each of her hands, she finds my nipples in the mass of hair. She slowly, carefully brushes away the hair until my nipples are bared. My nipples begin to harden, I can feel the hair on the back of my neck rising. Something else is rising, too. I wonder if she can feel it.

"Men do have these, too, do they not. I know women have more bosoms than men. My mother told me about it when mine began to grow. She bought me a soutien-gorge for my thirteenth birthday. I was so proud. If you want, Jacques, you may touch my bosoms, they are larger than yours but not so large as they were when I was a young woman. And right now they are getting hard as if they are cold but I am not cold at all. Your little nipples are growing bigger and harder right now, too; but they will never grow as large as mine, will they?"

Why am I so excited? Maybe because no woman has ever "discovered" me like this, or maybe they did and never told me. Lorrie, before Didier, was very shy about her body and mine. We almost always made love in the dark, like this, but this time, with Mirabelle telling me everything she feels, asking questions, it puts light into my mind.

"No, Mirabelle, nothing can ever make my bosoms large as yours."

"Mine are not so large anymore. I would love to have had a baby and have it suckle on my nipples. There are so many things I would like to have had that have never been."

She leans her head down on my chest and runs her face back and forth in the hair on my chest. Her hands slide down the sides of my chest onto my ribs just to the point where I almost jump with a feeling of ticklishness.

"Jacques, may I suckle on your bosoms? Is that a silly thing to do? I would like it very much. Also, I want to taste you. Taste is such an important thing for one who is blind."

I stay quiet as she first touches my nipples with her tongue and then closes on them with her lips. I didn't know I could sense the difference between her tongue and her lips, but I can. I feel very "sensitized" in a way I've never been.

She sucks first on one nipple, then the other, licking around the tip with her tongue. The nipple not being sucked is cool in its wetness and becomes even harder each time until I have some notion of what a woman must feel when a man fondles, caresses, kisses her breasts. The sensation of prickling moves forward over the tops of my ears.

Mirabelle pulls herself up closer to my head. She begins with her lips, her tongue, to taste my neck and then around the side of my neck to my ears. She kisses all around my ears, softly pushes her tongue deep into my ears so sometimes she blocks each ear completely and I can hear my own swallowing. I lie still, my hands at my sides. She has her hands at the back of my head now, turning my head from side to side as she carefully "tastes," licks me. It's like a mother cat with a kitten. I try to relax, to let it happen. She lifts her head, kisses me lightly on the lips with her lips, the point of her tongue.

"Is this all right, Jacques? I so much want to taste you. I enjoy very much the taste of you. There is something of salt and of leather and a taste which is like the bass-keys sound on my harpsichord, soft and resonant. I have great pleasure in tasting you. Does it give you pleasure?"

"Yes, much pleasure, Mirabelle."

She snuggles into the space under my left arm with her head.

"May I stay here and sleep with you tonight, Jacques? You can tell me to leave if it is uncomfortable. It would be so wonderful for me."

"Of course, Mirabelle, if that's what you want. I would like very much to have you sleep with me."

She has one arm across my chest and burrows closer to me. I feel so comfortable, so natural with her. I've never experienced this kind of sensual arousal without drive, direction. I know all we have done has not been toward sex but a way of knowing each other, experiencing each other, a coming closer.

I could never explain what has happened this night to Lorrie or anyone I know. They would either laugh or not believe me. I can almost not believe it myself but I know it's true. With that thought I drift off into sleep.

When I wake, she's gone. There's sunshine coming through the window. I'm surprised, at first, to find I'm not wearing my sweatsuit shirt. Then I remember.

I decide it will be a great day to run without my sweat suit. It might be cool outside but it can't really be cold with that sunshine. I look at my watch; it's almost eight o'clock. It's been a long time since I slept this late.

I pull on my running suit and shoes. I slip out quietly into the main room. I hear Mirabelle in her music room practicing on her harpsichord. The door is closed; she probably pulled it shut so I could sleep. I wonder what time she left my bed, maybe just after I went to sleep, or maybe when those six o'clock bells rang.

I palm the key from the rack by the door, pick up some change from the end table by my bed, and go out the door. I run down the steps and across the Quartier des Canettes to the Luxembourg Gardens. I'm feeling very light, fast. I run at almost full speed and don't tire. It's a great sensation, almost like flying. I run that way the entire time, not tiring, seeming almost impossibly smooth and quick with my fast pace. When the clock rings the third time, I run back down the rue Férou, across the Place Saint-Sulpice, scaring the pigeons by the fountain, down rue des Canettes, where we've been painting. I stop and buy croissants at the boulangerie, there at the corner, and wait for a chance to cross the rue du Four. The traffic is much heavier at this time of day than earlier. I sprint into the rue des Ciseaux and up the steps. Mirabelle is waiting on the landing for me.

"Did you have a good run?"

"Very invigorating."

I'm hardly even panting. I close the door behind us and lean forward to kiss her on both cheeks. I'm dripping with sweat. She reaches out to touch my arms as we kiss.

"But is it raining outside? I have not heard it."

"No, this is only perspiration."

She touches my shirt, reaches up, touches my beard, my face, my hair.

"You are completely wet. I have drawn a bath for you but you do not need it. Do all men perspire like this when they run?"

"If they run hard and fast enough, they do."

"Are you sure this is good for you? Might it not affect your heart?"

"It's supposed to be good for the heart, Mirabelle. It strengthens it."

I hand her the croissants. My dripping sweat has begun to weaken the light paper sack again. I look into the bathroom, the bath is full and steaming.

"You really spoil me, Mirabelle."

"It is my pleasure. Please give me your wet running clothes. Did you sleep well, Jacques?"

"Like a baby. I slept like a baby."

"I thought so. When I woke this morning, I felt your face softly, it seemed so relaxed, your breathing on my hand was soft. You were like a baby."

I sit down to take off my running shoes. I slip off my wet shirt and running pants. I have on just my jockstrap. It's one advantage of Mirabelle's being blind, I don't need to worry about modesty and all that.

"Jacques, have you taken off your wet running clothes? Are you standing there naked before me?"

God, she's impossible.

"Well, almost, but not quite, Mirabelle. Does it bother you? Am I taking advantage?"

"Oh no. I only wish I had eyes to see you. If you do things like this often, I might just start seeing again."

She turns away and is close to one of her giggles. I go into the bathroom, realize there's no real reason to close the door. It gets too hot and steamy with the door closed anyway. Also, I can watch Mirabelle, watch her carefully take out the croissants, bring the hot coffee over from the stove, put the pot of strawberry jam between our places.

I rub myself dry with a towel, let out the water, wipe out the tub, go into my room, and dress in my work clothes. I come back to the main room and we start to eat. It's all even more delicious than before. Mirabelle has heated the croissants in the oven so they're crispy on the outside and buttery inside. God, it's the little things that count. I don't know how I let myself forget that.

We start working on my room again after breakfast. First I do the third wall with the cork, that doesn't take long. Then I scrape, and paint white the wall with the door to the bathroom and around the corners all the way to the wall on the court. With the acoustic tile on the ceiling and this white wall, it's really light in here now. I decide to pull up the old dark carpet and see what's under it. If the floors are okay, I'll just paint them, or maybe leave them natural wood.

Mirabelle has been a big help all along. She can't do much while I'm painting, so she cleans up the breakfast dishes and starts lunch, then goes out to take care of her pigeons. It's still a beautiful day. I think for a minute of going out to join her, but decide to get on with the project first.

I'm just cleaning out my brushes when I hear the bells ringing. I've got everything away, and am peeling off the rug to look underneath, when I hear her coming up the steps. Living with Mirabelle seems to have made me more sensitive to sounds. The floor under the rug looks beautiful, natural oak, tongue-and-groove.

I'll pull up the rug and wax that floor till it gleams. This room is really going to be beautiful.

Mirabelle comes in the door. In my excitement, I almost say, "Look at this, Mirabelle, look at this beautiful floor," but catch myself in time.

"I'm finished painting, Mirabelle, and I've taken up the rug. The rug is so worn and old I think we must throw it out."

"Whatever you say. I know if you like it, I shall like it."

"But come over here and feel this floor, Mirabelle, it really is beautiful." She comes near me and I reach up to take her hands, help her onto her knees. She kneels beside me. I rub her hand under mine over the boards.

"They're so smooth, Jacques, are they painted?"

"No, this is the natural wood with only an old coat of varnish on it. They're beautiful oaken floors. It would be a shame to keep them covered. I can wax these and make them shine, reflect the light, make this room beautiful."

"You are right, Jacques. I think it was not the way in the time of my parents. They wanted rugs

in all the rooms. I think for them it was a way of showing they were truly bourgeois, bare floors were for the poor and country people."

I help her to her feet.

"Oh, Mirabelle, I wish you could see how this room is now, how even more beautiful it is going to be."

"I wish I could, too."

She pauses.

"But I guess not hard enough yet, yes; or I could see it if I really wanted to. Perhaps it will come. Being with you, having you tell me how beautiful things are, is making me want to see; if only I were not so afraid."

I look at her. She has her head turned up to me, to the sound of my voice. Her face is flushed from climbing the stairs but she isn't breathing hard. I hope I'll be in as good condition as she is when I'm her age.

"Come, Jacques, we are having filets de harengs for our entrée and then a beautiful coq au vin I've been allowing to cook all morning. Would you help me by setting the table?"

She's set out all the dishes, silverware, salt, pepper on the table. I take our napkin rings and napkins from the counter in the kitchen, spread the dishes and the rest at our places. I haven't set a table in years. I have a hard time remembering which goes on the outside, the knife or the spoon. Mirabelle comes and places the dishes of herring with warm boiled potatoes on the plates I've set. She brings a bottle of white wine from the refrigerator. It's a Sancerre, perfect for this meal.

We're really eating like royalty. I open the bottle with the opener on the table, wipe the inside of the neck, using my little finger, to get the bits of cork out. Mirabelle sits down. It's amazing how she remembers everything to put on the table and is never jumping up and down for something she's forgotten. She just doesn't seem to forget. I pour the wine.

She puts out her glass to me. I clink with her.

"To us, to our happy days."

We both take a sip; it's like clear fresh water.

The herring is room-temperature with little rings of onion over it, potatoes warm, not hot, sitting in the oil. With the cold wine it's delicious. We eat quietly. I realize how much Mirabelle enjoys eating by watching her face, she really glows.

We finish at about the same time and Mirabelle takes our dishes and silverware away. She brings back fresh silverware. She's so quick I can't think of anything to do without getting in her way. She turns to me.

"Perhaps it would be best if we serve ourselves from the pot. It is hot and the pot is heavy."

She makes room for me. I carry my plate in and dish out two good-sized pieces of the chicken plus a large dollop of gravy. Mirabelle uncovers another pot and there are boiled potatoes, what the French call pommes anglaises. I take my plate to the table and bring Mirabelle's over. She reaches for it but I pull it gently away.

"Tell me what you want, Mirabelle. What parts do you prefer?"

"I like to be surprised. One thing about being blind is you are often surprised by everything. I have learned to prefer it."

"Okay. I'm going to surprise you."

I reach in and pull out a good thigh, then another piece from the back of the chicken. I put two potatoes on her plate, dip gravy over the whole thing with the ladle. I carry her plate to the table.

"My, how you spoil me, Jacques. I can do that myself and your meal is getting cold."

We sit and eat again. This time we talk more. Mirabelle is telling about how she can feel some of the pigeon hens are beginning nests. She says they are very slim, lively, and restless. She can hear the cocks courting round and round in circles at her feet.

"You know, Jacques, every year there are new baby pigeons born in the nests and one would think the flock would grow bigger and bigger but it remains almost the same. What do you think happens to these young? I know some of them stay in the flock but most of them will disappear before summer ends. I think many of them do not survive the late-summer molt, it is very hard on them, and often they do not have enough food after the tourists have left."

"It must be difficult for pigeons living in a large city such as Paris."

I hadn't thought much of it before, but all the carbon monoxide, the smog, the noise would make it tough for the pigeons to breed, to survive; it's hard enough for humans.

"Yes, there are always birds disappearing, even some of the healthy adults. I get to know them and then they do not come back. It can be sad."

"But then, that's life, Mirabelle. It's like that for all of us."

*"Yes, I know, Jacques. We all must leave some-
time, but it still seems sad."*

I want to ask her what she feels about death, about her age, but
I don't. We're so comfortable and so happy together, it seems
strange to consider such a thing on a beautiful day. I don't want
to think about it myself, either.

I carry the dishes into the kitchen and Mirabelle washes them
in the sink. We just leave them on the dish rack to dry. We're both
anxious to get out painting. Today, I'm hoping to finish our painting, up Canettes, with the Place at the end. It's really great having
the good sun.

We're settled in and painting before two o'clock. At first I don't
know where to start, but once I'm into it, explaining to Mirabelle
what I'm doing as I go, it takes off on its own. It's five o'clock and
I'm finished almost before I know it. I've been up and down the
street about ten times, sometimes dragging the box, sometimes
just checking a detail where I'm doing the blending. I manage the
shadows falling across the buildings in the right foreground exactly
the way I want it. I even bring one flash of sunlight down onto the
street like a décolletage. It helps hold the foreground, left and
right, together.

When I've definitely decided it's finished, we go up and take a
place at the café. This time, because it isn't so cold, I have a demi,
a beer, and Mirabelle orders a verveine, a kind of herb tea. It's a
great joy sitting in the last sunshine.

That night, Mirabelle comes to my bed again. I was expecting
her, and open the covers so she can slide in with me. Her feet

aren't cold because she hasn't sat on the edge of the bed for so long. I hold her in my arms and we're both very still. I wonder if we're just going to sleep and I'm starting to doze off when I feel her soft hand brushing lightly over the top of my hair. She shifts and puts her head on my chest.

"Do you want to sleep, Jacques? Are you tired?"

"Whatever you'd like, Mirabelle. Are you tired?"

"No. I do not think you can know how much it means to me when you allow me to touch you and taste you, to come to know you the way I do. I cannot think of anyone else in the world who would be so kind."

"I told you, Mirabelle. It's a pleasure for me. I never knew anyone could be as gentle, as caressing as you are. I've not known that hands could touch so lightly, lips so tenderly."

"I am very happy, Jacques. Would you mind very much taking your sleeping shirt off again? I have been remembering all day how your hairy chest felt against my face and I would like to feel that again."

I lean forward slightly, tilting her head and body, pull my shirt over my head. In so moving, I smell myself. I'd bathed in the morning but with the whole day of work, both painting the walls and painting my painting, I smell of perspiration and turpentine.

"I'm sorry if I smell, Mirabelle. I should have washed up before I came to bed. I didn't think."

"Oh no. I am glad you did not wash away your

smells. I told you I like the way you smell, it is so real, so like a good healthy animal."

She nuzzles her face into my armpit. Then I feel her lips and tongue as she begins to lick me down the side from the armpit to the hairless sides of my trunk. Now she really begins to tickle. I jump.

"*Did I hurt you, Jacques?*"

She lifts her head onto my chest again.

"No, you only tickled me."

"*Tickle? Oh yes, I remember when I was a little girl, Rolande would tickle me and we would tickle each other. It was a very strange feeling. I have discovered one cannot tickle oneself. When you know where someone is going to touch, there is no tickle. I think it is partly the surprise.*"

"Perhaps, Mirabelle. But *I* knew where you were, what you were doing, and still it tickled me. However, there is one place any person can tickle himself, you know."

"*Is there? Tell me. Where is it?*"

"In the top of the mouth. If you take your finger and lightly rub it along the roof of your mouth, you will have a very strong feeling of tickling."

I demonstrate, then realize she can't know what I'm doing. I tickle the top of my mouth, anyway, and she puts her hand on mine. I pull my finger out of my mouth quickly when the tickling becomes too much, then massage the place with my tongue, rubbing hard, to stop it. It really is a strong sensation, between pleasant and painful. It's almost like the itch of athlete's foot.

Mirabelle takes her finger and puts it in her mouth the way I had done. Quickly she pulls her hand out of her mouth and makes the noises of rubbing her tongue against the tickle.

"Oh my, Jacques. Is that a tickle? It has been so long, I had quite forgotten. It is a most strange sensation, is it not?"

She tries again, pulls out her finger, and shakes her head.

"That is really most peculiar. Do most people know of this?"

"I don't think so, Mirabelle. I had an uncle who showed me when I was a little boy. I haven't told anyone except you."

"Is it possible for me to tickle you like that? Or must one do it oneself?"

"I don't know, I've never had anybody try to tickle me there."

"May I try?"

"All right, but be careful I don't bite you."

She turns her hand and gently, with her forefinger, rubs against the top of my mouth. It is so strong I need to pull her hand away. It's more powerful than when I did it myself. I rub vigorously with my tongue.

"Yes, Mirabelle. Somebody else can tickle the mouth of another. It is very strong."

"Oh, please, would you tickle me in the mouth, Jacques?"

I reach out my hand and she opens her mouth. I reach in and rub my middle finger against the ribbed roof of her mouth. Almost immediately she pulls away. She pushes her tongue back and forth, in and out, shaking her head for several seconds.

"But it will not stop. I cannot make it go away."

We're both laughing, with Mirabelle interrupting to rub her tongue against her mouth some more.

Finally we settle down. Mirabelle lowers her head to my chest again. I rest my hand on her head and run it carefully over her hair to the point where it begins twisting into the braid.

"So we have our little secret, Mirabelle. We won't tell anyone else, will we."

"No, I think not. We do not want to drive the whole world crazy."

She lies still for several minutes, then her hands begin to move slowly down my ribs again, slowly, tentatively, creeping along the soft flesh.

"You tell me when it starts to tickle. I would like to know just where it begins."

I wait and nothing happens. I do not feel ticklish, only a pleasant stimulation something like when she kissed and sucked my nipples, a tingling at the back of my head. Then she brings her one hand, the one on the far side, away from her, across onto my stomach where the hair grows thickly down the middle.

"You were not ticklish this time, Jacques? Perhaps we used up all your tickle in your mouth."

"I think it is because you moved so slowly, Mirabelle, you didn't take me by surprise, I was expecting it."

"Do you mind my hand being where it is now?"

"I'll tell you, Mirabelle, when I am not happy."

She lowers her head onto my chest and with her other hand smooths away the hair and begins to suckle on my nipples again. I'm between being very relaxed and highly excited. She moves from one nipple to the other.

"I wish I had two mouths, Jacques. I think each of your nipples tastes a little differently but I can't be sure. By the time I move from one to the other, I forget."

Her hand on my stomach has found my navel. She carefully, like someone exploring the edge of a crater, circles her fingers around it, going deeper each time.

"I have a navel, too, but it is not so deep. I do not think there is a bottom to yours."

She inserts her finger deeper. She comes to the puckered skin at the bottom and explores more.

"Oh yes, there it is. It is like mine but it is so hidden in your stomach and by your hair, it is hard to find."

She slides her body down, going deeper under the covers. I feel her tongue enter my navel, cautiously ringing the sides and going deeper. It's such a strange feeling, I didn't realize the navel was so sensitive, it's not ticklish but still is just on the level of sensation I can bear. She lifts her head.

"I can put my entire tongue in. I did not realize men had such deep navels. And you have a wonderful taste here, the same as behind your ears but stronger. It is absolutely delicious."

"I think my navel is deeper than most men's, Mirabelle. Sometimes I need to clean it out because bits of lint and dust gather in there. I don't know about other men, but this could be exceptional."

"Yes, it is very exceptional, I am sure. Is it painful for you when I put my tongue in here?"

"No, it's only a very peculiar feeling. I've never felt anything quite like it."

I'm also beginning to feel a tumescence in my penis. It isn't exactly an erection, but the growth and swelling, which is still such a marvel to me, has started. I try to concentrate, to stop it.

This is a switch. The trouble in my sex with Lorrie over the last few years has been that I haven't had spontaneous erections. With Lorrie's stimulation, I would usually respond and we could then have sex. Especially after Didier, I had this trouble, but then Lorrie became so adept at stimulating me, it didn't matter much. But rarely in the last years has any of it been spontaneous.

The last time I can remember trying to keep an erection down must have been twenty years ago. Of course, this isn't exactly an unstimulated erection that's happening. We haven't kissed and she hasn't touched me there, but what she's been doing has made me very excited. Perhaps it's because of the long time without sex at all, or because, with the running, I've gotten into better shape physically. Whatever it is, this stiffening is out of control. If I'm not careful, it's liable to pop right up and clobber poor Mirabelle on the cheek. I try to think of my painting, anything, but nothing helps. Mirabelle takes her tongue out of my navel.

"Jacques, is that your penis I feel moving? I know men have penises but I did not know they could move by themselves."

"Yes, Mirabelle, that's my penis, and usually they don't move by themselves."

"May I touch your penis? Would it annoy you if I touch it?"

She pauses, pushes the covers away from her head so I can see her face. I reach down and take her hand, move it gently down toward my erection. She slowly continues to move her hand downward herself, until her fingertips carefully, sinuously touch it at the base where the penis comes out of the pubic hairs. I feel her fingers wrap around it.

"It is so large! Is this what a man puts into a woman to plant the seeds for babies? It is impossible. I know I am ignorant about such things. How can this be?"

"It happens all the time, Mirabelle. But my penis isn't this big all the time. You have aroused me sexually and my penis has swollen because of that. Normally, it is much smaller than this."

"Have I truly aroused you, Jacques? Are you angry with me? I did not know."

"Yes, dearest Mirabelle, you have aroused me. I didn't think this would happen but it has. I am not angry, it is very pleasant for me."

"May I touch it some more? I want to discover more about it. You have been so kind, would this be all right?"

"Yes, Mirabelle, but I warn you, if you stimulate me too much I could very easily have some of my seed come out, so do be careful. If it's going to happen I'll tell you so you can move away."

"Do you have enough seed? Would you be angry if some of your seed spills out?"

"No, I wouldn't be angry, Mirabelle, there's much seed in me. But I only want to warn you, so you won't be frightened."

Finding how unknowing she is of these things is almost harder to believe than accepting that she's blind. When I think about it, being isolated with her sister, who didn't communicate with her all that much, through all those years of her adulthood, combined with her not being able to read, having no access to other people who would speak of such things, I shouldn't be surprised. She is like a child, a very naïve fourteen-year-old from another time, two generations ago.

She has slid under the covers again. I reach down and push the bottom of my sweat suit off, kick it to the end of the bed with my feet. I'm just about bursting with the pressure to ejaculate.

As a married man of twenty-five years, I've had some experience with holding back, but this is, for some reason, the most difficult I've known. She has one hand still around the base of my penis and with the other she is, in her tentative way, "exploring," running the tip of her finger up its length.

"The skin is so soft, Jacques, and there are lines like veins, and it curves. Is this normal?"

"Yes, Mirabelle."

"And the skin at the end is loose, with extra skin at the very top, the skin feels almost like the skin in the bottom of your navel, only it is softer."

"If you want, you can pull back that skin and discover the true head of the penis, Mirabelle, it's called the glans. The skin is only a cover, such as the eyelid that protects the eye."

As I say it, I wonder if that is a good simile. I wonder if her blind eyes have the same sensitivity as seeing eyes. Of course they do, she isn't really blind, her eyes are like mine.

Gently, with both hands, she slides back the skin so the glans is exposed. I'm having an impossible time holding back. I can feel her finger now gently exploring the head of my penis. Usually, because I'm not circumcised, this part of me is so sensitive that finger touching can be almost painful, but her fingers are touching so tenderly, there is only the slightest feeling of them passing over, like the weight of a fly walking on my skin.

"It is an amazingly strange feeling, your glans, Jacques. It is shaped almost like a heart, with a split on one side and a small hole in the split, it is somewhat like an acorn from which an oak could grow. Is this the hole from which you urinate?"

"Yes, it's also the place from which my seed can come. It is very sensitive, be careful."

"Am I hurting you?"

"No, you are very gentle."

"I did not know men would be so sensitive; they are not much different from women, are they? It must be wonderful when a man can put this sensitive part of himself inside the very sensitive parts of a woman. I understand now why there is much talk about sex and love. It truly is a miracle, is it not?"

"That's right, Mirabelle, a miracle."

The miracle is I'm still hanging in there. I didn't know I could do it. I'm beginning to wonder if somehow I've changed over the past year, that all the alcohol and sleeping on the ground, maybe the running even, have changed me so I can't ejaculate. I know I'm probably going to have one of the worst cases of hot nuts I've had since I was fifteen if I hold this erection much longer.

"May I taste your penis, Jacques? I can smell it. It smells very much like a man smell. I never knew that was what I was smelling when I smelled

men. *I would like very much to taste your penis."*

"You must be careful, Mirabelle. I am very excited and I could spill my seed at any minute. It is getting more and more difficult to hold it back."

"I will not bite you, Jacques. I will be very careful."

"I'm not worried about you biting me. It's only that most women are afraid of tasting or swallowing a man's seed. They don't want it to happen. It seems wrong to them."

"Why, Jacques? Is the seed of a man poisonous? It would seem that anything that when mixed with a woman's egg will create a new person must be very good, it is an important part of life itself. Why are they afraid?"

She's lifted her head out from under the covers, holding tight on to my stiffened penis with both hands.

"I don't know, Mirabelle. I've never thought about it. I've never had a woman who drank my seed but I've heard about such women. There are also men who drink other men's seed. Lorrie would never put her mouth around my penis until that last year when she was with Didier. And, even then, she never drank my seed."

I can feel my impossible erection starting to settle down some, it's still stiff but I don't feel as if my testicles are about to be sucked into my body.

"People are very strange, are they not, Jacques? They are so often afraid of the best things. Have you ever tasted the seed of a man? You could have tasted your own seed. What does it taste like?"

"I've never tasted the seed of a man, Mirabelle, not even my own. I guess I've been afraid just as almost everyone else is. I don't know why."

"I am blind, and as you know, tastes and smells mean much to me. I think I can smell your seed, it smells very good to me. If you will not allow me to taste your seed, it would be as if someone would not let you see something beautiful, such as a sunrise or a sunset, or the light coming through the trees. Do you think that is right? I promise if I do not like the taste of your seed, I shall tell you; if you prefer, I shall spit it out. Would that be all right?"

"You may taste my penis if you want, Mirabelle. If I feel I am going to give off some seed I'll tell you and I'll pull away. Would that be all right with you? It can be very stimulating to a man to have someone taste his penis, so do be careful."

"I shall be very careful. But I would like to taste your seed. It would be marvelous to have some of your seed inside me. It is not poisonous, it will not make me ill. Why are you so worried?"

She begins by tasting, running her lips, her tongue up the shaft of my penis from the bottom where it springs from my pubic hairs. I can feel the tender stroke of her tongue as she moves it all around the length of my penis. I spread my legs to make more room for her. She stops.

"Under the penis there is wrinkled skin with some hair on it and something inside. Is that where you keep the seed, Jacques?"

I feel her hands gently exploring my testicles. She moves her fingers back almost to my anus.

"Yes, those are the testicles, Mirabelle. It is there where a man stores his seed."

"They feel like the stone on the inside of a peach, it is a strange feeling. They are so different in texture from the penis, one so smooth, the other so wrinkled and hard."

"If the penis is soft, then that part is soft, too, Mirabelle. It is the way a man is."

"I never knew men could be so interesting."

She moves her hands back down the shaft of the penis, pulling the skin all the way back. Holding it tightly, she brings her mouth, her lips, her tongue farther up until she begins to touch the glans. My penis is stiff and hard again, I feel the texture of her tongue, rough and at the same time wet and flexible, as it licks around the top of the glans and then into the split. I can't stop myself from squirming and only barely suppress a moan of passionate delight.

"Is is all right if I put my mouth around the top of your penis? I promise I will not bite."

I can't say anything, I'm only feeling, my entire body is at the point of convulsing. I feel the hollowness of her mouth as she closes it over the top of my penis. The warmth of her comes from her mouth into me and I start the slow pumping of ejaculation, she holds her mouth tight over me as I feel myself losing control.

"Mirabelle, careful, I'm going to let out some seed. I can't help myself!"

She only tightens her mouth over my penis, holds on tight with both hands as I turn this way and that in a paroxysm of passion and delight. Her braid of hair brushes against my thigh, and I ejaculate with a force to match the twisting of my body. I feel her sucking it in, hear her swallowing, running her tongue against the source, licking, sucking, swallowing. It seems she's drinking the very life out of me.

As I gradually come back, breathing hard, my penis shrinking, softening, she keeps licking like a child finishing the last part of some favorite dessert. By now I'm totally relaxed. Her fingers, her mouth still gently stroking me, she takes my testicles into her mouth and now she's tasting them. She stops and settles her head on my stomach.

"Jacques, you taste so delicious, I do not know when I have ever tasted anything so beautiful. It is a taste such as I have never tasted before, like the best kind of béchamel but with something of a very good demi-sel butter on toast, too. But that does not describe it either. Thank you for letting me taste your seed. I am certain it is very good seed. I hope sometime you will allow me to taste it again. But now your penis and testicles are growing smaller and softer, is that because the seed has left them? Will the penis become big again?"

I'm almost asleep. I reach down and pull Mirabelle up over on top of me until her face is above mine. I kiss her on the lips, she holds them tight. I realize she doesn't know how to kiss; we call it "French" kissing and here she is, she who's just given me so much pleasure, totally unknowing in this most common of sexual activities.

"Open up your mouth, Mirabelle. I want you to taste my tongue. I think you will like it."

She opens her mouth. I press my lips to hers and feel them tighten with mine. I slowly put my tongue between her teeth and feel her tongue. I stroke her tongue, then the roof of her mouth with mine. I'm tasting the seed of a man now, my own seed. I breathe out into her mouth and then breathe in, pulling the breath through her nostrils. Her body tightens, we break away.

"Is that what kissing is really like? Or is this only your own special way of kissing? It makes me dizzy, I feel as if I could faint. Were you trying to tickle the roof of my mouth? It felt good but it didn't tickle."

"Did it feel good to you?"

"Oh yes! After I recovered from the shock, it was very good. You have a wonderful-tasting tongue but it is not as good as your seed. Could you taste your seed in my mouth?"

"I think so, Mirabelle. May I taste your tongue and then let us go to sleep."

I turn so she is by my side and we kiss again. This time, very shyly, tentatively, the way she'd tasted the rest of me, she explores the inside of my mouth, moves her tongue over mine, across the roof of my mouth. I pass her tongue with mine into her mouth and we caress tongues, top and bottom. It's very soft, loving. There's nothing of thrust, much of trust. I never realized how loving someone this way could be such a quiet feeling. We aren't going anywhere, we're already there.

I wonder how this night in bed is going to affect the rest of our relationship, how we will feel when we face each other in the light of day. Then I realize there's no light of day for Mirabelle. She's always blanketed in the soft cover of darkness and night. I begin to understand something of why she doesn't want to see. In so many ways she doesn't need to, and realizes how much of her life, as she knows it, would be lost with sight.

Blind Reverie

I shall never be the same again. When I went to sleep in Jacques's arms, it was as if I were falling into a warm deep hole. How could I have lived so long without knowing?

He is so bashful and kind, yet so strong and feeling. It was wonderful to feel his thick penis pressing against my leg, then actually touching it with my hands, my fingers. To taste his seed is to know how good life can be.

What must real sex be like, when a man slides his large penis into the soft parts of a woman? It is hard to believe it could be any more exciting than this. I think my poor old heart would stop if something more stimulating happened to me.

I hope this closeness we have felt can continue. I feel Jacques is somewhat concerned for me. I wish I could convince him of how beautiful every-

thing seems, how I am not afraid of dying a virgin now. I do not think I actually care so much as I did before. I have known so much, experienced such pleasure, how can anything be better? I must speak with Jacques about this, perhaps he can help me understand. I love life more than ever but am not afraid at all of leaving it, because he will always be with me.

Chapter 11

Our days blend one into the other. I'm falling more in love with Mirabelle each day and I'm not fighting it anymore.

During the days, we work on finishing the apartment, painting, taking up old linoleum, hanging drapes, getting rid of old furniture that can't be refurbished, taking the paint off some furniture that is painted over, and is often oak or cherry underneath.

I consult Mirabelle about every decision I make and most times we're in agreement. She helps with whatever she can. She re-upholsters the chairs and an old couch, virtually without assistance. The whole place is really starting to look light and airy. I'm so sorry she can't share it visually with me.

Every few days she asks me just how it looks, asks for me to take different positions in the apartment while she sits beside me. I put my arms around her or hold her hands and explain in great detail everything I'm seeing. I can almost feel her vision being constructed in her mind. In some ways it's like putting information into a computer, knowing it will remember all and integrate it into some special pattern according to a program. The program is Mirabelle.

We continue our painting. We are coming to the end of the places Mirabelle definitely remembers, her special places. I keep describing what I'm doing, what I'm painting, how it looks, how the light is falling, how I'm composing. She listens carefully in her wonderful concentrated way, smiling, seeing in her special private world. I paint more and more from inside myself. I listen as Mirabelle shares her vision and it is integrated with mine, but now I'm beginning to have a vision of my own. I've learned to see with more than my eyes. I'm becoming an artist.

I keep hoping Mirabelle will see my paintings, that she will have such confidence in me she can allow herself sight, but it doesn't happen.

Every night she comes to my bed. Gradually I become active in our lovemaking, caressing her, giving her pleasure in return. Mirabelle wants me to really make love to her, to enter her, but she is too small. Even with the most tender loving I can give her, she remains dry and tight. It's the one thing about her being older which is frustrating. I don't see her as an older woman anymore, in so many ways she's younger, more vibrant, experimental, than I am.

We try different lubricants and I "taste" her long and lovingly with all the love I feel for her, but she remains too small and there is no natural lubrication. Even my finger or my tongue, carefully inserted, gives her pain. Mirabelle cries in her discouragement.

"It seems I shall die a virgin after all, Jacques, my love. I have waited too long."

But our lovemaking is not blocked by this mere mechanical impossibility. Mirabelle is so passionate in her desire to please me, so fearless and imaginative in the pleasures she gives, I feel guilty. I also feel awkward, not knowing how I can possibly give her anything in return for what she gives me.

During all the time since I've left home, I've kept my promise to Lorrie. I've gone to the American Express every other Tuesday to look for mail. Then, while there, using a small counter by the window, I have written, telling how I am well, how I think of them often, how I love them.

Only twice have there been letters to me, both from Lorrie, none from the children. Early on, only two months after I'd left, she told me she was going home to Minneapolis. It seems Didier couldn't abandon his family and didn't want to see her anymore. I felt she was accusing me of abandoning her and I asked in my letter back if this were so.

But she didn't answer my letter. I was, at that point, gradually going downhill, was not in my real mind, wandering all over Paris. Perhaps, it was only in my own drunken stupor, this idea she was accusing me existed.

I told Mirabelle about that letter and she said it would be hard to tell, but she didn't think so, she was only telling me what had happened and was probably very, very unhappy about losing Didier.

The second letter I received was almost a year after I had left. It came just as I was beginning to pull myself together, when I was living in my attic, a few weeks before I met Mirabelle.

Her letter told me she was selling the house. She said it was too big for her with all the children gone now. She was going to rent a condominium where there would be an extra room in case one of them wanted to visit. She went on to tell me she was all right and that she was working. She was doing the kind of work she'd always wanted, personnel management, for a small firm in St. Paul. She said it was challenging, difficult, but she liked the work. She finished by saying she hoped I was happy.

I wrote a long letter back explaining how I was painting and that, although I wasn't yet painting as well as I wanted, I was making progress. I didn't tell her how I was living. I told her I still loved her and asked if she would tell the children I loved and missed them, too. I wanted to ask her to have them write to me, but decided I didn't want to put any pressure on them, it was probably very hard for them as it was.

When I moved in with Mirabelle I told Lorrie where I was living. I told her how I was living with a seventy-one-year-old blind Frenchwoman who was a wonderful person. I told her if she wanted to, she could write me there, and gave her the address. I said I would also still check at American Express. I told her my painting was coming along very well.

Every two weeks during the months I was with Mirabelle I wrote Lorrie long letters telling everything. I told of how my paintings were improving, how I felt that, at last, I was becoming a real artist. I told about fixing up the apartment. I told her my feelings about Mirabelle and how I thought I was falling in love.

I didn't want to be cruel and I was afraid Lorrie wouldn't understand, but one thing I'd learned is that when there are secrets, it is hard to keep love alive. I told Lorrie as much about Mirabelle as I could, about her music, her many languages, even about her pigeons. I hoped she'd understand.

It's a late-summer morning when I come in from running. Mirabelle is still in her tights. Either she worked out longer or I ran faster. She immediately goes into her bedroom to change. Despite all our intimacy, she is still very proper in her dress. I've never seen anything of her clothing left around. Even in her bedroom, all is in order, perhaps that's the only way you can really survive when you are blind and alone.

And her bedroom, now, is just the way she wanted it. I'm surprised how beautifully it came out. The white four-poster bed in the center, with a deep wine-colored carpet over the entire floor, complements beautifully the two tones of deep maroon in the damask-covered walls. I painted the ceiling as white as her bed so the room isn't dark. This doesn't matter to Mirabelle, of course, but my own aesthetic demanded it. I've never had any interest in interior decoration, but I'm enjoying this experience.

Most nights, Mirabelle comes to my bed, but she is always up and gone before I wake in the morning. I've thought of going to her bed, but for some reason have not. There's something magical about the way it is and I don't want anything to change.

This morning, Mirabelle comes out of her bedroom beautifully dressed in earth colors, the colors of my bedroom. She walks to the table and picks up a letter.

"Could you tell me from whom this letter is, Jacques? I cannot think of anyone in the world

who would write to me on such paper. The only letters I receive are official ones and they are always on much different kinds of paper, slippery paper or paper with very thin windows in them, and no timbres."

It's a letter from Lorrie.

"It's a letter from my wife, Mirabelle."

She smiles.

"I thought it might be."

She moves into the kitchen area. This kitchen now is bright and gay. The reflections from the many yellows in the sitting area light it and I built small hooded lights over the sink. None of this means anything to Mirabelle, so I did it for myself. I'm convinced, also, that if the apartment is the way it would be if she could see, Mirabelle might actually see someday. With my encouragement, she's even begun to turn lights on and off in each room when she enters or leaves. She thinks this very amusing. At first, she'd accidentally turn a light off when I was still in a room, and this could be disturbing but amusing. In the beginning, I'd wait awhile and then surreptitiously go over and turn the light back on. But there was no fooling Mirabelle. She knew immediately what I was doing and insisted I just say "Light!" when it happened. It doesn't happen very often now.

I decide to take my bath, which Mirabelle has drawn as usual, before reading the letter, although I'm anxious to know what it says. I pray everyone is all right. But I'm dripping sweat, it is a hot day, and I ran hard.

I don't linger too long in the tub. Then I rinse myself off with a cold shower. I dress in my room and come out. Mirabelle has just put our coffee and fried eggs on the table. She has melted Camembert over the eggs. It's something she's taught me to eat and I've practically become addicted. She knows just when to put these things out, because she knows exactly what I'm doing from the sounds I make.

I sit at the table and open the letter. My hands are shaking. I take a deep breath, hold it awhile, then let it out. It's the longest letter I've received from Lorrie. I read through it quickly, afraid of what I'll find. But everyone is fine. Still, I'm distressed by the letter. I look up at Mirabelle. She's eating the croissant I brought her, carefully sipping at her coffee.

"Do you want to hear the letter, Mirabelle?"

"Do you want to read it to me? Would your wife be angry if you read her letter to me?"

"No, I don't think so. But first I'll eat this beautiful breakfast before the eggs grow cold."

I enjoy the food, trying to concentrate on it as Mirabelle has taught me. I finish and take my last sips of her wonderful coffee. Mirabelle is finishing hers, too. She's looking up at me, unseeingly, and tears are forming at the corners of her eyes.

"Is it bad news? You seem so quiet, and there is something of tenseness in the air. Is it all right?"

"Let me read and you tell me what you think, Mirabelle."

I take the letter out of its envelope again and start reading. Actually this is the first time I've really read the letter. Before, I was so anxious, so scared something bad had happened to Lorrie or one of the children, I scarcely understood some of it.

I read:

"August 21, 1975

"Dear Jack,

"I'm sorry I haven't written for so long. It is not that I don't think of you, because I do, often. It is just I want you to feel as free to do what you want, as you allowed me to feel when I thought I was in love with Didier. It seems so long ago, is it only a little more than a year?

"I have asked the children not to write you for the same reason. I wanted you to feel there was nothing hanging on to you. It has been hard for them because they love you and worry about you. I share all of your letters with them. So, in a way, you have been writing to them, too. I can't say it hasn't been hard for me.

"Sometimes I think you don't feel I understand what you are going through, that I don't care, but this isn't true. It is a terrible thing to *feel* you have wasted a good part of your life, even if it isn't true. There is a terrible feeling of emptiness. It's especially difficult when it isn't so, and you come to know it, as I did."

Here I have to stop reading because I can't go on. I feel my throat tightening and tears swell into my eyes. I stop. I take deep breaths again.

"Jacques, you do not have to read this to me if you do not want to. It must be very difficult for you."

I look across at her and the tears are running down the outside of her face again, the way they always do when she cries. I look away and up at the beautiful day outside. I look down at the letter again, finally I can go on.

"John graduated last year in structural engineering. Your dad is so proud of him, Jack, imagine, a real engineer in the family.

"He has what looks like a good position working for the state, road and bridge building. He has his own apartment, too, and a girlfriend. They're sort of engaged the way young people do. It's so much better the way the young arrange those things now, they know each other before they get married, share things more, I think.

"Albie is another artist in the family. He's in the art department at U. of M. and is torn between ceramic sculpture and stonecutting. He's an absolute maniac. When I sold the house, I put away part of the money so he can have a studio when he finishes his graduate work in June. You'd be proud of him, he doesn't let anything get in his way and is covered with mud or pieces of stone dust all the time. His hands always look as if he's been in some terrible fist fight. He has girlfriends but there doesn't seem to be anyone special. His sculpture is everything.

"Helen is our reader. With all those boys around her, she had to be. She's an English literature major and wants to teach. I think she'll make a good teacher. You remember, she was always so easy to get along with. She's one of my best friends. She writes letters to you all the time and gives them to me so I can hold them and mail them when I think you'll want to have them. Maybe the time is coming soon.

"And Hank, our baby, is our first and only athlete. I don't know where it comes from. He was the star at ASP in Paris in just about everything and he made varsity baseball and the cross-country team at U. of M. in his sophomore year. He's no great shakes as a student but gets his C's and a B once in a while to keep his eligibility. He thinks maybe he'll be a P.E. major and teach, too.

"So, all are well. You don't have to worry. I just received a promotion at work last month and now do more personnel work and less secretarial. I even have my own secretary, part-time. I go out now and then but there isn't anyone special. I guess I'm burnt out with men. I have some women friends and we do things together like museums, theater, or go to the movies.

"I write this partly to wish you happy birthday. It's hard for me to think you'll be half a century old in a few weeks. It's even harder to think that next birthday I will be, too. Time seems to fly.

"The other reason I'm writing is because I feel

you're building a new life there in Paris. I want you to know if you want a divorce I wouldn't make any scene. I'd like to be as generous with you as you were with me in my difficult time. This does not mean I want a divorce myself. I do not. I miss you terribly.

"Would you give my best regards to Mirabelle and wish her every happiness. She seems such a wonderful person and so good to you and for you. I only wish I could have been the one. I think we were too young, Jack, too easily seduced by all the nonsense people come to think makes up a life, but probably actually keeps people from really living. I don't think either of us appreciated how lucky we were to have our health, our home, each other, and our four beautiful children. Perhaps no one knows how lucky they are with what they have. I don't think either of us did.

"Could you take some photographs of your paintings and mail them to me? I'd like very much to see what you are doing. You had such a big talent and it was going to waste. What a shame you had to wait so long to develop it. I feel so guilty.

"I've been having your mail forwarded from our old house but here is my new address:

Ms. L. Laughton
4610 Stevens St.
Apartment 3B
Minn., Minn. 55409

"If you'd like Helen's letters, and if you'd like the other children to write, let me know and I'll tell them. Please keep writing. I look forward so to your letters.

> "Fondly,
> "Lorrie"

I put down the letter. We're sitting across from each other, crying. I'm crying for so many things, I can't think straight. I'm crying for Lorrie and the kids, for myself, for my stupidity; all I had to do was wait. But mostly I'm crying for us, for Mirabelle and me. It's as if we've built a whole city, a civilization, on top of two old ones, hers and mine. The remnants, the remains, keep jutting up through the surface every time we try to dig, to build. No matter how beautiful the world we create for ourselves, the old ones are always there, ready to erupt. I reach across and take Mirabelle's hands. She squeezes mine.

"She loves you very much, Jacques. I did not know that."

"I don't think I could make myself believe it anymore, Mirabelle, and therefore couldn't get it across to you. I didn't really *know* until right now with this letter. I was blind."

"No, do not say that. I am blind. You still love her very much, too, do you not."

"Yes, I do. I don't think I ever said I didn't. I've always loved her. I know I did a wrong, stupid thing to her, but I was blind then, blinded by my own selfish emotions."

"Perhaps, but I think you behaved better than most men would have. You did give her the freedom

she thought she wanted. Even she did not know what she really wanted then, did she?"

I find myself about to break down and sob. I hold tighter on to Mirabelle's beautiful, sensitive hands, then let up, afraid I'll hurt them. Must I hurt everyone I come near?

I swallow the sobs, try to control myself. We sit like that for what seems a long time. The tears have run off or dried on Mirabelle's face. She smiles at me.

"What will you do now, Jacques?"

"I'm trying to think that out. First I'll write to Lorrie, thanking her for this lovely letter. I'll tell her how much I'd love to hear from the kids, especially Helen's letters over such a long time. I'll ask her to write more often to me here."

I look into Mirabelle's eyes. She's so calm, radiant.

"I'll tell her I don't want a divorce. It doesn't make sense."

I pause. She definitely smiles at me.

"And will you go back home to them?"

"Not now, Mirabelle. I'm not ready. I'm happy here, with you. I'm not sure I want to live in a condominium in Minneapolis, even with Lorrie. I've changed. My life is here now, with you, my painting, this quartier, this apartment. I'm not sure she'd have me back anyway."

"She will take you back, Jacques; she loves you. I know I would want you back, no matter what."

She pauses, squeezes my hands again.

"When is your birthday? You said nothing about it to me. I think this letter is Lorrie's special birthday present for you."

"I guess it is what I've wanted, Mirabelle. You're right. But as

Lorrie says, we don't always know what we want, not really. My birthday is less than two weeks from now, on the seventh of September. I'd forgotten it. I didn't mean to keep it secret from you. In a certain way, I've almost forgotten what time is, how much time I've lived, how much I haven't. Our life seems 'out of time' somehow. I don't think I could ever leave it."

"My birthday is the tenth of September, Jacques, we have almost the same birthday. I have been keeping it a secret from you; I shall be seventy-two years old. I cannot believe it myself. I have felt like a young girl these days with you. In my mind you are only slightly older than I am. We are children together, playing house. It has been like that, has it not?"

"Why don't we truly celebrate our birthdays, Mirabelle. Let's go to the fanciest restaurant in Paris and dine in style. You wear your best clothes and I'll buy myself some new clothes for my birthday present. All right?"

"What a wonderful idea, Jacques. We can pretend we have been married a long time and are celebrating our twenty-fifth anniversary or even our fiftieth, and enjoy each other."

I quickly reopen the letter from Lorrie and look at the date. She wrote it on the twenty-first of August, our anniversary, our twenty-fifth anniversary. That's *why* she wrote it and she didn't even say anything!

"What is the matter, Jacques, you moved so fast and are now so still?"

"Mirabelle, she wrote this letter to me on our twenty-fifth wedding anniversary. I didn't even remember it. God, I feel terrible. I guess I'm still my old self."

Mirabelle seems to stare at me, absorbing this information.

"Why do you not telephone her, Jacques? Tell her you forgot but that does not mean you love her any less. You could use the phone in the box by Le Drugstore. She would understand."

"I don't even know her phone number, Mirabelle. I've gotten so out of touch. Besides, what's the difference of a few days, now. I'm going to sit down here now and write her a long letter, I have too many things I want to say to ever say them on a telephone. I hate phones anyway."

Mirabelle rises and brings paper and a pen to me. She puts her hands on top of my head.

"Be kind to her, Jacques. Tell her everything you think you must say, but be kind."

She takes down her little sack with the grains and her leather satchel with her tools for the pigeons.

"I shall come back when the bells ring."

She leaves. I read Lorrie's letter over again several times. It's the letter I thought I always wanted, thought I'd never get, and now I don't know what to do.

I stare at the blank sheets of paper, trying to put things together in my mind. It is so hard to try to be honest.

28 August 1975

Lorrie dearest:

Thank you for your wonderful letter. It has brought me back to life. This does not mean my life here has not been pleasant and rewarding but it has brought back to my inner being, the life we lived together.

I'm terribly sorry I forgot our anniversary, our twenty-fifth anniversary. I've lost all count of time, so that, until I read your letter, I did not know my fiftieth birthday was so near, either. It is difficult to explain how far I am in my mind now from clocks and calendars. When one lives intimately with someone who is seventy-one and blind, minutes become so precious they are not counted, it takes too much time to count.

Please ask the children to write, and I would very much appreciate Helen's letters. I promise to answer any letter I receive.

I'm sorry your life has not been more happy. I thought I did what I could to make it so, make it possible, but now I see I was mistaken. It is so difficult to know what is right, even when one's intent seems right.

I won't be coming back to you for a while, Lorrie. I hope someday this will be, that you can accept me, and the children will forgive. For now I must stay here, it is where my life is. My work, my sense of worth, is tied in with where I am, what I'm doing.

Mirabelle is out feeding her pigeons and I'm writing on our kitchen table. It is warm and the sun comes bouncing into the courtyard window. As I've already written you, we've fixed up this apartment so it is most pleasant. I hear the sounds of Paris outside and wish I could share them with you.

Mirabelle thinks I should go home, try to reintroduce my-

self into your lives. I don't think so. I think all I have gained
these past hard long months would be lost if I left now. My
artistic development is at such a delicate, fragile point, it
could all collapse easily and I would be as nothing again.

So, please bear with me, all of you. Know that I love you
deeply and hope someday to be with you again. My fondest
dream is to have you here with me, but I know that is not
possible. It is an impossible, unrealistic dream.

It was so rewarding to hear the progress all of you have
made in your lives. It makes me very proud of you. It's wonderful that each of you is discovering yourself and carving
out a place where you belong. Doing that, knowing what you
want and then doing what is necessary to achieve it, is the
main thing at this time in your lives, at any time, in anyone's
life.

I stop. I don't know what else to say. So many things I want to
talk about are private between Mirabelle and myself, it would be
a violation of her. I reread what I've written and end the brief
letter "with love and admiration" and sign it both "Jack" and "Dad."
I'd thought it would be a much longer letter and am surprised
how quickly it was written.

I fold it and slide the two sheets of paper into one of Mirabelle's
envelopes. I write the address Lorrie gave me on the outside, stick
stamps on it, print PAR AVION in the lower right-hand corner of the
envelope. I write my name and this apartment's address up in the
left-hand corner. I almost write "Jacques." It's become my name.
I go out and drop the letter in the mailbox of the post office at
the corner of rue du Four and rue de Rennes.

I find Mirabelle out under the statue with her pigeons. She turns to me.

"Did you decide not to write the letter?"

"It's done, Mirabelle, written and mailed."

She has two pigeons on her hand and she's feeding them grains. She turns her attention to them.

"So what will you do?"

"If you want, I'll stay with you, Mirabelle. Nothing is changed except I am a much happier man. If you will have me, I would like to live as we've been living."

There's a long pause. I watch as she goes through all her motions with the pigeons. They aren't afraid of me anymore at all. I think if I put out a finger they'd actually try to land on it.

"I would like that very much. Are you certain?"

"I'm not sure of anything anymore, Mirabelle. But for now I know what I want."

Just then the bells begin ringing. The birds fly around in circles. The combination of the birds' wings rustling and the bells ringing drowns out the sound of traffic. August in Paris is mostly tourists. A good part of the French are gone and won't be back for another few days when the grande rentrée begins.

Mirabelle rolls up her kit, tucks her sacks and kit into her satchel, stands up, brushing off some of the grains and husks that have fallen on her lap. I take her arm, lean down, and kiss her on the side of the neck.

"What marvelous food have you prepared for us to eat, loved one? Maybe I don't love you after all, maybe it's only the food you cook."

Mirabelle holds tight on to my arm, her cane between us. She squeezes my arm.

"Jacques, I have a camera that belonged to Rolande which you can use to take photos of your paintings. I shall give it to you when we are home. We are having a blanquette de veau, if you really want to know."

She smiles up into my face, the sun is on hers, lighting the transparency of her skin, showing in its harsh glare the fine network of lines, the pale brown spots across her forehead, some tiny veins that have broken out in her cheeks. I lean down and kiss her again.

"Jacques! You are getting worse than the pigeons."

She can't suppress a giggle. Who would think a seventy-one-year-old woman could giggle like that. I hold her closely and we enter the rue des Ciseaux just as the last bells sound behind us.

After we eat, Mirabelle gives me the camera. It's a real oldie. It has a snap-open lid with a bellows to give it some focal length. I check, but there don't seem to be any light leaks. There will be some problem with parallax taking photos of paintings, but I can work that out. It takes 120 film. I haven't bought anything but 35mm since I was a kid.

But I buy some film, make some estimates from the ASA and DIN readings, along with the charts on the descriptive material which comes in the box, and decide to take my chances without a light meter.

I stand the paintings in a shaft of sunlight just coming into the room, lighting the paintings so the texture and stroking of the impasto will show. It takes me most of the afternoon to take the pictures. I have almost twenty paintings and there are eight more I've sold. I'm wishing I had those eight back. God, it's hard not to be possessive of the things and people you love.

When I get the pictures all taken, I carry the rolls down to the photo shop. They say they'll have them ready in three days. Maybe then I'll have things more in mind and I can write a better, more complete letter. I know I'm still in a state of shock.

That afternoon I don't feel like painting. Mirabelle and I go over to a shady part of the Luxembourg Gardens and spread out on reclining chairs in the dappled sunshine near where the beehives are. It's great being relaxed, listening to the buzzing of the bees, feeling the sun, smelling the grass and different flowers. We don't talk much. It's so intimate just being quiet and alone together. I reach over and take her hand, pull it across my lap.

"We are like lovers in the park, are we not, Jacques?"

"We *are* lovers in the park, in the Luxembourg Gardens in Paris, France. Don't forget it."

"I will not forget it but I cannot believe it either."

We walk home in the beautiful summer evening. The sky is silver-gray, with thin streaks of mauve. I've never tried painting in this kind of light but I think of it now. The problem is the light in a sky like this changes so fast, is so temporary. I look down at Mirabelle, holding my arm. She didn't bring her cane.

That night we make love long and lovingly, slowly becoming each other. I'm over her, my weight on my elbows and knees, my hands on the side of her face; Mirabelle is fondling my penis, my testicles, softly stroking them. She's already tasted me, brought me to a soft sweeping conclusion, but now she's bringing me back again. She pushes the head of my penis gently against her vagina. She tenderly tucks me in, as if she's making a bed, tucking in the covers, and then I feel myself start to harden and simultaneously slowly slide into her. Mirabelle pulls the lips of her mouth tight, her eyes are open, staring past me.

"Do not move, Jacques, dearest! Do not move, please!"

I try to hold still but can feel the incipient, insistent engorgement, the warm tightness of her surrounding me. I hold still. Mirabelle is breathing shallowly, short breaths, almost gasps. It excites me even more. She moves her head back and forth on the pillow.

"Oh, Jacques, I could never have imagined it would be like this. How can anyone ever feel alone when they have known this closeness? No, do not move! Please, stay still!"

"Does it hurt, Mirabelle? I don't want to hurt you."

"No, it does not hurt, it is only more than I can bear, the sensation, the feeling, is so strong. Stay, please."

I stay. I try holding still but the flood of energy is building inside me, concentrating, forcing, and then I can't stave it off any longer. I come. I come without moving, feeling the soft flow through me, the strong spurts of my semen pumping themselves out. Mirabelle is quiet under me. She seems pale in the dim light of the candle I have left burning beside my bed. I gradually become soft but I don't come out. I lower myself gently from my knees onto her. She's crying.

"We did it, did we not, Jacques, loved one. You planted your seed in me. I am no longer a virgin, am I? I am a real woman."

"You've always been a real woman, Mirabelle."

"Oh, how I wish I had something in which your seed could grow. Oh, how I wish I could have a child with you. Is it not foolish? I am always wanting more, even what is impossible. But I want to be honest with you."

I lift myself away, settle beside her, and hold her close to me. Her heart is pounding so fast, so hard, I can feel it against my chest.

"Are you all right, Mirabelle? Do you feel all right?"

"I shall be fine in a minute, only hold me tight."

We stay like that a long time; just when I think she's asleep, Mirabelle speaks.

"Dearest, there is something I must tell you. It is a secret I have kept from you."

I wait in the near darkness, smelling the clean smell of her hair, she has the smell of a baby.

"Just a year after Rolande died, I had some trouble with my heart, also. I needed to be taken to the hospital. I was told by the doctors that my heart is weak. This is why I do all my yoga and exercises. It is also why I play my harpsichord, to calm myself.

"I have never again had any more trouble, but I just felt it now. It was not bad the way it was the first time, but there was a tightness in my chest

*which was frightening. It went away, perhaps I
am cured.*

*"Jacques, I tell you this because last month I
made my testament. With Rolande gone, my parents
gone, there is no one in this world I know of who
is my family. I want you to have this apartment
and any money of Rolande's that is left when I
go. I hope you do not mind. Perhaps your wife
will come and live with you here. I do not know.
I only wanted to tell you this, in case something
happens."*

I'm frightened deeply. I can't think of anything happening to
Mirabelle. I don't want to know she is not strong, that her heart
could fail. I know I could never live in this place after she is gone.
I really don't know what to say that won't hurt Mirabelle.

"Please, Mirabelle, don't talk about those things. I don't want to
be here after you are gone. You know that. And nothing is going
to happen to you anyway. We'll just live each day as it comes and
hundreds of days will come, one at a time."

*"Yes, Jacques, you are right. I only wanted you
to know. Are you angry with me?"*

"How could I ever be angry with you? I love you. You're the
most wonderful person in the world. And I'm so happy you are
not a virgin anymore. Now we're both full-grown people, happy
with each other."

And we go to sleep.

Usually, when I wake, Mirabelle has already left my bed quietly.
I have become accustomed to this, it is what makes everything

seem so new, it's not as if we're married, but as if I've had a visitation in the night or that I'm a child and my mother is up heating the house, making breakfast for me.

This morning I wake and Mirabelle is gone as usual. I put my hands behind my head on the pillow and slowly open my eyes, remembering the night before.

At the foot of the bed I see Mirabelle sitting on the floor, in her nightgown, her legs folded in the lotus position, staring at the wall.

I have the walls in my room covered with our paintings, from ceiling to floor. I like to look at them. I like to run them through my mind as if I'm counting gold or diamonds, gold I mined and refined with Mirabelle. I learn from them and gain great pleasure. And here is Mirabelle staring at our walls of paintings in the early morning light. I clamber across my bed to the foot and come close to her. She speaks without turning her head.

"They are beautiful, Jacques, more beautiful than I could ever have imagined or dreamed. You are a great artist."

I'm stunned. I slide down to the floor beside her.

"What do you mean, Mirabelle. What is it?"

"I can see! When I woke this morning and the light came into the room, I could see the paintings on the walls. I have been here looking at them for a long time. I had forgotten how beautiful it can be for eyes to see, and I am not frightened at all."

I can't believe it. But Mirabelle wouldn't do a thing like this to me, she wouldn't pretend, it's not her way to play tricks, or tease.

"What are you seeing now, Mirabelle?"

She speaks in a very low tone but with great emotion, there are tears on her face and tears are still coming from her eyes.

"I see the wonderful invention you made of the Place Saint-Sulpice for me. It is so true, so much more beautiful than anything only real. Thank you."

I find myself speaking in a low voice, also. Part of me is confused, trying to integrate my amazement that Mirabelle can actually see. I can hardly believe it.

"And the one beside it, can you see that one, too?"

"Oh yes, it is the place where the pigeons come down to eat in the little streets near the Place Furstenberg. I remember very well when you painted it. And these are even more beautiful than my own vision. You truly have put us together in these paintings, have you not, Jacques? I can never thank you enough."

We sit for a long time there on the floor. It is a warm day, so we are not cold. She tells me about all the paintings. She makes no mistakes, she remembers the painting of each one, she can tell me where I have made her vision even more clear to her. I move my head in front of her.

"And me, Mirabelle. What do you think of me? Are you disappointed in the way I look? I know I'm not a handsome man."

"I am certain you are beautiful, Jacques, but I cannot see you."

"What do you mean, Mirabelle? What is it?"

"I can see nothing but the paintings. When I turn my eyes from them, toward the window, or

toward you, or anything else, a fog starts to rise and all is red, then black again. I am sorry, I know how much you would like me to see, and perhaps I shall, someday, but not now. I do not think I am quite ready, my mind is still frightened."

At first I can't accept it. I keep making her focus on the paintings, gain her sight there, and then turn slowly or quickly, with her eyes open or closed to look at me, but there is nothing. She's still not prepared to see me or anything else.

But it's a big step. I hope it will last. I'm interested to see what happens when we go out to paint together and I tell her what I'm painting, when will it be that she will see a *new* painting. I lean forward and put my arms around her.

"Are you all right, my love? Is all this too much of a shock? Maybe you should go back to bed and rest."

She stands and I stand with her.

"No, Jacques, let us get on with our normal lives. It is what I think we must do. Things will come as they must, we cannot force them."

She goes into her room. I pull off my sleeping suit and slip on my running togs. My hands are shaking. Having her able to see my paintings is like losing some blindness myself. She comes out and takes a half-lotus position on the floor, one leg out, smiling toward me as I cross in front of her, go out the door, and down the stairs.

After breakfast, she goes into her music room. I pack my box and prepare to go out and paint. I hope to paint a scene up on the rue Mabillon, where there was once a bear pit, where bears used to be exhibited in the nineteenth century. There's a tree growing in the pit and a beautiful projection of a concierge's loge with steps down into the pit. Mirabelle turns to me.

"This morning, I want to work some more on a special concert I am preparing for you. Tonight, I would like to play it for you as a special thank-you for your paintings. Then I shall go take care of my pigeons. Can you be back here when the bells ring?"

"Sure. If you're doing the cooking I'll crawl back on my hands and knees if necessary. Just because you can see my paintings now, you can't get rid of me."

She smiles her quiet smile and turns away. I go down the stairs. It's a great day to paint, warm and not humid. It's tremendous painting when there isn't so much smell of automobiles as there is the rest of the year.

I get the drawing and underpainting done. I wonder if Mirabelle will be able to see it. I hear the bells ringing just as I'm putting the caps on my tubes. I'm home, going up the stairs, before the bells stop. Mirabelle opens the door for me. I put the box just inside the door with the painting visible. I watch her. I can see her looking but can also see she isn't seeing it.

It's another great meal. But too much has happened. We don't seem to have the same easy relationship. I miss it. I don't know what to do.

"I'm over painting the fosse des ours on rue Mabillon, Mirabelle. I think I have a good painting started. Do you want to come with me this afternoon?"

"I should work on Monsieur Bach some more

this afternoon, Jacques, I am trying to tie in the third and fourth voices to the first two I can now do, and it is not easy. But, yes, I would like very much to paint with you. Will you tell me what you are doing as you go along, as you always do?"

"Of course, I need your help, you know that."

"No, I do not think you need me to paint anymore. You are quite a complete and wonderful painter by yourself now. But I would like very much to be with you."

So, after we get the dishes done, we go over to the rue Mabillon with our two folding chairs. It's very close by, not more than three small streets away. I've set up for my painting on a narrow foot-bridge across one end of the fosse; I find a place for Mirabelle and get back to work. While I'm setting up, I describe what I've done so far.

"You see, Mirabelle, more than half the painting is the fosse itself with the deep hole, the tree growing up and out, the leaves blocking out most of the sky. Coming down into the center of the fosse I've painted the stairs from the concierge's loge, making them bigger and more solid than they really are. I have a deep, exaggerated perspective along the wall of the fosse next to the street. On the left side I don't show much of the wall, except behind the loge.

"Up on the street level, I have people walking away from me, not developed much, more shadows of people so far. I don't have any automobiles. The student restaurant across the street I've only roughly sketched in.

"At the back of the painting, and with the most light, is the rue du Four. I've worked that up with bright yellow, Indian yellow, and some ochers and I'll make it even brighter with direct paint at the end."

I go on describing the painting until I'm ready to start the impasto. I tell her exactly what I'm trying for, what I'm actually doing with the paint, what I'm hoping will be the overall effect, the contrast of the two levels with the sky, the enclosing effect from the leaves of the tree, blue and green, light blue and violet, like the Furstenberg trees, only these leaves are older, beginning to get tired, even having some touches of yellow and orange as they begin to feel summer ending. But they're still big, soft; casting slow-moving shadows. I tell her how I'm treating the shadows, differently in the fosse, smaller, darker than on the street.

I've gotten so I can paint and talk about it at the same time, as in all the paintings I've done with Mirabelle. In fact, my talking about it makes things clearer for me, helps me know what to do next.

When Mirabelle doesn't quite understand something, she'll ask a question and that helps, too. I would never have believed I could paint this way. I'm hoping it will help Mirabelle see the painting. I think if she can see it here, where it's actually happening, instead of on the wall of my room, it would be another great step forward.

Toward six o'clock, just when I'm listening for the bells to start ringing, and I'm beginning to think the painting might even be finished, she leans forward and whispers in my ear.

"I can see it, Jacques. It was so strange. I stored it all in my head from what you told me and then I began to see my painting on your easel and gradually, almost without my knowing it, my painting blended into yours and then became the painting

you have been painting, not just the one you were telling me about. It was magic. It is a beautiful painting. I shall never know how you do it. I know you tell me everything but I still do not know. It is like a dream."

"You can really see it, Mirabelle? Tell me about it! Can you tell what kind of light we're in? Tell me!"

"The bells are about to ring, so the light is not bright here now. I do not think there is any sun, it feels too cool, but there is sun in your painting, especially in the distance, on the rue du Four, just as you said. The sky is blue in the painting but it does not feel blue now in the real sky. There are few people in your painting but I hear many rushing past us now, going home to souper.

"Do not ask me if I can see you, Jacques. I know I cannot. I cannot even see the real scene you have been painting, right in front of my eyes. I can smell it, hear it, almost feel it, but I still cannot let myself see. I am sorry."

I swing around in my chair, wipe my hands clean with a paint rag, and take her hands in mine.

"Don't feel sorry for me, Mirabelle. I'm only disappointed you can't experience with me all this which has brought this painting into life. I would so like to share it with you."

"You have, in the best way possible, in your painting. Can you not understand, I do not need to see, especially with you to see for me."

"Mirabelle, that makes me feel part of your blindness, part of the reason! Try! Would you please try some things for me! Let me help you to see!"

"I shall do what you ask, Jacques."

"All right, I want you to see just me, it should be easier than this whole street. I want you to look at the painting until you have it focused in your mind, then close your eyes and open them again."

She stares at the painting. I can see her tracking the picture. Then she closes her eyes. I shift so my head is in line with her face and the painting.

"Open your eyes, Mirabelle. What do you see?"

"I see nothing. I felt you move and I see nothing."

"I know the mind is quicker than the eye, Mirabelle; but this is too much. Next time we'll try it slowly."

As I finish saying this, the first resounding bells of Saint-Sulpice, just up the street, begin.

"This time, look at the painting until you can really see it. Move your eyes around it as if it were the real world, let yourself go into the deepest and farthest-away places on the painting. Pretend it is a real place you're looking at, not just some canvas I've spread paint on. Look at it as if you've done the painting yourself and have only now finished it. Can you do that?"

"I can try."

I sit quietly beside her, listening to the bells, hearing the bells of Saint-Germain-des-Prés answering from farther away. Mirabelle is really concentrating. I wait. I start speaking softly.

"Now, Mirabelle, slowly turn your head toward me, try to relax, just let me become part of the painting; don't force yourself."

She slowly turns her head until she's facing me, looking into my eyes. She holds her head still, then slowly smiles.

"It is so strange, Jacques. As I turned my head, at first it is as if there is a fog again, then at the edge of the painting it is red and then there is only darkness. I am sorry I cannot see you. But it does not matter. I do not need to see you."

The bells have stopped ringing. I don't want to press. It's so strange.

"You're just not ready yet, Mirabelle; I'm sure you'll see me and, afterward, everything. We can wait."

I start packing up. I look at the painting myself. It's a good one. It's almost as if I can't fail. I'm not sure if I've lost my critical faculties and don't see what I'm doing wrong anymore, or if these paintings really are as good as they seem to me. After all, my only critic is blind. It doesn't say much for objectivity when I painted them myself, and the person who loves them with me can't see anything else and loves me to boot. I have her eyes prisoner, prisoner to our love.

After dinner that evening, Mirabelle leads me into her music room. I sit down in my usual chair. I watch Mirabelle go over to her harpsichord. I've rigged a small light where the music would normally be, as a part of my desire to have her living as if she had sight. She takes her cover off the harpsichord, makes a few other adjustments.

Then she walks over to a large armoire against the wall on the other side of the room. Carefully, she lifts several objects from shelves, each covered with a small cloth, and spreads them out on top of the harpsichord lid. There are nine of them.

"Jacques, I promised you I would tell you what it is I do with the newspapers. You have been most kind and not pressured me into speaking about it, but now I am ready to show you. Perhaps it is only another of my little folies but it is something I enjoy doing very much.

"You see, I make papier-mâché with the old newspapers. I soak them in a pan with paste and glue and knead them until it is all a fine, even mass. I dry it out some and then I shape this mass into objects."

She smiles. She turns and uncovers one of her "objects." It is a solid with soft curves and stands about eight inches tall.

"You see, when I play my music, I see the music in my mind. I do not see it as notes, of course. I see it as one of my visions. Each piece of music is for me a certain form and color. As I have mastered different suites, preludes, fugues, or more complicated pieces of music, I have tried to form my vision of each and make it real. These are my sculptures of music."

She runs her hands softly over the piece she's exposed on the harpsichord. She looks toward me.

"This one I tried to paint a dark purple, almost black, for me it is 'Le Tombeau de Monsieur Blanc-rocher,' which I played for you. In this 'Tombeau,'

I have tried to show the freedom I feel playing it and at the same time the calm sadness. I cannot see, only feel my 'objects.' There is a man at the paint store who is kind enough to listen and give me the colors I describe to him. But, of course, I cannot feel color. You know much about the Baroque music, Jacques. Have I made clear what I am trying to do?"

I'm floored again. It's a beautiful little sculpture. I go up and run my hands over it. I wouldn't know without her telling me, but it is a good representation of the undulating quality, order without measure, the way it sounds to me.

Mirabelle begins unveiling her other little statues, one by one.

"See, this is my gigue, it is orange to me and filled with action, that is why I have it so twisting and turning. And this one is the sarabande, red and with long, twirling turns and soft curves. Here is my allemande, the browns of earth and somewhat slow and flatter. You see, each of them is different. Is it not peculiar, Jacques? I have never shown them to anyone else but I am happy for you to see them; I had great pleasure forming them. It somehow made me feel not quite so blind to make these little objects that could express how I feel about the music."

I put my arm around her. I really don't know what to say. She continually surprises me.

"Mirabelle, miracle woman, you've done it again. These are incredibly beautiful. I'm amazed no 'seeing' sculptor has ever tried to do this. Probably, because you are blind and such an accomplished musician, only you could do this so well, translate the music into form. Each of these really is music, frozen music. Thank you for showing them to me."

I spend almost half an hour going from one to the other, letting my hands, fingers as well as my eyes wander over the surfaces. Sometimes I close my eyes to know them the way Mirabelle has known them, trying to put them into my mind as she's taken them out of hers.

"Now I want to put these away and play my concert for you."

She takes each of the sculptures in turn, covers them, puts the sculptures back into the armoire. Then she lifts the lid off the harpsichord, pulls her chair under her, spreads her right hand horizontally in front of herself, reaching to the harpsichord with her little finger, pulling the chair until her stomach is against her thumb, just that spread hand's breadth away from the harpsichord. I go back, turn off the lights, and settle into my usual chair.

"*You see, Jacques, since I cannot see, I must always be the same distance away from the keys. That is why I do this with my hand. It must seem strange to you, that is why I explain.*

"*Tonight I want to play a concert going from the simplest music up to the most complicated I can play. It will start with François Couperin, then Johann Sebastian Bach. I think you will enjoy the progressions in the music. I shall play François Couperin's little preludes, all eight of them. Try to think of my statue for prelude as you listen. I should have left them out and you could hold them and feel them as I play each one. Perhaps another time.*

"If you become tired listening, only tell me. I am trying to develop my own style of playing. It is a blend of all the different tapes I have heard of different performers playing this music. Perhaps you can tell me if I am succeeding."

With that, she begins to play. She plays beautifully, uniquely, the timing and touch of these simple preludes taking on a new dimension, precise, but with a lilting wave of continuity I'd never heard in them before. Some of the eight I don't even recognize. When she's finished, she puts her hands in her lap and turns toward me.

"Now we shall hear almost the same thing from Monsieur Bach. He was much more the pedagogue, you know. Sometimes I think he did not really like music for the way it can dance and enter the heart but for the way it fits together. It is as if he is always trying to show us what he can do, how clever his mind is, how agile; but, still, it is beautiful in its own way. Now listen to these 'Six petits préludes pour les débutants du piano.' I think you will enjoy them. I shall play them in the order of the keys. The first will be C major, then C minor, D minor, D major, E major, E minor.

"It is like listening to someone building a staircase to a personal musical heaven. It is very kind of him to take us with him."

She begins to play again. I close my eyes and listen. How true she is to the music, but still I can hear Mirabelle in it. I'm sure

Monsieur Bach wouldn't approve but it is good for me. It seems no time at all when she is finished.

"Do you still want to hear more?"

"Yes, please, Mirabelle, it is beautiful."

"Bien. Next I am going to play a series of simple dances Monsieur Bach wrote for his wife Anna Magdalena to play. He must have been a kind man, but he is always teaching. Ah yes. These are all kinds of dances, menuet, polonaise, musette, marche. I hope you like them, I enjoy very much playing them. It must be like dancing, and I have never danced."

She starts again. These are charming, most of them I know. They have a wonderful childlike quality. I think how much fun it would be to dance with Mirabelle, if her heart could take the strain. I imagine she would dance with grace and dignity.

I listen and let my mind move with the various movements. Time passes magically and she's finished. I open my eyes and her hands are on her lap again.

"Did you enjoy that? Sometimes when I was first starting to play, whenever I would be depressed or unhappy, I would play those little dances and all would be fine and good again.

"Now our teacher, Monsieur Bach, asks more of us. These are called by him inventio et sinfonia. There are fifteen of each. It was here I began to realize how difficult it could be to play well. The inventiones were not too difficult because there is only one voice, but the sinfoniae have three. I had

to listen very hard, very often, to separate the voices and then put them together. I thought of going to a special school here in Paris where they teach the blind to play, but felt I was too old, and also, I wanted to learn by myself. So I worked hard. Now you can hear and tell me if I did well. This will take a longer time to play because there are so many. If you become fatigued from listening, tell me."

There is only the light over her harpsichord. It is completely dark out the window. I feel I could stay like this and listen forever. It is such a perfect thing to do after a full day of painting.

"Mirabelle, I don't think I could ever become tired listening to you play. Please play again if it is not too much. Many evenings I have listened to my records and tapes for hours, it makes me feel some things in the world make sense. Lorrie would often go to bed because she said it was too much. And this is far superior to any of the tapes I had."

She begins and pauses briefly between each of the inventiones, they are exquisite. Then she comes to a full stop, takes a deep breath, and begins the sinfoniae. My mind shifts with the voices. In a way, because she had to separate them, they are almost as they were written, different voices, only carrying on the same conversation. They seem to toss the lead back and forth, over-lapping, carrying through with each other. When she stops, I can't believe what I've heard.

"Mirabelle, that was incredible. I have always listened too passively now, I know. You have made it all seem so real, so natural, the logic of the music came to me."

"Yes, Monsieur Bach is very logical. I am glad

you could hear it with me. You must know that you do the same for me with your paintings. You make so much so clear that even my personal visions become pale. I feel I know what you were thinking when you painted, why you do, did, the things you have done to make the world seem united, whole. Are you ready to hear some more?"

"Yes, please. Are you sure you aren't tired?"

"I could never tire playing for you, Jacques. I learned all this music only for myself, never knowing what a joy it would be to share. Now I am going to play Monsieur Bach's 'Suites Françaises.' I do not know why they are called that because they do not sound française to me, but that is not the question."

She pauses a minute, lifts her hands from her lap, straightens her shoulders, and begins. Some of these she has already played for me. This time I watch her face as she plays. She remains perfectly calm except for the movements of her shoulders as she makes an extra long stretch, or when the movement is slow and she rocks gently to the music. After each "ordre" she stops and asks if it is enough or should she stop. Each time I assure her, beg her to go on. She plays as if there is no end until she finishes with the last of the *Suites Françaises*.

"Now we should stop and go to bed. But first, after all that Bach, I should like to play one of my very favorites from Monsieur François Couperin. There are eight morceaux, and this is the fifth piece in the sixth ordre. It is called 'Les Barricades Mis-

térieuses.' This would be called 'The Mysterious Barricades' in English, I believe. I think of my affliction sometimes as my personal barricade mistérieuse, perhaps this is why I like to play this one so much. Listen."

She begins to play. I know the work but I'd never heard it played as Mirabelle plays it. There is the deep, dark mystery of the unknown. I can almost experience her blindness in those sections. The contrast with the lighter sections is strong and the continual recurrence of the low tones is beautifully executed. I'm enthralled. I almost lose contact. Then she is finished. I get up, turn on the light, go over, and put my arms around her from behind. She clasps her hands over mine. They are warm and must be tired.

"Thank you, Mirabelle. This has been the most complete evening of my life."

"It is only small thanks to you for all you have given me, dearest love."

She stands and I hold her in my arms. I help her lower the lid of the harpsichord and spread the cover over it. She holds the switch on the light until I'm out of the room and then turns it off. She is coming to act as if she can know what it is to be a seeing person, even though she sees nothing herself.

That night we make love in a slow, almost musical way. I can still hear the dances of her hands on the harpsichord and we seem to be playing cadences with each other mutually, bringing out the bright, clean notes sometimes, then the soft, dark, deep ones. I enter her and it is easier than the last time. I hold back and hold tight as she pulls me to her and then I come again, a soft flow into her, trying not to move, not to hurt.

I watch her face to see if she is all right, but there is no pain, only joy, delight, pleasure. She repeats my name over and over, Jacques, oh, Jacques, je t'aime, comme je t'aime. It's the first time she's spoken in French to me since we first met, except for a word now and then. We fall asleep together with her on top of me as my penis slowly slips out and I slide into a deep sleep.

Blind Reverie

Jacques is so concerned that I see him. Can he not know I <u>do</u> see him? Can he not feel in my music, when I play for him, that I can play for no one else?

I see him in <u>his</u> paintings, too. I am certain I see him much more clearly than if I let myself see his face. He is all there, his interest, vitality, strength, and kindness. I could not love him more than I do now.

But we are each part of the way we are. I am a blind woman, and what means so much to me does not mean so much to others. Dear Jacques is a man of his eyes; if he does not see, or feels he is not seen, in his own mind he does not exist.

It is so difficult for him, not knowing how to respond to his wife's lovely letter. I know he loves me, but he loves her, too. Love is not exclusive, it is inclusive; I wish I could help him know that. I think I would love Lorrie and the children if I could know them. But there is no use thinking of that. I must think more of how I can handle these days we have together, make the most of them.

I am afraid. Sometimes when we make love, I feel on the edge of something that could slide away and take me with it. I am not afraid for me, but for Jacques. I want him to stay here with his painting life if it is possible.

Chapter 12

The next day is Saturday. After our workout and breakfast, I go visit with Mirabelle while she feeds her pigeons. She wonders why I'm not painting.

"When you're finished here, Mirabelle, I want you to come with me to help buy clothes for our big evening out to celebrate our birthdays."

She turns her head toward me and smiles.

"What joy that will be, Jacques. I mean buying the clothes. Of course, it will be beautiful celebrating, too."

She hurries herself, scattering grains on the ground and on the bench. Even I can tell the pigeons are confused. After more than thirty years of ritual, thirty generations for these pigeons, the pattern is broken. I wonder if pigeons think. I doubt it; learn, maybe, but think, no. I don't say anything about this to Mirabelle.

I have two métro tickets, which are good for the bus. We get on the 86 bus, just a few steps from where Monsieur Diderot keeps watch on the pigeons for us. The tickets will take us to the Bastille. I help Mirabelle up the steps into the bus and we find a seat. This is where the bus starts out, so it's still practically empty. I take my favorite seat just behind the driver. I sit by the window because it doesn't mean anything to Mirabelle. When we start she leans toward me.

"Tell me everything you see, please, Jacques. It has been a long time since I have taken a ride on the bus. It is always so difficult asking the conductor to tell me when I arrive at the place where I must descend. When I must go somewhere far in the city, for example, the eye hospital on rue de Charenton, I always take a taxi. Rolande and I would take the bus, though. It was this same bus."

I tell Mirabelle about everything we pass as we go down the boulevard Saint-Germain. I tell her about the Carrefour de l'Odéon, then the Place Maubert. Then we go over the Pont Sully. I tell her about the boats going under us, about the green of the water and the gray sky with little spots of blue and a few fluffy white clouds under the gray. I try to describe Notre-Dame from the back with its huge spiderlike arms holding on to the ground. I tell her about the little park at the back tip of the Ile Saint-Louis.

Then our bus wends its way up the boulevard Henri IV and we come out onto the Place de la Bastille. Again, we could go farther for another ticket each, but I want to walk with Mirabelle down the Faubourg Saint-Antoine. This is my old neighborhood, this is where I lived in my attic. I'm taking her to the Marché d'Aligre, my favorite place to shop.

We push our way through the crowds up the rue d'Aligre to the marché itself. Mirabelle is holding tight on to me. I have my hand on hers. I hold her cane over the crook of my other arm. I hunt around looking for the used-clothing section. Mirabelle squeezes my arm.

"Really, Jacques, are there as many people here as there seem to be? I have never had so many people crash into me, it is worse than the market on the rue de Seine."

She giggles. I've been trying to protect her from people bumping her but it's a real crush. I wonder if I'm not asking too much. I know she had to tell me about her weak heart, but at times like this I wish I didn't know.

"There are so many smells, people smells, smells of fruits and vegetables and meat; and so much noise. I never knew there could be so much noise made by just the voices of people. It is wonderful! I feel so alive!"

I find the clothes racks. I paw through them. Mirabelle is feeling the cloth. There's a guy haranguing us but I ignore him. It's all part of the game.

Finally, I come upon what I'm looking for, a full-dress evening suit, a tux. I spread it out looking for holes, impossible stains. There doesn't seem to be anything. This suit has been kept in mothballs in some attic or closet for at least thirty years. It's so old-fashioned it has become beyond mode or style.

I try on the jacket and it fits almost perfectly. The pants are a bit big in the waist but the leg length is right. Mirabelle is feeling the cloth, bringing it up to her face. She leans toward me.

"This is very good cloth, Jacques, the kind my father wore at his wedding. For a long time, we kept that suit when he did not come back, but then Rolande gave it to the poor at Saint-Sulpice. There's a door on rue de Vaugirard where you can turn in such things."

Now the guy who's been bugging me starts talking about what a wonderful suit this is. I throw it back on the rack and start to turn away. I look back, ask, as if I'm indignant, "Combien?"

He gives me a price of forty francs. I saunter away. Mirabelle leans near me.

"Forty francs is very inexpensive for that suit, Jacques; you must buy it if you like it."

"I'm going to, Mirabelle, don't worry, but not for forty francs."

We wander around the market, looking at different things, or at least with me looking and telling Mirabelle what I'm seeing. We do this for another ten minutes, then stroll casually past the suit rack again. The seller sees me, as I figured he would. He's probably had his eye on me most of the time, most likely knows exactly what I'm doing. These are professional hagglers. I hate to haggle myself but have gotten used to it. He pulls the suit off the rack, holds it over his arm as if it's a coronation robe. I stop, look at it, shake my head. He grabs down an old-fashioned opera hat, reaches out, and plops it on my head. My God, it fits! I'm lost.

"Trente-cinq francs, monsieur, avec le chapeau. Vous serez comme le roi d'Angleterre."

I could probably bargain some more but I can't resist; it's the hat that does it. I take it off my head. It's impeccable, one of the kind that can be collapsed and snapped out, silk. I put it back on, look in a little cracked mirror he has hanging on the side of his truck. I wish Mirabelle could see me.

I reach into my pocket and pull out three ten-franc bills, and a five-franc coin. I give them to him and take the suit with the hat. We move away.

"I am so glad you bought the suit; you will be beautiful in it."

I have the hat on my head still. I lean down.

"Mirabelle, I bought the suit to go with my hat, feel my new hat."

She reaches up and touches it quickly with her fast, sensitive hands.

"Mon dieu, Jacques, you could be le ministre des finances himself, not just le roi d'Angleterre. You must look most impressive. Are you doing this so I will want to see you so much I must just let myself? Is that it?"

"Maybe, partly, Mirabelle. Now the minister, or the king, whichever, must look for a pair of shoes. I'll not pay more than ten francs and they must fit comfortably because, after our 'gala,' I shall use them for painting shoes."

We find an old pair of what look like dancing shoes, the kind Fred Astaire used to wear, thin-soled, patent leather. I could never use them for painting, but they fit and cost ten francs. One can't have everything, so I buy them.

We get back from our shopping expedition and enjoy a great lunch. Mirabelle makes me put on my suit and measures me for alterations like a tailor. It's another skill I didn't know about.

"Do you not know, Jacques, all blind women can sew? It is one of the things we are supposed to do, like making baskets or repairing the paille in chairs. Oh yes, Rolande always claimed I had les mains d'or, golden hands, master hands. You shall be very handsome."

When she's finished measuring, I dress in my comfortable painting clothes, heft my box on my back, pick up a stretched canvas, and head out to paint. I can probably only get the drawing done, but I don't want to lose the day completely. There's a spot just on the street where the Place Furstenberg comes out, on the high side, where, by looking up and to the left, I can see a whole pileup of buildings, with a complex mix of windows, rooftops, walls, indentations, mansards, and chimney pots at all different angles. It could make a good vertical painting on a 25 Figure.

The next days we are busy readying our costumes. After Mirabelle has altered my tuxedo, I have it dry-cleaned. This costs more than the suit, but Mirabelle insists. I sold that painting, the one looking up at the buildings, straight off the easel, for another fifteen hundred francs, so I'm feeling flush.

I call Le Grand Vefour, an incredibly fancy restaurant, one of the best known in Paris, which is located in the archways of le Palais-Royal. I make reservations for two on the ninth of September. We do much talking about what we hope to order. For a wine, we settle on a simple Côtes du Rhône. It's here, with the wines, they can really blast you away in a place like this.

At night, every night, we make love. It's gotten so natural and we don't lose any of the other pleasures we had before we could actually have intercourse. I'm wondering if Mirabelle is having any orgasm. It's difficult, maybe impossible for me to tell. I could never be sure with Lorrie. I decide to ask.

"What is orgasm, Jacques?"

Jesus! How do I tell a woman what's orgasm? How could she have gotten this far without knowing? I wonder if she's never masturbated, but I don't want to ask.

"Well, when I have my seed come out, Mirabelle, that's a man's orgasm, but it's different from a woman's."

"Would I have seeds or eggs come out of me?"

"No, it's different. Nothing comes out. You just feel as if you're so excited you can't control yourself. You feel all warm and happy and it's as if your body takes over and gives you pleasure itself. It's something like that, I'm told."

"It sounds wonderful, like music. It feels beautiful when you come into me and my body feels warm and I am very happy, but I do not think that is orgasm. What must I do to have an orgasm like that? I would like it very much."

"You don't have to do anything, Mirabelle, it will probably come by itself. You'll know when it does."

I'm beginning to back up in my mind. Maybe a real "four-star" orgasm might be just enough to wreck her weak heart and kill her. Besides, I don't want her to start thinking of orgasm so much she blocks herself from having one. I'm wishing I'd kept my big mouth shut.

"Oh, I do hope so. Help me if you can."

"I will, Mirabelle."

We leave it at that.

Most nights now, before we go to bed, Mirabelle gives me concerts. They can be anywhere from half an hour to two hours and they have become part of our lovemaking for me and I think for her, too.

She moves on to more difficult work, especially the Bach compositions she calls *Le Clavecin Bien Tempéré*. She's working on a series of preludes and fugues in three and four voices from the *English Suites* in preparation for the more difficult pieces from *Le Clavecin Bien Tempéré*. She also plays one evening some Scarlatti and some more Couperin, such as "Double de Rossignol," and "Le Petit-Rien."

Another night she plays Duphly's "Le Forqueray." For me it's such a joy. And Mirabelle, despite her knocking Bach because he was always teaching, teaches me beautifully, gently, sharing her incredible knowledge of Baroque music. When we're in that music room and I'm listening to her, she's completely in charge. It's the reverse of the way it is when she's with me painting and I'm explaining what I'm seeing and doing.

And, every morning, when I wake, I find her at the foot of my bed, sitting, looking at the paintings. She can't seem to get enough; it's as if she's drinking them in. Sometimes I wake and just watch her, her head turning slowly from one to the other. Every artist should have such an audience, someone sensitive who loves your work and can't, literally, *"see" anybody else's*. I know the paintings are a part of our lovemaking, too, just as her playing her music is.

On the evening of the ninth, we decide to walk to our rendezvous at Le Grand Vefour. It's a lovely evening and we've spent almost an hour bathing, dressing, inspecting each other. Mirabelle has even given me a haircut and beard trim. I wouldn't believe a blind woman could do such a thing, but her hands drift over my head, feeling, touching, measuring, and when she's finished I have a hair and beard cut such as I've never had before. Of course, except for hacking away at my own beard, I've *never* had a beard cut. I didn't have a beard before I started living in the streets.

She also insists I carry a beautiful umbrella which had been her father's. It has a carved handle in the shape of a duck's head with a gold collar. It's beautifully furled and I'm not about to unfurl it for fear it might fall apart, after more than fifty furled years. Mirabelle also rustles out a beautiful white silk scarf and drapes it around my shoulders.

"Jacques, I do wish I could see you, I think you must look very handsome."

She runs her hands over my face, my clipped beard, down the front of a slightly fragile white dress shirt she also found, and along the silk lapels of my evening coat. She's probably actually seeing me better than I can ever see myself.

I talk Mirabelle into wearing an old boa we find hanging in the closet. She also wears the dark dress she'd worn once only, at Rolande's funeral, along with a black Persian lamb coat which had belonged to her sister. On her head she wears a cloche hat with a little black veil, also left over from the funeral.

When I look at us in the mirror in her parents' room, now mine, we look as if we've stepped out of an old daguerreotype. With the mirror fading, the silver backing chipped off, I'm not quite sure we're even *alive*. But we look damned impressive. I stand straight and tall, very aristocratic, while Mirabelle carries herself with her usual grace. It's too bad she can't see the scene we make. She'd probably go into a fit of giggles.

We figure we'll walk till we're tired, then call a taxi. We definitely don't want to *walk* up to the door of Le Grand Vefour.

We start by walking across the boulevard Saint-Germain, then down the rue de Seine. I swing my umbrella jauntily, like a boulevardier, and point out to Mirabelle the things I'm seeing. I'm having a great time and I think Mirabelle is, too.

We cross the Pont des Arts to the Right Bank and I'm trying to *see* for Mirabelle, trying to plant the beauty of the city that night in her mind, in her private collection of "visions."

"There are shining, golden lights on the Conciergerie, Mirabelle, and amber lights along the river. The cars are like a stream of amber on one side of the river and a stream of red on the other."

We're standing in the middle of the bridge, leaning over, looking at the point of L'Ile de la Cité.

"The front of the island resembles the prow of a ship with a lovely weeping willow tree growing on the front deck. Farther on is the Pont Neuf with its beautiful lamp lights shimmering in the river. Buses, cars, and people are crossing it; I can see the illuminated towers of Notre-Dame.

"There are young people on the quai of the island enjoying the softness of this evening. And, if we turn to our left, we see the golden, lit façade of Le Louvre, a great wall of stone, new and shining after its cleaning."

Just then, one of the huge Bateaux Mouches comes from behind us, under the bridge, lighting the water deep green with its large spotlights. There are the sounds of diners and the multilingual spiel of a tour guide. I try to explain how mysterious, almost frightening this large, shark-shaped boat appears to me, at the same time how the soft lights on the tables inside give it a friendly, almost cozy look.

We continue over the bridge. We walk across in front of the Louvre and past the Arc du Carrousel. I try explaining what I'm seeing but feel inadequate. It isn't the same as when I'm painting, then I'm forced to really see things, not just look at the outsides of them. I feel frustrated.

"What is the matter, Jacques? Please do not stop. I am getting such a glamorous picture in my mind. I was never here as a child, or if I was, I do not remember. I was here with Rolande sometimes, but she did not much like to walk and she did not talk about what she was seeing. Please tell me more."

We decide to forget the taxi. We'll take one home. So we enter under the arcades of the Palais-Royal somewhat surreptitiously. We take advantage of a moment when the doorman is escorting people out of a huge Rolls-Royce to insinuate ourselves into position and saunter slowly up the steps to the door. We wait until another doorman opens it for us and we go in.

The maître d' comes toward us quickly, probably wondering out of what time machine we've stepped. I give our names and he shows us to a wonderful location, where I take the bench against the wall. He motions Mirabelle into the chair across the table but I insist she sit beside me. We'd decided on this ahead of time. She wants me to help her with the menu and also describe what there is to be seen. I actually get a French shrug, authentic, from the maître d', but no real objection. He gives rapid-fire instructions to a waiter, and the silverware, glasses, dishes are rearranged to our liking. Before Mirabelle sits down, there is the cloakroom attendant standing beside her, waiting for her coat.

"Mirabelle," I say in English, English-English, "I don't believe it is too cold in here, you might want to give the gentleman your coat."

She flashes a smile at me and proceeds to unbutton her coat, as he helps her slide out of it. She unpins her hat and hands it to him as well. Then, feeling the edge of the table, she moves around it and slides in beside me. So far, so good.

"That was wonderful, Jacques, I should have thought about the coat. But it went off beautifully, did it not?"

"Oh yes. They might well be beginning to think we really are some of the British royal family after all; aristocrats left over from last century. We could be out slumming. This is great fun."

When the sommelier, a self-satisfied, heavy man, comes to ask if we would have something before dinner, we casually order Kir Royal, another precast decision. He bows and moves away. A waiter hands me a menu. Since we're sitting beside each other, I presume he thinks we'll only need the one, and I can order for us both. That fits our plan exactly. So far, I don't think anyone has any idea Mirabelle is blind. They probably have me figured as a gigolo escorting an older woman for money, and that's fun, too; almost as good as being members of the royal family.

I've been to this restaurant a few times for high-level luncheon conferences. I was so busy trying to impress my boss, or outwit our competitors, I didn't have much chance to notice the quality of the food. I did remember the excellent French quality of the

decor, though, and I'm sorry Mirabelle can't see it. To someone
just casually looking at us, we seem to be huddling over the menu,
but I'm actually giving her a blow-by-blow account of what's happening around us, what I'm seeing. They'll figure we're having a
difficult time making up our minds, but let them think what they
will.

"There are high ceilings, Mirabelle. Beautiful crystal chandeliers
hang from those ceilings. The floor is carpeted with a dark wine-
colored rug almost the same color as the one in your room. We're
sitting on deep red velvet benches with dark wood trim."

I look behind her. There's a small plaque attached to the dark
wood. I lean over to read it.

"I'm sorry to tell you this, Mirabelle, but you are *not* a member
of the British royal family. You are sitting in the same place the
Empress Josephine sat a few years ago."

*"I always knew I was not British, Jacques.
It is so good to find my true place."*

She says it without even a hint of giggle. We're really into it
now.

I go on describing the crowds sitting around us at the impec-
cably white tables, beautiful linen with napkins big enough for any
normal tablecloth. I describe how the glassware is all so bright,
shining, the silver glittering in the light from the chandeliers. Mirabelle leans close to hear me, her eyes seemingly fixed on the
menu.

*"It sounds wonderful, Jacques. Are you doing
all this just so I will be forced to let myself see? Is
that why you are so kind to me?"*

"Of course. You think I'd spend money like this on just anyone and for a mere meal? I have 'designs' on you, my dear."

"Dessins? What does that mean? Do you intend to make a dessin, a drawing, of me? I do not understand."

"Aha, but you will, my dear."

I twist my mustache like a classic villain. Then I describe what I'm doing and what I mean by "designs" on her, that I'm not about to tattoo her. This is too much. She brings her napkin up to hide a giggle, just as the Kir Royal is delivered.

I lift mine and, without help, Mirabelle finds and lifts hers by the thin stem. She holds it out, looks, or pretends to look, into my eyes. We tap the glasses.

"To our continued success and a long life, Countess."

"Oh, Jacques. This is too much."

"Nothing is too much for the Comtesse de Rochambault."

"Stop it, Jacques, and drink your Kir."

We sip. I haven't had this in over two years. There was actually a time when it seemed no American could seem to think of any other drink before a fancy dinner. Now it tastes fresh, unique, the fruity quality carried beautifully by the bubbles of the champagne.

"This is delicious, Jacques. I do not think I have ever tasted champagne like this."

"It's a lovely pink color, Mirabelle, and the bubbles rise in the glass like balloons going to heaven."

"I think you are drunk, Jacques, and we have not even started."

"I *am* drunk, Mirabelle. Let us be drunk together."

I reach for her hand under the table. It is cool and dry. I wrap it in my warm hand. With my other hand I tilt up the menu.

"Shall we begin with les escargots, my dear, or would you prefer some other hors d'oeuvre?"

"That is what we decided before we came, was it not, Jacques? We would have six escargots each for hors d'oeuvre?"

"That's right, Mirabelle, and you are going to have a blanquette de veau, while I shall have a boeuf bourguignon. I'm looking for them on the menu now, but I don't see them. If I remember this place correctly the food is all very fancy. They wouldn't have peasant food like my boeuf bourguignon, but they could have another fancy name for it. Oh, there it is, I see your blanquette de veau. We are in luck."

Just then the waiter comes up to us. He stands on the other side of the table, face blank, with his pad and pencil in hand. I tell him we'll start with les escargots, deux fois six. He writes it down. "Et ensuite?" says he, smiling an artificial smile.

"We'll have la blanquette de veau for Madame, and I shall have un bon boeuf bourguignon."

I snap shut the menu. He stands there, his smile frozen.

"Nous n'avons pas le boeuf bourguignon, monsieur."

Well, at least he's honest. I open the menu again. I see a coq au vin. That's low-down, good rib-sticking food for me, and I go for it. I know it won't be as good as Mirabelle's but it's something I like. I tell him that's what I want. He scribbles and leaves.

"Jacques, tell me more of what you are seeing."

I look around some more and start pointing out the more ridiculous characters at some of the tables. I must admit I'm doing something of a caricature on a few of these people, sort of a verbal Daumier. Mirabelle is torn between giggling and trying to shut me up. The sommelier comes back.

"Qu'est-ce que je peux vous offrir comme vin, monsieur?"

He hands me a wine list. I don't even open it. I answer in English.

"What do you have in the way of a simple Côtes du Rhône, monsieur?"

He leans over me and opens the wine list, paging through till he comes to the page with the Côtes du Rhône. He now speaks in reasonable, heavily accented English.

"Here is a simple but robust Côtes du Rhône, monsieur."

He points with his pencil at a wine costing a hundred and seventy-five francs. That's robust all right. I barely glance at the wine list. Let him think I'm illiterate.

"Good. Bring us a bottle. It should do."

He retreats inside himself, marks on his pad, leaning back on his heels, then swoops the wine list from my hands. I smile at Mirabelle.

"Jacques, I feel from your voice that you are angry with these people. Have they done something wrong?"

I take both her hands. They're definitely cold.

"No, Mirabelle. They're fine and I'm having a wonderful time in my own way. It's only all this seems so wrong when I think of the way I lived, the way we live, the trueness of our lives. This is so artificial, unrelated even to the food, it is all form and doing the right thing. I guess it reminds me too much of the way I lived most of my adult life and I'm actually angry at *myself*. I promise to stop."

"Perhaps we should leave. What could they do

to us? We could pay for our Kir Royal and walk out the door."

"Don't tempt me, Mirabelle. No, let us celebrate. I want to enjoy this with you and not ruin everything. I promise, we shall have a wonderful time for our mutual birthdays."

And we did. We laughed, and we laughed at the right things. I stopped laughing at the people around us, and we had our own private funny things, mostly about us and the clothes we were wearing. I began to feel sorry for the waiters, the maître d', even the sommelier. Hell, they were only trying to make a living. They probably didn't believe in all this googah any more than we did.

We finished off with some mousse au chocolat and a coffee.

"Jacques, with this chocolate and the coffee, we'll never sleep tonight."

"Do you really want to sleep, Mirabelle?"

I squeeze her hands, then her leg under the table. I wonder if anyone else in the room is doing the same. It doesn't look like it. They're taking the whole thing seriously.

"No, Jacques, I do not want to sleep. I want to taste you. I know you taste better than anything they could ever cook or think of in this restaurant. Your taste is so natural and there is such variety. Am I a shameless woman?"

"I think you're a wonderful woman, and besides having good taste, *you* taste good, too."

We walk back in the night. Mirabelle doesn't want to take a taxi. She says they always smell of cigarette smoke and the perfume and sweat of other people. So we walk. I don't know what time it is, but the lights on the buildings are still lit. There's less traffic on the quais. We walk slowly and feel the bottle of wine, the mousse, and the coffee fusing into our bodies and making us soft and vulnerable.

When we arrive home, we undress each other and go to bed. We make love, just as Mirabelle wanted, and then go to sleep. We have no trouble sleeping despite the chocolate, the wine, and the coffee. Our lovemaking has melted them all into one totality and it's just the two of us. As we go to sleep, Mirabelle whispers into my ear.

"I do not think I had an orgasm, Jacques dear, but I am beginning to think I might know what it could be."

In the morning when I wake, Mirabelle isn't at the foot of the bed as usual. When I go into the main room she's standing on her head. I know, now, this is about the third position she takes with her yoga. I go back into my room and dress for running.

When I return from my run, breakfast is being prepared and my bath is ready, hot as usual. I kiss Mirabelle on the back of the neck as I walk past. She turns to me.

"That was wonderful last night, Jacques, all of it. I hope you had as fine a time as I did. It is as if I have lived all my life preparing for that particular birthday. I still cannot believe I am seventy-two. It does not seem possible."

"That's right, Mirabelle, today's your birthday. Happy birthday.

Let me cook the meal today. Would that be all right? I can make something very American, something you've never eaten, I'm sure."

"Is that what you want, Jacques?"

"Yes, if you want it, too."

"You know I love surprises."

"All right, you go out with your pigeons and when the bells ring come back and I'll have a surprise for you. It will be better than Le Grand Vefour and much less expensive, too."

After breakfast, I go shopping. Mirabelle says she'll practice some, then go out to her pigeons.

I hunt all over before I find what I want. Even finding the name for them is a trick in itself, but I see some hanging in a butcher shop and from then on, it's easy. I also find the other ingredients I need.

This is something I know how to make. It was sort of my specialty around the house. I enjoy cooking. In the years at MBI there just wasn't much chance for me to do any. God, what a waste, it was as if I had been trying to destroy the quality of my own life, of those I loved.

I do the last basting and tasting just as the bells start ringing. A few minutes later Mirabelle comes in the door.

"What are you cooking, Jacques? I have never smelled anything like this. It smells delicious."

"You just sit down, Mirabelle, and it will come."

First I serve half an avocado each with a regular vinegar, oil, and garlic dressing in the hole where I took out the pit. Mirabelle had never tasted avocado before. I show her how to eat it. She carefully munches down on the avocado flesh and at first is surprised, but then I can tell by her face she's experiencing the wonderful nutty flavor of avocado.

"But what is this? It is delicious. Is it a fruit or a vegetable or did you make it yourself?"

"It's avocado, Mirabelle. They have them in many of the markets now in France. In California, people eat them all the time. These come from Martinique. It's one of my favorite foods."

My pièce de résistance is some irresistible American spareribs with a sweet and sour sauce. I also have ears of corn. Mirabelle just sits there. She touches the tops of the food gently with her fingertips.

"What is it I am eating, Jacques, and how does one eat this food? I feel like a baby."

"This is finger-lickin' finger food, Mirabelle honey, and there are no waiters watching; pick up the corn or the meat and eat the way it seems best. If you feel too messy, use your napkin. You might like some butter and salt or pepper on your corn. You eat the kernels right off the cob."

"Are you making fun of me, Jacques? Do not be cruel."

"No, really, Mirabelle. If you could see me, you'd see that's exactly what I'm doing myself. Try it. I think you'll like it."

And she does. We munch along, not talking much. I hadn't thought of how it would be a new experience for a blind, older person to eat with fingers, but she works it out quickly.

"I feel as if we have gone back thousands of years into the past, eating with our fingers, no forks or knives, just tearing meat and corn off with our teeth. And it is so delicious. Maybe this is what makes

Americans the way they are, eating the food of angels as if they were devils."

She wipes her chin. I'm really enjoying myself. I managed to get the sauce on the spareribs to have just the right blend of sweet and sour so one can taste the tomato but it isn't acidic. It goes beautifully with the corn. Mirabelle is searching, with her fingers, over her ribs and cobs for bits of food she hasn't found.

"Jacques, that was one of the best meals I have ever had. You could really put that restaurant last night out of business. You will have to cook us some more of your American cooking."

"I'm sorry, Mirabelle, I don't know how to cook many things, but I'll try. It was fun."

It's then I spring my surprise.

"Mirabelle, let us drink some more of your wonderful drink with the pear. It would be the perfect way to end this birthday meal together."

"But there is none left, Jacques, I saved the bottle where it always was before, but it is empty."

"Please, Mirabelle, for me, let us pretend."

She stares at me a second in her perceptive blind way, then slowly stands up and goes over to the cupboard where she keeps the bottle. As she comes to me, a smile comes on her face.

"What have you done, Jacques? It is full now. Did you put water in it, are you trying to change water into Poire William for me, as Christ did for his Mother with the wine?"

"Do you want me to take down some glasses, Mirabelle?"

She places the bottle on the table and turns back to the cup-

board; gently, in that special way she has with her fingers, she
holds two glasses by their short stems and puts them beside the
liquor. She sits down.

*"Please, Jacques, open the bottle again as you
did before. I pushed it down hard so the pear would
not be rotted in the air."*

She hands me the tire-bouchon. I push it into the cork and pull
it out easily. I pour generously into our two glasses. She's listening.
We say nothing. Then I lift my glass to hers and she senses it. She
holds out her glass.

"To Mirabelle, the most wonderful woman in the world, for
whom, as with this pear in the bottle, time does not pass. Happy
birthday."

We drink. I'm anxious to hear her reaction. It is a long chance
I took. I didn't want to desecrate; at the same time, the coincidence
was irresistible. She sips, seems to look into the glass, sips again.

*"It is very good, Jacques, but it is not the same.
It has another flavor completely. I know nothing
of these things."*

"Well, Mirabelle, I wanted to buy, as a birthday present for you,
a new bottle with another pear in it. I searched all over Paris for
such a thing but could not find it.

"Finally, I was in a small specialty wine shop for these types of
liquors near the Panthéon. He had Poire William but without the
pear. I told him something about us. I said I was buying it for a
wonderful woman named Mirabelle.

"His eyes sparkled. He turned quickly and went down a trapdoor
he had behind his counter. He came up with a dusty bottle and
put it on the counter between us.

" 'Sir, this is a twenty-year-old bottle of Mirabelle made by my father. I'm sure you will find it exquisite. To make the Mirabelle properly, it is necessary that one allow the fruit to mature on the tree until it is just ready to fall, then one must carefully pick these fruits, store them in a wooden barrel, and allow them to ferment. Fruit picked like this scarcely needs any sugar.

" 'It is just so that my father made this Mirabelle. This is the last of over eighty bottles he bottled. Here, see the date in his own handwriting, 1953.'

"So, Mirabelle, I bought that bottle, then I brought it here. I was going to give it to you for your birthday present. Then I had the idea to pour the Mirabelle into your bottle. It seemed the right thing to do. I'm sure the man at the shop wouldn't be too happy with what I was doing to his father's wonderful liquor, but I hope you approve. Your approval is all I really need."

Tears are rolling down Mirabelle's face again. She comes around the table and for the first time sits in my lap. Intimate as we've been, I'm still shocked at how light she is, it's as if she has hollow bones like a bird. She has her glass in her hand.

"Please, Jacques, drink from my glass while I drink from yours. It would make me very happy if you would do this. It is an old custom, one my mother and father practiced every birthday I can remember."

We drink and then Mirabelle tucks her head in the hollow of my neck and shoulder. We stay a long time like that.

In the evenings, while Mirabelle is practicing her harpsichord, I write to my family. Mirabelle's still working on the *English Suites*.

Lorrie's sent on the letters from Helen and I've been reading them one at a time in the sequence they were written. Some of them make me cry, some laugh, all of them reveal her in a way I've never known; as a very serious person with a great sense of humor. For the most part, she treats Lorrie's and my separation with a light hand for such a young person. But sometimes her resentment and Lorrie's, so well concealed, comes through. She calls me "the outcast." In these letters I begin to see how she loves me, wanted to be closer to me, but I was never really available to her.

I answer each of her letters as I read them. I try to explain what was on my mind when I left, the sense of having lost myself and of going on a search, sort of a personal crusade. I tell her how I think I've found something of what I really am, and am much happier for it. I tell her in as much detail as I can the progression of experiences I've been through.

Many of her letters are about the things she's been doing at school or about boyfriends or girlfriends. I know it is all not particularly au courant now, but I respond as I would like to have responded at the time. They were important to her, so they're important to me.

I also receive letters from each of the other children. Jack is somewhat reserved. I guess as the oldest and the most formal of the children he resents me the most. But he's cordial and talks some about his new work. The other two spend half their letters explaining why they haven't written, but don't ask why I left. I imagine Lorrie primed them to be nice.

I try answering them as I've done Helen, hoping to bridge the gap in our lives. I find it takes me hours with paper and pen explaining, without complaining or begging. What I want most of all is to make up for some of the lost time, not just these last long months but all the years when I was only there physically, and not very much of that.

I write more intimate letters to Lorrie. I start at the very beginning of my saga and tell everything that happened. Just getting down the main experiences and what I was feeling at the time fills twenty-five pages and takes three evenings.

Then I try to tell her about Mirabelle and me. I tell about buying the suit and top hat at the marché and going to Le Grand Vefour. I tell her about Mirabelle's pigeons, how she can handle them, about her harpsichord playing and the way she learned so many languages by herself, just with tapes. I tell about her doing yoga and how she exercises every morning while I run. I tell how she became blind, the terrible shock of it, and how she can see my paintings now but still can't see anything else.

I don't tell how Mirabelle got so she could see. I do tell how we started by painting together, how she opened my mind and heart to the beauty of the world so my painting began to make sense.

It's hard to write all this and not hurt her. But I'm convinced it must be if we're ever to be together again. I don't want to hide what I am, what I've become, from her.

For example, in telling about our visit to Le Grand Vefour I mention Mirabelle cutting my beard before I realize Lorrie doesn't even know I have one. So I back up and tell how I've had a beard for some time now and enjoy it. I ask if this would be too difficult for her to take, to become accustomed to. I tell her also that I'm going quite gray. In this time that's passed, I've gone from a man with gray temples to a man with pepper-and-salt hair receding at the forehead. My beard is, if anything, even whiter.

Lorrie writes back the most beautiful letters, telling me about her life, the children, assuring me that there are no hard feelings with any of the kids except perhaps for Jack.

It feels wonderful to be in contact with all of them. I worry about Mirabelle. We don't have much time alone together; the writing takes so much time in addition to my painting. Also, after I've finished, I'm dead tired. I can feel myself drained in a way not even painting has ever done.

Each evening, as I finish, Mirabelle always knows. She'll come out of her music room, stand behind my chair, put her hands first in my hair, gently massaging, then massage my neck and down my back. Her hands, so small, so gentle, are also strong. She rubs and strokes the tension out, across my shoulders and down my arms.

Often, then she'll invite me into her music room and play for me. She has a tremendous repertoire, including Scarlatti, Handel, and others I've never heard. It is as if strength from her pours back into me through the music. I guess it's because I don't play. Music, more than anything, is nourishment for my soul. I take it into my heart and it flows through my body.

Sometimes, especially if I've been painting all afternoon, I drop off to sleep with the music. Mirabelle says she doesn't mind because she knows it's what I need. Always, if I've fallen asleep, she comes to me, gently strokes my forehead and kisses my closed eyes, my nose, my lips with soft featherlike kisses until I wake and she leads me almost drugged to my bed.

Sometimes I'm asleep again when she comes in beside me. She'll touch me softly all over, knowing with her sensitive fingers if I want to sleep.

Usually, no matter how tired I might have thought I'd been, she can arouse me and our lovemaking proceeds almost as in a dream, soft, drifting, slow movements, practically uninterrupted with the moment of my insertion and careful, gentle movements almost as if we're underwater. I fall asleep sometimes after I've come, especially now she's learned to be on top of me and control the movements of our sexual union herself. She's so light, I scarcely feel her weight, only her intensity.

My painting is going well. On some days when it rains, I paint inside the apartment, first looking out the window, then setting up small still lifes in my room by the window. As a student I'd always disliked painting still life. But now, with what I've learned about one's personal inner vision being more important than the subject matter itself, I find still life an interesting challenge. It's nice for Mirabelle, too. She can be comfortable beside me without the noise and confusion in the streets.

One day when it's raining, I start another portrait of Mirabelle. The reason I do this is because the portrait I painted of her when we first met is the only painting she can't see. If it's in her field of vision she automatically becomes blind to everything. It's really strange. The morning when she saw the paintings for the first time, I had it hanging on the wall over my bed, separate from the rest. I like looking at it as I'm undressing for sleep. That's why she couldn't see it. Now I want to try painting with my new vision, my new skills, my knowledge and love for her revealed.

When I'm finished, I compare it with the first painting. It's so different. I can't tell how much Mirabelle has changed and how much of the change is due to change in me. In the first painting she seems so still, so stiff, with little feeling of the life and joy, the young girl, I've come to know in her. In the new painting, the brush and its movements are more evident as such, also functioning better in describing Mirabelle, at least the Mirabelle I know now. Neither painting has anything of a blind person about it. I suspect I've just never really seen her as blind.

But when I finish it and show it to Mirabelle, even though I'd put up a mirror behind me so she could, if she wanted, see the whole painting as it came into being, and even though I've explained everything I did, and why I did it, so she could participate in the painting with me, she still can't see it.

"I am sorry, Jacques. I think I just do not want to see myself as an old lady. You make me feel so young and happy, I know there is something inside me that is afraid."

"But, Mirabelle, I've painted you as I see you, with all my love, my deep admiration and respect for you, my passion. It's all there. How I wish you could let yourself see it."

"I know, Jacques. Perhaps it will come. I am afraid I will not see myself as you do, even though you painted it as you say, I must see it with <u>my</u> eyes, and I am frightened.

"It is difficult to explain, but I sometimes have the feeling I am surrounded by a bubble which keeps me alive and happy. Seeing your paintings is like having the terrible world out there filtered through *the screen of your love; but my bubble remains intact. I am still safe. I do not yet have enough confidence in myself, or everything out there, to actually be a part of the outside world. Please be patient."*

One thing we like to do is go up to the Church of Saint-Sulpice at about eleven-thirty on Sunday. Saint-Sulpice has one of the great organs in the world and has had some of the greatest modern organists, including Marcel Dupré, to play it.

Just after eleven-thirty, a mass is usually letting out and the organist plays classical music, not just hymns or simple liturgical music. He plays Bach mostly and the high vaulting of that ugly church has wonderful acoustics. Mirabelle has found the perfect place to sit so the thundering rumble of those big pipes and the dainty treble of the small ones come together right there, in all their integrated complexity.

We sit quietly and it thrills us both to hear and share it. This is a free concert and only those who know about it stay on to listen. We linger until the first bells at noon start and the concert is finished. My great joy is walking the length of the aisle toward where the organ is located up on the balcony in front of the rose window. Then we go through the open doors and out on the Place with the fountains playing. The wondrous change of sounds from the organ to the bells and then the water is magical.

And it's something Mirabelle and I can share. I only wish she could look up into those high vaults lit by stained glass, then move out of the dimness, onto the high stone porch of the church, and look out over the sparkling Place with the statues of bishops sitting back to back; huge lions crouching at their feet as water splashes all around them, reflecting sunlight. But then, probably she enjoys those sounds even more than I do, there's no distraction.

Life goes on and it's beginning to get cooler. We've passed All Saints' and All Souls' Day. On All Souls' Day I take Mirabelle to the cemetery in Montparnasse and we find Rolande's grave beside the grave of her parents.

Mirabelle hasn't been there since her sister died. We find the location of the graves by asking the curator of the cemetery. He locates them in a large ledger with small blue horizontal lines and a few red vertical ones.

Mirabelle leans over the graves and traces the names of her parents and Rolande carved on the gravestones. We put the pot of flowers we've brought with us at the foot of the graves. It's all terribly overgrown and the stones are covered with moss. I start weeding around the edges between the monument and the pebbles. Mirabelle joins me, and we spend two hours pulling weeds with our bare hands until it looks loved and cared for.

"Does it look all right now, Jacques?"

"It looks fine. You can be proud of it. To my taste it's the most beautiful grave in the cemetery."

And I'm not lying. So many of the graves are made of smooth, massive marble with gilt writing and are decorated with plastic flowers or small black-on-white enameled plaques saying things like *Souvenirs à notre père et mère*, or *Nos regrets*.

"This is where I am supposed to be buried, Jacques, with my family; but I do not want to be buried here. Is that terrible?"

"Don't think about being buried, Mirabelle. Enjoy this beautiful autumn day with me."

"I am enjoying it very much. But I can think about being buried and still enjoy it, maybe even more. Do you know where I would like to be buried? I would like to be buried in the sky somehow. I do not mean I want to be burned, that is a horrible thing, but I wish I could some way just be taken up into the sky and left there. I am not talking about heaven either. I want to be in the air where all the music seems to rise and disappear. Do you understand?"

I hold her close to me. We're lovers in a graveyard, now. I think of the Brontë sisters, how romance and graves can be so intricately woven, the closeness of the two.

"I think I understand, Mirabelle. If we could only be degravitated, or shot up into space so we would float around forever, untouched, alone; it would be so clean, so detached from everything, as you say, like music."

"You do understand, Jacques. I think sometimes music is like the stars. I would like it to be that way."

November 19 will be Lorrie's birthday. It will be her fiftieth, too. She wrote a wonderful long letter telling how much she enjoyed the photographs of the paintings I'd mailed her. She said she really understood now what I must have felt all those years when I was working to make everything easy for the family, while I had such a tremendous vision festering inside me. That's the word she used, "festering."

I thought a long time about it, I guess that's the way she feels. It's probably the best word for it. But I know it wasn't all her fault and I try to tell her how pride and competition, needing my bosses' special attention, was as much a reason for my sticking with MBI as making money for the family. I was behaving like a child. Many times, I know I even forgot I once wanted to be a painter. Sometimes I'd joke about it with my colleagues, sort of on a "would you believe" basis.

I tell Mirabelle I'd like to send one of our paintings to Lorrie for her birthday.

"That is wonderful, Jacques. I am certain it will make her very happy. We have so many here and we should not be selfish, should we."

But it turns out to be harder picking one than we thought. On the one hand, we want to give her one we think is the best, one we think she'll really appreciate. On the other hand, we have a hard time giving any of them up.

We sit all one afternoon trying to make up our minds. It's such fun when I'm sharing sight with Mirabelle. It's almost as if we're watching television together, some magical television in which we're the main actors and everything together. It's like living the same dream.

"Jacques, you shall need to decide yourself. I cannot be strong enough. I still do not know how you can sell them. I know you want to be independent, have your own money, but it is so hard to let any go. You yourself must decide."

She stands and goes into the main room. I sit there and finally decide on one I painted looking down the rue Princesse. It has the house where Chardin lived. I know he is one of Lorrie's favorite painters. It's a good painting, and knowing it's Chardin's place would make it very special to her.

I use a screwdriver to take the tacks out, then roll the canvas with the paint on the outside, so when it's unrolled it won't crack. I put the tacks in a small plastic sack, then break down the stretcher and slide the pieces inside the painting. I slip the whole thing into a tube for mailing, write IMPRIME—POSTER on the outside, take it down and mail it at the post office. On the custom form I just write AFFICHE, which means "poster." Trying to get paintings out of France can be a lot of red tape. But this way, if you're lucky, it's easy.

The next day, I start a self-portrait. It's raining again and even with the curtains pulled back to let light into my room and with a hundred-watt bulb concentrated on me and the canvas, it's hard to see.

I get myself all set up and just look for a while, the way I've learned to do. I haven't been looking at myself much lately. In some ways I look older; in others, younger. I definitely look much healthier and I think I'm beginning to put on some weight. Even with all the running, we do eat fantastically, and the old metabolism is slowing down.

I paint all afternoon, until there's no light. I set up the next morning and there's better light. I work on it while Mirabelle's taking care of her pigeons. We're making a coq au vin and every once in a while I go in and give the pot a stir. No wonder I'm getting fat. Just the smell could put on a few pounds.

After we eat, and Mirabelle washes up, she comes in and sits on the bed behind me. I try to explain what I'm doing, where I'm having trouble, the parts I like. I'm getting to the end of the painting and I'm wondering if Mirabelle will be able to see this one.

I know I'm finished but I keep working, hoping to hear her exclamation at seeing it, but nothing comes. I put down my brushes.

"You are finished, Jacques?"

"Yes, Mirabelle, I think anything I try now would do more harm than good."

"Then you are finished. I am so sorry I cannot see it. I thought for a moment there I would, that the clouds and darkness would clear, but just when I thought it would happen, my mind closed down and there was nothing. I think it is something like trying to have an orgasm. It probably just has to happen to you, you cannot try."

I decide that since Mirabelle can't see it, I'll send this portrait off to Lorrie and the kids when it's dry. It's one way a part of me can be with them. I look at the painting for a long time before I pack up my paints. It's like looking at somebody else, even the face in the mirror looks like someone else. In a certain way, the painting looks more like the "me" in the mirror than it looks like the way I think I look. But then, no one knows how they look and we all look different at different times to different people, even ourselves.

That evening I don't write. I haven't received any letters for a few days and painting the portrait was my way of saying how I'm doing, what's happening in my life, my real way.

Mirabelle says she's ready to play some of the work from *Les*

Suites Anglaises for me. I take my chair in the darkened room and she plays. The difficulty of the piece is lost in the controlled restraint and personal fervor with which Mirabelle plays. Her concentration is incredible. I'm transported into a world of music, stars, mathematics, progressions, repetitions, elaborations until I don't even feel my body. I can't believe it when she stops. I have no idea of how much time has passed. I stagger over behind her.

"Mirabelle, that was so beautiful I can never tell you what it meant to me. You took me with you into your mind, introduced me to Bach in a way I've never known. I don't know if I've ever felt so close to you. Thank you."

"I played it especially for you, Jacques. It was the best I have ever played and I knew it would be because I was playing for you, for us. I think I could feel your mind in mine as well as that of Johann Sebastian Bach. It was such a pleasure to feel us together in the music."

That night when she comes to my bed, the music is somehow still with us. We become each other, floating in our own music, plucking songs from each other's bodies, lifting our hands in titillating crescendos, stroking long notes as we feel our mutual vibrations.

I've left a candle burning on the night table by my bed as usual, mostly for me, so I can see Mirabelle when she comes through my door, softly walking, staring at me, unseeing, then sliding under my lifted covers. It is a part of our ritual.

I push away the heavy covers and explore her body in the dim light. We always make love to each other simultaneously, giving cues for what we wish for ourselves by what we do for each other. There isn't much talk, mostly only sounds of our delight. I come into her and slowly roll, still hard, tight, inside her, until she's on top of me, her braid falling over my face. I can see she's on the edge of going to another place. She begins to move more strongly against me, thrusting in a way she's never done.

"Oh, Jacques, I think it's happening. The music is growing louder, stronger. Je suis perdue. Je suis . . . Hold me tight, Jacques! Don't let me go; ever! Hold me."

And then she gives a loud moan, almost a shriek except it is deep in her throat. She pushes herself up on her arms so she hovers above me, a light, white-faced imp hovering with dark shadowed eyes in the night. I begin thrusting back in unison and feel myself spasm, spill my seed, come, inside her. I sense myself joining in her quiet frenzy.

I watch her face. She's had her head tilted up, her eyes closed. Then she looks down at me. The candle reflects on her eyes. A look of horror comes onto her face. She whispers.

"Jacques, I can see you! I can see you! Mon Dieu, you are an old man! You are older than my father! How can this be?"

I do not know how to react. I am so happy she can see, but this was the last thing I'd expected, yet I should have known. I stare back at her.

"Are you sure, Mirabelle?"

"Yes. You have gray hair and a white beard, the face of a grown man. I did not know."

"You knew I was fifty years old, that I have a wife and four grown children. You must have known. I mean are you certain you can see?"

"Of course. But I did not know. I had such a different picture of you in my mind. Please do not be hurt. Give me time to grow accustomed. It is so strange."

She lowers herself onto my chest with her head turned away. I can feel the tears coming, rolling in the hairs on my chest. I begin to suspect she'll never see again.

"Are you all right, Mirabelle?"

"Yes, I am fine. And you are right. I am a silly old woman with the mind of a little girl. It is so difficult for me putting it together."

She raises herself again, staring at my face.

"Turn your head back and forth so I can see all of you. Please, Jacques."

I roll my head back and forth slowly on the pillow.

"Yes, you are really quite handsome when I try to see you as I really am, not with my little-girl eyes. You must know, Jacques, this is a great shock to me. I am surprised I can still see."

She turns her head carefully, looking around at the room.

"And you have made it all so beautiful. It is much more beautiful than I remember."

She starts giggling, then laughing out loud. She laughs so hard I'm afraid for her. She tries to speak several times, but has to stop because of the mirth that ripples up from her throat.

"Oh, Jacques . . . I am so sorry . . . It must

have been terrible for you when I called you old when I am the old woman . . . It is so funny, so strange. I am truly sorry. Can you understand; can you forgive me?"

The humor of the situation begins to unlock me. I'm past the fright, the shock of it all; I begin to laugh. This makes Mirabelle laugh even more. I hold her tight to me and we shake, vibrate with each other's laughter. I don't know how long it is before Mirabelle speaks again.

"Jacques, if I think you look old, what must I look like? You must promise to hide your portraits of me and take away all the mirrors in this house. If not, I am sure I shall be blind again. I do not think I could possibly look at myself."

"Don't be foolish, Mirabelle. I wouldn't be here if you weren't a very attractive woman. Isn't it enough that I think you're beautiful? What do you want?"

"You are an artist, Jacques, you see me in a dream. I am not an artist. I am afraid I would see myself for just what I am, an old woman. I do not want that."

She settles quietly on my chest, her heart beating like butterfly wings against a window.

"I am very tired now, Jacques; could we please go to sleep? We can worry about my seeing in the morning. Until then, just be my beautiful, wonderful, handsome, kind, loving man and hold me tight against all the hard things in this world, please."

With that she becomes quiet. In a few minutes she's asleep and I slowly ease her off me and onto the bed beside me. I prop her head on a pillow. Her eyes are closed. She's so beautiful. She's always slept with her eyes closed, even when she couldn't see. I wonder if all blind people do.

Reverie

I am ready. All I could have dreamed in my
blindness I have. Jacques will be mine forever in
my heart and in my mind.

We had such wonderful days, playing, working
together, loving. Has any woman ever had such a
beautiful concentration of love? And he knows I
love him, how much he means to me. It does not
matter about our age. When I saw him that first
time tonight, I knew immediately how much older
he is than I, in his heart. He carries such sadness
and is so brave to face life as he does. I can never
be like that.

I hope he will do as I ask him when it happens.
It cannot be far from now. I try to hide it, but the
soft, fading feeling inside comes often. I know he is
strong enough to lose me in this way, because he

has so much: his work, his wife, his children. There will be just enough time for us.

How long will it be before he finds my message? I was afraid he might discover it before I left, so I hid it carefully. It is very difficult for a blind woman to hide something from the sight of someone who sees. Blindman's buff is what the English call the game played by children. This is more like "blind woman's bluff." I must sleep. I am so very tired.

Chapter 13

When I wake, everything seems so still. I lie there with my eyes shut and listen. Then I realize it's because I don't hear Mirabelle moving around the house. She usually moves so quietly it's hard to hear her, but if I listen closely I often can. I listen.

Then I open my eyes and become aware she's still in bed beside me. It's the first time she's stayed on, most times she leaves without my even knowing it. I look across at her and she's sleeping on her back, so quietly, so calmly, with a slight smile on her face. I feel a strong swell of emotion for her. She seems so frail, so small, so vulnerable; it's hard to believe her tiny body could contain so much power. I wonder if she'll still be able to see when she wakes. It would be wonderful, incredible.

I lean across and kiss her gently on the lips. They feel cold and there is no response. I look more carefully. She doesn't seem to be breathing! I spring to my hands and knees on the bed beside her.

"Mirabelle? Mirabelle! Are you all right?"

There's still nothing! I place my hands on both sides of her head and run my thumbs gently over her closed eyes. It doesn't seem possible; even her eyes are cold. My heart has started thumping so badly it shakes my entire body. Impulsively, I cover her with myself, wrap her in my arms, pull her to me. She's cold through and, although not stiff, unresponsive. I begin to cry.

I'm crying uncontrollably and I know I'm crying as much for myself as for Mirabelle. I don't know why I don't feel more sorry for Mirabelle; I'll never know. She's the one who's dead, she's had *her* life taken away in the night, just as she'd begun to see, to live in this world. Could it be that in my heart I knew that by seeing, she was doomed? I don't know. I'm almost going insane; selfishly drowning in my own grief. It doesn't seem possible.

I stay like that, holding her, stroking her, sobbing, knowing something of how it must have been for her as a child when she found her mother. I have never had any direct experience with death; even my parents are still alive. It's impossible to accept. One moment she was here, with me, sharing the most intimate of moments, and now she is gone, can never return.

I don't know how long it is I stay there in the bed, holding her tight to me; alternating from impossible sobbing to a deathly silence, a silence where I want to stop my own heart from its vulgar beating, to join the calm, the quiet, of Mirabelle.

Then I carefully lay her out, centered in the bed, my bed; she looks so alone. I smooth her white, eyelet-decorated nightgown, carefully fold her hands on her chest, one hand over the other as she would so often hold them when she was moved by something. I'm still crying but I can feel acceptance, numb, dumb acceptance coming over me. As I straighten the sheets, the covers, I carefully cover her, just her body, not her face, as if she's asleep alone. I begin talking to her. I'm down on my knees beside her.

"Mirabelle, I know from your face you died happily, as you lived. I must believe that. You will live on in me and in our paintings. I'll tell my children and Lorrie about you so you can live in them, too, and help us all live better lives. I'll try to tell everyone I can what a wonderful person you've been. Most of your life you've lived in darkness, and so if it is to darkness you go now, it will be home for you. I want to think that.

"If it is not, then, as in your dreams, you can see again. I hope you will see me. I hope you can know what is in my heart, how much I've loved you, will always love you. Mirabelle, I am surprised to find how I am feeling now. I am almost quiet, happy to be with you, to know I shall be with you all my life, no matter what may happen."

I stay on my knees on the floor beside the bed a long time. Finally, I rise and dress. All the time, I keep talking to Mirabelle. There is much to be done. It's almost as if she is talking to me, too, telling me those things I must do.

It is hard to abandon her, alone in the room. I leave the door ajar. I go to where Mirabelle keeps our francs for our daily use. I'm surprised to find there are over sixteen thousand francs in that little enameled sugar box. I've never opened it before. Any money I earned when I sold paintings, money I didn't need for materials, I gave to Mirabelle and she put it in there. For Mirabelle, money was only something to be used when you needed it, like soap. She didn't really save money or depend on it. I know she'd approve of the way I'm going to use it now.

Then I see a small envelope in the bottom of the box. It has one word on the outside: JACQUES. I open it. Inside is a letter. I walk, holding it, back to the room with Mirabelle. I kneel again beside the bed, memories of saying my prayers as a child. The note is printed in capital letters. I read:

SEPTEMBER 11, 1975

DEAREST JACQUES,

IT IS EARLY IN THE MORNING AND I STILL FEEL THE COOL OF NIGHT AFTER OUR WONDERFUL WARMTH IN BED. I WANT TO WRITE THIS NOTE TO YOU NOW, AFTER OUR WONDERFUL BIRTHDAY DINNER. YOU ARE ASLEEP. THE PROBLEM WITH MY HEART IS MORE SERIOUS THAN I TOLD YOU. I CAN GO AT ANY TIME, SUDDENLY. IT SEEMS THE RIGHT THING TO DO, TO BE FAIR TO YOU, TO WRITE NOW, AT THIS MOMENT.

IT IS DIFFICULT FOR ME TO HANDWRITE, I AM USING A RULER AND A CONTRAPTION I INVENTED TO KEEP MY LINES STRAIGHT. I DO NOT WRITE OFTEN, AND SIMPLE LETTRES MAJUSCULES ARE EASIEST FOR ME.

IF YOU ARE READING THIS, I AM PROBABLY DEAD. I DO NOT THINK YOU WOULD LOOK INTO THIS BOX IF IT WERE NOT THE CASE. YOU ARE SUCH AN HONORABLE PERSON. I LOVE YOU SO VERY MUCH, JACQUES.

IF I AM DEAD, DO NOT BE SORRY. I KNOW IT WILL BE HARD FOR YOU, HARDER THAN IT IS FOR ME, BUT WE HAD SO MUCH, LET US NOT FOR-

GET. YOU HAVE GIVEN ME EVERYTHING IN THIS LIFE I COULD EVER HAVE DESIRED. THESE LAST MONTHS WITH YOU HAVE MADE ME ALMOST GLAD TO HAVE BEEN BLIND ALL THESE YEARS, SO I WAS SAVED JUST FOR YOU, SO WE COULD COME TO KNOW AND LOVE EACH OTHER AS WE HAVE.

YOU PROBABLY HAVE DIVINED THAT IN MANY WAYS, I AM STILL THE LITTLE GIRL WHO CAME HOME TO FIND HER MOTHER DEAD IN THE BATH-TUB AND HER FATHER DEAD IN SOME FARAWAY MUDDY PLACE. AFTER THAT, I DID NOT WANT TO GROW UP. THE HORROR OF BEING AN ADULT, AND SUFFERING AS MY PARENTS HAD, WAS MORE THAN I COULD SUSTAIN. FOR THAT REASON, I BE-CAME BLIND. IT HAS ALWAYS SURPRISED ME I DID NOT BECOME DEAF AND MUTE AS WELL. I DID NOT WANT TO GO ON WITH LIFE AS IT IS USUALLY LIVED.

I WANTED TO REMAIN AN "INNOCENT," AT LEAST AS INNOCENT AS A FOURTEEN-YEAR-OLD GIRL IN PARIS CAN BE. AND I WAS REMARKABLY INNOCENT, EVEN FOR MY AGE AND TIMES. MY IN-NOCENCE WAS THE MOST VALUABLE QUALITY I HAD.

I HAVE LEARNED TO CONCENTRATE ON TRUST AND TOLERANCE. I HAVE DISCOVERED THESE ARE THE MOST IMPORTANT COMPONENTS OF INNO-CENCE. THERE CAN ONLY BE GUILT WHEN ONE DOES NOT TRUST ONE'S OWN TRUEST IMPULSES,

OR DOES NOT TOLERATE OTHERS WHEN THEIR
IMPULSES ARE DIFFERENT FROM ONE'S OWN.

I LEARNED MUCH FROM THE PIGEONS; THEY
HAVE BEEN MY MOST IMPORTANT TEACHERS.
THEY ARE SO TRUSTING, MOST PEOPLE ARE CON-
VINCED THEY ARE STUPID; I THINK MANY PEOPLE
BELIEVE ALL INNOCENTS ARE STUPID OR CRAZY.

THE PIGEONS ALSO TAUGHT ME MUCH ABOUT
TOLERANCE. SOMETIMES, OUT THERE ON THE
PLACE, I COULD HEAR LITTLE CHILDREN CHASING
THEM, BUT PIGEONS DO NOT COMPLAIN, THEY
ONLY MOVE OUT OF THE WAY. JACQUES, YOU WILL
NEVER KNOW HOW CLOSE I WAS TO MY PIGEONS.

WHEN I MET YOU, I FELT YOU WERE STRUG-
GLING FOR INNOCENCE. YOU WERE SEARCHING
FOR A WAY TO SEE "CLEARLY," "CLEANLY," WITH-
OUT PRETENSE. AS YOU PROBABLY KNOW, MY MU-
SIC, AS I HAVE LEARNED IT, AS SOUND ONLY, HAS
BEEN VERY IMPORTANT IN MY PERSONAL SEARCH
AND IN MY LEARNING TOLERANCE FOR MYSELF.
IT ALSO TAUGHT ME TRUST, TRUST IN THE MUSIC.

I THINK THAT, TOGETHER, WE HAVE BEEN AT-
TAINING A HIGH STATE OF "INNOCENCE." WE
HAVE BEEN CONFIDENT, ONE TO THE OTHER,
THAT WE WOULD NOT HURT. WE ALSO KNEW
FROM THE FIRST, I BELIEVE, EACH OF US, THAT
WE WOULD DO EVERYTHING POSSIBLE TO KEEP
THE OTHER FROM BEING HURT. AND, MORE POS-
ITIVE, WE EACH WANTED TO GIVE THE OTHER

PLEASURE, MAXIMIZE, WHERE POSSIBLE, OUR POS-
SIBILITIES, AND SHARE OUR THOUGHTS, OUR
PRESENT, OUR HOPES, OUR PAST TRAGEDIES.

I AM SURE, SITTING THERE, SOMETIME IN THE
FUTURE, READING THIS, IN LIGHT OF LAST NIGHT
AND ALL THESE WONDERFUL NIGHTS, CONSID-
ERING MY SEEMING "UNHOLY" DESIRE TO MAKE
LOVE WITH YOU, TALK OF INNOCENCE COULD
SEEM BIZARRE. IT WOULD TO MOST PEOPLE. BUT,
YOU SEE, JACQUES, I HAVE BECOME CONVINCED
THAT SEX, PASSION SHARED, WITHOUT GUILT, IS
A VERY HIGH FORM OF INNOCENCE. I BELIEVE IT
IS ONLY BECAUSE PEOPLE HAVE INVESTED THIS
ENTIRE WONDERFUL EXPERIENCE WITH RITES OF
OBLIGATION, OF POSSESSION, OF RESPONSIBIL-
ITY, THAT IT HAS BECOME ALMOST THE SYMBOL
FOR LACK OF INNOCENCE.

PERHAPS IT IS BECAUSE SEX IS RELATED TO RE-
PRODUCTION AND ALL THIS IMPLIES. ONLY WHEN
YOU PUT YOUR SEED IN ME THE FIRST TIME DID I
DEVELOP A TOLERANCE FOR PEOPLE WHO TURN
THIS GRACIOUS ACT INTO WHAT HAS BECOME RIT-
UAL. WHEN I KNEW I DID NOT HAVE AN EGG FOR
YOUR SEED, THAT THERE COULD BE NO THIRD
PARTY IN OUR SEX, I FELT THE TRAGEDY. IT WAS
THEN I BECAME TRULY AWARE OF THE IMMENSITY
OF SEX.

I BELIEVE YOU ARE CAPABLE OF GREAT INNO-
CENCE, JACQUES. I HOPE YOU CAN CONTINUE

YOUR SEARCH FOR IT; I AM CERTAIN YOU WILL. I
SHOULD LIKE VERY MUCH THAT YOU STAY ON LIV-
ING HERE IN OUR APARTMENT, PAINTING AND RE-
MEMBERING ME. BUT, OF COURSE, THAT IS
SELFISH AND NOT INNOCENT AT ALL.

I ALSO WANT YOU TO GO HOME TO YOUR FAM-
ILY. I KNOW YOU CAN NEVER FEEL INNOCENT IN
YOUR HEART UNTIL YOU DO. YOU STILL LOVE LOR-
RIE AND YOUR CHILDREN, BUT YOU DID NOT
TRUST YOUR DEEPEST FEELINGS OF LOVE FOR
THEM.

MOST OF ALL, I WOULD LIKE YOU TO LIVE HERE
IN OUR APARTMENT WITH LORRIE, HELP HER TO
FIND SOME KINDNESS IN HER HEART FOR DIDIER,
IN HIS WEAKNESS.

I HAVE MADE ARRANGEMENTS WITH THE NO-
TAIRE WHOSE NAME IS AT THE BOTTOM OF THIS
LETTER, SO ALL I OWN BECOMES YOURS AT THIS
TIME, THE TIME OF MY DEATH. BUT I TOLD YOU
THAT. YOU NEED ONLY GO TO HIM WITH THIS LET-
TER, HE DOES NOT KNOW YOUR NAME, BUT WE
ARRANGED IT SO THIS LETTER WOULD BE YOUR
CACHET, WHEREBY YOU WILL BE RECOGNIZED. I
HAVE ARRANGED CONTRIBUTION DIRECT AND
PROPERTY TAXES WITH THE PEOPLE AT THE BANK.
THE G.D.F. AND E.D.F. WILL BE PAID, AUTOMATI-
CALLY, BY THE BANK ALSO. THEY ARE QUITE KIND
TO A BLIND OLD LADY.

IF YOU DO NOT GO TO THE NOTAIRE, THEN ALL

WILL REMAIN AT YOUR DISPOSAL, WITH ONLY THE PRESENTATION OF THIS LETTER NECESSARY, ANYTIME WITHIN THE NEXT TWENTY YEARS, TO OBTAIN YOUR RIGHTS. IF YOU DO NOT CLAIM IN THAT TIME, IT WILL BE SOLD, WITH THE PROFITS TO GO TOWARD THE PROTECTION OF OUR PIGEONS IN THE CHURCH TOWER AT SAINT-GERMAIN-DES-PRÉS.

I KNOW IT IS TERRIBLE TO WRITE OF THESE THINGS, BUT ONE MUST SOMETIME. I HAVE PUT IT OFF FOR SO LONG. THERE IS ENOUGH MONEY IN THIS BOX TO BURY ME. I DO NOT WANT TO BE BURNED. I CAN BE BURIED IN THE FAMILY PLOT WE VISITED, IN A SIMPLE WOODEN BOX. I WISH THERE WERE ANOTHER WAY, AS WE DISCUSSED, BUT SO BE IT.

NOW I END THIS LONG LETTER, JACQUES, I SHALL START MY EXERCISES AND SOON THE BELLS WILL RING AND YOU SHALL WAKEN. I AM WRITING AT THE TABLE WHERE WE HAVE SHARED SO MANY WONDERFUL MEALS AND GOOD TIMES. I CAN NEVER THANK YOU FOR ALL YOU HAVE BROUGHT TO MY LIFE. I HAVE FELT LIKE A REALLY GROWN WOMAN, IN THE BEST WAY, WITHOUT FEAR, FOR THE FIRST TIME. AND STILL I HAVE FELT MORE INNOCENT THAN I WOULD EVER HAVE BELIEVED POSSIBLE.

YOU ARE A BEAUTIFUL PAINTER AND A BEAUTIFUL PERSON. I AM SO HAPPY TO HAVE BEEN

BLESSED WITH THE VISION OF YOUR WORK. IT IS
THE PROOF OF INNOCENCE TO SEE "CLEARLY"
AND NOT BE TRAPPED INTO SEEING ONLY WHAT
IS THERE. THANK YOU FOR SHARING THIS WITH
ME.
REMEMBER, I LOVE YOU FOREVER.

YOURS,
Mirabelle

After that, there's the name of the notaire. I lay the letter and
my head on the bed beside Mirabelle and cry again. It's all so like
her, loving, and yet intelligently arranged. I feel as if she has talked
to me from the bed in front of me. I look up and try to absorb her
quiet, beautiful face into my mind for all my life.

I put her letter back into the bottom of the box and then place
the box in the cupboard where it has always been. I fold the sixteen
thousand francs in my wallet with my carte de séjour and carte
de travail. I walk back into the room and stand, my eyes riveted
again on Mirabelle.

"Mirabelle, I'll do what I can. I hope you approve of what I'm
going to do. It's probably illegal and some people might think it's
even immoral or perhaps crazy, but it *is* innocent. It is what my
deepest feelings tell me must be done."

I lock the apartment and go downstairs. The most shocking thing
is how everything seems the same. If I didn't know Mirabelle was
up alone in that bed, cold, I couldn't believe her dead. All that we
shared is here, unchanged.

I go to a phone across from Le Drugstore and phone American
Express. I manage to reserve a seat on a flight to Minneapolis early

the next morning. I arrange to pick up and pay for my ticket at the airport.

I go back upstairs. I make myself a pot of coffee and pull our table from the main room into my room, and set it up beside Mirabelle in the bed.

"Mirabelle, I'm going home to my family. I know that's what you want me to do. I cannot stay here alone without you. I know you want that, too, but it is not possible. Now, first, I must write to my family and tell them what has happened."

I have the feeling Mirabelle hears and understands me. The smile on her face is so enigmatic, yet so expressive. I do not feel alone at all.

Lorrie,

I want you to share this letter with our children. Mirabelle has died. My intensity of sorrow cannot be expressed. There is also a transcendent joy which suffuses me. Mirabelle will never be dead to me; her spirit and all she gave will live on in me, in my painting, in our paintings.

I want you to know how I feel about myself. The tight selfish bindings, which have always held me within my ego, that made me isolated, alone, have been broken forever. I now feel an integrated part of the world, not fighting, not struggling, just part of it. And, as Mirabelle said, in some way, more innocent.

I cannot possibly tell you how much I love you and our children. I shall forever be sorry I caused all of you so much pain. But another part of me is convinced it has been for the best; that now I can be a true husband and father to our family, show my love, and not be a mere "breadwinner" and provider. As I write this, I'm sure of it. As I'm part of everything now, I am even more part of you.

I'll be coming to Minneapolis within the next week or so and I'll phone from a hotel when I arrive. I don't want to impose myself on you, just share what we can. I hope to bring my paintings home so you and the children can see what I've been doing. I promise I'll try to answer any questions any of you may have.

I look forward with great joy to our meeting and hope it will be a joy for you, too.

There are so many other ideas I want to share, but there are things to do here and I want to spend as much time with Mirabelle as possible.

I hope to see you soon.

Love,

Jack

When I'm finished, I read the letter to Mirabelle. Perhaps this seems macabre or weird to someone who has never had a close loved one die, but it's perfectly natural for me. I hope, all my life, I'll feel free to speak with her, and intend to. I've lost some of my respect for the apparent.

Any painter who really discovers his art comes to this point. And Mirabelle, almost because of her blindness, knew it, too. In her music, she dealt with sounds, not the visible written music, by which most musicians are blocked. When she listened to speech, it was sounds, with meaning, she heard, not substitutes for print. For her, there was only one real language. I think that's why it was so easy for her to learn so many forms of other language, including her music. Even her ears were innocent.

The bells of noon start ringing. I get down on my knees beside the bed again and lay my hands over hers on her chest. I stay quiet there, with my eyes closed, I hear not only the bells but the wings of the pigeons rustling as they swoop and fly from the tower and over the street. I wonder how it registers to them that Mirabelle isn't there. Perhaps they've been conditioned in all these years to expect her, but do they have a memory of her? Would it take her presence to stimulate their tiny brains into the old rite of coming down to be groomed and fed? I think for a minute of going out to try taking her place, but then decide against it. No one can take Mirabelle's place, not even for the pigeons.

I pull out my old duffel bag where I kept my clothes and things when I was living in the attic. It's made of heavy canvas with a canvas strap and grommets at the top. A hook on the end of the strap closes it. This is the duffel bag I came home with from the war, the bag I walked away from home with. I pull the chair closer to Mirabelle's bed and lay my duffel bag on the table. I search out the small screwdriver I used to repair and replace some of the light switches here.

Then I take down from the walls all the paintings. There are twenty-eight of them, almost all 25F, the size that seems to fill my vision but isn't too unwieldy on the back of my box. There are nine I sold, so that makes a total of thirty-seven in the past more than six months. I hadn't realized I had painted so much. But then that's only quantity, I believe it's the quality of these paintings which makes them important.

I start removing tacks from the sides of the stretchers to which the canvas is attached. There are forty tacks in each stretcher, so it's going to take some time. The secret is to dig the edge of the screwdriver under the head of the tack and then tip it back so it pries the tack out of the wood. Most times I get it first time. I start talking.

I try to tell Mirabelle about how hard it is for an artist to be innocent. The very act of seducing people into believing that color smeared on canvas represents something else, sky, light, air, space, can never be innocent.

"Yes, you are right, Mirabelle. Here in Paris, when we met, I was approaching a minor innocence. Those days of wandering through Paris, letting the city happen to me, were the inception of my new life. From them, I gained the courage to try making sketches, watercolors, as homage to the beauty I felt flowing into me.

"But, even when we worked together, and you unleashed my emotions in painting, so that scenes floated in my mind as personal visions, I was still not true. I was purposefully trying to create an object which would stimulate, facilitate another person to an experience of innocence. But it was not innocence itself."

I continue talking and prying the tacks out of the paintings, rolling the canvases, putting the pieces of stretcher sticks inside, filling the duffel bag.

"In my paintings I want to express the awe and excitement I feel from what I see, how what I see relates to what it seems I am."

I stop and concentrate for a while on the tacks. I finish several more canvases. I'm having a hard time telling Mirabelle and myself what I mean. I pull over another canvas, it's one looking down the rue des Canettes toward the rue du Four.

"You see, Mirabelle. No, of course you don't see. First, you're dead, and even if you were alive, I'm not sure if you could see. It doesn't matter."

I come to the edge of breaking down again. I take deep breaths. There's no way I can dismantle these canvases with shaking hands and tears.

"It's like this. I want people to look at my painting so they can share joy with me. Also, there are things I'm doing with composition, with texture, lighting, brushstrokes, to make this little piece of canvas seem magic, like a window onto another world, a world related to one moment in time and one place, as seen by one person, me. But more than that, a window onto a place of imagination, of beauty, of excitement. It's a tiny illusion of light and space I'm trying to make seem true."

I'm a little closer now. I look at the canvas still half-attached to the stretcher, curling down on itself. Did I ever really believe in the place I'm suggesting here, is it all some kind of self-hypnosis that doesn't mean anything except it gives me pleasure? Is all art just that, a form of self-delusion, self-gratification, self-serving pretension?

I turn the painting around, stretch it out. No, I can still fall into it. For me it still works, even after over a month. But that's the problem, does it work for others?

"Mirabelle, every time I painted our paintings, I had you in mind. I wanted *you* to see them. It wasn't enough that I could please myself, I wanted it to be a place where we were together. And because you are blind, could share *your* inner vision, it seemed to happen. I felt, *knew*, that, if only for the two of us, the painting was a special object which brought us together. Then, beginning with the couple who bought the painting of the Place Furstenberg, I began to feel our vision meant something to others, alone, by itself.

"But how many people can see these magic things? I want to share with as many people as possible, but still be true to myself, to the subject. There's the trap, Mirabelle, I find myself, sometimes, painting the painting to attract others, like putting feathers on bait for fish. It happens. Perhaps I want too much, or perhaps I've had too much training, or perhaps it's only that I want adulation, money, success. I don't think so, but I don't know. It's here, too, where I can never be innocent, Mirabelle. I need your strength.

"I'm afraid when I go back to America, live with all the others, our friends, who value success more than anything else, and success, for them, means making money, or being recognized, I'll fail, fall into contrivance again, lose the magic.

"Will I be able to continue what we've started, our private, soft, free involvement with the paintings we've made? I really don't know, and it frightens me."

I look over at Mirabelle, quiet, smiling in the big bed. The walls around us stare down, empty now, without the paintings. At least they were good decorations. But if that's all there is to painting I'd rather go back to MBI. I take another canvas from the stack, stare at it for a few minutes, try to pretend I didn't paint it, that I've just seen it for the first time, in a gallery or a home or on the chevalet of some other artist. I can't do it. These paintings are so much a part of me, or I'm a part of them, I can't really see them anymore as objects.

"Oh, Mirabelle, I miss you so. In your blindness you taught me to see. And now that I can see, not just passively, but actively, as a painter, I'm not sure if I have the strength to carry on alone.

"I know Lorrie will like my paintings. Her reaction to even the photographs was so rewarding. But *why* does she like them? Is it only because they look like 'paintings'? How is a painting supposed to look? Painters can't agree. It seems to change with time, almost like the styles of clothing or houses.

"But some painters have crossed the boundaries of time and mode, Mirabelle. Rembrandt, Chardin, Titian, van Gogh, Monet, many others, were just true to themselves in their best work, so true it was almost impossible for anyone to follow in their footsteps. And now I can look at their work and somehow become them, in their time, in a mystical communion.

"Yes, there is something there, but will I ever attain anything like that? Is it worth it? I've already caused so much pain to my family, can I justify this mad search for a dream that seems so unattainable one can begin to doubt its existence? Do I make any sense at all, Mirabelle?"

I work all afternoon as the cup fills with tacks and the duffel bag begins to swell with the rolled paintings. It's so strange to think that all my joy, my creations, can be rolled so easily and packed into this sack like a pile of dirty clothes. When they were on the wall, they seemed so much more, they gave me a sense of elation, of completion, I'd never known, and now they're as nothing. I could put them out by the poubelle and they'd be thrown into the grinding truck and mauled into so much more compacted trash.

I hear the six o'clock evening bells ringing. I'm not hungry, although I haven't eaten all day. I don't even want to think about eating without Mirabelle across from me. It would be an admission that she really is gone. I still don't feel I've told Mirabelle why I'm so concerned about my innocence, my ability to keep on with my painting, painting as she taught me.

"What worries me more than anything else, Mirabelle, is that I might be painting for only a small elite group of people, mostly moneyed people, who have the time and interest to look at, or even buy, paintings. This would seem to be the exact opposite of the reasons why I want to paint. If painting is going to separate people along economic or class lines the way music or theater or literature does, then I don't want to be part of it. Since I was a student, this has been a problem for me. The kind of people who dominate the world of art, who have access to the galleries, to the museums, to the publication of paintings in books, or even postcards, are not the people I'm interested in.

"They gain control of paintings as possessions, huckster them, promote, hustle, sell them, like any other commodity. They gain control of the distribution, so that anything unique, tender, true to itself and the artist, has virtually no chance of being seen.

"With almost all the great painters this has been the case. Rarely does the artist live to know that thousands, millions of people have their lives improved by the insights he's sacrificed to share. Am I strong enough to live and die as Vincent van Gogh did, without selling one painting, the debtor and ward to his brother? He obviously wasn't, and I don't think I am. He was a true innocent, Mirabelle, and he died one. I don't think I'm innocent, trusting, tolerant enough, to be so magnanimous. Do you understand?"

I give up. I'm not even sure what I'm trying to say myself. I turn on a light and continue dismounting the paintings. It's dark when I roll the last one and squeeze it in beside the others. I slide the bag from the table and the end swings to the floor. It's heavier than I thought it would be but I can lift it. I thump it a few times on the floor so the paintings slide to the bottom, then pull the grommets together and slide the hook at the end of the strap through the U-shaped latch. I hoist it onto my shoulders, it's heavy but I can manage. It and my paint box will be all my luggage home.

There's one painting, the last one I was working on, a view across the Place Saint-Sulpice, that is too wet to dismount and pack. I leave it leaning against the wall. I also leave the first painting I did of Mirabelle. The second portrait I'm taking with me.

Then I start cleaning out the paint box. I use my palette knife to clean off my palette down to the wood. I squeeze all the paints with the tops on so the paint is in the upper part of the tube. I wash all the brushes thoroughly, first with turpentine, then rubbing them into a bar of soap under hot water in the kitchen sink. Because I've been painting so consistently, I've gotten somewhat sloppy about keeping my materials in order. One painting just seemed to lead to another and I was always in such a hurry to be painting.

There are several brushes which are so worn there are only a few short bristles or hairs left. These I throw away. I dump the turpentine and varnish medium from my little containers into paper towels and scrub them out.

All the time I'm doing this I'm talking to Mirabelle. Mostly I'm remembering the good times we had, sometimes crying, sometimes laughing. She's always been such a good listener to my rantings, it's almost as if she's hearing me, registering, nodding, laughing quietly inside herself. I still can't let go.

When I'm finished, I put it all together and tie a piece of rope around my paint box so the legs won't get detached and bent or broken in the luggage bay of the plane.

By now it's dark. I go back into the bedroom and stretch out beside Mirabelle in the darkness. I try to pull myself together. I know I'm doing almost everything automatically and I need to make sure I don't make mistakes.

I roll over on my side toward Mirabelle and stroke her forehead, letting the tips of my fingers rest lightly on her eyes, the sides of her nose, her lips, her chin, her neck. I remember how she explored me, and then start crying again. I put my arm across her stiffening body and my face into the pillow. It's all so impossible.

Finally, I pull myself together and start cleaning house. First, I turn on all the lights in all the rooms. I just walk around for a while, enjoying the lovely home we've shared these months. Next, I take away everything I own, every piece of clothing, including my tux, fancy shoes, even my toothbrush. I throw them all into a plastic trash bag. I take out all the food from the refrigerator, any perishables from the shelves, put them in another bag. I only keep the clothes I'm going to wear on the airplane.

I draw a bath, remembering Mirabelle drawing one for me each morning. Then I lower myself into it and try to relax. I scrub my whole body as if I'm trying to shed my skin. I'm red and tingling when I pull the plug, wash out the tub, and dry myself. I think of

Mirabelle's mother, of Mirabelle pulling what was probably that same plug to let out the bloodied water.

I dress again in the clothes I've been wearing during the day, and spread the clothes I plan to wear on the plane across the bed beside Mirabelle. I look once more around the apartment, then tie the bags shut, using the plastic string dangling from the bottom. I walk back into the bedroom.

"I'll be right back, Mirabelle. I have a few things that must be done."

I take the keys from their place, both the apartment key and the key for the church tower. I pick up a small dust broom, and another plastic sack. I go into Mirabelle's music room and open the armoire which holds all her works of musical sculpture. I lower each one carefully into this sack. They aren't heavy, they're like Mirabelle, so much of love and concentration in such a small space and weighing so little. Then I gather up some of my reserve candles, some matches, and the painting of Mirabelle that I didn't pack. It's about ten o'clock in the evening, but it's a Monday, so there shouldn't be too big a crowd out in the street.

I go down the stairs after closing the door. The streets are busy, but nothing exceptional. Except for the painting, I could look like one of the street sweepers out a bit early for the night's work, or a clochard with my trash bags.

I walk a block away from the apartment, then stuff my plastic bags with the surplus clothes and food in them into one of the trash cans at the curb. I then cross the boulevard Saint-Germain to the church. I look around carefully and slip over the fence around the presbytery to the side and in front of the church. I easily discover the door to the tower. The key turns in the lock, stiffly, and the opposite way I would have thought, but the door swings open. I close it behind me. I'm in total darkness. I decide not to light a candle yet; I can feel my way up the worn stone steps.

It isn't as far as I thought it might be. I come to a trapdoor, push it open, there's a counterweight, and I'm in the belfry. I look down through the slits in the arches and see the traffic and crowds below. I look across the boulevard and see the building in which Mirabelle's apartment is located. I think of her stretched out on my bed. Enough light comes in through the slits in the arches so I can see where I am, what I'm doing.

I climb up onto the huge oaken beam supporting the bells. I hope there's no reason for them to ring bells now, I'd probably lose my hearing, become the deaf artist taught by a blind woman. There shouldn't be bells, not at ten in the evening, no wedding, no baptism, and only one quiet, unannounced funeral.

I disturb several pigeons and they fly crisply, frantically, in the dark, stiff wing feathers beating against the walls, then they settle down. I find, as the bell tower cleaner had said, several dead pigeons on top of the broad beam. I gather them into a pile in the corner by the trapdoor. The beam is at least three feet wide. The gray-blue-green bells loom in the dimness below me. Below them is a dark hole. I crawl out on the beam, brushing it clean as I go, brushing the dirt into the hole. In the years since it has last been cleaned, considerable dirt has accumulated.

When I'm finished, I crawl backward to where I can secure my footing again. I'm dripping wet from perspiration, a combination of exertion, fear, and anxiety. I crawl once more across the beam and put the painting of Mirabelle at the other end, away from the trapdoor through which I came. I store the sack of sculptures and the candles in the near corner with the dead pigeons.

I quietly descend the steps. I go out the door, peering carefully for anyone, then close it quickly and lock it again. I climb over the fence, step out on the street, hurry across and past Monsieur Diderot, then down the rue des Ciseaux and home.

I wash off thoroughly in the bathroom, then go back into the bedroom with Mirabelle. I'll probably need another bath before I'm finished. There's the slight flashing from a flickering neon light outside, which seems almost to animate Mirabelle's face; strange I never noticed it before. I stretch myself on the bed beside her again, to prepare for the next step of what I intend to do.

"Mirabelle, I hope you will be happy with what I'm planning. We never exactly talked about it but this is the closest I can come to what I think you said you would like."

I really don't want to make an extra trip but, at the same time, I want to do this right, wrong as it all probably is.

There's still another painting against the wall, the one of Place Saint-Sulpice that isn't dry. I gather it under my arm, being careful not to smear it. I also take from its place in the cupboard our bottle of Poire William, almost empty again now, except for the pear. I hurry across the street, over the fence, and up the tower, deposit these things, then hurry back again to the apartment without any problem. Now it's only a question of waiting, and some luck.

I lie in the semidark talking quietly to Mirabelle while we wait. I go over all I can remember with her, from when she crashed into me, until that last wonderful night. Was it only last night when she could actually see me for the first time? I almost laugh remembering how we laughed.

It must be almost four in the morning when I decide the time has come. It's after most of the tourists and revelers have left the street, before the street cleaners start. It's the quietest time.

I wrap Mirabelle in a sheet first, then enfold her again in a blanket. I allow just a small flap of the blanket to cover her head, the way it would if a father were carrying his child in the night. If anyone sees me, I hope I can pass it off as that. In a way, she is my child as I am hers.

I have no trouble scurrying across the boulevard. There's practically no one out. I hurry but try not to seem hurried or harried. I enter the small yard of the church, swing Mirabelle up onto my back while I climb over the fence, step into the vestibule, and open the door. I have the key in my hand and it locks automatically behind me. I've made it through the hard part. In the dark, it's difficult maneuvering Mirabelle, who is quite stiff now, around the corners of the twisting stone stairs, but I manage to arrive at the top, where I've left the trapdoor closed.

I push it open and close it behind me with my foot. I lower Mirabelle carefully onto the end of the beam beside the dead pigeons. Again I disturb a few sleeping pigeons, they flutter some, then quiet down, making their cooing nighttime noises. Can they possibly know who it is who is coming to stay with them?

I light one of my candles. I carefully crawl across the beam to the other end. I place the candle in front of the painting of Mirabelle, sticking it in its own drippings. I then stand the painting of Saint-Sulpice at the other end of the beam and light a candle in front of it. There's no danger of the candles lighting the oak beam, they'll just be extinguished in their own meltings.

Then I slowly, gently arrange Mirabelle until she's stretched out on the oaken beam in its center. I uncover her face. The light from the candles lights her so there are deep shadows on her face and her eyes seem open and watching me. In the moving from the apartment, her smile seems to have widened, yet still there is approval. I think she begins to find all my theatrics somewhat amusing. I'm talking to her all the time as I arrange things.

"You are in the tower against the sky, Mirabelle. You are with your friends the pigeons. It seems like the right place."

I take the dead pigeons and arrange them around Mirabelle as if they are a cortege. Between each two pigeons I place one of her sculptures. In the flickering light, I swear I can almost hear the tinkling of her harpsichord as she plays the music they represent. I don't think I'm going crazy, but I could be.

I light two of the other candles and place them on either side of Mirabelle. Then I light the last candle and put it at her feet. Beside it, I stand the almost empty bottle with the pear inside. I settle myself on the floor for a last look. I stay there in the dark at her feet on my knees for a long time. I'm trying to create a vision of her for myself, for the long years ahead. Finally it is time.

"I hope you like this, Mirabelle. I think it will be years before anyone comes and finds you. You are close to home and with those you love. I wish I could stay here with you but I must go."

I stand and look down at her. She seems so small, so alone, but it is all I can do.

"You will hear the bells, Mirabelle. I can always think of you listening to the bells, being part of them. No one else will know what those bells mean, only us. I'll never forget you, my love. Goodbye, Mirabelle, goodbye. You know how much I love you."

I open the trapdoor and begin backing down the stone steps. I close the door behind me. I can barely make it down, my knees are shaking so, and I'm crying. I open the door to the tower, go through, and lock it behind me. I look at the key in my hand, I decide to keep it, I'll carry it always as the key to all we had together.

I climb back over the fence and run across the boulevard, back to our apartment. I take another bath, change into my clothes for the airport, roll the clothes I was wearing into a ball, and stuff them into yet another blue plastic sack.

I go around and close all the shutters and windows. I look one last time at Mirabelle's beautiful harpsichord, then at her lovely white bed floating in her red room, at my room where she so recently was on my bed. Tears are streaming down my face, I'm sobbing. I turn off all the lights, pick up my paintings, the paint box, and my last plastic bag. I back out the door and lock it. I put the key to the apartment on top of the box for the electric meter. It's so high I need to jump. Nobody will ever find it.

After I dump my bag of sweaty clothes into yet another trash can, I stand and wait for a cab at the taxi tête de station in front of Le Drugstore. I wait quite a while before one comes. It is growing lighter. I have my box and duffel bag of paintings on either side of me. I look up at the tower of Saint-Germain-des-Prés. I think of Mirabelle up there. I think I see the slight glow of the candles. I lean into the taxi and tell the driver I want to go to the airport at Roissy. He nods for me to get in. He climbs out to help put my box and bag in the trunk. I stay out to help him.

Just then it starts. The bells begin to ring for six o'clock. It's the bell to wake Mirabelle. I take the bags from the hands of the taxi driver. He stares at me. I shake my head no, still staring at the tower, listening.

Someone else commandeers the cab. I listen through all the bells as they ring and then to the distant answer of Saint-Sulpice. It's time to go, I know, but not quite yet. I need more time. I watch the sun rise.